KU-556-250

7/23

Praise for *Glasshopper*

Observer Best Début Novels of the Year
London Evening Standard Best Books of the Year

'Tender and subtle, it explores difficult issues in deceptively easy prose. Across the decades, Ashdown tiptoes carefully through explosive family secrets. This is a wonderful début – intelligent, understated and sensitive.'
Observer

'A disturbing, thought-provoking tale of family dysfunction, spanning the second half of the 20th century, that guarantees laughter at the uncomfortable familiarity of it all.'
Juliet Nicolson, *London Evening Standard*

'An intelligent, beautifully observed coming-of-age story, packed with vivid characters and inch-perfect dialogue. Ashdown's storytelling skills are formidable; her human insights highly perceptive.'
Mail on Sunday

'I love it. It's a book that's very fast and really rewarding for the reader. There's a wrenching end to the first chapter that switches the mood and absolutely hooked me for the rest of the book.'
David Vann, author of *Legend of a Suicide*

'An immaculately written novel with plenty of dark family secrets and gentle wit within. Recommended for book groups.'
Waterstone's Books Quarterly

'It's very subtle, and subtlety is the key to this. The tragedy is happening behind the words, and you could be forgiven for wanting to read it again to catch all the nuances. It reminded me of Iain Banks. If you enjoyed *The Crow Road*, you'll get lots out of this book.'
Simon Mayo Show, BBC Radio 5 Live

SURREY COUNTY COUNCIL

'This stirring coming-of-age novel evokes the strictures of the '50s and the tacky flamboyance of the '80s brilliantly. It's a heartbreaking, redemptive tale of family secrets that will take you on an emotional rollercoaster. Arm yourselves with a box of Kleenex as you'll be weeping into your pillow by the end.'
Glamour

'Carefully observed, unexpected and mesmerisingly beautiful.'
Easy Living

'A brilliant début.'
Sainsbury's Magazine

'In Jake, Ashdown has created a beautifully realised character, totally believable as a 20th-century boy but imbued with qualities which should resonate with any reader and will surely stand the test of time. The prose is succinct and smooth, the dialogue crisp and convincing. An intriguing, atmospheric read with a healthy dollop of realism.'
Argus

'Skilfully written and difficult to put down... this novel is a page-turningly good read.'
Drink and Drugs News

'Ashdown's début novel is accomplished, accessible and absorbing.'
NewBooks Magazine

'The beauty of Ashdown's writing is that readers are able to connect to the real characters presented and understand that life isn't always all that easy. Her character representations, no matter what sex or age, are flawless, and her descriptions create superb images to match the story. It's hard to know who to recommend this to without encouraging everyone to go out and buy it. Ashdown is a definite one to watch in British literature.'
The Bookbag

To read an extract from Glasshopper, turn to p.262

ISABEL ASHDOWN

Hurry up and Wait

Myriad Editions

First published in 2011 by

Myriad Editions
59 Lansdowne Place
Brighton BN3 1FL

www.MyriadEditions.com

1 3 5 7 9 10 8 6 4 2

Copyright © Isabel Ashdown 2011
The moral right of the author has been asserted.

All rights reserved. No part of this publication may be reproduced, stored in a retrieval system, or transmitted in any form or by any means without the written permission of the publisher, nor be otherwise circulated in any form of binding or cover other than that in which it is published and without a similar condition being imposed on the subsequent purchaser.

A CIP catalogue record for this book is available from the British Library.

ISBN: 978-0-9562515-5-8

Printed on FSC-accredited paper by
Cox & Wyman Limited, Reading, UK

For my mother, Jane, with love

'The breaking of a wave cannot explain the whole sea.'

Vladimir Nabokov

January 2010

Sarah waits at the kerbside, her winter coat buttoned up tight against the cold night air. The tang of sea spray whips through the lamp-lit High Street, as the distant rumble of clawing waves travels in from the dark shoreline, up and over the hedges and gardens of East Selton. It's an ancient echo, both soothing and unsettling in its familiarity. She checks her watch. She's early.

At the far end of the Parade, an old Citroën turns the corner and rattles along the street, drawing to a stop alongside her. She stoops to peer through the window, and sees John Gilroy smiling broadly, stretching across to open the passenger door, which has lost its outside handle. She slides into the seat, pulling the door shut with a hollow clatter.

'It's good to see you, John,' she says, returning his smile, not knowing whether to kiss him or not. She runs her fingers through her hair. 'This is a bit weird, isn't it?'

John pinches his bottom lip between his fingers and frowns. 'Yeah, *really* weird.'

There's a moment's pause as they look at each other.

'I suppose we'd better get it over with, then?' he says, releasing the handbrake and pulling away.

They cruise slowly along the deserted Parade as the wind buffets the faded canvas roof of the car, whistling out across the night. Sarah draws the seatbelt across her body, clunking it into place between the seats. A disquieting recollection rattles her, a sense of having been here before, with John at her side. She studies his face as he struggles with the gear-change from second to third, a slice of mild irritation still lodged between his black eyebrows. 'Sticky gearbox,' he mutters as it grinds into gear.

Sarah gazes out at the shop windows as they pass through the High Street. She remembers old Mr Phipps from the tobacconist's. Every Saturday morning Dad would take her there on the way back from the paper shop, and she'd choose something from the jars at the back of the counter. It was a tiny vanilla-smelling store, its walls adorned with framed black and white photographs of the screen greats: Clark Gable; Bette Davis; Victor Mature. She notices the estate agent's, on the corner opposite the war memorial, although the name over the top has changed.

'I couldn't believe it when I got your email,' she says. 'It's been years.'

'Twenty-four years,' John replies.

She nods.

'I worked it out. It was just before your sixteenth birthday, wasn't it?'

'You've got a good memory.'

He keeps his eyes fixed on the road ahead. 'Well, one minute you were there, and the next you'd gone. It sort of sticks in your mind.'

Sarah shivers against the cold. 'The town gives me the creeps, to be honest. When I checked into the B&B this afternoon, the woman who owns it seemed familiar, but I don't know why. I guess she's just got that Selton look.'

'What's a "Selton look"?'

'Don't know. But it puts me on edge, whatever it is.'

John scowls, feigning offence.

'Not you, though!' she says quickly. 'You don't count.'

She notices he's wearing a knitted waistcoat under his jacket. It's a bit hippyish but she's pleased to see he's no longer in the black prog-rock T-shirts that seemed to be welded to his torso throughout the eighties.

They turn into School Lane.

'So, who are you dreading most tonight?' John asks.

'Oh, God, what a question! It would be easier to say who I'm not dreading.'

'OK, then. Who?'

A light mist of freezing fog has started to descend, and the windscreen wipers squeak into action.

'Actually it's the same people. I'm looking forward to seeing certain people but dreading them at the same time. Tina and Kate are the obvious ones.'

'Dante?' John asks, briefly turning his eyes on her with a small smile.

She blinks. 'He probably ended up in some rock band in LA. That was the trouble with Dante. Too cool for school.'

John laughs, rubbing his chin.

They pull up in the new car park at the rear of the girls' building, a few rows back from the large open double doors of the gym. Sarah scans the area, trying to make sense of the layout. 'This bit used to be the netball court,' she says. 'Can you believe they've built a car park on it?'

John shrugs. 'Well, I suppose the schools are even bigger now than in our day. I'm surprised they haven't merged the boys' and girls' schools into one. It would make sense, wouldn't it?'

Sarah's fingers fiddle nervously with the charm bracelet beneath the sleeve of her coat. She rolls a small silver conch between her thumb and forefinger. 'Do you mind if we just sit here a moment?' she asks.

John shifts in his seat. 'We can sit here as long as you like.' He reaches inside his jacket and brings out the postcard-sized invitation. 'I wonder who designed the cheesy invites? Look at this: "*Wanna know what your old school friends have been Kajagoogooing? Then put on your leg warmers and Walk this Way for a Wham Fantastic night out…*"'

'Stop!' Sarah laughs, clapping her hands over her ears. 'I can't believe I let you talk me into coming.'

'It'll be fine,' he says, slipping the card back in his jacket.

A taxi pulls up outside the entrance to the gym and a small group of men and women disembark. The men are clutching cans of lager, and they stumble on to the pavement, laughing and shouting to each other. Sarah recognises one of the women as a girl from her class, but she can't quite grasp the name. Melanie? Or perhaps it was Mandy.

'Bloody hell,' says John, grimacing. 'Look at the state of them.'

Sarah blows air through pursed lips, watching her white breath slowly drift and disperse inside the car. Her eyes rest on the funny little gearstick, poking out of the dashboard like a tiny umbrella handle. 'Is this a Citroën Dyane?'

John leans into the windscreen to wipe the moisture away with a sponge. It's a stiff synthetic sponge, and all it does is turn the condensation to water, which runs into a pool on the dashboard. 'Yep. My trusty old Dyane. It's a bit of a renovation project.'

'Thought so,' she says. 'It's freezing. Just like my dad's old car.'

He sticks the sponge under the dashboard. 'I know. I really liked his car. Used to see it chugging through the town sometimes, and I thought, one day, when I've got a bit of money, I'd like one of those.'

Sarah leans across and kisses him on the cheek. It takes them both by surprise, and she draws her hand to her mouth.

'Sorry,' she says from behind her glove. 'I'm a bit nervous.'

John shifts in his seat so he's facing the windscreen. 'Me too.'

Two screaming women run down the side of the car towards the school, click-clacking on high heels. Sarah tries to make them out, but they're strangers to her. She draws a smiley face on her misted side window.

'We'd better go in,' says John, 'before the car steams up completely.'

Sarah stares ahead, her fingers curled around the still-buckled belt strap. 'Just five more minutes.'

Summer Holidays 1985

Sarah considers the possibility that her father could be lying dead in his bed upstairs. She looks over her shoulder, to the first floor bedroom window, where the curtains are drawn and unmoving. He's in his sixties now. It's possible.

The soft drift of decaying seaweed floats over the streets and gardens, in from the shoreline, salted and sharp. She crosses the lawn in her bare feet, feeling the slow heat of morning break through as she inspects the neat poles of runner beans that line the edges of the garden. A violet morning glory has attached itself to the beanstalks, and twines elegantly up and round, its vine head bouncing lightly in the still air. She collects a handful of beans and returns to balance them on the windowsill beside the deckchair. Her feet are damp with dew; she stands motionless, alert for human sounds from within the house. Nothing. He only retired in May, but already he's got himself stuck into more research work. She heard him up late last night, working on his new project. Maybe he never even made it to bed. Perhaps he's in his study now, slumped across his papers and history books, his skin pale and lifeless.

Sarah plucks a daisy from the lawn and drops back into the deckchair, causing her heavy fringe to puff up momentarily. She gathers a handful of hair and checks it for split ends, noticing how the sun has bleached the top layers to a soft tawny brown over the summer. Where would she go? Maybe she'd be sent away to Swiss finishing school, like Jane Tyler's cousin. Or to some distant relative, perhaps one she's never even heard of.

But there are no relatives. She's on her own.

The sun's heat washes over her as the cloud cover thins in the wide blue sky. 'One – two – three – ' She pulls off the white petals one by one, discarding each with a casual flourish. They flutter briefly before spiralling to the ground, bruised and broken. ' – thirteen – fourteen – *fifteen*.' Sarah blows the last petal from the palm of her hand, just as Ted pads out through the back door, fanning his tail and grinning.

'*Fifteen*, Ted! That's how old I am today. Yes, it is! And that's how many kisses you have to give me!'

Ted's tail goes into overdrive, and he stamps his little paws rhythmically, like a wind-up toy. Sarah snatches him up on to her lap, where he wriggles and snorts happily as she ruffles the whiskery fur of his chin. She hears water running through the pipes at the side of the house as the toilet flushes inside.

'So where's the Birthday Girl?' her father bellows as he makes his way down the stairs. You'd think he sounded annoyed if you didn't know him. 'Well? These presents won't open themselves, young lady.'

Sarah turns to look up at her father standing in the doorway in his chequered gown and slippers, his bright white hair pushed up wildly on one side. With his gently rounded belly and sleep-creased face, she sees the boy in him.

'I suppose you want a coffee?' she asks, pushing herself out of the deckchair.

'Naturally,' he says, placing two gifts on the concrete path beside her seat. He takes her face in his hands and kisses the top of her head.

They decide to have breakfast outside, and, while Sarah makes coffee and toast, Dad drags the garden table and chairs out into the middle of the lawn. He arranges the two parcels and a single card in the centre of the table.

'Right. There's jam and marmalade. And butter.' Sarah carefully lowers the laden tray on to the table.

'Marmite?' Her father pulls a disappointed face.

'Oops. Sorry. Hang on.' She runs back inside.

When she returns, she drops the morning post on the table and places the Marmite on his plate.

'You can't beat a bit of Marmite on toast,' he says, thumbing through the envelopes on the table. 'Bill. Bill. *Reader's Digest*. One for you. Bill. That's it.'

He spreads a thick layer of butter across his toast. Sarah pulls a disgusted face and opens the envelope, easing a clean knife under the corner and slitting it gently along the fold. The card is a Monet print, of the bridge at Giverny.

'No signature,' she says, as she looks inside. 'Just a kiss. Look.'

She holds it open to show him the little handwritten 'x'. Her father raises his eyebrows and takes a drink of coffee.

'*Dad*. It'll be Kate or Tina. Kate probably. She's always taking the mickey out of me for not having a boyfriend. She's winding me up. I'll phone her later, so she knows I know. Cow.'

Sarah's sure it's a joke, but the card unsettles her and she slaps it on to the table face-down. Dad picks it up and turns it over in his hands critically.

'So. Are we going to open these presents, then?' He passes Sarah the first one, clearly a book.

She carefully opens the wrapping, smoothing out the paper as the book cover is revealed.

'*I Capture the Castle*. Dodie Smith.' She smiles gratefully. 'Looks good.'

'It's a classic,' he replies. 'You'll enjoy it, I'm sure.'

The other present is perfume, Anaïs Anaïs, neatly hand-wrapped in the store.

'How did you know I like this one? I love it!' She immediately sprays it on her wrists, holding it out for him to smell. The sweet floral fragrance hangs in the air between them, confusing the scent of honeysuckle which wafts over the garden fence.

'Very nice. Very you. Deborah helped me to choose it.'

Sarah pulls a face. She's certain he's blushing behind his white beard.

He takes a bite of his toast. 'She's an old colleague, from Stokely University days. An old friend. She's got a daughter, you see, so she knows about buying presents for young women.'

'So you didn't choose it yourself, then.' She busies herself, folding the wrapping paper into neat squares.

Gulls fly over the garden squawking and screeching; Dad looks up as the birds pass by and soar over the rooftops out of sight.

Sarah carefully balances the Marmite jar on top of the pile of paper, to stop it unfolding. 'Have I met her?'

'No. No, I don't think so. No.' He starts to clear the plates.

'What about this one?' Sarah asks, holding up his card.

'Oh, yes, of course,' he says, perching on the edge of his seat, still clutching the plates.

She wipes her knife clean, and slides it beneath the seal. 'Ten pounds! Brilliant. That's great. Thanks, Dad. That's really great.' She smoothes the note flat. 'And say thanks to Deborah, for, you know, helping with the perfume.'

She kisses him quickly on the cheek, and gathers her gifts and cards into a little collection on the table in front of her.

Dad rises and strides towards the house with the plates. 'Will do!'

'So, what shall we do today?' she calls after him.

He pauses in the doorway, and turns back, gazing past her into the garden.

'Dad?'

'Oh. Well, I've got to get some work done this morning. How about a walk later on, then back here for birthday cake?' He's frowning.

Sarah follows him into the house. 'I'll get baking, then. Victoria sponge?'

'Naturally,' he replies, and he leaves her to clear up.

As Sarah weighs the caster sugar and pours it into the mixing bowl, she hears the click of his study door and she knows she won't see him again until teatime.

Autumn Term 1985

The first Monday of the new term is a bright September day, and Sarah walks to school briskly, looking forward to seeing Kate and Tina after the long summer break. They both live over at Amber Chalks, at the opposite end of town to Sarah, so she never gets to walk in with them in the mornings.

When she arrives, there's a notice pinned to the wooden door of their hut, advising of a room change. Other girls from 5G stand around in clusters, blinking at each other under the sun's glare.

'Wood rot,' says one of the girls. 'In the floorboards. Or it might be the heating.'

Sarah scans the courtyard for Kate and Tina. She's hardly seen them over the holidays, as she spent most of the time working in the chemist's. Kate popped in to see her once, but Sarah was nervous about chatting for too long when the shop was so busy. Kate had topped up her lipstick at the Outdoor Girl counter and gestured to Sarah's navy pinafore. '*Nice*,' she mouthed as she backed slowly out of the shop door, causing the under-mat monitor to go bing-bong more than once.

The group of girls meanders along the corridor towards their temporary form room.

'Have you seen Kate?' Sarah asks one of her classmates over the noise.

The girl shakes her head.

When she arrives at Room 121, Sarah finds Kate and Tina huddled comfortably in the pair of back-row window seats.

'How'd you know we'd be in here?' she asks, slinging her army bag over the back of the chair in front of them.

'Got here early,' says Kate, brushing her hair in long, elaborate strokes.

'Your hair's grown,' says Tina to Kate, barely acknowledging Sarah's arrival. She scratches at the eczema between her fingers. Sarah notices how pale Tina's skin appears next to Kate's golden tan. Kate always looks healthy.

'Looks nice,' Sarah adds.

Kate gathers her hair into a bunch and releases it, so that it fans out like a peacock's tail. 'Yeah. Gonna get it cut soon – like Siobhan from Bananarama. Not her old style; the new one, short at the sides and long and spiky on top.'

'That'll really suit you. And coloured?' Tina starts fiddling with her own mousy hair.

'Yeah. I reckon I'll henna it. Here, Sar, can you get it cheap at the chemist's? You get a discount, don't you?'

Mr Settle enters the front of the classroom, looking sallow and depressed. When Sarah had him for English last year, they nicknamed him 'Doughnut' because he brought one into class every lesson. Without fail, he'd place it in its bag at the front of his desk, where gradually the grease and softened sugar would seep through and spread across the white paper. Then, exactly ten minutes before the end of class, he'd carefully open the bag and devour the doughnut in three mouthfuls. Always three. Now, he holds up his briefcase, horizontally, where everyone can see it, and lets it drop to the desk with a loud slap, sending chalk dust billowing through the streaks of sunlight. A few of the girls shriek in surprise.

'Welcome back, 5G!' he booms. 'Now, SIT!'

'Pillock,' Kate whispers to Tina.

Sarah looks over her shoulder to grin back at them.

'So,' Mr Settle starts, as he clears the debris of chalk and drawing pins from his desk. 'You were all expecting the dishy Mr Gardner as your form teacher this year, weren't you?'

Some of the girls snigger and nudge each other. Sally Richards wolf-whistles across the classroom. Mr Settle shakes his head despairingly.

He opens his briefcase, and Sarah sees a flash of white paper bag as he removes a faded blue A4 folder. She looks back at Kate and Tina. '*Doughnut*,' she mouths with a smile. Kate licks her lips suggestively.

He snaps the briefcase shut. 'Well, Mr Gardner is no longer with us. So, for now, you'll have to put up with me. Or vice versa. Believe me, I'm no happier about it than you are.' He pulls out his seat and opens up the register. 'Zoe Andrews...? Sharon Buller...?'

When he's finished taking the register, Marianne puts her hand up from the front desk. She still looks the same as she did in the first year: plebby and a bit too heavy for her age.

'Yes, Mary-Ann,' says Mr Settle.

She doesn't correct him on her name. 'What about our form room?'

'You'll be in here for now, while the caretakers sort out the heating in your hut.'

'Thank God for that!' Kate says loudly. 'Last year the heating *kept* breaking down. We nearly died of *hypothermia*.'

'That's enough!' Mr Settle shouts towards the back wall. 'Right, timetables out. You were all given your schedules at the end of last term. Anyone who's not sure what they're doing, come to me. The rest of you, make sure you've got your books ready for first lesson.'

Seven or eight girls straggle up to his desk to find out where they should be. He gives them each an exasperated look, before running his finger down a large chart to tell them which lessons they have to attend.

'Have we got Assembly today, sir?' Tina calls over Sarah's head. She cradles her bony fingers together and pushes outwards, cracking her knuckle joints.

'Yes!' he bellows again, without looking up.

Tina and Kate snigger behind Sarah, and she turns to join in.

'*That* big,' whispers Kate, and she wiggles her little finger, nodding her head towards the teacher. 'That's why he has to shout all the time. To make up for it.' She wiggles the little finger again and sneers.

Sarah turns to look at Mr Settle in his brown suit and crumpled tie. 'Yeah. Look at his tiny shoes. *Teensy weensy feet*,' she squeaks in a little mouse voice.

'Sarah Ribbons! Where are you for first period?'

'Oh! English, sir.'

He runs his finger down the sheet. 'Correct! Alright – Assembly. Off you all go! And NO talking!'

5G streams along the corridor in an untidy line, joining other classes on the stairs, a slow procession of green V-neck jumpers, shuffling towards the hall. Tina looks tiny walking beside Kate, who's almost a head taller. Kate sashays along with a bored swagger, sucking on a long strand of hair and rolling her eyes.

Sarah counts the months on her fingers. Ten months till July. 'I'm going to burn my uniform when we get out of this place,' she whispers to Tina.

'Yeah, and the school. I'm gonna burn the bloody lot down!'

A teacher shushes them at the open doorway to the Assembly Hall. Row after row files in, until all sixteen classes of the upper school are lined up facing the stage. Mrs Carney, the Head, walks along the side of the hall, past the teachers who flank the passageways on both sides. She ascends the stage in front of the dark red curtains, and positions herself behind the central podium.

'Good morning, girls,' she says. Her voice sounds as if she has a mouthful of mashed swede.

'Good morning, Mrs Carney,' the pupils chorus.

'You may sit.'

There's a scuffle and murmur as the girls try to sit in their lines on the grubby parquet floor without exposing their underwear. Sarah notices that Kate's wearing a new pencil skirt, long and straight down to her calves, with a slit up to the back of her knees. She has to ease herself down sideways on, or the skirt would rip. Sarah inspects her palms and dusts them off on her green jumper.

Mrs Carney pats her short grey hair with the flat of her hand, then gracefully gestures towards the teaching staff. 'This year we are pleased to welcome two new teachers: Miss Welsh and Mr Morton. Mr Gardner is no longer with us, but the excellent Mr Settle will fill in until we find a suitable replacement.' She stresses the word *suitable*, then hurries on as if she regrets the inappropriate inflection.

Sarah leans over her crossed legs, making a quizzical face at her friends. Kate forms a circle with the finger and thumb of one hand and pokes at it with the forefinger of the other. '*With a sixth former*,' she whispers.

Tina's mouth drops open, before turning into a mischievous smirk. 'Dirty git.'

After the school announcements, everyone stands to sing 'All Things Bright and Beautiful'. As always, Kate, Sarah and Tina descend into hysterics at the line, 'the purple-headed mountains', and by the time they file out of the hall for their first lessons Sarah's stomach muscles are bunched up like fists.

'See you at break?' she asks the others.

'Yeah,' shrugs Kate. 'I'll be round the cloakroom, or something.'

The three girls go their separate ways, Tina and Kate arm in arm in one direction, Sarah alone in the other.

Sarah meets Kate and Tina at the cloakroom at lunchtime. Kate's taking an old Madonna poster down from the inside door of her locker, replacing it with one of the Style Council.

'Lush,' she says as she presses the Blu-Tak into place.

Tina is fiddling about in her own locker, stacking her books in size order. She's still got a magazine cutting of Andrew Ridgeley on the inside door, which frays at the edges with age.

Kate nudges Sarah, pointing at Andrew's highlighted quiff. 'Sad,' she says with a curl of her lip. 'You're always about three years behind everyone else, Teen.'

Tina grabs the picture off the door and screws it into a ball, which she drops and kicks along the length of the corridor. 'There – better?'

Kate raises her eyebrows and turns the key in her lock with an efficient snap. 'I'm busting for a wee – let's stop off at the loos on the way.'

They take the stairs through the central foyer, passing through shards of sunshine which break through the ceiling-high glass panels of the lower corridor. Other girls move about, making their way towards the canteen or out on to the field at the back of the school where they'll eat packed lunches and recline like cats, hitching up their skirts as they take in the last rays of late summer.

Mrs Whiff passes them in the corridor, heading towards the front office. Her real name is Smith, and she gained the nickname not because she smells bad, but because she can sniff out trouble at a hundred paces. She glares at the girls as they go by, pausing at the front office for a quick word, before disappearing through the staff room door with a stiff turn of her sturdy little ankles.

'Cow,' says Kate, sticking two fingers up at the closed door as they pass.

As usual, the toilets are filthy. There are six toilets in the block, all choked up with sheets of tracing-grade loo roll and God knows what else.

Tina's hopping from one foot to the other. 'I can't wait,' she says, dumping her bag by the sinks and slamming a cubicle door behind her.

'Disgusting,' says Sarah, pushing the doors open one after the other to inspect the insides. 'Someone's done that on purpose.

Idiots.' She finds the least revolting one and enters, closing the door. She holds her breath against the bleachy stench.

'Hurry up,' squeals Kate on the other side. 'I'm *busting*.'

Sarah hovers above the seat, careful not to touch any of the surfaces. She unzips the inside pocket of her bag and removes a small wad of toilet tissue. She can't bear the school stuff; it's so non-absorbent, you might just as well use nothing at all.

Kate growls outside the door. 'Come on! I am *actually* going to wet myself!'

Sarah pulls the chain and exits rapidly, letting Kate rush in to take her place. 'I wouldn't touch the seat if I were you,' she warns. 'You might catch something in this place.'

Tina joins Sarah at the sinks. She washes her hands briskly then moves them in wild little waving motions to shake off the water. 'Like your shoes,' she says, indicating Sarah's new white slip-ons.

'Yeah, they're nice, Sar,' Kate calls out from the cubicle. 'I had some like that last year. Here, did you see the way old Whiff looked at us in the corridor? Like we're doing something wrong, just by being there. She's such a bitch.'

Sarah faces the mirror and pulls down her lower eyelid, lining it with thick black eyeliner. 'I know,' she says. 'She's got a face like she's just eaten something foul.'

Kate giggles on the inside of the cubicle. Tina and Sarah frown at each other as they hear the sound of marker pen squeaking across the Formica surface on the other side of Kate's toilet door. 'Go and take a look,' she smirks when she comes out, posing in front of the cloudy mirror to adjust her fringe. She looks really pleased with herself.

Inside the cubicle Sarah pushes the door back and reads Kate's message, written in large permanent capitals: *MRS WHIFF EATS COCK*. She screams with laughter. 'Tina, you should see this! Brilliant!'

She realises that it's suddenly quiet on the other side of the door. Thinking the other two have gone on without her, she peers out cautiously, to see Mrs Whiff standing in the entrance, hands on her wide tweedy hips, rage in her expression. Kate and Tina stand sheepishly against the basins, staring at the lino floor.

'And what, may I ask, is *so* funny, Sarah Ribbons?'

Sarah comes out of the cubicle fully, and looks at the other two. She readjusts her bag strap and rubs her nose, trying not to look guilty. 'Nothing,' she says as lightly as possible. 'Someone just said something funny, and I was laughing – '

Mrs Whiff looks her over with that nasty-taste look she has, and pushes past her through the toilet door. When she re-emerges her expression is altered, the anger replaced with a look of unsettling serenity.

'You two – get off to lunch. *Now*,' she hisses, pointing towards the corridor with the sharp flick of a Nazi salute.

Tina and Kate scurry off without a backward glance, leaving Sarah and Mrs Whiff alone in the toilets.

'So, Sarah Ribbons. I don't want you to think for one moment that I'm shocked. Not in the least bit – do you think I haven't seen and heard worse in my years at the school? You're just a silly little girl with a dirty mouth.'

Mrs Whiff marches Sarah down to the library and locks her in the cupboard-sized office beneath the gallery. It's a tiny room, with a small glass window which looks out across the books from behind the librarian's desk. If Sarah stands on her chair she can see pupils and teachers passing through the room, in and out of the bookshelves and seats. Apart from Mrs Whiff, no one knows she's there. There could be a fire – what then?

She sits in her makeshift cell, writing out lines as her stomach grumbles and complains about its missed lunch.

I apologise for writing filthy obscenities.

Bloody Kate. Bloody Whiffer. Bloody school.

The study door is shut when Sarah arrives home from school. She closes the front door quietly and walks through the dim hall and into the kitchen to get herself a snack. Ted follows behind, batting her calves with his scratchy paws.

'You hungry?' she asks, passing him a slice of cheese.

He takes it in his teeth and runs through the house and out into the back garden through the open door. Sarah follows him, nibbling on her own slice of cheese as she goes. The dog crumples into a triangle of afternoon sunlight, chomping awkwardly on his treat. At the end of the long, thin garden, the willow tree sways gently, creating a soft murmur. Leylandii stand like sentries along one side of the garden. Sarah hates them, and wishes they could be cut back, to let in more light. But Dad likes it the way it is. She hunches down to stroke Ted. She can see her father through his study window, bent over his desk in concentration. His white hair flops over his forehead, too long for a man of his age. Today in Biology they were studying the heart, and Sarah wants to ask him about her mother, to learn more about how she died. But she's tired of asking. 'She had a weak heart,' he told her last time with visible irritation. 'What more is there to know?'

She unpegs the washing from the line, dropping each piece into the laundry basket without folding. Ted follows her back and forth between the line and the basket, hoping for another treat. As she gathers the washing, Sarah keeps watch on the window, wondering when her father will acknowledge her presence. He knows she's there. She carries the basket towards the house, pausing on the patio close to his window. She drops the basket, and it hits the concrete with a loud crack. Dad sits upright, alarmed, and frowns at her through the glass.

'Cooeee,' she waves with a half-smile.

He hesitates, untidily closes the pages of his newspaper, then pushes himself out of his seat, running his fingers through his snowy hair. 'Want a hand?' he asks, taking the laundry basket from her as they meet in the hallway.

'All done,' she replies. 'How's the work going?'

'Not bad. I'm working on the history of women's roles in agriculture, for an after-dinner speech next month. For the Country Landowners' Association. All rather dull, truth be known.'

'Looked like you were reading the paper to me,' she says as she walks into the kitchen.

He laughs, putting his hands on his hips. 'Nothing gets past you, eh? Actually, I was looking at those photos of the *Titanic*. There's a super article – you must read it. The pictures are spectacular; like something from the lost city of Atlantis. You know, it's been down there, undisturbed, for over seventy years, and now they've finally found it. Amazing.'

'*Amazing*.'

'Well, you should at least take a look. How was school?'

'Same as usual.'

'Mmm.'

Sarah fills the kettle. 'You need some new trousers, Dad.'

'Don't be ridiculous,' he says, opening the cupboard doors above the sink. 'Haven't we got any biscuits?'

'You look like a tramp.' Sarah jabs his balding corduroy trousers with her white shoe. 'And you need a haircut.'

'If I needed a new wife, I'd go out and find one,' he grumbles, as Sarah reaches into the top of the cupboard and brings down a packet of custard creams.

'I'm just saying,' she says, passing him the packet and rolling her eyes.

Her father walks back down the hallway, and Sarah hears the study door shut behind him.

'What about your tea?' she yells after him.

'You've got legs, woman!'

'Miserable old bugger,' she mutters under her breath, feeling a sudden bubbling rage. She snatches Ted's lead from the hook. 'Make it yourself!' she shouts back down the hall, slamming the front door behind her.

When she reaches East Selton seafront, Sarah sees the new boy from up the road, standing on the end of the great iron flow-pipe, throwing stones out into the still water. She spots him as she walks along the wooden ledge that separates the lower beach from the stony bank where the wooden huts stand. The beach feels strangely empty now the summer holidays are over, and the haze of autumn coming floats above the water, obscuring the horizon. The boy has his back to her and she slows down, wanting him to turn and see her standing there with Ted by her side. When he doesn't, she keeps on walking, pushing her wind-blown hair from her eyes, whistling every now and then for the dog to catch up. She wants to know where the boy comes from; what brings his family to their dull street. She saw him walking to school this morning. He has a nice face. The stones he throws appear to sail out for miles and miles, before breaking the sea's surface with their force.

When Sarah was little, her father took her to the water's edge one evening, perhaps at this very time of year, and taught her to skim pebbles. 'You have to choose the right shape,' he told her, 'to get maximum bounce.' After what seemed to be hours, Sarah mastered it, and now she's better at pebble-skimming than anyone she knows.

She crunches over the pebbles, collecting stones as she walks, and stands at the tide line, several breakwaters along from the boy. Ted sits at her feet, gazing up at her expectantly. Sarah squats on to her heels, squinting one eye at the smooth line of water ahead. She launches her missiles one after another, *bam-bam bam-bam*, and they bounce across the surface, chasing each other like jumping beans, until they disappear from view. Sarah stands and turns back towards the boy. He's facing her now, his feet planted squarely on top of the giant rusty pipe, his head tilted.

Sarah feels her heart slowing to a steady thud as she looks at the strange boy, out there on the pipe. Ted jumps at her legs with his soggy paws, and she turns to walk back up the beach towards home.

Back at Seafield Avenue, her father has already laid the table for supper. He's had a bath and a shave; she can smell the Old Spice the moment she enters the hallway. The kitchen is thick with steam, which pours out into the hall, giving the house a damp, clammy atmosphere.

'Did you have a nice walk?' he asks, taking the potatoes off the hob.

'Yep,' she replies, returning the dog lead to its hook.

'Did you see anyone?'

'Nope.' She passes him the butter as he starts to pound away with the masher.

'Did you miss me?' He smiles, and slops the creamy potato on to two plates, as Sarah serves up the fish fingers from under the grill.

'Nope. Grumpy old man.' She tries not to return his smile. 'Did you do any baked beans?'

Her father holds out his arms, and she reluctantly enters his embrace.

'I love you, Sarah-Lou,' he says, kissing the top of her head. 'I'm sorry. I *am* a grumpy old man. I'll try harder.'

'Hmph,' she says, but she's smiling into his sweater, and she knows he can hear it in her voice.

'It's my artistic temperament,' he says, giving her a squeeze.

'You're senile, more like.' Sarah picks up her plate and takes it into the dining room.

'Nothing wrong with my brain,' Dad says, tapping his temple as he sits in the seat opposite. 'It's all just fine in here. Just fine.'

~

After a couple of weeks of walking the same route to school on opposite sides of the road, they speak to each other.

'You live up my road, don't you?' he calls over.

Sarah turns to look at him.

'I'm Dante,' he persists, breaking into a jog to cross the road and join her. 'Jones. Do you go to Selton High?'

'Yep.' Sarah's face feels hot. She notices that the hair on the sides of his head is cropped close, right round and under the longer top layer of dark hair. 'What about you?'

Dante isn't wearing a uniform, but a baggy grey T-shirt, black jeans and Converse boots. 'Lower sixth at the boys' school. We just moved here from Canada.'

'Canada? You don't sound Canadian.'

'We were only there for a year. But I can do a pretty authentic Canadian accent when I want to,' he says, slipping into a soft lilt as he kicks a pebble along the pavement.

Sarah smiles.

'Want a Polo?' he asks, offering her the packet.

Sarah takes one, trying to avoid touching the skin of his fingers as she hands the packet back.

'You lived here long?' he asks.

'All my life,' she answers. 'Too long.'

He laughs.

'How come you were in Canada?'

'My folks are in the music industry. Dad was producing a few albums out there, and Mum does hair and make-up. You know, for music videos and stuff.'

'Wow,' says Sarah. 'That must be amazing.'

Dante shrugs, looking at her under his fringe. 'Maybe we could go out? Where d'you go round here?'

As they near the school gates, Sarah spots Kate and Tina leaning against the railings, eyeing up the sixth formers as they pass through the boys' school entrance. Kate's gone back to wearing her short-short skirt again, which is rolled up to mid-thigh. Her shirt is unbuttoned enough to clearly show the swell of her breasts. She puts her hands on her hips and cocks her head to one side, smugly casting a silent question out to Sarah.

'So what d'you think?' asks Dante. 'About going out?'

Kate nudges Tina, squaring up to Sarah and Dante as they approach.

'Maybe,' Sarah answers hastily before Kate can hear.

'Well, I'll walk with you tomorrow, then?'

Sarah smiles, a closed-mouth smile, and Dante gives her a thumbs-up and jogs through the boys' gates. Kate and Tina are upon her like hyenas, pawing her, greedy for information.

'Well? Dish it!' Kate presses. '*Who* was that?'

'Dante. He's moved in down my road.'

'Oo-ooh,' says Tina, raising her eyebrows and linking arms with Kate. '*Dan-te.*'

'Lush,' says Kate, rolling her skirt back down as they walk through the corridor towards their form room. '*Lush*. You have got to introduce me to him, Sar!' She preens herself in the glass of the corridor windows.

'Oh, I don't know,' says Sarah. 'I don't even know him, really.'

Kate punches her on the arm, near her vaccination scar. 'Of course you do. He's walking with you in the morning. I'll be waiting at the gates. Introduce me then. Easy.'

Sarah spends the rest of the morning preoccupied with thoughts of Dante. He looks like a film star. She'd like to run her fingers under his hair, to feel the fuzzy-felt rub of his crew-cut scalp.

At the end of the day she rushes out ahead of Kate and Tina, anxious to avoid the usual twitter and trivia of their homeward conversation. She thinks about Dante all the way home, replaying their conversation over and over, trying to visualise everything about the way he looked. He's nothing like the other boys round here; there's something special about Dante Jones.

And the next day, there he is, waiting on the corner just as he'd promised.

After school on Friday, Dante takes Sarah into town and buys her an ice cream from Marconi's kiosk on the Parade.

'Want a flake?' he asks, raising his eyebrows.

She blushes. 'No, thanks.'

'Course you do.' He turns to the ice cream man. 'She does.'

Sarah smiles as the man presses the flake into the ice cream and hands it to her.

'Aren't you having one?' she asks Dante.

He shrugs. 'I'll have a bit of yours.'

'No, you won't!' she says, snatching it out of his reach as he tries to take a lick.

'Go on, then,' he says, fumbling around in his loose change to pay the ice cream man. 'I'll have the same.'

They walk along the Parade in the autumn sunshine, eating their cornets and chatting. The town is buzzing with kids in Selton school uniforms, many of them new starters whose crisp blazers hang long over their small arms. One girl shrieks when her friend points out Dante, and they both blow him a kiss as they pass. He grins knowingly, flicking his fringe aside and rolling his eyes at Sarah. 'Kids,' he says.

Sarah looks back at the girls, who are falling about outside the newsagent's, laughing into their hands. She smiles to herself and bites into her wafer cone.

'It's been like that all day,' she says. 'Over-excited first years all over the place.'

Dante finishes his ice cream and brushes off his hands. 'Mind you, they can't help it,' he says, holding out his palms. 'I mean – look at me.'

Sarah gasps, letting out a single, 'Ha!'

'What?' He flicks his fringe again.

'You!' she replies. 'How much do you love yourself exactly?'

He gives her a serious look and runs his fingers up through the back of his hair, turning his head this way and that for Sarah's inspection. His nose is beautifully aquiline, his cheekbones sharp and high. He laughs and gives her a little bump with his shoulder as they reach his house at the top of their road. 'Only kidding.' He shoves his hands into the back pockets of his jeans.

'See you, then,' Sarah says, backing away.

'Your treat tomorrow?' he calls after her.

'What?'

'The ice cream. We can meet up tomorrow and you can buy me an ice cream.'

'But I'm working tomorrow.'

'I'll meet you after work, then. You owe me that ice cream!'

'Ha!' she laughs as she watches him walk up the gravel path towards his house.

He looks back at her from his front door. 'Deal?'

She pulls her best incredulous face and starts to walk away. 'OK,' she shouts back once he's out of sight. 'I finish at 5.30.'

'Cool,' she hears him reply. She smiles all the way home.

~

It's Wednesday afternoon, and Tina and Sarah have Geography together, while Kate's in German just across the corridor. She barely spoke a word to Sarah before they went to their different lessons. Tina arrives in the classroom a few minutes late, having dashed off to the loos after lunch. She scribbles a note and passes it to Sarah.

Kate knows you're seeing Dante, it reads. Tina widens her pale blue eyes for impact.

'*What*?' Sarah whispers, the colour rising up her neck.

She's really mad about it, Tina scribbles at the foot of her notepad. She underlines the *really*.

Sarah shakes her head and tries to concentrate on Miss Tupper at the front of the class.

Miss Tupper claps her hands twice, above her head like a flamenco dancer. 'Tina Smythe! Look at me, not Sarah, thank you very much.'

'It's *Smith*, miss.' Tina licks her thumb and tries to rub away a felt tip doodle on the back of her hand. 'Smith not Smythe.'

Miss Tupper frowns. 'It says *Smythe* on the register.'

Tina tuts. 'Yeah, it's spelt *Smythe*, but it's pronounced *Smith*.'

'Fine,' says Miss Tupper, looking annoyed as she turns away to rub the blackboard clean.

When the next lesson bell rings, Sarah rushes out ahead of the other girls.

‘Kate!’ she calls when she spots her among the crowd leaving the classroom opposite. She catches up and falls in step. ‘Walk with you to Maths?’

Kate walks as fast as she can in her tight skirt. The daylight catches Kate’s shiny new hair, making it gleam like the coat of a red setter.

‘Slow down a bit,’ Sarah laughs, her voice almost drowned out by the noise of chatter in the corridor.

There’s an awkward gap as Kate continues to hobble along stony-faced.

‘You know Dante asked me out before you even saw him.’

Kate throws her a spiteful glance. ‘Yeah. *Right.*’

‘Yes, right, actually,’ Sarah mumbles. ‘He asked me out that morning. And before I had the chance to tell you about it, you were going on and on about how I should introduce you. That’s not my fault.’

Kate stops short of the Maths room, and turns square on to Sarah.

‘Well, Sarah. I just happen to think more of my friends’ feelings than I do about the first pathetic boy that comes along. He’s no big deal anyway. I wouldn’t go out with him if he asked me. I was taking the piss when I said I liked him. Haven’t you ever heard of sarcasm, *Sarah*?’

Sarah stares at Kate for a second. She doesn’t know whether to laugh or scream. ‘You were ready to ditch me and Tina for him if he’d been interested. You don’t get first picks of everyone, *Kate*.’

‘Ha! I wouldn’t touch him with a bargepole.’ She starts to walk away.

‘You don’t even know him,’ Sarah whispers as they enter the classroom.

‘Oh, fuck off, Sarah,’ Kate hisses. ‘I’m sick of you hanging around me anyway. I mean, look at you.’ She runs her eyes over Sarah critically. ‘So, no loss to me, then.’

Sarah sits down beside Marianne as Kate flounces across to a desk on the far side of the room.

Sarah shakes her head again and opens her Maths book.

Halfway through the lesson, a crumpled note is passed across the classroom. Marianne reads it and gives Sarah a sympathetic frown before handing it over.

Sorry, Sar. It all came as a bit of a surprise. It's just I had you down as a lezzer. No hard feelings. Hope you and Mr Spaz are very happy together.

Sarah looks back along the row of girls to Kate, who's sniggering into her green sleeve. Everyone else along the line has read the note, and they nudge each other and smirk. Zoe Andrews is nearly wetting herself laughing. Kate looks up and blows Sarah a kiss.

Sarah and Dante lean against the huge brick wall which runs around his house at the top of Seafield Avenue. They'd stopped off at the park after school, and spent an hour on the roundabout, lacing fingers and talking about Kate.

'She'll get over it,' Dante says now, squeezing her hand gently. 'And if she doesn't, you've still got me.'

Sarah bashes her head against his breast bone, letting out an annoyed little growl. 'She's such a cow,' she says.

Dante lifts her chin with his forefinger and plants a kiss on her lips.

'Honestly, this time next week you'll have forgotten all about this. Promise.'

Sarah walks a few backward steps, giving a little wave as she goes. Dante remains at the wall, watching her, and as she walks the few hundred yards back home alone her mood lifts. He's right. It's not a big deal. Soon Kate will set her sights on some other boy and forget all about it. And when that one goes wrong, she'll come running back for a shoulder to cry on. You can count on it.

As she turns into the front drive of her house, Sarah's breath catches in the back of her throat. There on the doorstep is Kate, chatting away with her dad, tossing her head and laughing.

'Ah, here she is now! Sorry, my dear, what's your name again? Dreadful memory for names, I'm afraid. Hopeless.' Sarah's father rubs his deeply lined brow.

'It's Kate,' she chirps, touching his wrist lightly.

The shingle crunches beneath Sarah's shoes, spitting out little shots of gravel as she walks up the drive towards them. When Kate turns to face Sarah, there's menace playing around her mouth.

'*There* you are! I needed to ask you about our Maths homework, Sar. Can I come in and look at your textbook?' She stands expectantly beside the doorstep, nodding subtly to Sarah, who stands dumbly looking on.

'Come on, woman! Where are your manners?' Dad scowls, beckoning Kate in. He wanders ahead of them, back up the dark hall and into his study.

As the door clicks shut, Kate raises her eyebrows and skips through the house ahead of Sarah. Before she can stop her, Kate darts into each of the downstairs rooms, looking them over and wrinkling her nose.

'Urgh. Your kitchen. It hasn't even got a window!'

There are dirty pots piled up beside the sink, where Dad hasn't washed up from breakfast and lunch. In the fruit bowl, an apple on the top has gone off, deeply cratered with a white floury mould.

Sarah guides her out of the kitchen, out of earshot. '*Shush*! Dad's working.'

'Where's your room, then?' Kate stands at the foot of the narrow stairwell. 'Up here?'

Sarah's eyes are drawn to the damp corner of wallpaper that hangs limply at the ceiling joint. Tiny black spots gather on the plaster beneath.

'Let's go up.' Kate has her hand on the banister.

Sarah can feel the pulse racing through her neck. She's afraid that Kate can see it, throbbing above her white shirt collar. Kate turns and sprints up the diamond-patterned carpet, towards Sarah's bedroom.

'Who's that?' she asks, pausing with her finger on the small black and white portrait outside Sarah's room.

'My mum,' she replies, and she urges Kate inside the room and closes the door.

'She's dead, isn't she?' Kate sits on the edge of the bed and bounces vigorously. 'Bet this bed hasn't seen much action.'

Sarah stares on, puzzled.

'Oh, don't worry, I don't really want to talk about Maths. I just wondered why you've never invited me back here before.'

Her face is challenging. There's a pause between them, and for a tiny moment Kate's eyes waver, flickering towards the floor and back.

'I don't know, really,' Sarah says, trying to keep her voice even. 'I've never been to yours either.'

Kate shrugs. 'I've been back to Teen's place loads.'

'But you only live round the corner from Tina.'

'So?' says Kate, standing abruptly and brushing off the back of her skirt as though it's picked up dirt.

Sarah takes a backward step towards the door. 'And you only moved here last year, so I just haven't got round to it, I suppose.'

Kate surveys Sarah's room with disdain. 'Nice décor,' she says, running her hand along Sarah's faded floral curtains. '*Nice*. See you at school, then.'

She breezes down the stairs and out of the front door without looking back. Sarah stands motionless on the landing, her head cocked to one side, listening as Kate crunches across the shingle driveway and clanks the gate shut behind her.

~

On Dante's birthday, Sarah tells her father she'll be home later than usual. She's joined the drama group, she tells him as she kisses him goodbye and swallows her deceit.

Their place is the beach. A couple of weeks back, as the evenings drew in, they prised open the door of one of the beach huts, brushing out the dead sand flies, chasing the spiders out into the cold. Sarah brings something new for the hut each day: a cushion, a torch, a hessian sack for a doormat. Dante places an upturned orange crate in the corner, and Sarah's paisley scarf makes a tablecloth. They talk about decorating the hut in the spring, and imagine balmy summers spent together, lying on the sand at the water's edge.

Tonight they have longer together, and she and Dante curl around each other, making covers from their jumpers and coats. The light from the torch throws a soft amber glow into the room, sending long, deep shadows up the salt-bleached wooden walls.

'This is nice,' Dante whispers into Sarah's hair. 'I love my presents.' She's given him a bottle of Aramis aftershave, bought with her discount at the chemist's, and a new black and white Afghan scarf from the market in Tighborn. 'Do I smell good?' he asks, offering Sarah his cheek. His hand moves over the small bumps of her chest, and she lets him slip it under her shirt to unhook her bra. She stiffens briefly as she fears his disappointment at her tiny breasts, but he murmurs into her hair to convey his pleasure.

Sarah pulls herself up sharp, startling Dante.

He retracts his hand as if bitten. 'What?'

'You'll never believe what Kate's been saying about me.'

'*God*, Sar. I thought you'd heard someone coming in or something.' He exhales, relieved.

'Tina told me that Kate's been going round telling everyone my dad's a pensioner, and that he's a snob. She doesn't even know him. Just because he speaks well, it doesn't mean he's a snob. And she said my house is creepy, like the Munsters' house. She told Tina that it's definitely haunted, because she reckons she's got "the gift" for that kind of thing. She said, most likely it's the restless spirit of my mum, trapped between this world and the next. And that it's no wonder I'm a complete freak, living like that – ' Sarah's voice cracks with emotion.

Dante pulls her close again. 'Why would Tina tell you all this stuff? For Christ's sake, they're just stupid little girls, Sar. Forget them.'

'*You* don't have to see them every day.'

'Thank God,' Dante says, gripping her wrist firmly. 'So,' he says, shadowing her small frame with his broad shoulders. '*For–get–a–bout–it.*' He kisses Sarah, pressing her into the cushions beneath. He runs his fingers up her thighs, hovering lightly at the cotton edge of her knickers. An involuntary thrill trickles along the back of her knees.

'I can't,' she tells him when he starts to unbuckle his jeans. She feels him pressed into her hipbone, hard and unmoving. 'I *can't*, Dante.'

Dante nuzzles into her neck. '*Sar.*'

'*No.*'

She pushes her palms against his chest and he flops against her shoulder, defeated. 'I just thought, you know, as it *is* my birthday.' He snuffles her ear playfully.

'Just not yet,' she says quietly.

Dante props himself up on one elbow and smiles down at her in their warm bed of cushions. 'The "yet" gives me some hope. You're gorgeous, Sarah Ribbons. Gorgeous and sweet and innocent.'

Sarah sits up indignantly. 'I am not "sweet and innocent"! I'm just – not a tart.'

'I didn't mean it like that, Sar.' He sits up and rearranges his T-shirt, looking worried.

Sarah pouts at him.

'You're gorgeous. That's all I meant.' He kisses her, and she smiles her forgiveness. 'Come on, we'd better get you back home.'

Outside her front gate, Sarah holds him tight. 'Happy birthday.'

He rubs his fingers into the small of her back. 'You said, "not yet". I'll sleep well thinking about that.' He closes his eyes blissfully.

'"Yet" can mean "ever", you know,' she says, prodding him in the chest.

Dante laughs, salutes her, and walks back along the street towards his own home, his new scarf floating over his shoulder in the lamplight.

'I love you,' Sarah whispers, and she watches him until he's out of view.

The night is humid, fractured with restless images which Sarah struggles to prise apart through the fog of sleep. Her father waves from the top of the beach, as she wades out into the still water of the sea. The sun is bright and hot overhead, and the beach is crowded with pale bodies and rolled-out towels. Gulls screech and soar in the clear blue sky, their chatter moving in and out of focus. Dad is gone now, and Sarah launches out into the water, balancing herself in the centre of the lilo, feeling the sun stroking her bare limbs. She lies back and closes her eyes against the light. The cool water in the grooves beneath her back warms and ripples around her, as the lilo rocks gently on the calm tide. She knows she's sleeping, can feel the weight of the sheets on her body. But she can't quite rise from the dream. The sounds of the beach become distant as the lapping water gently slaps at her arms and legs; morning gulls squawk and squabble outside her window. As she's falling, lulled, into a heavy doze, a rogue wave seizes the lilo. It sucks her back, up, up, to a terrifying height, before it sends her crashing towards the stony shallow water and the noise of the shoreline. She wakes, her breathing momentarily paralysed, her body damp with sweat.

~

On Saturday Sarah rises early for work at the chemist's shop on the High Street. She creeps about the house, quietly making breakfast, rushing out into the cold, dull morning before her father wakes.

Seafield Avenue is deserted but for the milk van she can see disappearing into a cul-de-sac at the far end of the road. The sea air is sharp, and she pulls her coat collar up, pinching it closed at the neck with a shiver. She's glad she wore her thick tights because there's always a cold blast coming in through the shop door at work, which is firmly wedged open throughout the year, whatever the weather. A trio of seagulls glides overhead, dipping down beyond the big house on the corner. Dante's house. She hears the gulls' cries travelling off into the distance, their piercing echoes bouncing through the empty streets and avenues. Sarah looks in through the gates to Dante's home, and imagines him sleeping in his bed, his heavy fringe fallen back to reveal the smooth lines of his jaw and his laughing eyebrows. With a furtive lurch of pleasure, she recalls the sensation of the crew-cut plane just above his neck, its coarse resistance pricking the smooth of her timid fingertips as they kissed beneath their coats in the hut last night.

Eventually she turns into the High Street, the sight of the chemist's shop across the road breaking into her private thoughts. She can see Mrs Gilroy, the owner, through the shop window, preparing the tills and pulling up the blinds. She's a trim little woman who wears her hair in a tight grey twist, working briskly in the pharmacy at the back of the shop, casting wafts of powder and L'Air du Temps as she weighs and counts and checks off her prescriptions. Mrs Gilroy tends to stay in the pharmacy area, just popping out to hand over medicines to her customers. The old dears seem to appreciate her personal touch, her refined reserve. After Sarah had worked in the chemist's through the summer holidays, Mrs Gilroy had offered her a regular Saturday job. 'The customers like you,' she said.

Sarah walks along the alleyway at the side of the shop, and in through the fire-escape door at the back. She hangs her jacket on the coat stand beside a teetering pile of Imperial Leather soap cartons. 'Morning,' she calls into the tiny kitchen, where Barbara and Kerry are making tea.

'Morning,' replies Kerry.

Barbara grunts without looking up. Sarah pretends not to notice, as she steps into her blue pinafore, popping the fastenings closed with sharp little clicks. The sounds from the kitchen are acute: the teaspoon against the side of a mug, the squeak of the fridge door, the whispers between Barbara and Kerry.

From the kitchen, Barbara raises her voice a little, going over the same old topic. 'I've worked here for fifteen years,' she complains. 'And Mrs Gilroy knew my Kim was after a job.'

'Oh, I know,' says Kerry.

'And she goes and gives *her* the job.'

Sarah picks up a notebook and pen, and brushes her hands down her uniform to smooth out the creases. 'I'm going out front to start stocking up,' she calls into the kitchen.

On the shop floor, Mrs Gilroy unlocks the front door and straightens the doormat. Barbara and Kerry arrive behind the tills, smiling self-consciously as Mrs Gilroy walks past them and into the pharmacy. Sarah fills a shelf halfway down the shop, while Barbara leans on the main counter, heaving into her ridiculous bosom, still moaning. Sarah will have to put up with this until the two part-timers arrive at eleven, to help cover the lunchtime rush. Barbara's always more careful what she says when it's not just her and Kerry.

Her daughter Kim is in the same school year as Sarah, but Sarah hardly knows her at all. She wears her hair in a pineapple bunch, with her eyes thickly lined with bright blue pencil and mascara. On her fifteenth birthday she'd come into the shop to show her mum the brand new, genuine gold half-sovereign ring that her twenty-year-old boyfriend had bought her.

Kerry flips open the cash register to replace the till roll, and it makes a loud cracking sound in the empty shop. Sarah looks up.

'Thinks she's something special,' says Barbara.

Sarah continues to fill her shelf, hoping that Mrs Gilroy can hear them in the pharmacy. A customer enters the shop, and hands Kerry a prescription, breaking up the gossip.

'Hello, Mrs Brading. Just your repeat, is it?' Kerry takes it into the pharmacy.

Barbara polishes the counter and glares at Sarah every now and then.

Sarah's filling the sanitary towels section, lining them up neatly in order, from 'Light' to 'Super Super Plus'. At first Barbara made Sarah look after Feminine Hygiene just to humiliate her, but now she keeps on top of it without being asked. And the contraceptives drawer. She figures that if she puts herself in charge of the most embarrassing sections, Barbara will run out of ways to torment her. After tampons, she'll probably move on to the haemorrhoid shelf behind the till.

She glances back over at Barbara, who is squeezed so tightly into her blue uniform that the poppers stretch and strain all the way down her fleshy chest.

Sarah flattens a Dr Lillywhite's carton and takes the rubbish into the stock room. Mrs Gilroy's son, John, is up on the racking as she climbs the steps for a container of Tampax.

'Alright, Sarah? How's tricks?'

'I'm OK, thanks,' Sarah answers, pointing to the box she's trying to reach.

John tucks his long hair behind his ears. 'The old banshees still giving you a hard time?'

'Who?' asks Sarah, brushing a cobweb aside.

'You know. The old miseries. I see and hear a great deal from this lofty vantage point.' He puts on a mock voice of wisdom. 'The Scottish one's the worst. Tongue of poison,' he adds, aping Barbara's accent flawlessly.

Sarah smiles. 'She really hates me. Have you heard her?'

'Ignore them. They're just jealous. Of your youth and beauty.'

John clucks his tongue and passes down the bumper box of tampons. 'How old are you, Sarah?' He holds on to the box for a second.

'You know how old I am. Fifteen.'

'Oh, yes,' he says, letting go.

'Thanks, John!' Sarah calls up, and she returns to the front of the shop.

As she's putting the last few boxes in place, Tina and her mum come through the front door.

'Sar! Forgot you were working here!' Tina looks really pleased to see her. She's wearing tight white leggings and her knees look wider than her thighs.

Her mum hands a prescription to Barbara over the counter.

'That'll be ten minutes, Mrs Smythe,' Barbara tells her.

'It's pronounced *Smith*,' Tina corrects over her mother's head.

Barbara's brow wrinkles.

'I'll wait,' says Mrs Smythe. She smiles at Sarah, before turning to browse through the Yardley display.

'You'll never believe this,' Tina whispers, tugging Sarah behind the sunglasses stand. 'You know Jo Allen? You know she hasn't been back at school since the holidays? Guess why?'

Sarah shakes her head. 'Why?'

'It all started down the youth club, apparently – screaming in agony, she was. At first they thought it was food poisoning so they rushed her to hospital, but when they got there the doctor put a stethoscope against her and said, "There's another heartbeat in there." Then Jo had another screaming fit and knocked herself out on the bench. And gave birth!'

Sarah stares at Tina. 'You're kidding me. It can't be true.'

Tina sucks in her gaunt cheeks. 'God's honest. My mum knows her mum. It's a girl. Toyah they called it. Honest to God. Ask her!'

'Wow,' Sarah says, shaking her head in disbelief.

'She should be more careful, what with AIDS and everything. My mum said it's not just gays and drug addicts who can get it now. I mean, look at Rock Hudson.'

Sarah can see Barbara creeping around the edges of the shop, staring at her for chatting.

'I've got to get on, Teen. She's giving me the evils.'

Tina twists round conspicuously. 'Fat cow,' she mouths to Sarah.

'Fat *ugly* cow,' Sarah whispers back.

At lunchtime, Sarah wanders along the High Street, window-shopping to kill time. She tries to imagine Jo Allen with a baby. Back in the summer term, she'd been asked to walk Jo down to Mrs McCabe's office at registration, because she looked as if she was going to pass out. Mrs McCabe asked Jo to take a seat, then turned and rubbed Sarah's shoulder, smiling gently. She thanked her for bringing Jo to the office; Jo had smirked, despite her fainting fit, and Sarah thought she must be putting it on. No one suspected she was pregnant, although everyone at school knew what she was like. Once, in the second year, Sarah had overheard Jo Allen telling Bev Greene about her boyfriend. When she was *twelve*. Jo and her friend were sitting in front of Sarah in Maths and Mr Nolan had popped out to fetch a new box of chalk.

'Oh, my God,' Jo said loudly. 'You should see Will's dick. It looks like a saveloy! Tastes a bit like one, too.'

The two girls had howled hysterically. At the time, Sarah had only just started wearing a training bra, and she was horrified. She'd seen a saveloy in the chip shop. It was a big, angry-looking sausage, unnaturally smooth and red. Jo looked over her shoulder and laughed.

'What's up Sarah? Never seen a knob before? *Virgin*.'

But now, Jo has a baby girl. And concussion. Poor Jo. Poor baby.

~

Art is the only subject in which Sarah, Kate and Tina are all together. They're taught by Mrs Minor, who's been at the school for decades. Sarah is petite, but Mrs Minor only reaches her nose in height. In their first lesson after half-term,

Mrs Minor reads the register slowly, looking over her half-moon glasses at each girl in turn, rolling her Rs and smacking her lips in scorn. Where she is able to, she passes a personal comment on the girls she's taken a particular dislike to.

'Have you been busy over the weekend, Marianne?' she asks.

Marianne looks up, holding her large frame self-consciously. 'Erm. Yes, miss?'

'Busy *eating*, by the look of you.'

A gasp ripples around the classroom. Marianne flushes a deep red and stares at her hands.

'*Bitch*,' hisses Kate.

Mrs Minor continues through the register. 'Kate Robson. Well look at you. *Nat-ur-al*, is it?' She points the end of her pen towards Kate's newly dyed hair.

'Yes, miss,' Kate replies with a challenging curl of her lip.

'Mmm. Well, the sun shines funny where *you* live.'

Tina keeps her head down when Mrs Minor reaches her, choosing to pass up the opportunity to correct her on her surname. The class are set a pastel still-life study. It's a vase, filled with orange and yellow carnations. The girls sit around the table with their artist boards on their laps, concentrating on the terracotta vase. Kate still isn't talking to Sarah, but Tina has been updating her on everything nasty that Kate has said. Marianne is also in their group, and Sarah can't help looking over at her, wanting to say something. She appears crushed.

'She's such a bitch,' Kate whispers to Tina, nudging her head in Mrs Minor's direction. 'Like she's a right looker, or something. She's about fifty – and look at the mad ginger bowl haircut!'

'And she's a dwarf,' adds Sarah. 'Or a midget. Which is smaller? Even I'm tall next to her.'

Kate laughs, reluctantly. Mrs Minor turns and glares at their group.

'Is she married?' asks Tina.

'Well, she's a Mrs.' Kate pulls a retching face. 'Urgh. Imagine. Poor bastard. Mind you, bet he can rest his cup of tea on her head, so at least she'd be of some use.'

Sarah puts her board down and goes to the back of the room to find an orange crayon. As she digs through the pastels box, bony fingers pinch her ribs, making her leap back.

'Looking a bit *scrawny*, Sarah.' Mrs Minor stands motionless by her side, speaking quietly. 'Your mum not feeding you?'

She gasps at the mention of her mother. Mrs Minor's expression is pinched and Sarah stares down at her, feeling her pulse racing.

'Well?'

Sarah grips the orange pastel and pulls herself up to maximum height. 'Well, you're looking a bit short, but I'm too polite to say so.' She marches back to her seat, her heart thudding in her chest.

Sarah's group turns to look back at Mrs Minor, who pretends to be tidying up the pastels box.

'What happened?' asks Kate. 'We saw her put her arm round you.'

'Nothing,' says Sarah, cautious of Kate's change of tone.

'You said something to her,' says Tina, fiddling with a hole in her thick black tights.

Sarah starts filling in her carnations. 'I told her she was a bit short.'

'Classic!' laughs Kate, leaning over to slap Sarah on the knee. 'Oh, man. You're brilliant.'

Tina snorts and gives Sarah a dry smile, and Marianne nods at her gratefully. I didn't do it for you, Sarah wants to shout, and she looks away, avoiding Marianne's gaze. The girls get on with their sketches, scribbling away at their drawing boards, smudging orange into yellow into green. No one talks much, but the group is unified in animosity towards Mrs Minor. She knows it, and she sits quite still behind her desk at the front, looking smug and raising an eyebrow to any girl stupid enough to look up and meet her eye.

When the bell rings, Sarah's group are last out of the door. They're still moaning and making fun of Mrs Minor, when suddenly she's right there among them, her black eyes moving from one girl to the next.

'Eek!' Kate cries out, startled to find her right up close at her side. Mrs Minor drops back, smirking like a midget Mona Lisa. The girls turn the corner and clatter down the wide wooden staircase. They pass Mr Settle on the stairs, in his depressing brown suit. He stands back against the handrail to let them pass, clutching his white paper bag and frowning disapproval.

'*Doughnut*,' whispers Sarah as they rush past him.

Kate laughs, looking back up the stairs to see his polished shoes disappear beyond the last rail. 'Doughnut,' she repeats, still giggling to herself.

The sun is out, so they collect their coats and lunchboxes from the lockers and head for the field where they can eat under the oak tree. Sarah's lunch is usually the same: cheese in white bread, a packet of crisps, an apple and a bottle of tap water. Kate always seems to have plenty of money on her, and most lunch breaks she races off to the canteen and returns with a synthetic cream bun, which she eats before she has her sandwiches.

'Where d'you get all your money?' asks Tina, as Kate drops her bag against the tree trunk. It's a favourite spot of theirs, far enough away from the main building, and edging on to the boy's field next door.

'My dad.' Kate runs her finger down the length of the bun, watching the strawberry jam and cream concertina up to her knuckle.

Tina nibbles away at her Ryvita and Marmite. 'Is it pocket money?'

'No. I get pocket money at the weekend. This is just for food and stuff.'

It's a wonder Kate looks so good, what with all the junk she eats. She never even has a single spot on her face.

'You're lucky,' says Tina. 'I just get two pounds a week. What about you, Sar?'

Sarah is rubbing an apple against the nylon of her green skirt. It shines up nicely. 'I've got my job at the chemist's, so I don't get pocket money.'

Kate stuffs the last of the cream cake into her mouth and stretches out her long legs. 'What d'you spend it all on?'

'Not much. Magazines. Chocolate. Clothes.'

'You buy your own clothes? You're kidding!'

Sarah bites into her apple, a satisfying wet crunch. 'At least I get to choose whatever I want.'

Kate kicks her shoes off and looks at Tina, who's still gnawing away at her cracker. 'You on a diet or something, Teen? No wonder you're so bloody skinny if that's all you're having.'

'Yeah, but I had an orange this morning. It's not like I'm starving myself.' She chucks the last corner of her Ryvita into her lunch box and snaps it shut irritably. 'My dad's just bought us a SodaStream.'

'God, they're so old hat now,' sneers Kate. 'And the Coke tastes like treacle. You're better off buying the real thing. Do you remember when your dad bought that CB radio? That was about two years after everyone else got one. What was your "handle", Teen?'

'Hong Kong Phooey,' Tina mumbles, rolling her seagull eyes.

Kate snorts with laughter. 'Hong Kong Phooey! Oh, my God, and what was your dad's? Oh yeah! I remember – '

'Kojak. He said it was 'cos he liked lollipops.' Even Tina breaks into a smile now as she folds her thin arms across her flat chest. 'But my mum said it was because he was an ugly baldy.'

'Go on, Teen – give us a bit of the lingo.' Kate leans back on her elbows, smirking.

Tina picks up her yoghurt spoon for a microphone. 'Breaker – breaker. This is Hong Kong Phooey, coming at you from Sundale Avenue. Do you read me? Over and out. 10-4, 10-4. Message received, loud and clear.'

The three girls sit side by side around the trunk of the tree, looking out across the field.

'Well, at least you've got your career all mapped out, Teen,' sighs Sarah.

'What's that, then?' asks Kate.

'Dirty trucker.'

Tina gives Sarah a soft thump with the heel of her hand, and for a few moments the three of them are harmonious, happy to be together again.

~

When they return to school after half-term, Dante and Sarah walk in together, hugging openly outside the school gates in the last few minutes before the bell rings.

'Meet you here after school?' she asks.

Dante lets go and pauses at the entrance gate to the boys' school, twiddling his ear hoop. 'Sorry, can't. I said I'd go back to Ed's tonight. We're gonna do some taping and stuff.' He holds up the carrier bag of albums he's carrying.

'Tomorrow, then?'

Dante gives her the thumbs up. 'Yeah, I'll see you in the morning. Same time, same place.' He hugs the bag of albums to his chest. 'Better go,' he says, checking his watch, and he sprints through the gates and out of sight.

When Sarah finds the others, they're in the toilets next to their form room. Kate is talking about November Night at the local youth club. Her dad runs it with a couple of the other parents, and he's given her four free tickets.

'You and Teen can have one, then there's one spare. Dunno who to give it to, though.'

Kate stretches over the sink, bringing her face up close to the mildewed mirror. She reapplies her lipstick, rotating it over the 'O' of her mouth, once, twice, three times. 'Twilight

Teaser,' she says, smacking her lips. 'My new lipstick. It's called Twilight Teaser.'

It's been raining for days now, and heavy drops rap loudly against the toughened glass windows.

'What about Marianne?' suggests Sarah, pulling down her lower eyelid and drawing on to the inner rim with her black pencil.

'You are joking!' Kate snorts. 'Teen, did you hear that?'

The sound of flushing comes from the far cubicle, and Tina comes out to join them at the sinks. She holds her mouth beneath the tap, rinses water around her teeth, then spits. 'What?'

'Sar reckons we should invite Marianne next week.'

'No way! She's so embarrassing. And completely square.'

'She's not that bad,' says Sarah. 'She's just a bit shy, that's all.'

'And completely sad,' adds Kate. 'I'm not having her dragging around, showing us up. Have you *seen* her shoes? They're like Cornish pasties!'

Kate and Tina cackle.

'Loik an old Cornish fisherman!' says Kate in a West Country accent.

'Yeah, all meaty and chunky!' adds Tina.

'And not that tasty.'

'Oh, my God,' gasps Kate. 'I'll never be able to look at her again without seeing a big meat pasty.'

Sarah half-laughs with them. 'All right, I get the picture.' She closes her bag, slings it over her shoulder and leans back into the sink with a huff. 'Who're you going to ask, then?'

'Dunno.' Kate hitches up her skirt and readjusts it in the mirror. 'Thought you might wanna ask Dante?' she says, with her eyes firmly fixed on her reflection.

Sarah looks sideways at Kate, then back at the floor. 'Yeah?'

'Mmm,' Kate ponders as she rearranges her hair in the dirty glass of the mirror. 'I suppose I could let him have a ticket.'

She turns to look directly at Sarah. 'But he'll have to buy me a Coke when we get there.'

'Are you sure?' Sarah asks the back of Kate's head as they exit the loos and amble down the cold tiled walkway towards their afternoon lessons.

'Sure. Why not?' replies Kate. They reach a fork in the corridor and go their separate ways.

~

The weekend before November Night, Sarah cooks her father one of his favourite meals.

'Superb!' He inhales deeply as she places the dish on the table in front of him. 'Poor man's banquet. Bangers, mash and a glass of good wine!' He pats his round stomach and pours himself a glass of burgundy. It glows like a jewel under the light of the overhead lamp. He swills the wine in its glass, holding it up for examination, before taking a first sip and flushing it around his mouth appreciatively.

'Care for a small glass, *mademoiselle*?' He always offers Sarah a glass, and she always declines.

'Salt?' she asks, holding it out to him.

'Naturally,' he replies.

'How's school?' he asks. 'Looking forward to your exams?'

She gives him a sarcastic smile across the table. He's in high spirits, which usually means that his research work is going well. Sarah can map out his progress through the highs and lows of his moods. Without asking, Sarah picks up his plate and fetches him the last two sausages from the kitchen.

'*Magnifique*,' he says, slicing them up into mouthfuls before stabbing a piece with his fork and holding it above the table. 'My compliments to the chef! Is the chef in the house? Chef? *Chef*!'

Sarah puts her hands over her ears and shakes her head. He's so embarrassing, even when they're alone. 'No more!' she screams, watching him pop the sausage slice into his mouth elaborately.

He stretches back into his chair to savour the last mouthfuls in silence. 'Divine,' he says eventually, closing his eyes as he links his fingers together, resting them on his full stomach. He looks like Father Christmas when he's happy like this, all white-haired and round-bellied.

Sarah clears the table and returns with two bowls of Arctic Roll. 'It was on special offer,' she tells him as he cuts into it with his spoon.

'Very good,' he says.

After a few moments' silence, Sarah rests her spoon in her bowl and looks across at her father. 'Kate's got tickets to November Night. On Friday. She's asked Tina and me to go with her.'

He licks his spoon clean and places it carefully on the table beside the bowl. *In the bowl!* she wants to yell at him, *Put it in the bowl!* His eyebrows are bunched towards each other in concentration.

'And where exactly is this November Night?' He stresses the last two words, as if they're ridiculous.

'The youth club,' Sarah mumbles, watching his face change as she speaks the words.

He shifts in his seat and props himself up on his elbows, mirroring her own posture. 'And have you seen the kind of "*youths*" that hang around outside the "*youth club*"? The "Borstal club" would be more appropriate in my opinion.'

Sarah stares into her bowl. 'They're not all like that,' she says, eventually looking up, desperate to keep the emotion from her voice.

'You're not like them, Sarah-Lou.' His voice is plaintive now, almost apologetic. 'You're a classy girl, and I don't want you throwing that away on the wrong crowd. God knows, if I'd had the money, I would've sent you to a better school. But we don't have that kind of money, and I can only thank God you've weathered the storm of Selton High.' He pauses, waiting for Sarah's response, but sees only the rage rising into her face.

He slams his fist on the table, hard enough to bounce Sarah's spoon right out of her bowl. 'The *youth club*,' he whispers, suppressing his voice. 'For Christ's sake, Sarah. The *youth club*!' He pushes his chair away from the table and strides furiously from the room.

Sarah gulps back the scream which clings to the pit of her stomach. She leaps from her seat and violently kicks her shoe at the open doorway her father just passed through.

'I'm going!' she shrieks down the hallway.

'You're not!' he booms back from his study.

Ted cowers next to the sideboard, viewing Sarah through his guilty-sad eyes. She clips the dog lead on to his collar and marches to the front door, pausing briefly with her hand on the latch.

'I am! And I'll get drunk, take drugs and have sex! Because that's obviously what you think I'll do anyway!' She slams the door behind her, and flees, down to the dark sea-front, shivering though her thin blouse and school jumper. There, beside the rusted mass of the great water pipe, she rages into the wind, drowned out by the crashing waves which smash against the gleaming pebbles, dragging them up and out before casting them aside once more.

The next morning, Dad concedes. Sarah may go to the youth club on the condition that she leaves at 10pm, at which time he will be waiting for her on the bench across the road. He agrees that under no circumstances is he to enter the club. She must keep ten pence aside for the phone box, to use in the event of an emergency. He must learn to trust her to make sound judgments when it comes to friendships. Both consent to the terms grudgingly, each equally fearful of the other's potential to punish.

When Tina and Kate call for Sarah on Friday night, her father remains in his room.

'10pm!' he shouts through the closed door to his study.

'God,' whispers Kate. 'What's up with *him*?'

'Just ignore him,' grumbles Sarah. 'He's in a foul mood.'

Kate's dad is the DJ for discos and party nights like tonight. It's not his real job, more a hobby. 'He's an estate agent,' Kate told Sarah when she first arrived in Selton. 'When we were in Branham he was the top agent in his office, which meant he always got the best bonuses. He makes an absolute fortune some weeks.' Sarah didn't really know what to say to that.

Once the girls are through the entrance, Kate rushes straight over to her dad, with Sarah and Tina in tow. He's fiddling with the disco lights at the front of the mixing desk, and he seems pleased when he looks up and sees the girls there.

'Hello, ladies!' He smiles widely, hooking his thumbs into the front pockets of his jeans. Sarah notices the small silver hoop in his left earlobe. 'Glad you could make it.' He kisses Kate and nods at Tina, before turning his slow smile towards Sarah. 'Now, I know *Tina*, of course. So that means you must be – '

Sarah feels self-conscious under his gaze. She's struck by how young he seems compared to her own father.

'You must be – *Sarah*.'

Sarah smiles back. 'Hello, Mr Robson.'

His face drops into a frown, and he shakes his head deliberately. '*Sarah*. I'm not *that* old, you know. You can call me Jason. Or Jase. Your choice, sweetie.'

Sarah turns to Kate, who rolls her eyes. Tina giggles.

'So, my lovely ladies! Give me your requests. Two each, and I'll be sure to play them for you.'

The girls huddle around the mixing desk for twenty minutes or more, debating which singles they most want to hear. The hall begins to fill up, and, having sorted out the disco lamps, Jason sprints over to the far wall to shut down the overhead strip lights.

Small clusters of boys and girls are dotted around the hall, the younger ones congregating at the tuck shop.

'That's Jo Allen's mum running the tuck shop,' Kate says, her voice lowered. 'My dad reckons she's a right tart.'

They all turn to get a better look, and see her standing behind the sweets and Tip Tops, chatting with the kids like anyone's mum.

'How does he know?' whispers Tina.

Kate shrugs. 'He just does. How do you think Jo Allen ended up like she did, knocked up at fifteen?'

'But her mum looks alright,' says Sarah.

'Well, that's what my dad says, anyway,' says Kate, as her father walks back across the hall and takes the list from her hand. They've scribbled their names next to each track. 'You'd better play them,' Kate growls, pulling a mock fist under his chin.

'Or what?' He gives her a little shove.

'Or I'll knock yer block off!' she says.

'You and whose army?'

Kate runs her fingers up through her backcombed quiff and leads the girls away, with Tina giggling uncontrollably.

'D'you think he'll play them?' Tina asks, twisting the cord strap of her shoulder bag, first this way then that. She looks back over towards Jason.

'Of course he will,' replies Kate. 'Or there'll be trouble.'

The first of Kate's requests comes on almost immediately.

'This is for a feisty young lady I know... Katie Robson! It's "Cruel Summer" by Bananarama.'

The girls cheer and sprint on to the dance floor, adjusting their outfits as they go. Sarah's wearing a black Lycra miniskirt with wool tights and a striped T-shirt. Her purple suede ankle boots are new, and the plastic soles slip on the polished floor as Kate drags her over to dance.

'Whoa!' she laughs, righting herself by grabbing at Kate's clothing.

Kate's top slips off her shoulder, revealing the black lacy bra strap underneath.

'Arghh!' shrieks Kate, pulling it back up, and the three

girls scream and dance and scan the room to see who might be watching.

By 9pm, Dante still hasn't shown up. The girls sit on the plastic seats in the far corner, munching on smoky bacon crisps. Kate and Sarah have been laughing at Tina, who's just eaten a Mars Bar and two packets of crisps.

'Bloody hell, Teen. It's all or nothing with you!' says Kate, digging her in the ribs. 'Won't make any difference, though. You're still a stick insect.'

Tina brushes the crumbs off her lap.

Kate gives Sarah a knowing look of pity when she asks if the clock above the door is accurate.

'Face it, Sar. You've been stood up.'

'*Kate*,' urges Tina, 'Don't make her feel worse than she already does.'

'I'm fine,' insists Sarah, with a casual wave of her hand. 'He'll be revising or something. Or he forgot.' She claps her hands together, aware of how false she seems. 'Anyone want a Coke?'

Jason's voice cuts across the room into their dark corner. 'I met a smashing young lady tonight, and I have a special request from her. Her name is Sarah Ribbons; the track is a classic from the seventies, and an old favourite of mine – "Sunday Girl" by Blondie!'

The girls rush to the dance floor, linking arms as they chant the lyrics together. The brightly coloured disco lights flash across the darkened room, and Sarah feels intoxicated; alive. Together they dance and spin and sing and laugh. And when the track ends, Jason plays it all over again.

Just as she promised her father, at 10pm Sarah waves goodbye to her friends from the edge of the dance floor. She stops at the coat rail in the shadowy foyer to collect her jacket. As she reaches for her khaki parka, she feels a warm hand gently stroke the curve of her neck. She turns sharply, to see Jason standing close behind her, his face half-lit by the outside lamplight.

'Thanks for coming, Sarah. I hope we'll see you again, sweetie.' His blue eyes sparkle as his face moves in and out of the shadows.

Sarah nods and runs across the empty street towards her waiting father.

~

The clock reads 08:50. Sarah is drained of energy, having been woken in the early hours by a horrible dream. In the dream, she was peering out from the covers, and she had to reach Ted, who lay on the floor of her bedroom, cut in half, alive and bleeding. She could clearly see the white wisps of fur between the toes of his paws as she tried to reach him through her paralysis. She struggled to breathe as she rose from the fog of sleep, until she realised it wasn't real at all.

Today is her first Saturday off work in weeks. She stares at the ceiling, wondering what happened to Dante last night. He'd said he was going to meet her at the youth club, but now she wonders if he hadn't wanted to go at all. With a sick lurch, she realises how young everyone was at November Night. There was no one below her year there, and no sixth formers at all. If he had been there, Dante would have been the oldest by far. Embarrassment rises to her cheeks and her stomach shudders.

'*Shit*,' she mouths at the ceiling, before kicking off her sheets in one violent motion.

In the dull November light of the downstairs hallway, Sarah bends to pick up a pale blue envelope from the doormat. She recognises Dante's handwriting immediately. She wants to rip into the envelope, but can't bring herself to open it so carelessly. She finds the little vegetable knife on the draining board in the kitchen, and uses it to carefully slit open the letter. Inside is an A4 sheet of lined paper, with a few neatly written words from Dante.

Sorry. See you at the hut at 3pm? D. x

Her blushes return as she thinks of the youth club, and she vows she'll never go there again. It's for kids, not for someone like her. She'll tell her dad later; let him enjoy being right. It's good to let him win, sometimes.

She creeps around the kitchen, so as not to wake him. She doesn't hear Ted patter in as she butters her toast, and she nearly drops the knife when he licks her toes with his small smooth tongue.

'Hello, boy! I suppose you want a walk before I go into town.' She scratches beneath his chin to make his eyes close and his mouth smile. 'Well, I think I can just about fit you in. Yes, I do!' She picks the terrier up and pulls him close, listening to him snuffle against her neck, as she recalls her nightmare dream with a sickening lurch.

She seizes him tight in her panic and whispers into the warm grey hair at the back of his collar. 'You'll be alright, boy. You're not going anywhere.'

Her father moves about upstairs, coughing and clearing his throat. Ted's ears prick up and he leaps from her arms to sprint up the stairs.

'*Hello*, boy!' says her dad up on the landing. Sarah shakes her head and turns back to the toast.

She unplugs the kettle and fills it at the sink. 'One – two – ' she counts, re-plugging the kettle and flicking the red switch down, 'three – '

'Kettle on?' Dad bellows through the house.

'Yep,' she calls back. 'Want a coffee?'

There's a pause, before he answers. 'Naturally!'

She reaches into the cupboard for a mug. One and a half teaspoons of coffee, two of sugar, one third filled with milk. Mix it before adding the water.

'Good girl,' he says as he enters the kitchen. He kisses her on the top of her head, and watches as she pours in the boiling water and stirs it rapidly. He takes the mug from her before she's even removed the spoon. 'Mmm,' he says sipping it. 'Very good.'

She leans against the sink and watches him take a few more sips before he crosses the hall and shuts the study door behind him.

'I'm going out in a while, Dad!' she calls through the door.

'Mm-hmm.'

'Into town with Kate.' She waits for his response. 'I'll be back about six?'

'Yup! OK.' Pause. 'Have you walked the dog?'

'Just about to. I'll let you know when I'm off.'

'Mm-hmm.'

Sarah sighs and returns to her bedroom to get dressed.

Kate slips a Heather Shimmer lipstick inside her fingerless glove as she and Sarah are leaving Woolworths. 'You know it's my sixteenth coming up? Well, we're having a bonfire party – next weekend.'

Sarah resists the urge to look over her shoulder for the shop staff. She wishes Kate would do her shoplifting when she's not around.

'Mum says I can have you and Tina over for the night.'

'Brilliant!' says Sarah, fumbling with the top button of her donkey jacket as they turn down a cobbled alleyway into Needle Street. 'Do I need to bring anything?'

'Nah. Dad'll do hotdogs – and I'll get Mum to buy some marshmallows.'

'Sparklers?'

'Oh, we'll have tons of them.'

Sarah shivers, clapping her gloved hands together and smiling through her chattering teeth. 'That's great. We didn't do anything on Bonfire Night this year.'

'You'll have to stand well back, though. My dad can be a bit mental with the fireworks. Reckons he's still a teenager.'

'I can't wait,' smiles Sarah as she pushes against the glass door to the Coffee Garden. They sprint up the narrow staircase and into the tiny café on the first floor. It's more expensive than

Marconi's, but the superior hot chocolate and cakes are worth the extravagance. Tina rarely joins them at the Coffee Garden, saying she prefers the atmosphere at Marconi's. But Kate and Sarah both know it's because she can't afford it. Sarah wouldn't have suggested it if Tina had been coming.

They choose one of the snug seats that look on to the side street below, in the smoking section of the café. The usual middle-aged woman takes their order. *Wendy – Proprietor*, her name badge reads. They spy out of the window as they wait for their drinks to arrive.

'Want one?' Kate holds out a packet of Benson & Hedges.

Sarah shakes her head. 'I'll have a puff of yours.'

Halfway through Kate's cigarette, Wendy places the hot chocolates on the table, with an inch of squirty cream brimming over the top. With delicate long-handled spoons they silently scoop away at their mugs, until the warm cocoa is revealed beneath.

'Man, my mum is being a bitch at the moment,' Kate sighs, laying down her spoon.

Sarah can't imagine calling her mother a bitch. 'How come?'

'I think it's since Jen left home. So now it's just me and Dad for her to have a go at. Honestly, she's either asleep, because of those bloody sleeping pills, or blowing her top at us.'

'How long is it since Jen went?'

'Almost a year – not long after we moved into the Amber Chalks house. As soon as she turned seventeen. She never wanted to move here in the first place, so she shacked up with her boyfriend, who's a complete dope-head.'

'Doesn't your dad mind?'

'He's not her dad, is he? Mum had Jen before she even met Dad.'

'Does he get on with her OK?'

'No way! She hates him, says we only moved here because of him. And she's so jealous of me, even though he's always tried to treat her like his own. She calls me "Princess Kate".

Jealous cow.' Kate runs her finger across the top of her coffee cake, making patterns around the three walnut halves. 'Some people are never happy.'

'I'd love to have a sister,' says Sarah, mopping up a spill of hot chocolate.

'It's over-rated,' Kate snorts. 'Believe me. Anyway, Mum's on at Dad non-stop now she's gone. She reckons he drove her away. I reckon it was Mum's fault, myself. Miserable cow.'

Sarah glances up at the cuckoo clock above the till. 2.30pm.

'I've got to go!' She swigs back her drink and hurries into her coat. 'I'm supposed to be meeting Dante at three.'

Kate looks incredulous. 'Even after he stood you up yesterday?'

'He didn't "stand me up". That's why we're meeting. He's really sorry. He just forgot.' Sarah digs around in her purse and places the exact money on the table. 'See you Monday!'

Kate smiles grudgingly, piling the coins up beside her plate. 'Alright. See you Monday.'

Dante's already waiting when Sarah arrives at the hut, sitting cross-legged among the cushions, listening to his Walkman.

She smiles uncertainly as she pushes the wooden door closed behind her, feeling the flush rise to her cheeks again. She reaches into her bag and pulls out a handful of dusty old nightlights she found in the camping equipment under the stairs.

'Oh, well done – I'll light them,' Dante says, jumping up to arrange them around the room. 'I've brought another blanket from home – it's freezing.'

Sarah nods and stands awkwardly in the centre of the hut. 'It's almost dark already, and it's only just gone three.'

The wind sings and whistles wildly around the hut, sending pebbles scattering loudly past its wooden walls.

Dante takes a step towards her. 'Sorry – ' he says, reaching out. The door crashes open, as wind howls through the hut, extinguishing all the newly lit nightlights.

Sarah screams.

'Bloody hell!' Dante forces the door back and pushes a heavy rock up against the frame to prevent the wind from blowing it in again. He relights the candles and flops down into the cushions. 'Right,' he says, patting the pillows beside him, 'where were we?'

Sarah folds herself down under the covers.

'I made you this,' he says, and he hands Sarah a compilation tape. 'To say sorry about last night.'

Sarah reads the back of the cassette case, which lists all the tracks he's recorded in careful black block letters. 'It doesn't matter,' she says. 'You'd have hated it anyway.'

Dante scratches his chin, then kisses her on top of her head. 'There's some classic stuff on here,' he says, taking the tape back. 'Nick Cave, Visage, Siouxsie and the Banshees. Took me hours. Actually – I might keep it – '

'No! It's great. I love it!' says Sarah, snatching it from his hands and kissing his neck. She wriggles down under the covers.

'Good,' he growls. Then he laughs madly, like Count Dracula from *Sesame Street*. '*Good*! Ha-ha-ha! Velly, velly *GOOD*! Ha-ha-ha-ha!' They wrestle under the blankets, laughing and squealing as the wind whips around the hut, hurling shingle and flotsam and brackish weed against the flimsy wooden defences of their sanctuary.

~

On Monday morning, Sarah sleeps late, only woken by the dog whining and scratching at the bedroom door.

She steps into her slippers and pulls her dressing gown tight, breathing white air into the icy hallway as she heads down the stairs to the kitchen. Her father still refuses to install central heating, insisting that a log fire and hot water bottles are more than sufficient when there's only the two of them to worry about.

'What are you doing here?' Dad frowns as Sarah squeezes past him to reach for a bowl. 'It's gone ten o'clock.'

She tuts, waiting for him to finish with the milk. There are coffee rings all over the worktop, which she knows he'll leave for her to clear up.

He takes a sip of his coffee and talks over his shoulder as he idly butters the toast. 'Shouldn't you be at school?' His white hair curls wildly around the collar of his faded dressing gown.

She looks him up and down from behind. 'Haven't you ever heard of exam revision?' she huffs.

He turns and raises his eyebrows at her, taking a bite from his toast.

'Your hair needs cutting,' she says sharply, turning back to pour a bowl of Rice Krispies.

'So you keep telling me.'

'Well, it's true. You look like a tramp. Or an old hippy. That's it. A leftover hippy from the sixties. God, it's embarrassing.' Sarah scatters sugar over her cereal, and scoops a large spoonful up into her mouth. '*Really*.'

Dad stares at her for a moment, then smiles knowingly. 'Someone got out of bed the wrong side this morning. And you don't *look* as if you're doing much revision to me, you stroppy madam.' He picks up his toast and coffee and leaves the kitchen.

'God! Can't I even have any breakfast? *For God's sake*!'

He laughs heartily from his study. 'Women! Bloody temperamental, the lot of you! It's all those complicated female hormones. An absolute mystery to us mere mortals.'

'Arghhhhhh!' she screams, hurling a teaspoon out through the doorway and into the hall. 'You – you OLD GIT!'

He laughs even louder. 'Have a good day. *Revising*.' And with that he shuts the door to his study, leaving Sarah to stew alone.

She pokes around in her English literature books, flinging them aside to fetch biscuits and chunks of cheese, reopening them to scan the words without commitment. She considers walking Ted, just for a change of scene, but decides that she can't be bothered. She turns on the TV but it's just news and some primary school programme about the journey of a baby kangaroo from its mother's womb to the pouch. The baby looks like a little grub. She watches it for a while, as she nibbles a chunk of cheese into a near-perfect circle, with her feet up on the coffee table and Ted on the sofa beside her. He stares at her cheese, licking his lips every now and then to remind her he's there. When the baby gets to the pouch, Sarah switches off the TV and picks up her books again.

After a while, Dad puts on his coat and says he's popping out. He wanders out into the hallway, patting his pockets as he tries to locate his keys.

Sarah flicks a book across the table in irritation. Why would anyone give a toss about *She Stoops to Conquer*? She's so bored she could cry. 'Where are you going?' she shouts from the living room,

'Out!' he replies, clattering about in search of an umbrella.

'But where?'

'Just out! For coffee with a friend, if you must know.'

Deborah. Sarah chews on a loose bit of thumbnail. 'When are you back?'

'Later!' The door slams behind him, sending a blast of cold air up the hallway and into the room.

She shivers and pushes the books to the floor, patting her legs for Ted to stretch out on the sofa with her. He wriggles along the length of her body, resting with his face in the crook of her shoulder. He lifts up a front leg, inviting Sarah to rub his chest.

'Lovely Ted,' she whispers, lulled by the sleepy warmth of his body. The rain starts to fall more heavily, tapping solidly against the windows outside, and Sarah feels comforted by her small dog and the rhythm of his breath. *In. Out. In. Out.*

Last night, in the beach hut, Sarah and Dante had kissed for hours before drifting off under the heavy warmth of their blankets and cushions. When Sarah woke with his head still cradled in her arms, she thought she'd never felt happier.

'What time is it?' she whispered.

Dante stirred and looked up into her face. 'It's nearly nine.'

'No!' she gasped, pushing back the covers.

'You know, I can't wait forever, Sar,' he said, propping himself up on his elbows. His dark fringe fell across half his face, so he looked at her with just the one eye. 'I've told you countless times that I love you. You know that, don't you?'

'I'm still only fifteen,' she'd replied, avoiding his eyes, scrabbling around for her shoes. 'And anyway. It's not never. Just not yet.'

'But you're so gorgeous,' he pleaded, reaching out to pull her back down.

Sarah dodged out of his reach and started to pull on her coat. She didn't want this. 'Just not yet.' She smiled, expecting a smile in return.

But Dante flopped back against the cushions, fixing his eyes on the ceiling. 'I suppose you've got to get back before Daddy notices you're late?' There was acid in his tone.

Sarah returned an angry scowl. 'He'll go mental if I don't get back soon. It's alright for you. You can go back whenever you like, and your folks'll be cool with it. My dad's just not like that.' She stood with her hands on her hips, waiting for him to look at her. 'Aren't you going to walk me back?'

Dante shrugged, throwing his arm across his brow, closing her out with his eyelids. 'In a bit.'

'Forget it,' she muttered angrily, her hand on the wooden door.

Dante's eyes remained fixed on the panels above, and, unable to bear his silence a moment longer, Sarah strode out into the cold November night, leaving the hut door to flap and crash in the wind. As she reached the top of the black beach, she could still see the dim light from the hut, and no sign of Dante rushing after her…

She lies on the sagging sofa, thinking about her mother. What would she make of all this? Sarah has no living memory of her, nothing to go on but the little black and white photograph at the top of the stairs. She swings her legs off the sofa, waking Ted, who claws at her ribs in his surprise. He follows her up the staircase and sits at her feet as she takes the photograph from the wall and holds it close to her face.

'What would you do?' she asks the face in the frame.

The grainy portrait gazes back at her, still and indistinct. She wipes the dust from the picture and returns it to the wall.

~

By the time Kate's party comes round, Dante and Sarah still haven't made up. She knows he's avoiding her because she hasn't seen him on the way to and from school, and there's no sign that he's been back to the hut since last week. The phone rang earlier, just as she was getting home from work, but by the time she'd got the door open and sprinted up the hall it had rung off. Maybe it was him.

Her father insists on driving her to the bonfire party. It's a still, black night; perfect for fireworks. The car chugs along as Sarah quietly fumes, feeling irritable and embarrassed about being chaperoned. Sometimes he behaves as though she's nine or ten.

'It's not you I don't trust; it's other people,' he says as they turn into Kate's cul-de-sac on the new Amber Chalks housing estate.

'Not everyone is a rapist or murderer, Dad. I'd have been just as safe if I'd cycled.'

'Well,' he replies, squinting through the cloudy windscreen as if he's got a nasty smell up his nose, 'better safe than sorry.'

She persuades him to drop her at the pavement outside the house, rather than walking her to the door as he'd like to.

It's a large modern building on a large modern estate, with a big grassy play area opposite the house. Kate once told her that they got the biggest garden in the street, because of her dad's job at the estate agent's. 'Perks of the job,' she said. Sarah notices all the shiny new cars parked in the neat driveways along the road.

'Bloody Wimpey,' mutters Dad.

'What?' Kate's wrestling with the seatbelt, which is caught up between the seats.

'Wimpey homes. A blot on the landscape. Look at them. Little boxes.' He breaks into song. '*And they're all made out of ticky-tacky. And they all look just the same.*'

'Don't be such a snob, Dad!' hisses Sarah. 'God!'

'I'm not being a snob,' he replies, releasing Sarah's seatbelt with a simple click. 'I'm an aesthete. Which is an entirely different thing altogether.' He pushes his tweed hat back on his head and puckers up for a kiss.

Sarah growls, throwing open the door of the old Citroën and dragging her bag over from the back seat. 'See you tomorrow.'

When she slams the car door, flakes of rust scatter on to the road.

Dad calls out through the closed window. 'Mind the Dyane! She's a collector's piece!'

Sarah turns and walks up the path, hoping that they can't hear him from inside Kate's house.

'What time will you be back tomorrow?' calls Dad, leaning across and jerkily rolling down the passenger window.

'*I don't know*! By lunchtime.' She scowls as he winds the window back up. '*Go*!' she mouths at him, and she stands in Kate's front path until the rust-bucket disappears around the corner and out of view. '*Idiot.*'

The front doorbell plays a tinny version of Big Ben, which Sarah can hear ringing out in Kate's hallway when she pushes the little plastic button. The light above the entrance is bright white, and Sarah feels small and exposed as she waits for Kate to answer. She can faintly hear the sound of canned laughter through the door; perhaps they're all in the living room watching TV. Voices drift from the back of the house, and she wonders if she should just go around the side gate. But she's never visited before, so it might be rude. Just as she's about to press the bell again, the door opens and it's Jason, Kate's dad, looking as if he's on his way out.

'Jesus! Sorry, Sarah. I didn't expect to see you there. Come on in!' He steps back to let her through, fastening the buttons of his jacket with leather-gloved hands.

The hallway is small and light and comfortable, with soft carpet underfoot. Sarah shudders inwardly as she recalls Kate poking around in her own crummy hallway, with its ancient patterned carpet and woodchip walls. Kate's home is clean and new. No ghosts here.

'Right! I'm off to the Co-op to pick up some more Coke and crisps. Apparently we don't have enough. According to *Princess Kate*, that is.' He winks at Sarah, as if it's their little secret.

Sarah feels the creep of heat rising up her neck. 'Um,' she says, gesturing towards the stairs.

'Oh, yeah. Sorry, sweetie.' Jason leans on the banister and hooks one thumb in his jeans pocket. 'Katie! *KATE*! Sarah's here, darlin'!'

Kate's feet appear at the top of the stairs, trotting down in pink slippers.

'See ya!' says Jason, and he closes the door behind him.

Kate jumps off the third step and hugs Sarah. 'Sar! Hope the old man didn't embarrass you?'

Sarah's stomach judders.

'Who? My dad?'

'No, you div. *My* dad. Bring your stuff up. You and Tina can sleep on the floor in my room. I've got my own futon now, for when friends stay or just for lounging about on. It's cool. Folds down in seconds. It's a proper one from the Futon Company in London. Not one of those cheap fakes.'

Kate's room is exactly how Sarah might have imagined it. Primary-coloured bedsheets, her own dressing table and posters all around the walls. The room must be the size of Sarah's living room. Kate turns the volume up on her hi-fi, so that they have to shout over the music.

'Who's this?' yells Sarah, nodding at the hi-fi.

'*Dead or Alive*. Like my new poster? Morten Harket. Lush.' Kate jumps up on to her double bed and kisses Morten on the lips.

Sarah screams as the bedroom door opens abruptly. She stands frozen in the middle of the room, still clutching her overnight bag.

'Kate!' Her mother is leaning into the room, looking harassed. 'Kate! I've been calling you for ten minutes! Turn that bloody music down!' She doesn't even look at Sarah.

Kate leans over and turns down the music. 'What? Did you say something? I didn't catch any of that.' She's smirking. 'The music was too loud.'

Her mum looks ready to thump her. 'Come and help me with the food. *Please*.'

Kate points at Sarah. 'Have you met my mum yet?'

'Hello,' Sarah smiles awkwardly.

'Hi. Now, come and give me a hand, Kate!' She stomps out, running a hand through her unruly peppered hair. She's nothing like Sarah had imagined.

Kate puts her head to one side, listening as her dad comes back in through the front door.

'I'll get on with the fire, Patty,' he calls out.

'Do what you like,' she calls back.

Kate whacks up the volume again and jumps to her feet, bouncing lightly on the bed. 'Now where was I? Oh, yeah.' She starts licking Morten Harket from head to toe.

Sarah sings along to the music with her hands on her hips, punctuating each 'a-ha, a-ha' with a pelvic thrust and a toss of her hair.

Kate's screaming with laughter, joining in the pelvic thrusts. 'Please sir, can I have some more? More-ten Harket that is!'

'More! More! More!' chants Sarah.

The girls leap around the room, screaming, 'More! More!' until Kate's mum strides into the room, unplugs the stereo and drags Kate out of the room by her elbow. Sarah reins in her nervous laughter and follows them down the stairs to help with the salad.

'Sorry about the music,' she says as they enter the kitchen.

Kate's mum smiles briefly, and passes her a bowl to pour the crisps into. 'Hear that, Kate? You could learn a thing or two from Sarah.'

When Kate's mum turns her back the two girls pull faces at each other, stifling their laughter and chomping on crisps. Sarah can see Kate's dad through the back window. He's standing on the edge of the patio, leaning on a garden fork, drinking a can of lager. The light from the kitchen window illuminates his back, throwing a tapering shadow out into the darkness of the long garden.

Kate scrapes the chopped lettuce into the salad bowl and holds it out towards her mum. 'Do you think that's enough?'

'Suppose so.'

'What do you think, Sar? Is it enough, or do we need *more*?'

'*More*?' Sarah raises her eyebrows. 'More-ten Harket?'

'I don't even like salad,' shrieks Kate. 'But I'd like a bit of *Morten*!' Kate and Sarah descend into hysteria again, holding their stomachs and staggering into the worktops.

'Go on, then,' says Kate's mum. 'You might as well piss off outside.' She turns back to the sink to wash her hands.

Sarah looks at Kate in surprise, but Kate doesn't even flinch.

'Come on, then. Let's see if Dad's got the sparklers.'

In the garden Jason's stoking a bonfire at the far end of the lawn. It's almost as high as their shed, and Jason leaps back as sparks burst out in his direction. He jogs towards the girls, silhouetted by the orange blaze, and stops in the middle of the lawn, leaning on his garden fork.

'Come to give me a hand?'

'Yeah,' says Kate. 'Don't think Mum wants us hanging around in there.'

Jason gives the fork a wiggle. 'Right, then. You two can help me with the seating plan.'

'Seating plan?' asks Sarah, looking at Kate as if her dad is a bit touched.

'Why not? Follow me, girls, follow me!' He marches between them towards the house and stops beside a pile of sliced tree rounds.

'They're tree stumps,' says Sarah.

'*Exactement*! Got them from this house we just sold. The new owners wanted shot of the tree in the back garden. So when they had it chopped down, I said I'd get rid of the wood. Genius, eh?'

Jason flips three of the stumps on to their sides and starts to roll one back down towards the bonfire. The girls follow, rolling their stumps too, purposely bashing them into each other like giant bowling balls.

'About five or six foot from the fire, I reckon. You got someone else coming, Katie?'

'Yeah – Tina.'

'Then we need two more, one for her, one for your mum.' Jason goes back to tending the fire, poking and jumping back like a schoolboy at the hearth.

'I'd forgotten about Tina,' Sarah says to Kate as they go back for the last stumps. 'She's late, isn't she?'

'Yeah. She's always late.'

Always. 'Does she come over a lot?' asks Sarah, feeling an unexpected pang of envy.

Kate flips the log on to its side. 'Quite a bit. You know, she only lives round the corner. On the council estate at the back of our development. It's pretty rough round there; I feel quite sorry for her, really. She's always having to look after her little brothers, so I don't like to say no when she wants to come over. But she can be a bit of a pain sometimes, you know, if I want to be left alone. Anyway, she's always late.'

Sarah turns her stump over, mashing her thumb into a hibernating snail. 'Urgghhh!' she screams. 'Snail! Oh, God! It's a snail!' She holds her hand up to the light, to see the whole snail impaled on the end of her thumb.

Kate squeals. 'Arghh! You look like Little Tom Thumb!'

They both scream as Sarah runs back towards the house, shaking her hand violently to send the ruined snail hurtling to the patio with a little crack.

'Murderer!' shouts Kate. 'Snail masher! Murderer!'

Sarah's still got her thumb held out in front of her as if it's infected, laughing as Kate dances round her, pointing accusingly.

'Evil murderer! Snail slayer!' She crouches to get a better look at it. 'Best finish it off, I s'pose,' she says. And with that she rises and stamps on the quietly writhing blob with a simple sharp step.

'No!' shouts Sarah, bringing her good hand to her mouth, to cover her laughter and disgust.

The back door opens with a squeak and Kate's mum leans out, seeing Tina through to the back garden. Tina waves at the two girls with both hands and smiles over her shoulder as Kate's mum pulls the kitchen door shut. 'Thanks, Patty,' she says. *Patty*.

'Teen!' shouts Kate, rushing to hug her. 'You made it, then?!'

'Yeah, soz. My mum had one of her migraines and I had to wait for her to wake up, 'cos I was looking after the twins. D'you want your present?'

'Nah. Save it till later – we've got to roll these stumps down to the bonfire.'

As they place the last two logs around the fire, Jason comes round from the back, dusting off his jacket. 'Hello, Tina, love.'

Tina giggles.

'You're so weird, Teen,' mutters Kate, as they sit on their little gathering of tree stools.

'He just makes me laugh,' whispers Tina. 'I don't fancy him or anything dodgy like that. He's just funny.'

'Who said you fancied him?'

'No one. But you always make out like I do.' Tina's whining now.

'No, I don't! Urghh! That *would* be weird.'

Tina brings her knees up to her chest and wraps her arms around them, shivering. 'Keep your voice down! He'll hear you and then it will be weird.'

'Well, if you've got nothing to hide...' says Kate in a taunting voice.

'Yeah,' Sarah joins in. 'If you're sure you don't fancy him...'

Tina shoots her a sharp glance.

Jason sits on the stump beside them, holding his can of lager. 'Fancy who?' he says. 'I suppose you girls are talking about your many admirers, eh?'

Tina sniggers. Sarah and Kate exchange a blank expression.

'Bet you're beating them off with sticks. Blimey, I remember what it was like when I was your age. All I could think about was girls. Girls, girls, girls. It's a surprise I got anything else done at all. I was quite a hit with the ladies, you know.'

Tina can hardly look at him for giggling.

'You think he's joking, Teen, but he really means it. Saddo.'

'Oh, yes,' says Jason, standing and hitching up his jeans proudly. 'Queuing up round the block, they were.' He winks at Sarah and gives Kate a little punch on the arm.

'Oh, no,' moans Kate, putting her hands over her face. 'I can't bear it.'

'Right! I'll go and get myself another lager, then. Expect your mum'll have the food ready in a mo.' Jason strides up the garden and in through the kitchen door.

From where they sit, Sarah can see Jason and Patty together in the kitchen. Patty's still at the sink, and he kisses her on the cheek before opening the big fridge-freezer in the corner. Patty carries on at the sink without looking up. A few moments later, Jason calls the girls to fetch their food, and they load up hot dogs and crisps and cups of Coke before returning to their seats around the fire. Jason sits a little way from them, eating and stoking the fire in turn. He opens another lager and drops the ring-pull into the empty can by the side of his log.

'Your mum not coming out?' asks Sarah between mouthfuls.

Kate shakes her head, glancing at the empty seat beside her dad. 'She hates the cold. And she's a grumpy cow.'

Jason pretends not to hear as he lights up a cigarette with a loud click of his Zippo lighter. He inhales deeply and blows the smoke in a cool stream above his head, where it's whipped up and away with the smoke from the bonfire.

Kate looks back towards the house. 'God, I wish she'd do something about her hair. It's embarrassing.'

The others turn to look through the window at Patty, who's busy wiping down the worktops.

Kate pulls a disgusted face. 'She looks like Ken Dodd.'

Sarah gasps. 'No, she doesn't!'

Jason frowns at Kate with mild disapproval.

'Your mum's lovely,' says Tina, trying to wipe away the blob of ketchup she's squirted down her pale grey jacket. She glances at Jason to check he hasn't noticed.

'Lovely to you, maybe,' replies Kate. She stares into the flames.

Sarah watches Kate, following the reflection of the fire as it leaps and dances in the glass of her eyes.

No one speaks for a while, until Jason jumps up and dashes back towards the house, pausing to crush his cigarette stub under his heel at the edge of the patio. He returns carrying three cans of cider, dangling from his little finger by a plastic loop as he balances the cassette player and a pile of tapes in his arms. An extension lead trails behind him all the way back to the house.

'Disco mix, anyone?' He grins, handing the cans to Kate, and sets up the cassette player on the seat meant for Kate's mum.

'Nice one, Dad!' Kate tugs on the ring-pull of her can, passing one to Sarah and Tina. She bops up and down on her seat to Cyndi Lauper, and Tina starts giggling again as she joins in, singing along to the music with Sarah.

Their breath puffs out white into the cold night air, and the moon is just off the full circle, draped with wispy clouds. Sarah can feel every nerve in her body. Jason is eating another hot dog, leaning on to his knees, smiling at the girls. The next song is 'Joanna' by Kool & The Gang, and they know all the words to this one too. Even Jason joins in, and the girls make microphones out of their forks, swaying and singing with their eyes closed.

'Jason!' shouts Kate's mum, breaking into the calm of the night. She's flung open the back window and is leaning out looking annoyed. 'Jason!'

'Oh, blimey,' he says under his breath. 'Looks like I'm in for a bollocking.' He makes a fearful face behind his hand, then replies, 'What is it, Pats?'

'You've wedged open the back door with your bloody extension lead. While you're busy playing Prince Charming, I'm freezing my tits off in here!'

The girls snort with laughter and Patty looks even more furious than before.

'Oh, come on, Pats, it'll only be for a bit longer. I'll be doing the fireworks in a sec. Give me five minutes, OK?'

Patty pulls the window shut with a clunk and glares out of it while she tidies around the sink.

'Women, eh?' Jason says. 'Can't live with 'em; can't live with 'em.'

'Shut up, Dad,' Kate laughs. She turns to Sarah and Tina and whispers, '*Down in one.*'

They throw back their necks and swallow the cider in large gassy gulps, glug-glug-glug, until Kate crushes her can in her hand and throws it over her shoulder victoriously.

'Steady on, girls,' says Jason.

Sarah chokes and splutters, spraying cider out sideways and descending into giggles as she places her empty can by her side, discreetly covering her mouth to conceal a small belch. Tina nips off to the loo, tiptoeing across the grass like a long thin shadow against the light of the kitchen window. The fire roars and spits momentarily as a fleeting breeze passes through the garden.

Kate throws a crust of bread at her dad, bouncing it off his knee. 'So what about these fireworks?'

Jason finishes his lager, and stands, brushing himself down. 'OK. Tell you what. You go and get the fireworks and me and Sarah can move the logs back away from the lawn.'

Kate sprints off to find Tina and fetch the fireworks from the box room. Sarah bends and rolls her tree stump back towards the fence where Jason has indicated. As she flips it over, Jason bumps into her, catching her around the waist with one hand.

'Oops. Sorry, love,' he says, bringing his second hand to the other side of her waist. They're in the shadows.

'Oh,' says Sarah, stepping back.

He keeps his hands on her waist, and gives her a squeeze. 'You're a slim little thing, aren't you?' he says, then he turns and walks back across the garden to fetch another log. Sarah's glad the garden is in darkness, to disguise her blushes. She can still feel the imprint of his large hands around her ribs.

'Haven't you finished yet?' Kate calls out as they return with the fireworks.

'Nearly there!' Jason replies, 'We almost had a collision, didn't we, Sarah, love? Nearly there!'

Once he gets started on the fireworks the girls coo and scream as the coloured lights fill the sky. Kate's mum still doesn't come out and join them. They end the evening with sparklers and marshmallows on sticks, until Patty bangs on the window, beckoning them in.

Jason gives the dying bonfire a final prod, and throws a last stick into the embers.

'Alright, girls. It's half-ten. Time to call it a day.'

At the base of the stairs, Kate gives her dad a hug before she dashes up ahead of Tina and Sarah. 'Night, Dad,' she calls over her shoulder.

Tina follows her up, with Sarah behind.

'Night, girls,' says Jason.

She feels his hand pat her backside lightly, and she spins round.

Jason winks up at her boldly, leaning his elbow on the final stair post. 'Sleep tight,' he says.

Sarah runs up the stairs and into Kate's bedroom.

~

On the first Saturday in December Mrs Gilroy asks her to stay behind and help John to put up the Christmas decorations. When all the other shop assistants have left, Mrs Gilroy switches off the main lights and disappears into the back office to do the paperwork, leaving John and Sarah to get on with the front window.

Sarah starts to empty out the current display, while John fiddles around at the back till, loading a tape into the cassette player under the counter.

'What're you putting on?' she calls over her shoulder.

John walks back towards the window, carrying a big cardboard box full of tinsel and decorations. 'Christmas crap,' he says as the first track starts to play. It's Band Aid: "Do They Know it's Christmas?"'

'Brilliant!'

She takes the box from him and slides it up against the opening to the window display.

He laughs, sprinting back up the shop. 'How can you listen to this stuff? I can't believe you like it.'

'I don't! But it's compulsory listening for when you're decorating Christmas trees or wrapping presents. She sings purposely off key and waves her arms above her head.

'Nice,' says John, returning with a box of Maltesers and two cups of tea. Sarah helps herself to a chocolate and they get to work, putting together the little fake tree, bending its wiry branches out until it looks vaguely presentable.

'It's a bit shabby round the edges,' says John, balancing it on a small stool in the corner of the window. He stands back and stares at it critically. 'I think it's seen better days.'

She puts her hands on her hips and looks at the tree too, dropping another Malteser into her mouth. The tree creaks and falls back into the shop, snapping off a branch as it hits the floor. 'I dunno. I think it's fine.'

They manage to wedge it upright by tying a length of string from the stool to the base of the tree, before spreading the decorations out on the floor. After a while a comfortable silence descends, and John works at the tree while Sarah wraps empty boxes with gold paper and ribbon, to create a *faux* gift scene inside the window.

As John occupies himself winding the coloured lights around the little tree, Sarah stretches across him and ties a pair of big red baubles to the top of his ponytail, giggling to herself through a mouthful of chocolate. He stands up and reaches round to work out what she's done.

'Oi!' he says, trying to undo it. 'It'll look like I've got a big knob on the back on my head!'

She howls with laughter, spinning him round to take another look. 'It does!'

'Aarghh! Get these big bollocks off me!' he laughs, frantically trying to untangle the baubles. He hides his face in his hands as a group of kids walk by on the other side of the glass, pulling monkey faces and pointing at his head. Eventually, he gives in and they finish dressing the window, with John's baubles still in place, lightly clacking together every time he moves his head.

'Here,' Sarah says, when they've finished, putting her hand on his shoulder to turn him towards the window. She gently unties the baubles and smoothes out his hair.

'Thanks,' he says, taking one of the baubles from her and hanging it on the tree.

'Pleasure,' she replies, hanging the second bauble next to his so that they almost touch.

He looks at her uncertainly, as if he's about to say something important.

'*Parumpapumpum*,' she sings, turning away swiftly to avoid his eyes. She pops the last Malteser in her mouth and starts to pack up the leftover decorations.

'I'll get the dustpan and brush,' he says after a pause, and he walks back up the shop, his soft suede desert boots squeaking with every step.

~

It's the last day of term and Sarah, Kate and Tina meet at the school gates to walk into town for hot chocolate in Marconi's. It's full of Selton High School pupils, out celebrating the start of the Christmas break, and the queue along the counter stretches all the way to the door. The noise is instant, the moment they walk through the steamed-up door: a steady clamour of teaspoons on crockery, adolescent banter and kitchen clatter. A tidy group of sixth form boys sits just inside the door. The boys look up, assessing the girls and turning back to each other, casually raising approving eyebrows. They drink coffee, with no cakes or biscuits. Their returning gaze makes Sarah feel juvenile in her school uniform and flat slip-on shoes. The queue is slow, and as they wait she inadvertently catches the eye of one of the boys, who's pulling a vomit face at his friend and indicating towards Tina.

Sarah looks at Tina, who is oblivious to the attention, scratching away at the skin between her fingers. She's so pale. There's something about her that reminds Sarah of a Jacob's cream cracker.

'Is there anywhere to sit?' asks Sarah, pulling off her gloves and standing on tiptoes to see past the throng of green uniforms.

Kate is looking too, drawing her fingers down through her fringe, her eyes flitting from one boy to the next. 'Go down the back and see if you can bagsy a seat. We'll get the drinks in – want a cake?' She's noticed the boys to their right and her mouth turns up slightly at the corner.

'Flapjack,' Sarah replies, pressing some coins into Kate's hand, and she moves down through the crowded café until she finds a small table for four beside the alleyway window at the back. She hops up on to the chair to wave to the others.

Kate gives her a thumbs-up.

Sarah plucks a paper napkin from the stainless steel box on the table and runs it across the formica top to sweep the crumbs on to the floor. She can see some girls from her French group over on the other side of the café, giggling and dunking shortbread into their hot chocolates. There's tinsel draped around their necks like garlands and one of them has tiny silver baubles hanging from her earrings, which swing and rotate every time she moves her head. They all look so young. Make-up-less and natural-haired. She gathers up her own hair and inspects the ends, wishing they'd gone to the Coffee Garden instead.

Through the window in the alleyway, pedestrians walk back and forth with shopping bags and pushchairs. A young woman further along the path wrestles with her red-faced toddler, who rigidly screams and refuses to get up off the pavement. Eventually, the mother scoops the child up under her arm and marches along the path towards Sarah. As she passes, Sarah sees that she's only about nineteen or twenty, and her expression, nakedly exposed in the privacy of the alleyway, is one of pure despair. She disappears from view, replaced by a leisurely snake of school kids and sixth formers on their way home for Christmas.

Sarah realises too late that Dante is among them, strolling along the alleyway with his hands in his pockets. Her heart lurches momentarily. They haven't spoken since they last argued, and she's told herself that he will have to make the first move if he wants to make up. Everything slows down, and as he progresses towards her their eyes lock, but his expression doesn't alter. There's no smile, no warmth. He just looks at her straight and walks on past the window and out of sight.

Tina puts the tray down on the table with a rattle. 'Your hot chocolate's a bit spilt,' she says. 'Some plank knocked the tray when I was walking through.' She sits opposite Sarah and pulls the tray along, yawning.

'Where's Kate?' Sarah asks.

'Chatting up some sixth former down by the door,' Tina replies, licking the sugar off her jam doughnut.

'Really?'

Tina pulls an indifferent face and pours two spoonfuls of sugar into her hot chocolate.

'Hasn't it already got sugar in it?' asks Sarah.

'I like it sweet,' she says. 'It warms you up.'

Kate joins them, waving a torn piece of lined paper in the air with a satisfied smile. 'His name's Christian,' she says, taking her mug. 'What a great name.'

'Maybe he is one,' says Sarah.

'What?'

'A Christian.' She peers into Kate's cup.

'It's coffee,' Kate says.

'You don't drink coffee,' Sarah laughs.

'Who says I don't?'

There's a moment of silence between them, while they stir their cups and nibble at their cakes.

Sarah picks up the slip of paper. *Christian 677898.* Kate smiles and snatches it from her. 'He's lush, isn't he, Teen?'

Tina nods.

'And he's definitely not a Christian. I'd be able to tell. We might go out over the holidays. He's going to phone me, but I thought I should get his number just in case.'

'I just saw Dante,' says Sarah. 'Through the window.'

Kate drops her slip of paper and leans into the table. 'Who was he with?'

'No one.'

'Did he see you?'

'Yep.'

'And?'

'Nothing. He didn't smile or wave or anything. He just looked at me and kept on walking.'

Kate and Tina are wide-eyed. 'What a bastard. If he's finished with you, he should at least let you know.' Kate suddenly laughs. 'What a *bastard*.'

Tina scratches her eczema, shaking her head. 'That's really bad, Sar. You should forget about him.'

The crowd in the café is starting to thin out a little and Sarah can now see the sixth form boys down at the front. They're standing to leave. One of them turns and looks over to where they're sitting. Kate jumps up and waves; he puts up a cool hand and exits through the steamy front door. She sits down, her silly bosom jiggling excitedly as she bounces her knees under the table.

'So, presents?' she says, taking a swig of coffee and wrinkling her nose.

The girls reach into their bags and each place two presents on the table in front of them. They open Tina's first. She gives Sarah a bar of Fruit and Nut chocolate, and Kate a long jade necklace. 'I know how much you like jade,' she says. 'But don't wear it round my house, in case my mum sees it.'

'Did you nick it off your mum?' asks Kate.

Tina smacks her lips together. 'She never wears it.'

Kate puts it round her neck, wrapping it twice.

'Looks nice,' Sarah says.

Sarah gives them both the same thing, a handmade beaded leather pouch, containing a small bottle of perfume she bought from the chemist's. 'I made the pouch. They've got loads of really nice leather remnants in the bead shop. Thought you could use it for jewellery or something.'

Tina looks really pleased, and is already dabbing the perfume behind her ears.

'Sweet,' says Kate, dropping it quickly. 'Now *look* what I got you!'

Sarah can tell from the weight of the small tissue-wrapped parcel that it is a gift of greater value than those she gave. She unwraps the paper, to reveal a beautiful plum-sized silver frog, hinged at the back to reveal a secret compartment. Tina has a ladybird version.

'They're gorgeous!' says Tina. 'Where'd you get them?'

'Newcombe's silver department. Good, eh?'

'Thanks, Kate. It's *so* lovely.' Sarah turns it over in her hands, inspecting the smooth lines and delicate markings.

'Did you nick 'em?' asks Tina.

'Of course,' says Kate proudly.

They all laugh. Tina clears up the cups and plates and carries the tray back down to the counter.

Kate twizzles the necklace around her finger and gives Sarah a little nudge. 'It's not even real jade, you know,' she whispers, pulling a face at the back of Tina's head. She lets the beads fall back against her chest. 'It's bloody *plastic*.'

~

Sarah works in the chemist's every day of the holidays in the run-up to Christmas. On the first day, she passes Dante's house, furtively glimpsing through the metal gate as she slows her pace. There's no sign of anyone, and she can't see his dad's car in the drive. She wonders if they've gone away. It's over a month since they argued, and they still haven't spoken. She's still mad with him, but starts to wonder if she over-reacted. Or maybe he did. As she turns on to the Parade, she sees Kate and Tina outside Marconi's.

'Kate!' she calls out, breaking into a jog. The path is icy and she slips, throwing her arms outwards to stay upright.

Kate grins.

'Didn't expect to see you at this time in the morning. What're you up to?' Sarah asks.

'Christmas shopping! Thought we'd beat the crowds if we came early.' Tina shakes her purse in front of her. 'We're getting a drink first.'

'Wish I could come,' Sarah says, glancing over the road at the chemist's. 'I've got to work. I won't be buying *any* presents if I don't.'

Kate nods at the blue A-line pinafore hanging out from beneath Sarah's coat. 'Yeah, I saw you had your nice dress on. Never mind, we'll be thinking of you when we're in Dotty P's trying on our New Year's Eve outfits.'

'I've seen this amazing dress,' Tina says, stamping her feet on the pavement to keep warm. She doesn't have any gloves on and her little knuckles are almost grey. 'It's really short, Lycra, with electric-blue sequins all round the neck and bottom. It's gorge!'

'What're you doing for New Year?' Sarah asks, looking back over at the chemist's. It's nearly 8.45.

Kate raises her eyebrows. 'I reckon my dad might agree to a party at ours.'

'Really?' Tina and Sarah say together. They laugh.

'Maybe. You're gonna be late, Sar.' Kate pushes open the door to Marconi's. 'See you later!'

Sarah dashes across the road, checking her watch as she goes. She sees Barbara and Kerry a bit further along the pavement, also making their way to work. As she rushes into the alleyway at the side of the chemist's, she steps on to a thick sheet of black ice created by the leaky guttering overhead. She crashes to the floor, thumping heavily on to her side, spilling the contents of her shoulder bag across the pavement.

The two women turn into the alleyway and Barbara shrieks with laughter. 'Have a nice trip?' she asks Sarah, casting a wide shadow across the ground.

Sarah's arm is in agony, and she can't even feel her thigh. Barbara steps over her, smirking, whilst Kerry follows sheepishly. Sarah tries to push herself up with her other arm.

'Hey!' John shouts, entering the alleyway just before Barbara and Kerry disappear around the corner. 'Hey! You don't just leave someone lying there!'

The two women scuttle around the back and in through the fire door.

John hunches down and helps Sarah to her feet, taking her weight as she limps into the stock room at the back of the shop. 'Did they just step over you?' asks John, helping Sarah on to a chair. He's shaking his head. 'You wait till I tell my mum. Nasty, petty...'

Barbara comes out of the kitchen. She doesn't look in their direction, but stomps towards the front of the shop with her face turned absurdly high.

'Right, that's it,' says John, and he marches out to the pharmacy and returns with his mother, Mrs Gilroy.

Mrs Gilroy sends John out of the room and asks Sarah to roll down her tights so she can take a look at her injury. Already there's a dark bruise forming, the size of a saucer. Mrs Gilroy rubs arnica cream into it vigorously. She checks Sarah's arm, to make sure there's no break. Sarah can't remember such pain since she took a rounders ball in the shoulder in the fourth year. Mrs McCabe let her sit in her office for an hour with an ice pack pressed against the swelling, and they chatted together as the nurse pottered around sorting out her paperwork. Mrs McCabe had only just started at Selton High and she told Sarah about her last post at a small private girls' school where they taught lacrosse and polo. 'I'm used to these sorts of injuries,' she said, lifting up the ice pack to check on the bruising. Her neat blonde hair curled on to her face as she inspected the bruise and Sarah wondered how old she was. Her face looked so smooth and clear in the dusty light of the room. Sarah hadn't wanted to return to class for the afternoon, but Mrs McCabe smiled and said she'd be expected back. 'Believe me, I'd like nothing more than to keep you here chatting,' she'd said as Sarah stood up to go, and she gave her good shoulder a little pat as she left the room.

It's a shame Mrs McCabe's just a nurse at the school; she'd make a far better teacher than most of the ones they have to put up with.

'I think you should go home and put your leg up for the day,' Mrs Gilroy says, with her hand resting on Sarah's arm.

'No! Really, I'm fine. Really.' Sarah moves her arm around in circles to demonstrate.

'Mmm.' Mrs Gilroy puckers up her raspberry-lipsticked lips, before calling John back into the stock room. 'We've got the big Christmas order in today, haven't we, John?'

'Yup.'

'Need a helper?'

He breaks into a smile. 'Yeah – I really do, actually. I'll never get it all unpacked myself.'

'Fine. So, Sarah, you can work out here with John today. If you feel even slightly unwell, you're to go home. Understood?'

'Yep. I'm fine!' Sarah tries not to look too pleased, but it's hard.

'I'll let you get on with it, then.' Mrs Gilroy returns to the pharmacy, leaving the ghost of L'Air du Temps in her wake.

'What'll she do? About Barbara and Kerry?' Sarah asks John.

'Oh, nothing much. But they'll know she knows.'

When the delivery arrives, Sarah climbs into the racking as John passes boxes up to store away. She can feel her thigh bruise throbbing beneath her tights as she settles on to the top platform, and she gives it a sturdy rub as she adjusts her position to get comfortable. They make a good team: as soon as he climbs the steps with another package, Sarah appears at the edge ready to take it from him. The conversation is easy as they work, and John tells her all about his year at university, and his six months travelling after he dropped out.

'You'd love New Zealand,' he says. 'Everything's so simple there. We worked all day on the farm, and it's bloody hard work, then in the evening everyone came together in a big team to make the food. Then you've got the rest of the night to chill out, smoke, listen to music, write letters home. I want to go back next year, when I've saved up.' John passes Sarah a carton of disposable razors. 'They go at the back, top left.'

'What made you leave university?' she asks, pushing the box into place.

'My dad died.'

There's a pause between them. 'Oh. What of?'

'You know, cancer. It was pretty crappy really. He was ill for ages, it just went on and on. Then when he died, it was my first year exams and I screwed them all up, because my mind wasn't on it. So I thought, what am I even doing here? What am I wasting my life here for, when I could die tomorrow? We all could. You know what I mean? So I jacked it in, worked for a few months till I had my air fare, then off I went.'

When Barbara and Kerry come out for their tea break, Sarah and John remain up in the racking out of sight, laughing and whispering. Barbara and Kerry must know they're up there, because the conversation below is stifled and low. John opens and closes his mouth like a ventriloquist's dummy, in time with their talking, pulling gossipy faces and gesticulating with his hands. Sarah sticks her tongue under her bottom lip and crosses her eyes, flapping her hands limply as if she's lost all muscle control. Barbara and Kerry discuss the contents of their lunchboxes and *Coronation Street* and the weather, and when they run out of things to say they cut their tea break short to get back to the shop floor.

'Yay! Good riddance,' says Sarah, cheering with her fists.

'What about you?' asks John as he climbs down again. 'What's the deal with your folks?'

'My dad's retired. He's quite old, compared to all my friends' parents. He used to work at the university over in Tighborn. Teaching history.'

'And your mum?'

'She's dead. I never really knew her; I was just a baby.'

'Wow, that's heavy. You got a stepmum?'

'No. Although my dad's mentioned this woman a couple of times lately. *Deborah*. In fact, I think he's meeting her today, because he was all secretive about what he was doing. That's how I can tell. He goes all vague. If I ask him what he's doing, he goes, "*Um, well, oh, yes, I'm meeting a friend for supper*," and I can just tell it's not any old friend. He said he'll be back late tonight, and not to wait up. And he *never* stays out late. It's pathetic really. He's in his sixties!'

'Ahh, I think it's quite nice. To have a girlfriend at his age.'

'Urghh. I think it's disgusting!'

John laughs, and they climb down for their lunch break. As usual John's bought himself a tuna sandwich from Valerie's on the Parade, and he only eats one half before having his crisps and Club biscuit.

'Right, then,' he says, quietly rummaging through the coat rack. 'Which one of these is Barbara's?'

'The lilac one,' Sarah replies, frowning.

John sits at the bench with Barbara's coat on his lap, carefully unpicking a small section at the bottom of the lining. 'You keep watch,' he says.

Sarah watches as he breaks up the rest of his sandwich and pops the pieces in through the lining. He takes the stapler from the desk and closes up the hem with three sharp snaps, before turning the coat round the right side and holding it up to Sarah. 'No one would ever know the difference,' he says, and he gently hangs it back on the coat rack, exactly where it had been before.

'Brilliant!' whispers Sarah. She jumps up and down on the spot, clapping her hands and wincing at the throb in her thigh.

John stares at her intently. 'I wish you could work in here all the time,' he says.

'Me too,' says Sarah. 'So, what's next?'

The shop closes at 5.30, and, when Sarah and John leave together, Dante's waiting at the entrance to the alleyway.

'Alright, mate.' He nods to John.

'Alright,' John returns a curt smile.

'See you tomorrow, then?' Sarah says.

John gives Dante a last quick glance. 'Cheers, Sarah.' He sticks his hands deep into his pockets and breaks into a jog to cross the road, his ponytail bouncing against his back with every step. Sarah watches him as he skips up on to the pavement on the other side of the road and strolls along the Parade into the darkness.

'Who's that?' asks Dante.

'Oh, that's just John. Mrs Gilroy's son. He works in the stock room.'

'So,' says Dante.

'So.'

'So, I thought I'd come and meet you from work.'

'That's nice.'

Dante scowls. 'Haven't seen you for ages.'

'Weeks,' she says. She looks at her shoes and kicks a piece of gravel off and over the steps.

'Sorry. I'm an idiot. So you haven't got yourself a new boyfriend, then?' He nods in the direction that John just went.

Sarah tucks a loose strand of hair behind her ear and laughs. 'I thought you might have gone away for Christmas. Or left the country.'

'Nah, we're here for the holidays. Anyway, the old folks are out tonight and I thought I'd see if you wanted to come and watch a film at mine? I'll do us a pizza.'

'I'm not sure if I like pizza.'

'Alright, then, I'll get fish and chips.'

'You've never invited me to your place before.'

'Well, now I am. I've got to get some stuff from the Co-op. I'll see you round mine at seven?'

She folds her arms across her chest, and looks as if she's thinking about it. 'OK,' she finally says, and she kisses him quickly on the mouth.

He smiles broadly and saunters off along the Parade. Sarah rushes home to shower and get herself ready for the evening, relieved to know that they're alright after all.

The entrance hall of Dante's house is enormous, with a polished oak staircase sweeping through the middle. A beautiful floor-to-ceiling tree twinkles in the corner, surrounded with an array of brightly coloured packages, stacked up beneath its branches.

'Wow. How old is your house?' Sarah asks as he shows her through.

'Dunno. 1800s, I think. Come and get a drink.'

In the big country kitchen, Dante opens the fridge and offers Sarah wine, beer or cider.

'Um, cider, I guess,' she says, accepting a can of Merrydown. She watches Dante pour himself a glass of white wine. 'So what film did you get?

'*Bachelor Party*.' He returns the white wine bottle to the fridge and leads them back down the hall.

'*Bachelor Party*? You're joking?'

'Don't ask me. Ed chose it.'

'Ed?'

In the living room another lad sits on the sofa with his feet up on the coffee table, a can of lager in one hand, the remote control in the other.

Dante gestures towards him. 'Ed, Sarah. Sarah, Ed.'

'Nice one,' says Ed, looking up briefly. He's busy fast-forwarding through the adverts.

Sarah smiles politely, as disappointment floods in. Dante spreads out on the sofa next to Ed, leaving her the armchair.

'Grab a pew,' he tells her. 'I've stuck the pizzas in the oven. I didn't get fish and chips in the end. Thought you should try a pizza, Sar. There's oven chips too.'

She frowns at him.

Dante looks away. 'Yeah, I bumped into Ed in the video shop. You don't mind, do you, Sar?' He doesn't look at her, but bends down to unlace his Converse boots.

She's not sure why she even bothered coming. 'So what's the film about?' she asks.

Ed sniggers.

Dante gives him a shove. 'It's about this bloke, Tom Hanks, and he's about to get married, and he decides to have a stag party.'

Great. Sarah takes a swig from her cider. She feels the fizz rising up the back of her nose.

'Yup,' says Ed, raising his can and clinking it against Dante's wine glass. 'Yes, sireee!'

They start the film and Sarah tries to get into the spirit of things, knocking back her cider and almost starting to enjoy herself. Tom Hanks is even quite funny. The timer on the oven buzzes and Dante sprints out of the room to sort out the pizzas. There's an awkward space while Ed and Sarah don't speak a word, both of them fixing their eyes on the paused image on the television screen. Tom Hanks is in a mechanic's workshop, standing beneath an elevated car, working on it with a spanner. The picture is all fuzzy.

'How do you know Dante?' Sarah asks finally, leaning forward to put her empty can on the coffee table. It makes a hollow clink.

'Oh. Sixth form,' Ed says, still looking at the TV. He bites the corner of his thumbnail.

Dante carries in a tray of food and drinks, and slides it on to the middle of the table. 'Get stuck in, mate,' he says to Ed.

Ed presses play on the remote control and they fill up their plates and open more drinks. Ed takes a long slurp from his can and belches loudly; Dante lifts up one buttock and farts. They shake hands and laugh. She glares at them with disgust.

'Sorry, Sar,' Dante smirks. 'It's Ed. He brings out the worst in me.'

Ed guffaws and slaps his own legs.

'But feel free to join in if you like.'

Sarah continues to frown at Dante.

'*Joke*,' he mouths at her.

'Oh, man!' Ed abruptly sits up, so that he's on the edge of the sofa, straining his neck towards the TV. He's got a cluster of small red spots on either corner of his chin. 'Look at those women. Oh, my God. Look at her tits. They are *phenomenal*, man!'

'It's breast heaven, my friend,' says Dante, stretching across to pour himself another glass of wine. 'Titty utopia.'

Sarah stares at the side of Dante's face, silently urging him to look at her. She's never seen him like this before.

'Mammary Madness,' says Ed.

'Puppy Pandemonium.'

'Booby Bonanza.'

Sarah wants to say something clever to put the two of them down, but she's speechless. The TV screen is bursting with half-naked women with oily pneumatic breasts and Bonnie Tyler hairdos. The men in the film are making comedy lust faces and blinking hard.

Ed sits back in his seat. 'Pass me a pillow, mate.'

Dante hands Ed a cushion, which he places across his lap.

Ed glances up at Dante. 'Boner.'

Dante sniggers and shakes his head. 'Control yourself, man.' Then he looks over at Sarah, who's knocking back her second cider, and adds, 'Mind you, I've got a bit of a semi myself.'

'Sure Sarah'll help you out with that,' says Ed, still focusing intently on the shiny onscreen breasts. He moves his mouth mechanically, as if he's silently whistling.

Dante gulps back his wine in one mouthful. 'Doubt it, mate. Doubt it very much.'

Sarah puts down her can, and leaves.

~

Tuesday is Christmas Eve, and Mrs Gilroy asks Sarah to arrive half an hour earlier as it could be the busiest day of the year. There's still ice outside, and she takes extra care as she comes in through the alleyway.

'Before we open, I'd like you to do a nice display of all the fragrance sets down at the front counter – we're always run off our feet with panic-shoppers on Christmas Eve. And when you've finished there, perhaps you can do something with the window too? Freshen it up with some different gifts and perfumes.'

Sarah gets to work on the display, first moving the existing nail care unit to polish down the surfaces. She loves this kind of work, and never gets much of a chance to do it when Barbara's around. When she finishes at the front counter, she steps into the window and starts to remove the current display, brushing up the dust and fluff from around the little tree that she and John put up a couple of weeks back. She rearranges the shelf units, before fetching fresh tissue paper from the stock room.

'Morning!' John calls down from the racking.

'Hi, John,' Sarah replies, carefully easing half a dozen pieces of red tissue paper from the flat pack on the desk.

'What're you up to?'

'Window display. I'd better hurry up, we open in ten minutes.'

'So you won't be helping me out in here today, then?'

'Doubt it. Mrs Gilroy reckons we're going to be busy. See ya!' She rushes back to the shop front and starts to arrange the tissue.

From the window, she sees Barbara and Kerry crossing the road on their way in. Barbara looks furious when she sees her doing the display. She accelerates to a fast waddle, and marches up the steps into the alleyway beside the window. Sarah hears a loud wallop on the pavement beyond the glass, and can just see the edge of Barbara's head on the floor, sticking out from the alleyway. Kerry is flapping around like a spooked goose.

Sarah quickly steps out from the window display. 'Mrs Gilroy!' she shouts as she tugs at the locked front door to go to Barbara's aid.

Mrs Gilroy rushes through the shop and unlocks the door. Round the corner in the alleyway, Barbara is lying on the icy pavement, groaning. Mrs Gilroy asks her where it hurts. 'Best not to move her,' she says. 'Sarah, you get John to fetch out a blanket, and I'll phone an ambulance. Kerry, you'll have to stay with her until the ambulance comes.'

Barbara carries on groaning and Kerry looks on, helpless and pale. Inside the shop, Sarah overhears Mrs Gilroy on the phone. 'Yes, well, she's quite a large woman, so I don't think we should move her. You'll need a stretcher and two strong men.'

John returns from delivering the blanket, adopting a saintly expression as he passes Sarah. '*Karma*,' he whispers.

Sarah goes back to dressing the window as Mrs Gilroy opens up the front door. Kerry's still outside, shivering and moving from foot to foot. Every now and then she meets Sarah's eye and Sarah smiles, but Kerry looks away quickly, as if she's being disloyal to Barbara. Twenty minutes later, the emergency men come to scoop Barbara off the pavement, staggering slightly as they try to ease her into the back of the ambulance. They almost tip Barbara straight off the stretcher and into the road. Kerry gasps, clutching her handbag to her chest. *Karma*.

By mid-morning, Mrs Gilroy has made John change into a white shirt so that he can serve out front as they're short-handed. He looks really annoyed at first, but working behind the counter with Sarah quickly lifts his mood. Kerry has been asked to stay on the front till all morning, so Sarah hardly has to speak to her at all. Kate's dad comes in, looking for a present.

'Hello, Mr Robson,' Sarah says, when he approaches the counter.

'*Sarah*.' He waggles his finger at her. 'I don't know how many times I have to tell you! It's Jason. Or Jase. To my friends.'

She feels the discomfort of John's eyes on her.

'Sorry,' she says.

'I need a woman's touch,' he says, beckoning her to come from behind the till. 'Tell me what I should get for Patty. Something nice and smelly. Expensive.'

She leads him down to the display she created earlier, and picks up the biggest lavender gift set. 'These are lovely. Bubble bath, talc, bath salts, body lotion.'

Jason stares at her intently, as if he's studying her face. 'Mmm. What do you do with that, then? Body lotion?'

Sarah turns the gift over in her hands and picks up a tester bottle of body lotion. 'You know. Moisturise your body.'

'All over?'

'Um, yes. But not your face. Just your body. Do you want to smell it?' She opens the tester and offers it to him.

Jason puts his hand round hers and brings the bottle to his nose. He closes his eyes and breathes deeply. 'Mmm. That really is nice. Can you gift-wrap it for me?' He releases her hand.

She walks him to the gift-wrapping desk. 'How's Kate?' she asks. She's struggling to find the end of the Sellotape reel.

'Well, when I left the house she was busy pulling out all the contents of her wardrobe. Meeting some new fella, apparently.'

'Really?' Sarah measures out a length of gold ribbon. She can't believe Kate hasn't told her about it herself. Maybe it's that sixth former from the café. Christian. Christian the Christian.

'Wouldn't tell me anything about him, of course. Probably some spotty little oik. You got a boyfriend, Sarah?'

She glances up briefly, then starts to draw the ribbon over the blade of the scissors to make it curl. 'No. Not really.' She hands Jason the finished gift.

'What a waste,' he says, surveying the gift at all angles.

She frowns, worried he's not happy with the wrapping.

'I mean you not having a boyfriend. What a waste.' Jason pays and leaves, pausing to wave over his shoulder as he passes through the front door.

'Friend of yours?' asks John.

'He's Kate's dad.' She walks away to tidy up the make-up stand at the front of the shop.

All afternoon, her thoughts return to the warmth of Jason's hand around hers, the intensity of his blue eyes on her face. She wonders if Dante is missing her.

At five o'clock, Mrs Gilroy removes her lab coat and brings out mince pies and Buck's fizz to offer to the final customers of the day. The dark High Street outside is lit up with Christmas bulbs looping from shop to shop, with the town Christmas tree sparkling brightly beside the war memorial. Mrs Gilroy lights some cinnamon candles and turns up the Christmas music. There are still about a dozen customers milling about the shop, picking up prescriptions and last-minute presents. They all congregate around the back till to eat their pies and chat.

'Santa's on his way,' says John, nudging Sarah with his elbow as he walks past balancing a tray of drinks.

She can't help laughing as her real excitement about Christmas starts to break through.

Her dad calls in on his way back from the butcher's and he stops for a mince pie. 'I've picked up the beef,' he says holding up a white carrier bag. He's wearing his tweed trilby and scarf. 'It's a fine cut.'

'Would you like a drink?' asks John, offering him a glass.

'Good man!' he replies, raising his glass. 'Good man!'

'He's my dad,' Sarah mumbles, and Mrs Gilroy obviously overhears, because she rushes over to shake his hand.

'Mr Ribbons – lovely to see you.'

Dad shakes her hand vigorously. 'Charmed,' he says. He looks ancient.

Mrs Gilroy rests her hand on Sarah's shoulder. 'I think your father must be as fit as a fiddle, Sarah.'

Sarah turns to her dad, who looks equally puzzled. 'How can you tell?' she asks.

'Because he's an extremely rare visitor to the pharmacy.'

'Aha!' says Dad, touching his nose

Mrs Gilroy smiles graciously and moves on to see her other customers.

'Righto!' says Dad, brushing pastry from his cuffs. 'See you back home. I'll get the fire going!' He bustles out of the shop, the butcher's bag swinging at his side.

'He seems nice,' says John, watching him leave.

'He's alright, I suppose.' She looks at the clock over the back till. 'Fifteen minutes to go!'

She looks across the shop to see Barbara's daughter, Kim, pushing through the other customers as if she's a VIP. Sarah notices she's got a couple more gold chains around her neck since she last saw her.

'Mrs Gilroy in?' she asks Sarah, chewing gum and looking vacant. ''S'about my mum.'

Sarah locates Mrs Gilroy and brings her over to Kim, who's leaning against the prescriptions counter with her arms folded. The shop lights bounce off her gold rings.

'Hello, Kim. Any news?'

'Well, yeah, actually.' Kim's trying to sound dramatic, but it just comes across as surly. 'The docs say it's a broken hip.'

'Good lord,' says Mrs Gilroy.

'Yeah. She could be outta action for weeks, he said. My dad reckons someone oughta get done for that alleyway being icy like that. It's a death trap.'

'Well, you're quite right, Kim. Sarah fell on the ice days before, didn't you, Sarah?'

'It's really icy out there,' she agrees.

Kim's craning her neck to get a look at the mince pies and chocolates. 'Yeah, a death trap. Mum says maybe I could help out in the shop, what with her being laid-up.'

'Well. You give your mum our very best, and tell her not to worry about work. We've got it covered. And assure her that I'll get on to the council about that alleyway, as it's their responsibility.'

'Can I have a mince pie?' asks Kim. She's lost interest in the conversation.

'Of course! Take one for your mum, if you like.' Mrs Gilroy wraps two pies in a serviette.

'See ya,' says Kim, scattering pastry crumbs on the floor as she leaves.

Mrs Gilroy starts to clear away the empty plastic cups. 'Don't suppose you'd like to do some extra hours after Christmas, Sarah? Perhaps the odd hour here and there after school, to fill in for Barbara.'

John grins widely.

'OK,' she says, ignoring him. He's trying to make her laugh again. He does a silent cheering dance behind his mother. Sarah smiles and turns away.

'Good!' says Mrs Gilroy, clearing up the last of the plates. 'I think it's time to shut up shop, don't you?'

Outside, John and Sarah wish each other a happy Christmas. For an uncomfortable moment she thinks he's going to kiss her, so she moves away first, trotting down the steps to cross over to the other side.

'See you next week,' he calls out.

'See you!' Sarah is clutching her wage packet and a gift from Mrs Gilroy, wrapped in the shop's red tissue paper. She thinks it's one of the large lavender packs like the one she sold to Jason earlier. Sarah puts her head down and turns her collar up against the icy wind which blasts along the High Street, hoping that Dad has got the fire going at home. He's probably laying out the tin of sweets and polishing the silver nutcracker at this very moment. She loves their little Christmas rituals. The same things every year: stockings by the fireplace, satsumas in a wooden crate, chocolates on the coffee table. Buck's fizz in the morning, a late roast beef lunch. It's the one day of the year when Dad won't let her anywhere near the kitchen, when he does everything and she can lounge about looking at her presents and cuddling up with Ted by the fire.

She turns the corner at the end of the High Street and walks into Tina. 'Whoa!'

'Sar!' Tina looks troubled.

'What is it? Are you alright, Teen?' Sarah puts her hand on Tina's arm.

'No, I'm fine!' She scratches the palm of her hand through her glove.

'No, you're not. What's up?'

Tina looks at the floor, then back at Sarah again. 'Promise you won't say anything?'

'About what?'

'Promise? Kate'll kill me if she knows I told you.'

'Told me what? Just tell me, Teen! You're keeping me in suspense!'

Tina wipes her nose on the back of her glove. 'I don't know how to tell you this, Sar. I'm really sorry. But I just saw Kate and Dante together. Holding hands, going into the Coffee Garden.'

Sarah stares blankly at Tina. 'You can't have. You must have got it wrong.'

'No. I saw them. They were walking along the street together, holding hands. Then Dante went in first, and Kate turned round and saw me. She looked really pissed off. She ran over and said, "You'd better not say anything, Teen," then she ran in after him.'

Sarah's chest is throbbing.

'When did you last see Dante?' asks Tina. Her eyes are full of apology.

'Um. Saturday.' She blinks at Tina. 'We kind of argued. Well, not argued. But I walked out.'

'Kate said you'd split up.'

'Honest?'

'I swear.'

The two girls stand for a moment, Tina wringing her hands, Sarah gazing into the distance as her mind whirrs and judders.

'I've gotta go,' says Tina, finally. 'I'm really sorry, Sar. I shouldn't have said anything.'

'No. No. You're a real friend, Teen. Thanks.'

They smile awkwardly at one another and walk away, in opposite directions. Plumes of smoke billow out from the chimneys on Seafield Avenue, creating mist genies beneath the lamplight. Sarah passes Dante's house, all lit up, with the curtains open. Christmas lights sparkle in every window. She runs the last few hundred yards to her house, unlocking the front door with unsteady hands. Inside, she breathes in the mushroomy scent of the Christmas tree, feels the warmth of the fire from the living room, hears the uplifting carols of King's College Choir. Everything's just as it should be.

'Here she is!' bellows her father, appearing from the kitchen with Ted by his feet. He holds his arms outstretched, a glass of sherry in one hand.

She gives in to his warm, stout embrace as Ted pads around their legs in small excited circles.

'Here's my favourite girl in the world.'

After breakfast Sarah and Dad walk their traditional Christmas Day circuit from East Selton to Tase Head. On the outward journey they take the top path, passing the holiday bungalows and converted railway carriages of East Selton, which gradually give way to the grander houses and sweeping gardens of West Selton. The wind was up last night, and this morning there's kelp and mermaids' purses strewn across the grassy footpath, making it slippery underfoot. Sarah breathes in the salt air which whips around her pink cheeks, as she tries to push away thoughts of Dante and Kate.

Dad cups his hand against the bright sunlight. 'One of the Rolling Stones lives in that one,' he says, pointing to a vast hedge sheltering a large house.

'I know,' replies Sarah, giving him a shove. 'You told me last time we walked here. And the time before that. And the time – '

He puts his arm round her shoulder and pulls her close as they walk. 'I like my new hat,' he says.

'Good. It suits you.'

Eventually they come to the sand dunes, where they trudge up and over the grassy marram mounds with Ted running ahead, before turning down on to the seafront for the walk back again. The tide is far out, and the sunlight grazes over the gentle motion of the water. There are lots of other families and couples doing the Christmas Day walk, too. They all greet each other, '*Happy Christmas.*'

'It's weird, isn't it?' says Sarah. 'How people get all jolly and say hello to each other for just one day in the year. Normally people would just ignore each other on the beach. It's weird.'

'I think it's rather nice.'

'Yes, it is nice.'

As they near home, they stop to collect flat stones and crunch down to the water's edge for their annual pebble-skimming contest. Each has an arsenal of twenty stones, which they take turns in casting out.

'Yes! Did you see that one? Six bounces!'

Dad throws another.

'Useless!' Sarah shouts, preparing to throw. Her pebble leaps across the water twice and sinks.

'Foul!' calls Dad. 'A successful throw will bounce for a minimum of three full jumps, or be deemed a foul. It's in the Rule Book.'

'What rule book?'

'The Pebble-Skimming Rule Book. What else?' He throws his last stone and stands with his hands on his hips. 'I suppose we'd better get home to peel those vegetables.' He whistles and Ted comes running back from the hole he's been digging at the edge of the breakwater.

'I still won, though, didn't I?' says Sarah, happily dusting the sand from her gloves.

'That you did, that you did.'

Back at home, she builds up the fire, while Dad starts preparing lunch in the kitchen. Ted's chewing on a lamb bone that the butcher sent home with Dad last night. He's making contented little grunts as he tries to get his small jaws around the large knuckle.

'Need any help, Dad?' she calls from the living room.

'No! Have another chocolate!'

She smiles and lays out her presents in front of the fire. The Virginia Andrews box set; a Terry's chocolate orange; the *Meat is Murder* album by the Smiths; a satsuma; a selection box; some rose bubble bath; and some black and grey striped fingerless gloves. Her main present remains beneath the tree, waiting to be unwrapped after lunch. She opens her selection box and stretches out lazily, popping chocolate buttons into her mouth one at a time.

The phone rings. She jumps up, feeling inexplicably guilty, recalling Tina's worried expression as she scurried off into the night. She imagines Dante and Kate holding hands and her stomach lurches.

Before she can reach the phone, Dad strides in wearing his red apron, looking irritable. He runs a floury hand through his white hair. 'It's Christmas bloody Day,' he says, and picks up the receiver.

Sarah stands with her back to the fire, rolling her foot over Ted's white and pink belly.

'Deborah?' says Dad, turning away from Sarah to face the window. 'What is it? Just – just slow down a bit – what is it?' He listens quietly.

She strains to hear what's being said, but already Sarah knows that Christmas is ruined, now that that woman has invaded their day with her phone call.

Dad glances round at her. 'Could you go and check the vegetables aren't boiling over, Sarah-Lou?'

She goes to the kitchen as she's asked; the vegetables aren't even on the hob yet. She waits. It's cold in the kitchen, and her breath is white before her face. She closes her eyes and hugs her arms around her body as she waits for Dad to finish.

He clatters into the kitchen and picks up the vegetable knife to start chopping the peeled carrots.

She opens her eyes and stares at him. 'Is it cold in here?'

'Not really,' he replies, looking bemused. He puts down the knife. 'Now, Sarah-Lou. Don't be upset. But, that was my friend Deborah on the phone.'

'Mm-hmm.' She clenches her arms tighter around her body.

'Well, you know her husband only passed away a couple of months ago, so she was meant to spend Christmas with her daughter. But she's just had a hell of a row with her son-in-law. He's a complete swine by the sound of things, and he's told her she's not welcome.'

'So?'

'So, we can't let her spend Christmas Day on her own.'

'Why not? It's just a day. We never have visitors on Christmas Day. *Ever.*'

Dad starts chopping carrots again.

She kicks a stray bit of Brussels sprout across the broken tiles of the floor.

'Well, I've invited her to join us. You'll like her. She's great fun, and a lovely woman.' He looks at her sideways. 'Sarah-Lou?'

'It's Sarah, Dad. Not Sarah-Lou. Just Sarah.'

'Sarah, please,' he says, brushing his hands down his apron. 'Please, just do this one thing for me? Be nice?'

She shrugs. 'I don't suppose I've got any choice, have I?'

Dad slides the carrots into a saucepan and starts peeling the potatoes.

'Thought not,' she says. 'I'll be in the other room.'

Just after two, Deborah turns up with puffy eyes, clutching a bottle of red wine. Her dark hair is streaked with grey, and her large bosom sits confidently beneath a red mohair sweater. Dad introduces them in the living room, and Deborah hands him her coat and scarf as if she's done it a hundred times before. He seems stiff and unnatural.

'God, I'm *so* sorry about this, Sarah. What a way for you to meet me for the first time. You must think I'm completely *awful.*' She kisses Sarah on both cheeks, pulling her in by her shoulders.

Sarah smiles.

'I haven't even got you a present! If I'd known I was coming – '

'It's fine!' says Sarah, waving a hand in the air.

'Drink?' says Dad. He's frowning and scratching the hair behind his ear.

Deborah looks relieved. 'Yes. *Please*!' She collapses on to the sofa as if she's just run a marathon. 'I could really do with a sherry.'

Dad takes a glass from the cabinet and searches about in the drinks cupboard. 'I'll just check the kitchen,' he says, leaving Sarah and Deborah alone.

Sarah pokes the fire and puts another log on. She sits down on the sofa opposite Deborah.

'So,' says Deborah, crossing her legs. She's wearing black leggings with shiny little ankle boots. Sarah notices how thin her legs are, compared with her large bosom.

'Chocolate?'

'Mmm. I *love* the toffee fingers,' says Deborah, taking the tin from Sarah. 'And the toffee coins. Oh, I don't know which one to choose.'

'Have both. It's Christmas Day.'

'Which are your favourites?'

'The same.'

'Then I'll have a strawberry cream. Leave the toffees for you.'

Dad hands Deborah a glass of sherry and sits beside her on the sofa. 'Lunch will be in half an hour,' he says. He glances at the space beside Sarah. She can tell he's wondering if he should have sat next to her instead.

'How did you meet?' Sarah asks.

Dad rubs the skin above his lip.

'We've known each other for years, haven't we, James?' Deborah pats his hand.

Sarah's not used to hearing her father's Christian name said aloud.

He takes a sip of his sherry. 'Yes, years.'

'So where did you meet?' Sarah persists.

'Stokely University, back in the sixties, wasn't it, James? We worked together in the history department. Good times, eh? You know, Sarah, we used to work all morning, giving lectures and seminars, then take ourselves off for a long pub lunch. Then we'd return for an hour or so of marking, then tidy up our desks and head off home. Happy days. It's not like that now. Glad to be out of it.'

'So you must have known my mum, then? She worked there too, didn't she?'

Deborah turns to her father. 'Um, yes, I did meet her once or twice – ' She shifts in her seat.

'What was she like?'

Dad claps his hands together. 'Right, time to lay the table, Sarah-Lou!' Deborah starts to rise, but Dad eases her back gently. 'No, no! You stay right where you are. We'll give you a call when we're ready.'

She smiles at them both gratefully as they leave the room.

Dad pushes the door ajar between them and Deborah in the next room. A lump gathers in the hollow between Sarah's ribs. She glares at her father across the dining table, as he carefully lays out the best cutlery and avoids her gaze.

Eventually, he meets her stare, talking low. 'Don't look at me like that, Sarah-Lou. Deborah's a guest in our house. I don't want you to embarrass her with lots of questions. It wouldn't be fair.'

'Fair?!' Her blood is racing; she can feel it throbbing beneath her skin. She slams a serving spoon down on to the tablecloth.

'Shhh!' he hisses, looking over his shoulder towards the doorway. He pushes his white hair off his face.

'*God*,' she whispers. 'I'm not even allowed to mention her without you making me feel guilty. I know it upsets you, Dad, but how would she feel if she knew you were like this?' Sarah's waving her arms around now, feeling all control slip away. 'You behave like she never even existed!'

Dad is pressing on to the table with the palms of his hands flat against the cloth, his head bowed.

'Dad, it's just not normal. This isn't normal. She was my mother – and I deserve to know about her!'

Deborah has entered the room behind Dad. She's standing in the doorway holding her sherry, deep concern in her steady eyes. Sarah stands frozen, her hands gripped around the back of the dining chair.

'James?' Deborah says softly. 'James? Do you mind if we have a quiet word?'

Dad turns and leaves the room with Deborah, shutting the door carefully behind him. Sarah is left alone in the dining room, staring at the peeling wood panels of the closed door. She pulls out the chair and sits at the table, resting her head on her folded arms. She'd cry if she weren't so exhausted. She wonders what Dante's Christmas lunch is like. They've probably got Bono or Sting as dinner guests. Or Annie Lennox. It's no wonder he's gone off with Kate. She's far cooler than Sarah. And she'd do anything with anyone.

Sarah hears the soft thud of the front door opening and closing, and the sound of car tyres turning on the gravel drive.

After a few moments, the door to the dining room opens. She lifts her head to see Dad standing in the doorway. He looks weary, apologetic.

'Deborah's gone. We thought it was probably best. It's been a difficult morning for all of us.'

Sarah squints, trying to catch his thoughts.

'Are you alright?' he asks.

She sits upright. 'Actually, Dad, it's been my worst Christmas ever. It's been rubbish from Christmas Eve all the way through to now.'

Dad ruffles his white hair distractedly, then re-ties the apron bow behind his back. 'Well, we'd better try and fix it, then, hadn't we? Want to help bring out the veg?'

She nods and follows him to the kitchen, shuffling her slippers noisily over the tiles. 'Sorry, Dad,' she says to his back.

'Me too,' he replies, spooning Brussels sprouts into a china serving dish. He puts down the spoon, rests his hands on her ears and kisses the top of her head. 'Me too, Sarah-Lou.'

Late on Christmas night, Sarah hears footsteps crossing the gravel driveway beyond her bedroom window, followed by the brief snap of the letterbox in the hallway below. She throws back the covers and quietly sprints down the stairs to find a small envelope on the doormat, addressed to her with a neat 'x' across the seal. The little package is weighty, and as she takes it into the kitchen to slit open the seal her stomach tenses uncertainly. A leather corded bracelet slips into the palm of her hand, delicately strung with tiny silver seashells which sparkle in the half-light of the kitchen. She slips it on to her wrist and turns it over, thinking hard about Dante and Kate.

'Idiot,' she whispers, and she takes off the bracelet and drops it on the worktop beside the breadboard.

~

Tina phones early the day after Boxing Day.

'So have you spoken to Dante yet?'

Sarah picks the fluff off her jeans. She's been practising stitches on her new sewing machine. 'No. I don't really know what's going on with him. After what you said about him and Kate, you know, I thought – well, that it's all over. But then he put a present through the letterbox on Christmas Day, just as I was going to bed.'

'What was it?'

'A bracelet – it's lovely. I suppose that's his way of saying sorry. Coward.'

Sarah can hear kids screaming and shouting in the background at the other end.

Tina huffs loudly, and her voice muffles for a moment. '*For God's sake, Josh! Shut up and leave each other alone!*' She comes back to Sarah. 'I spoke to Kate yesterday.'

'Did you? Did you ask her about when you saw them together?' She glances towards the hallway, hearing Dad moving about upstairs. The phone must have woken him.

'Yeah. She said it was nothing. That they just bumped into each other in town and went to the café together.'

Sarah's mind leaps around. 'But what about the holding hands bit?'

'Kate said Dante did it as a joke, to wind me up. What a bastard!'

'Did you believe her?'

'Definitely. She said she'd never do that to a friend. She seemed to really mean it. So, are you still going to her New Year's Eve party on Tuesday night? She said we can sleep over if we want.'

'Oh, I don't know. Dante will be there. I won't know what to say to him. And I don't want to make an atmosphere.'

'Don't be a plank. It'll be a chance for you two to kiss and make up.'

Sarah brushes a cobweb from the corner of the telephone table and sighs. 'Maybe. Alright. What time shall we meet?'

'I'll see you at the top of Kate's road at eight? Kate said to bring some drink along. I'm gonna wear my new dress – you know, the blue one. What about you?'

'Dunno. I'll sort something out. OK, Teen. See you then.' She hangs up and stares at the receiver awhile. She'll go into town and choose some fabric and a dress pattern. She could even go in to Tressies and see if they can cut her hair before Tuesday. She pushes her overgrown fringe behind her ears and pats her cheeks.

'New Year. New me.'

~

Tina's already waiting on the corner when Sarah arrives at the top of the Amber Chalks estate on New Year's Eve. She's wearing her usual padded coat over a short bright blue dress, with grey stilettos and sheer black tights. Her knees look bonier than ever. A Bottoms Up carrier bag dangles at her side.

'Did you bring any drink?' she asks as Sarah approaches.

'Cider,' she says, opening up her bag to show Tina a four-pack. 'I like your dress, Teen. Is that the one you bought before Christmas?'

'Yeah, does it look alright?' She looks over her shoulder to check out the back of her wiry legs. 'I'm really chuffed with it.'

Jason opens the door at Kate's house. He gives Sarah a whistle as he takes her coat and hat. 'Wow! Love the hair, Sarah! Very Debbie Harry, if you don't mind me saying so.'

Sarah tries to cover her embarrassment, bowing her head and pulling her fingers through the fringe, trying to straighten it out after wearing the hat.

Kate skips in from the living room. 'Wow, Sarah!' she screams. 'It's so cool! And so blonde! Where'd you get it done? I'm so jealous!'

'Tressies. But the colour was agony. They put this mental-looking rubber hat over my head then spent about an hour pulling bits of hair through with a crochet hook. The hairdresser had to get me a tissue to wipe up my tears.'

'You've had loads off,' says Jason, cupping the back of her hair where it rests just above her shoulders. 'It really suits you. Very cool.'

'Alright, Dad!' Kate's pulling a face. 'Haven't you got a disco deck to sort out or something?'

He swaggers off towards the living room and fires a pretend bullet in Kate's direction.

'Right! Drinks!' says Kate.

The girls hand over their tins and follow her into the kitchen.

By nine, the house is almost full. Jason's turned the music up high, so everyone has to speak up to be heard. Most of the guests are neighbours and friends of Jason and Patty, with Kate's younger friends hovering in groups on the stairs and in the living room. The lights are turned down low everywhere except the hall and stairs, and there are bowls of crisps and nuts in each room. Kate has positioned party poppers all around the house, ready for midnight, and every now and then someone pops one early, leaving trails of multicoloured streamers draped over chairs and banisters. Dante arrives with Ed, carrying a box of lager. They pause in the doorway of the living room, where the girls are chatting on the far side of the room. The palms of Sarah's hands grow cold and clammy when she sees him through the growing crowd of guests. Kate rushes over to greet them, and Sarah watches as they follow her into the kitchen.

'He's here,' she tells Tina.

'I saw. Who's his friend?'

'Ed. Ed the Pleb.'

'He looks quite nice.'

'He's a sexual deviant. I think Dante saw me, but he didn't come over, did he?'

'He's probably waiting for you to make the first move.'

Sarah runs her hands down her new dress, to straighten out the hem. It's short and black, made from a furry, sparkly kind of material. The sparkly pile has been shedding all evening; she sees a few strands lying on the ground beside her baseball boots. 'I don't know what to say to him. I can't decide if I'm still mad at him, or if I even care. I'm just going to enjoy myself.' She strokes the inside of her wrist, feeling for the seashell bracelet. Perhaps she shouldn't have worn it. She finishes her cider, and pulls Tina along to accompany her to the kitchen for a refill.

'Yeah! Let your hair down!' Tina giggles as they pass Jason at his DJ desk.

His eyes slip over them like mercury.

'What's left of it!' laughs Sarah, letting her gaze rest on Jason as they leave the room. He returns a sly smile, and she shakes her hair on to her face to cover her pink cheeks.

They pass Dante and Ed at the entrance to the kitchen.

'Hiya,' Sarah says.

Dante looks surprised. 'Hi!'

'Sar! Over here!' Kate calls from the corner of the room. 'Ready for another?'

Dante and Ed are obscured from view as Sarah and Tina squeeze through the bodies inhabiting the kitchen. She reaches for two more ciders from the fridge, handing one to Tina. 'I haven't seen your mum yet, Kate.'

Kate pulls back the ring pull and takes a swig of her lager. 'And you're not likely to tonight. They had a big bust-up, and she's gone to stay at her sister's. Thank God. She's such a bitch.'

'What was it about?' asks Tina as she readjusts her bra strap.

'Oh, *God*. My sister phoned first thing this morning, and that was it; Mum was in tears, then Dad was on at her asking what the problem was, and before you know it it's World War bloody Three! See that dent over there in the skirting? That's where the sugar bowl landed when she chucked it at him. Then all of a sudden she's gonna cancel tonight, because she's got a bit of a headache! She's mental. All she ever thinks about is herself.'

Sarah takes a sip of her drink. 'She'll be back, though, won't she?'

'More's the pity,' says Kate, stretching back against the kitchen worktop with her elbows. 'It's no wonder he spends all his time down the youth club. What she doesn't realise is that he's just trying to get away from her. He doesn't even get paid for it. Tell you what, I'd find a volunteer job myself, if I was married to her.'

Her jade dress is Lycra-tight, clinging to every curve and dip of her body. Sarah can clearly see the mound of her pubic bone pressed against the stretched fabric. She looks about twenty.

Kate stands up straight and holds out her can. 'OK. Down in one?'

The girls huddle together against the sink, and on Kate's count of three they glug back their drinks, eyes upturned until the first one slams their can down on the side.

'The winner!' shouts Kate, holding Sarah's arm in the air. The silver shells of her bracelet jangle as her arm is thrust skyward, its dangling cowry charms twinkling in the kitchen light. 'And your prize is... another can of cider!'

Sarah belches unexpectedly and they fall about laughing as they open fresh cans.

'I'm gonna wet myself!' Tina clutches her sides.

'Me too!'

The two girls race up the stairs to the bathroom, slamming the door shut behind them.

'D'ya know what,' says Sarah, slurring slightly as she sits on the toilet seat watching Tina reapply her lipstick. 'I can't be arsed. You know. With Dante. But at the same time, I can be arsed, and I want him to come over, and – you know. Make up. Oh I dunno.' She pulls up her thick tights, stumbling as she flushes the loo. 'Glad I've got my baseball boots on. I'd never stay standing in your shoes.'

Tina hobbles over to the toilet and has her turn. 'I don't think I'll be standing for long,' she says. 'Here, what about Patty and Jase?'

'Who?'

'Y'know. Kate's mum and dad. She sounds like such a cow. I don't know how he can put up with it.'

'It's weird. D'you reckon she's older than him? She looks older. Quite a bit older with her grey hair and all that.'

Tina stumbles as she pulls up her knickers. 'Yeah, she's gotta be at least ten years older? Or maybe she just looks old. Anyway, he could do better, I reckon. God, that cider's strong stuff.'

'*Nice* cider,' says Sarah, wiggling her bum and rearranging her new hair.

Tina snort-laughs, which sets them both off again, and by the time they leave the bathroom they're hysterical.

Down in the hallway, Kate is talking to Ed and Dante among a group of other Selton High kids.

'Tina!' Dante calls out as they pass.

Tina frowns, but she looks pleased at the same time.

'Someone I want you to meet.' He beckons her over. 'This is Ed.' He moves aside to welcome her into the group, ignoring Sarah altogether.

Ed grins like an idiot, but Tina looks really keen to stay and talk to him. Sarah's opinion of him remains unchanged. He's a total pillock. She wanders away from the group and into the living room, where she looks around for familiar faces. Jason's friends and neighbours seem so confident, drinking their drinks with ice and lemon, their sleeves rolled casually up their forearms. One couple are seated on the sofa, kissing passionately. Their ankles intertwine politely and the woman's red shoulder-padded silk blouse has slipped over, exposing a little flesh across her collarbone. Some of the others in the room give a running commentary on the couple's movements.

'Look at them! They're not even coming up for air!'

The snogging man carries on kissing, but manages to put two fingers up to them.

'It's their first date,' says one woman. 'I'd like to see if they're so enthusiastic in a year's time!'

Sarah wanders over to the disco decks to see if Jason needs any help. She concentrates hard on walking straight.

Jason puts his hand on her shoulder and leans in to make himself heard over the music. 'Tell you what, love. You can scribble down a few tracks you'd like me to play later. Let's make it three. I'll put them on in a while. Get you and the girls dancing?'

Sarah's pleased to have the distraction. 'Can I have a look through your records, to choose?'

'Help yourself. Although one of them will have to be a Blondie track, now, won't it?' He ruffles her hair and she ducks away laughing.

'So, definitely "Sunday Girl". That's the best one. I love some of the stuff from the seventies.'

'Me too. Write it down.'

'Oh! I know – The J. Geils Band!'

Jason starts flipping through his singles. '"Centerfold"?'

'Yes! That's it! I love that track!'

He winks, sliding the single out of its cover and turns it over to check it under the light. He gives it a blow. 'It's a bit racy, isn't it?'

Sarah takes the sleeve from him. 'Is it?'

'Yeah! Not that I'm judging. It's one of my favourites, as it goes.'

She carries on looking through the records. 'Well, it's just one of those songs that Kate and Teen and I all like when we get together. Here you go – Visage, "Fade to Grey". That's my final choice.'

She hands him the single.

He rubs his chin slowly. 'Nice selection. I like it. You're what we in the business would call a woman of eclectic tastes, Sarah. Consider it done.'

Sarah tugs at the hem of her dress, unconsciously sprinkling more glitter fabric on the carpet. 'Thanks, Jason.'

'That's more like it,' he says as she walks away. 'No more of that "Mr Robson" stuff!'

The crowd has dispersed from the hallway. Sarah searches for Tina and Kate, eager to get them back in the living room before Jason plays her choices. She looks in the kitchen and all over the ground floor, but they're not there so she trots up the stairs, darting into the bathroom again to check her hair. As she stands in front of the mirror, she hears giggling from behind the floral shower curtain. She pulls the curtain back and Tina falls out of the bath backwards, spilling cider all over her new blue dress. She lies on the floor, laughing uncontrollably, her fingers still gripping the half-empty can. Sarah is struck by the dark circles beneath Tina's eyes, and absently wonders if it's smudged mascara. Tina's stockinged feet are still hooked up over the bath edge, giving Ed a full view of her knickers. He's leaning out of the bath, trying to offer her his hand, but he's pissed as a fart and swaying around looking as if he's going to go over on top of her at any moment.

'Teen!' Sarah cries out, hunching down to try to help her up. 'And I thought *I'd* had too much to drink!'

Tina carries on giggling. 'This 's Ed,' she says, still rolling around on the cork floor tiles. She points up at Ed who's now finishing off his lager as he hangs on to the shower rail. It looks as if it's going to break.

'We've met,' says Sarah. 'Are you coming downstairs, Teen? Jason's gonna put our records on in a minute?'

Tina manages to roll over on to all fours. 'No chance! When I've got a lush fella to chew the face off? Not on your Nelly, smelly! You don't want me to go, do you, Ed?'

Ed shakes his head like a dumb spaniel. *Prat.*

'OK,' says Sarah cautiously. She pauses with her fingers on the door handle, looking from Tina to Ed. 'If you're sure. I'll go and find Kate.'

Outside the door, Sarah's lips feel suddenly dry. She ambles along the hall towards Kate's room, to see if she can find some lip balm in her overnight bag. She flips the light on, walking unsteadily around the coat-laden double bed to search for her things. It smells musty and warm in here, like the girls' changing rooms at school. She bends to look along the side of the divan, unsteadily peering underneath. When she hears a gasp, she lifts her head and turns to look towards the bed. Her stomach twists as she finds herself face to face with Dante and Kate, who are lying on the bed among the mountain of coats and scarves. They are so close to her that she can see the shining black of their enlarged pupils. Sarah stands, taking a horrified step backwards. Kate is lying on her back with her hair splayed out across the pillow, multicoloured streamers caught up in its dishevelled strands. Dante is lying on top, firmly positioned between her naked legs. His jeans are pushed down far enough to reveal two inches of his softly downed buttocks, and Sarah can see the naked skin of their hips against each other. They both stare at Sarah in blank alarm, wet-lipped and flushed. Kate's tights lie beside Sarah's feet in a tangle of black nylon, rolled off in haste. She sways, backing away from the grotesque scene.

'Sarah!' Kate cries out, suddenly trying to extract herself from beneath Dante.

As Sarah rushes for the door, she glances back to witness Dante withdrawing from Kate's open thighs. His penis glistens briefly before he folds it into his jeans.

She runs down the stairs, her hand brushing lightly along the banister. Tina's at the foot of the stairs alone, sitting with her arms hugged around her knees, smiling at nothing in particular. '*Teen*,' Sarah hisses urgently. '*Come on*!'

Sarah darts across the living room, weaving through the dancing couples, and out through the French doors into the garden. Tina staggers along behind her. They lean against the closed glass doors, shivering in the sharp night air.

'What's up, Sar? You look awful – have you been sick? I thought I was gonna puke earlier, but I'm alright now.'

Sarah shakes her head, bringing her hand up to cover her mouth.

'Sar? What's happened?' Tina appears suddenly lucid.

Sarah looks back through the glass. They're not there.

'I just walked in on Dante and Kate in her bedroom.' She's not crying. She can't feel anything.

'What were they doing?'

'They were doing it,' Sarah replies blankly. 'He was actually lying there, on top of her. *Having sex.* They were *actually having sex*!' She shrieks these last words, feeling her hands beginning to shake in the icy cold glare of the living room lights.

'Are you sure?' Tina is scratching away at the palms of her hands, looking worried. 'Are you sure they weren't just snogging?'

'No! I saw it.' Sarah's eyes are wide and wet now. 'Don't you see? I saw *it*! I saw his poxy dick as he slid off her.' She stares at Tina, who returns a shocked blink. 'Teen, how could she do this to me?! She's supposed to be my *friend*.'

Tina stumbles forward to hug Sarah, just as there's a loud rap on the glass from the other side. It's Jason, gesturing for them to come back inside.

Sarah runs her hands across her face. 'I'm fine. Can we just forget about it? Let's go inside and dance.'

It's 'Centerfold' playing first and Tina and Sarah bop about, singing and making up silly moves to the lyrics. Sarah's laughing now, but her stomach is tensed. Jason joins Sarah and Tina on the carpet, taking their hands and waving them in the air as they sing along. Ed lurches into the room and sweeps Tina into the corner, where they prop each other up, swaying drunkenly. Jason goes back to the record deck as the track comes to an end, *na-na-na-na-na-na-na-na-na-na-na-na-na-na...*

Sarah's still laughing as he puts 'Sunday Girl' on. He stands behind his desk, singing along with the lyrics, pointing to Sarah as if the song is about her. She closes her eyes and tries to dance like Debbie Harry.

Opening her eyes, she stares at Jason, who stands behind his DJ desk singing hard. She's suddenly exposed, her legs shaking, the tears flooding her eyes. Jason stops singing, his face concerned. She turns and runs, slipping out of the French doors and into the garden, taking refuge in the far shadows of the shed, alongside the tree stumps that remain piled up beside the fence. She looks up at the sky, searching for stars. She's shaking, and her anger and humiliation merge like an explosion trapped in the core of her belly. She doesn't want to cry, but sobs rack her body and, no matter how she tries to still her mind, the tears run and run.

She hears the soft crunch of footsteps across the crisp grass.

'Here. Put this on. You'll freeze.'

It's Jason. She feels him wrap his sheepskin jacket around her shoulders as he pulls her against his chest, her body shielded by her crossed wrists.

They stand like this for some time, neither speaking nor moving apart. Sarah can feel his warm breath on the top of her head, and she wishes she could sleep now, standing here, just slip into a deep slumber and wake up with it all gone away. She knows Dad is seeing Deborah tonight, because he didn't ask lots of questions when she said she'd be staying at Kate's. She wonders if her father is having sex with Deborah. Could he be doing that, at his age?

Everything's wrong.

Jason pulls back and raises Sarah's tear-streaked face to his. She feels the light from the house cross her face. 'God, your eyes look beautiful when you've been crying,' he says. 'You poor love. D'you want to talk about it?'

He rearranges two tree rounds so that they nestle up behind the wall of the shed, side by side. Sarah takes a heavy breath and swipes the tears from her face, feeling foolish.

'Is it Dante?' asks Jason, reaching for her hand.

She doesn't answer.

He sighs.

'These lads, Sar, they don't know what they're doing half the time. I should know. I was one once. Believe it or not.' He nudges her and, when she smiles, he shifts himself to put his arm round her shoulder. He pulls her in, and she yields.

'I'm not a kid, you know,' she says. 'I know what boys are like.'

'No. You're a young woman. And you don't deserve to be screwed about, do you? If Dante is stupid enough to fuck it up with you, then he doesn't deserve you, I say. He's an idiot.'

She's stopped shaking. 'Yeah. He is a complete idiot, now you come to mention it.'

'I don't know what you were thinking, sweetie, to be honest.' Jason leans back to take a better look at her, his arm never leaving her shoulders. 'Some people are special, Sar, and you're one of them. You're not like other girls of your age. You're really mature. I'd never think you were only fifteen if I saw you in the street. Early twenties, I'd say.'

'Really? Well, the man in the off-licence didn't ask my age tonight, when I bought the cider.'

'See? But you're mature in the way you behave, too. That's what I like about you, Sar. You're special.' He kisses the top of her head, then moves his warm lips across her cheek, down towards her lips.

Sarah turns her face to his, letting him kiss her, allowing his tongue to slide between her lips, his hand to slip inside the sheepskin jacket, to search out her waist, the traceable ridges of her ribs. She feels him sigh against her, the pressure from his mouth growing firmer.

'Dad?' Kate's voice calls out from the kitchen doorway. 'Dad? Are you out there?'

Jason leaps up and out of the shadows so he can be seen by his daughter. 'Alright, Kate?'

'What you doing?'

'Sneaky fag. I was just coming in.'

Sarah hears his footsteps retreat over the frosty grass.

'I was looking for you everywhere,' Kate says. 'We can't get the record player going.' The door bangs shut, and Sarah is left alone in the shadows.

She sits a while, her body inert, her thoughts a drunken jumble. She can't stay here tonight. Easing open the creaking shed door, Sarah clumsily wheels out Kate's bicycle and props it against the logs. She removes the sheepskin coat and drapes it over the lawnmower, before running across the garden with the bike, slipping out through the side gate. Pausing at the front pavement, she sees lights on in all the box houses up and down the street. She hooks up her dress, mounts the bike and cycles off into the dark night, heading for home.

Spring Term 1986

By the time they're back at school Sarah has reduced her anger to a low level. At registration her face remains immobile, her gaze never lighting on Kate. Tina flits between the two like a sparrow, apologetically censoring their conversations. Sarah tries to appear unconcerned.

In Geography Tina and Sarah can sit together and talk without worrying about Kate.

'Kate said you sent your dad round to pick up your bag on New Year's Day.' Tina offers Sarah a Tic Tac.

Sarah nods. 'He was passing her place anyway.'

'She said you've still got her bike.'

'Not any more,' Sarah replies, lowering her voice. 'I sneaked it back round before school this morning. I saw Kate with her back to the window as I wheeled it across the garden and my heart was hammering away! But it was still dark – I don't think she saw me.'

'Like a cat burglar,' Tina says, laughing. She leans back in her chair and sighs heavily. 'Did I tell you I've gone vegetarian?'

'Really?' It seems strange to Sarah, because she's never seen Tina eat any fruit or veg. Ever.

'Yeah. I decided over New Year, really. I saw this film, about how they make sausages – it was disgusting. Honestly,

Sar, if you saw it, you'd go veggie too. The worst bit was how they kill the pigs, kind of electrocuting them and hanging them up. It's not true they don't feel anything. But you wouldn't believe the crap that goes into the sausage. Everything! The ears, the snout, the eyeballs and – get this – the nipples! They showed them slicing the nipples off the dead pigs and adding them to the sausage mix. *Disgusting.*'

'Urghh.' Sarah shudders. 'But not all sausages are made like that, surely?'

Tina gives her a knowing look. 'That's what they want you to think.'

She gets out her compass and scratches into the wooden desktop: '*Meat is Murder.*'

'How's it going with Ed?' Sarah asks. She feels a pang of embarrassment that she called him a sexual deviant. It's not the kind of thing you can easily take back.

'Really good. He's a brilliant laugh. And he knows everything there is to know about films. If you ask him any question about any of the Bond films or *Star Wars*, he'll know the answer. It's amazing. And he's so thoughtful.'

'I'm really pleased for you, Teen. What do you do when you go out together?'

'Usually we go to Marconi's, or the cinema. We all went to see *Pee-wee's Big Adventure* on Friday night. Dante said the bloke in it looked like a right perv.' She flushes a deep pink. 'Oh. Sorry, Sar. You must hate it when I talk about him.'

Sarah shakes her head and scribbles on her pad. 'It's fine.'

Tina reaches into her pencil case and pulls out the seashell bracelet. She drops it into Sarah's hand. 'Dante said it wasn't from him in the first place, so I'm to give it back to you.'

'Was he telling the truth, or just saying it to not upset Kate?'

'No, I think he was telling the truth. Kate wasn't even there when he gave it back to me. Sorry, Sar.' Tina turns her hands over and scratches the palms.

Sarah balls up the bracelet and slips it inside her school bag, an unsettled coil of tension building in her stomach. 'Your eczema doesn't look so bad these days, Teen,' she says, as the teacher slams the door shut at the front of the room.

'I know,' says Tina, examining her palms more closely.

'Must be *lurve*,' Sarah whispers, giving her a nudge.

'Must be,' Tina giggles.

~

As the weeks pass by, Barbara's hip is still keeping her out of action, and Sarah enjoys her work at the chemist's all the more. On her way in one Saturday, there's a sudden downpour, and she's soaked through by the time she arrives. She stands at the fire exit, shaking out her jacket, wondering if there's a radiator she can drape it over.

'Morning, Sar,' says John, sticking his head out from the kitchen.

'John!' she says, surprised to see him. 'I thought you weren't coming back to work at all.'

'No, I just had a few weeks off, visiting some mates in the West Country and chilling out. What about Phil Lynott, man? Tragedy. Absolute tragedy.'

Sarah frowns.

John shakes his head. 'Phil Lynott. Thin Lizzy. You must have heard – he died of an overdose at New Year. I couldn't believe it, man.'

'Oh, yeah,' says Sarah, nodding. She had heard something about it on the news. He had big afro hair and a funny little moustache, from what she can remember from *Top of the Pops*.

'You know. 'The Boys Are Back in Town'? 'Whiskey in the Jar'?'

Sarah nods. 'Yeah, yeah, I know who you mean. Really sad.'

John bobs his head mournfully for a moment or two, before breaking into a full smile. 'Anyway, you look particularly glamorous this morning, if I may say so. Drowned-rat-chic. Very *à la mode*.' He takes a camp stance and places his forefinger against his pursed lips.

Sarah's bedraggled hair hangs limply around her face. 'I rather like it myself.' She bends, then flicks her hair back over her shoulders, throwing beads of water into the air. 'What shall I do?' she says, suddenly worried. 'Mrs Gilroy won't want me out there looking like this!'

John laughs, then puts his finger in the air as if he's had a brilliant idea.

'Wait here,' he says, and he jogs through the passageway towards the pharmacy.

Kerry bustles in through the fire exit, turning briefly to shake her umbrella out of the door.

'Morning,' Sarah says cheerfully. 'Nice weather.'

Kerry smiles awkwardly. 'Disgusting, isn't it?'

She's surprisingly civil to Sarah when Barbara's not around. She even appears to be a little shy when she's on her own.

'How's Barbara?'

Kerry avoids eye contact, and looks around the stock room for somewhere to prop up her golfing umbrella. 'Oh. Well, you know it was broken? Her hip. They take ages to mend, hips.'

When John returns, his expression visibly alters at the sight of Kerry.

'Yes,' he says, fixing her with a stern glare. 'You know, Sarah was really fortunate that *she* didn't break her hip when *she* slipped in the alleyway. You remember? When you and Barbara stepped over her and laughed?'

Kerry is wriggling out of her winter coat, fumbling as she tries to hang it up. She scurries out to the front of the shop.

Sarah puts her hands on her hips. '*John*! Just stop it, will you? She's being alright now that Barbara's not here. You'll make it worse again.'

John's face is severe. 'You know what? I'm fed up with people thinking they can bully other people and get away with it. Barbara's a bitch, but that one, she's just as bad for going along with it.' He jabs the air to accentuate the last few words. 'I don't know why my mother doesn't just get rid of the pair of them. They're useless old witches if you ask me. It's women like that – ' he points his finger in Kerry's direction ' – that will drive this business into the ground!'

Sarah stares at John blankly. 'Blimey.'

'Anyway,' John says, waving away an unseen annoyance, 'forget all that. You're in here with me for an hour. I told Mum you got soaked, so she said you can help unload yesterday's delivery while you dry off. Result, eh?' He picks up the clipboard and studies it carefully. 'Let's start with the top shelves. If you climb up, I'll hand you the cartons.'

Sarah climbs up to the top shelf, and sits on the edge with her legs dangling.

'Cotton buds,' John says, passing up a box.

Sarah twists to push them into place, turning to receive the next box. 'Did you have a good Christmas?'

'So-so,' he answers. 'It was a bit boring, to be honest. Just me and Mum.'

'Did you see any friends over New Year?' She throws an empty carton on to the floor beyond him. He picks it up and breaks it down flat.

'Nah. My best mates all went back to uni early, and I'm not really interested in the rest of the losers around here.' He gathers his ponytail through his hand, and lets it drop to one side. 'I just sat in my room, listened to Pink Floyd and had a spliff. It was alright.'

'Wish I'd done that,' says Sarah. She clicks the heels of her shoes together as she waits for the next box.

'Why? What did you get up to?'

'Oh, nothing. It was a party at Kate's, and it was just crap, really. I left before midnight.'

John pauses to tick off some items on his clipboard. 'Wasn't your boyfriend with you, then?' He doesn't look up.

Sarah tugs a loose hangnail at the corner of her thumb. 'I left him there. And he's not my boyfriend any more.'

'Really?'

'You don't have to look so pleased! It was a rubbish party if you must know, and now he's going out with my best friend.'

'Your best friend?' John looks shocked. He gestures that they're moving on to the next shelf down.

'My ex-best friend, I should say.' Sarah descends the ladder to the shelf below.

John shakes his head, tutting under his breath. 'Well, sounds like they deserve each other to me. What an idiot.' The changing light from the stock room windows streams in behind him, creating a halo from the fuzz of his untidy hair. The sun's coming out.

'Can we change the subject?' Sarah asks impatiently. 'So, have you got a girlfriend, John? As we're telling each other our life stories today.'

John laughs and gives her a shove with the next carton. 'Sorry,' he says. 'Didn't mean to go on. No. No girlfriend. Can't understand why no one would want to go out with a skinny old hippy like me.'

'You're not that old. A skinny hippy, yes. But not old.' She grins.

'I'm nineteen, nearly twenty. That's fucking ancient, man. It's nearly dead, for God's sake.'

The hall is full of steam and the aroma of casserole when Sarah steps through the front door after work.

'Hello, Sarah-Lou!' Dad calls from the kitchen. He's been uncharacteristically jolly over the past month, spending less and less time in his study. It's driving her mental.

'Hiya,' she says, intentionally sounding depressed. She drops her bag in the hall with a thud, and hangs up her coat by the front door. Ted limps down the hallway to greet her, his sleep-stiff joints slowing him. Every wag of his tail seems an effort, and yet still he does it, smiling up at her and patting her shoes with his paw. 'Hello, Teddy-boy.' She scruffs him under the chin and, satisfied, he turns and trots back to his bed in the living room.

'How was your day?' Dad asks.

'Same as ever,' she replies, leaning on the door frame. 'Except the fat cow isn't back yet. So, I suppose it's better than usual.'

'Ah, yes. The buxom beauty from the Highlands! Never a smile, has she? Have you noticed? A severe and somewhat disapproving demeanour, which surely masks a heart of fire!' He waves his teaspoon in the air and bends over the pot to taste his cooking.

'Urghh. How can you talk about her like that? She's a nasty old cow. Believe me, all that beats in her chest is a heart of ice.'

Dad laughs, dropping the teaspoon on to the side with a plink. He pulls at the cords of his apron, as if to check they're still in place.

'Are you expecting someone for supper?' Sarah asks, trying to sound casual. He cooks so rarely, there has to be a reason.

'Only you.'

'What's with the cooking, then?'

'Well,' he says, placing his hands on her shoulders, 'I think we should spend some time together, and, as you've been at work all day, I thought you'd enjoy a wholesome meal.'

She looks at him suspiciously. 'Can we eat on our laps?'

'If we must.'

Sarah shivers as she steps back into the hall. 'D'you know what, Dad? It's colder in this house than it is outside. I swear it's true. It's *freezing*.' She blows out into the tile-floored hallway. 'Look! You can actually see my breath!'

Dad snorts. 'Don't be such a drama queen! This is England, not the bloody Antarctic. Go and have a bath if you need to warm up. Dinner will be about seven. I'll build up the fire if you're that ruddy cold. OK?'

'Yeah, OK. Actually my feet are killing me. They made me stay on the back till all afternoon. It's a nightmare. See you in a minute.'

Sarah runs the bath hot and deep. As she opens the door to fetch her towel, the steam billows out into the chill landing, partly obscuring the photograph of her mother.

She stops to rest her finger on the little frame, before kicking off her shoes and closing the door against the gloom of the landing.

Her body turns pink in the steaming hot water. She rests her head back against the cold, hard ridge of the ceramic bath. Like the kitchen, there are no external windows here, and the room is penned in by solid walls all around. The damp is a problem, but right now it's hidden by the plumes of steam created by the hot bathwater. The cold tap drips slowly and steadily, causing small outward ripples to run through the otherwise still water. When Sarah closes her eyes she can see the graphic detail of Dante, as he slides out and away from Kate, both of their faces turned towards her. She blinks her eyes open wide to shake it away. She hasn't seen him at all since the party, not even walking to school, so he's obviously staying out of sight. She plugs the tap with her big toe, holding it there for the count of ten, then releasing the backed-up drips in a cold stream. Kate has everything. She's got a warm, modern, heated home. She's sexy and cool. She's got a father *and* a mother *and* a sister. She's got Tina. And now she's got Dante too. Sarah raises the palm of her right hand and brings it down flat, *splash*, causing water to spray around the bath. She feels anger at the tears, knowing it's Kate she's missing more than anything; Kate, not Dante. Kate with her cutting wit and bubbling laugh. Kate with her dancing eyes and ridiculous bum-wiggle. It's Kate, not stupid Dante.

Ted scratches at the door, whining to be let in.

'Go away, Ted,' she yells.

Jason hovers at the edges of her mind. When he kissed her on New Year's Eve, the deep yearning he provoked was something she'd never felt with Dante. The hut, the holding hands to and from school was all kid's stuff, she realises now. Dante's just a boy. Sarah wraps her arms across her chest, cupping her small breasts protectively. She slips beneath the hot water until her face is fully submerged, allowing the memory of Jason's firm hands on her body to invade her thoughts, letting it grow into something more. He's gently laying her down in the dark, enclosed shed, among the fertiliser sacks and patio chairs. She smells the earthy scent of gardening and creosote. She lets him push aside the sheepskin coat he wrapped her in, to ease up her little black dress. He runs his hands across her slim, white ribcage and sighs into her neck, his breath hot and moist. With a burst of exhalation, Sarah ruptures the still film of water, grabbing the handrails to pull herself upright in the damp air. Her breathing is rapid, her heart pumping hard as her body restores its normal rhythm. She draws her knees up to her chin and stares into the grubby white tiles at the end of the bath.

'*I don't want you, Dante*,' she whispers.

~

By Monday morning, things have shifted again. When Sarah arrives at the lockers, Tina is already there, getting out her books for the morning lessons. She doesn't look up.

'Hi, Teen,' says Sarah, searching in her bag for her key.

Tina slams the locker door shut and hurries off along the corridor, her pace somewhat impeded by her long tight skirt. Sarah watches her retreat, and sees Kate waiting at the far end of the corridor, propped up against the wall with her arms folded over her chest. The two girls stop and talk; Sarah stands and watches them. Kate turns towards her with disdain, hooks arms with Tina, and the pair vanish into the toilets without a backward glance. Sarah turns and stares into the back of her locker. Tina was fine on Friday, sympathetic even. They'd laughed and joked in Geography, and Sarah had asked about Ed, showing an interest. She knows what's going on: Tina's chosen Kate. She stares blankly at the timetable pinned up inside the metal door. Typing. She's on her own in Typing.

The week grows progressively worse, as Kate and Tina start pursuing Sarah around the school at break times. They follow her wherever she goes, calling out her name and ducking behind doors and bookshelves.

'Sarah Ribbons!' she hears them echo wherever she goes.

She hopes they'll lose interest after a while, but they keep it going, gaining confidence all the while. '*Nice* hair, Sarah!' they call as she passes. 'Vir-gin!'

When she takes refuge in the toilets at the start of lunch break, they find her, following her in, guarding the outside of her cubicle, discussing her as if she's not there.

'Did you see her dress at my party? Oh, my God, it was sad. She said she made it herself. As if we couldn't see that for ourselves.'

Tina laughs.

'Honestly, Teen, I can't believe we even hung around with her at all. She's so immature, it's an embarrassment.'

Inside the dark cubicle Sarah stands rigid, clutching her school bag to her shoulder. She tries to decide what to do next. She wants a wee, but she's afraid they'll look over at her while she's on the toilet. She hears the sounds of fingernails drumming lightly against the door. Someone else enters; another cubicle slams shut.

'Anyway, Dante says her tits are so small you'd need a magnifying glass to find them.'

Tina screeches with laughter. 'Really? He said that? That's *so* mean.'

'Well, it's the truth, isn't it? She's completely underdeveloped. There's probably something wrong with her.'

Sarah's panic deepens. She wants to know who else is in the toilets with them; who else heard what Kate just said.

'I used to think she was alright. But she's a stupid cow, if you ask me.' Tina sounds less certain of her words, but still she says them. 'We're better off without her.'

The fingernails continue to tap on the door, gradually becoming a scrabbling noise, like scratching mice. They're both doing it now.

'And what about her Dad?' says Kate. 'Have you seen how *OLD* he is? Oh, my God!'

Sarah pulls back the lock and flings the door wide, barging between them so they have to lurch backwards.

Kate shrugs. 'Oh, *sorry*, Sar. Didn't know you were in there.'

The light in the room is dull, subdued by the thick black rainclouds gathering beyond the toughened glass windows high above the basins. Sarah stops at the sinks to wash her hands. Kate and Tina stay where they are, their arms folded like a pair of bouncers. 'Think we touched a nerve there, don't you, Teen?'

The toilet flushes inside the closed cubicle and Marianne comes out. Kate and Tina turn to look at her.

'Ignore them,' Marianne mumbles to Sarah as she washes her hands in the next basin along.

Kate gives Marianne a shove. 'What was that?'

She takes a step back.

Kate moves towards her with a sneer. 'What did you say, fatty?'

Tina looks ready to run.

'I said, ignore them,' Marianne replies, failing to look unruffled.

Kate shoves her shoulder with the tips of her fingers. Marianne doesn't respond. 'Oh, I get it!' Kate laughs, looking to Tina for back-up. '*Lezzers*.'

Kate turns to go and Sarah plants a flat-handed slap across her face, with such force that spittle sprays from the edge of her lipsticked-mouth.

Kate gasps, bringing her hand up to her cheek. A deep crimson mark rises instantly.

Tina clutches her own hands, the thumb of one scratching madly in the palm of the other.

Sarah's breaths are short and rapid, but her eyes are unblinking with rage.

'You stay away from me, Kate. And you stay away from Marianne.'

Kate's shock is short-lived, and she tugs Tina's sharp elbow and struts towards the exit, combing her fingers roughly through her crispy-gelled fringe. '*Bitch*,' she hisses as they turn the corner and clatter away along the corridor. Their footsteps fade to nothing.

'Sorry,' Sarah says to Marianne, who is now standing beside the sinks looking close to tears.

She shakes her head, suddenly breaking into nervous laughter. Sarah laughs too, uninvited tears rising in her eyes. She looks at Marianne's Cornish pasty shoes and A-line skirt, and thinks about Kate and Tina taking the piss out of her for being so straight.

'Thanks,' Sarah says as they leave the toilets. 'Thanks for sticking up for me.'

Marianne smiles shyly and walks off towards the library where she'll eat lunch alone. Her heavy limbs move awkwardly, as if she knows she's being watched at all times. She doesn't look back, but Sarah knows she knows she's still there. She breathes deeply and walks along the corridor in the opposite direction, wishing the week away with every nerve in her jangling body.

~

Dad's not in his study when Sarah gets in from school on Friday, and she wonders how his project is coming along. He hasn't talked about it for weeks.

'There's post for you on the mantelpiece,' he calls from the kitchen in a sing-song voice.

She leans into the kitchen and cocks her head to one side.

He raises his eyebrows and smiles. 'They look like Valentine's cards to me!'

She drops her bag in the hallway and saunters into the living room, trying to show him she's not that bothered. There's already an opened card on the mantelpiece, for Dad. It's big and frilly, with a horrible romantic poem on the outside. Yuck. Dad stands in the doorway with his hands on his hips.

'Alright, Dad, I don't need an audience, thank you.' She turns her back to him and inspects the handwriting on the envelopes. She doesn't recognise either. 'I need a knife,' she says without looking back at him.

'Righto,' he says, his jolly mood unaltered by her curt manner. He returns from his study with the letter opener.

'Here you go.'

Sarah feels him standing behind her, waiting to see who the cards are from. She turns to look at him. 'Dad!'

'Alright, alright,' he says, holding his palms up in surrender. 'I get the message. I'll leave you to it, Sarah-Lou.'

Sarah turns back to her envelopes.

'Cup of tea?' he calls back from the kitchen.

'No!'

'Keep your hair on. Only asking.'

Sarah slides the knife under the first envelope, and pulls out the card. There's a teddy bear on the front, holding a big squashy red love heart. It says 'I ♥ You'. It's really naff. She can't think who would send her a saddo card like that.

The second one is handmade from dark red card, the front carefully stencilled in black ink. Inside is a handwritten poem:

My heart beats like a drum
Whenever you are near
You're all that I think of
Whenever you're not here
You make me feel like a bumbling fool
'Cos Sarah Ribbons, you're so cool
X

Sarah raises it to her nose and breathes in the scent of card and ink, as if its secrets might be locked inside.

Dad reappears in the doorway holding a cup of tea. 'I made you one anyway,' he says, handing Sarah the mug. 'So, two admirers, eh?'

Sarah shrugs. 'Don't know who they're from. Probably a joke.' She sips her tea.

'Don't be ridiculous, woman! You're a rare beauty.'

'Dad, do you have to? I really don't know who they're from.' She nods at the mantelpiece. 'I see you've got one.'

'Oh, yes,' he replies, looking delighted with himself. 'Haven't had a Valentine's card in, well, years! Good to see

I can still charm the ladies, eh? Eh?' He tries to put his arm around Sarah, but she dodges away.

'From Deborah, I guess?'

'Well, I hope so! Can't imagine who else it might be from!' He laughs with gusto and leaves Sarah alone by the fireplace.

She hears the door to his study bang shut. The three cards on the mantelpiece ripple lightly with the vibration. She hates Valentine's Day.

As she walks to work the next day, Sarah glances through the gates of Dante's house. All the cars are there, and the curtains are still drawn. Yesterday, as she'd entered the classroom for morning registration, Kate was showing off the Frank Zappa tape Dante had got her for Valentine's Day. She'd clammed up when she saw Sarah, snatching the tape back from Tina and sliding it inside her pencil case. Sarah had pretended not to notice, and searched around in her bag for lip balm.

She walks along the alleyway and into the fire escape at the back of the chemist's. She's glad of her job now that she's fallen out with the others, and she resolves to put Kate and Dante out of her head entirely. It's no good dwelling on it, Dad would say.

Because it's Valentine's weekend, the chemist's is busy and they're still short-staffed with Barbara being off. Sarah quickly says hello to John and hurries out front to help serve on the tills with Kerry.

'We'll sell loads of smellies today,' Kerry says. She seems happier than usual, and Sarah wonders if she's actually pleased to see the back of Barbara. 'We'll get loads of men who've had an earful from their other halves for forgetting,' Kerry goes on. 'Though I'd be really narked off if my boyfriend waited till the day after Valentine's to get me something. It sort of defeats the object.'

At mid-morning, two of the part-timers arrive to help out on the shop floor, and Sarah decides to fill up the painkiller section whilst there's a break in the rush. She starts with the aspirin shelf, jotting down the quantities needed from top to bottom in neat, clear numbers. As she reaches for a shopping basket beside the main till, she sees Jason coming in through the entrance. She knows he has spotted her, and she rushes out past the pharmacy and into the stock room, where she stands a moment.

'Sarah!' John calls down from the racking.

She jumps. 'Oh, God, John!' she replies, breathless. 'You nearly scared me to death!'

'Sorry. So, how you doing?'

'Good. Um, I'm filling up the over-the-counter stuff – where's the aspirin kept again?'

He jumps down and shows her. 'Is it busy out there?' he asks, handing her the carton of Aspro-Clear she's looking for.

'Yeah. Loads of dopey blokes looking for dopey Valentine's presents.'

'Oi! We're not all like that, you know.'

'Yeah, yeah,' Sarah replies, 'I know.' She counts the correct number of packets into the basket and hands the carton back to him.

'Nice bracelet,' he says as he pushes the box back into its place.

'Thanks,' she calls over her shoulder, and she heads out front, hoping she's been long enough for Jason to have left.

Mrs Gilroy stops her as she passes through the pharmacy. 'Sarah – take this prescription to Mr Robson, please.'

Sarah reads the label: Mrs P. Robson. They'll be her happy pills. That's what Kate calls them. Sarah's heart is banging as she rounds the corner into the shop and slips behind the till. He's there, browsing through the Polaroid sunglasses at the front of the store. She's not sure what to say.

'Mr Robson?' she calls across the shop.

He looks up and swaggers towards her, still wearing a pair of the shop's mirrored aviator glasses. Kerry is busy serving Mrs Budge at the other counter, and she's having to speak up as the old woman is hard of hearing. Sarah's alone behind the till, and as Jason draws nearer she feels faint with fear. He smiles and gently places the sunglasses down on the counter.

'*Mr Robson*?' he says. 'What have I told you about that, Sarah?'

'Sorry,' she says, blushing fiercely. 'I mean Jason.' She hands him his little paper prescription bag.

'That's more like it. So, where've you been keeping yourself? We haven't seen you since you did your disappearing act at New Year.'

She stares at him.

'I can't tell you how disappointed I was when I went back into the garden and found you'd gone. I was really enjoying our chat, you know?' He stares at her intently, the overhead lights dancing at the side of his eyes.

'Me too,' Sarah says. What's wrong with her?

'Then we must do it again,' he says. 'Soon.' He pauses, holding her gaze. 'Bye, Sar,' he says, and he leaves the shop.

She stands quite still, her hands flat against the cool glass surface of the counter, her stomach turning over like a tombola drum. His eyes are so blue.

~

Mrs Minor puts Sarah in the same painting group as Kate and Tina after half-term, along with Natalie Simpson and Marianne. Kate sucks at a length of hair, her shoulder pointed towards Sarah. Tina stares at her feet, sighing loudly and fiddling with her 'Love Animals Don't Eat Them' badge. Mrs Minor moves about the room arranging daffodils in the centre of each cluster. Their group sits beneath the high sash windows, and the spring sunlight slices through the classroom. Sarah fixes her eyes on the rippling leaves of the silver birch tree through the glass, distracted by thoughts of her father. This morning as they skirted around each other in their tiny kitchen she saw him stumble a little, before steadying himself against the fridge. He turned deathly pale. 'What's wrong?' she asked him. He shook his head and rubbed his chest with the heel of his hand. 'Nothing, I'm fine,' he replied, turning away from her to pick up the butter knife. His knuckles appeared white as he gripped the handle, his other hand balled into a fist on the worktop. 'Have a good day,' he said, still not turning to face her.

Sarah had thought of nothing else since.

'So, Sarah, you've not had a chance to do your roots lately, I see?' Mrs Minor is in spiteful high spirits.

Sarah automatically brings her hand to her hair, drawing her fingers through to break up the thin block of darker roots that runs along her parting. She meets Kate's eyes, but instead of looking pleased at Sarah's humiliation she shoots an angry glance back towards Mrs Minor.

'You ever thought about dying *your* hair, miss?' Kate slumps back in her chair, chewing on a bit of thumb-skin.

Mrs Minor turns haughtily to face Kate. 'Oh, protecting your little friend, are you?' she sneers.

Kate meets Sarah's eyes. 'Or maybe if you backcombed it you might look a little bit taller? You might gain maybe half an inch or so?'

Mrs Minor stretches across the group to rearrange their flowers, even though she's already done it. 'What's that you're wearing?' She points at Kate's legs. 'Looks more like a belt than a skirt if you ask me, Kate Robson.' She smiles victoriously.

'I didn't,' says Kate.

'Didn't what?'

'Ask you.'

The volume of chatter has dropped to near silence, as every girl listens in on the exchange, poised, waiting for Mrs Minor's reaction. Sarah and Tina stare at Kate, who continues to chew her fingers and bounce her shoe around on the end of her toe.

Mrs Minor turns on her heel and marches to the front of the class, like a little wooden soldier.

'I fucking hate her,' Kate whispers to Tina, turning round to face the front. '*Midget.*'

As the lesson progresses, the girls chat, Kate clearly trying to draw Sarah into the conversation. Sarah is hesitant at first, wondering if it's one of Kate's jokes. She'll pretend to be nice, then whip it away again. They're talking about the book that Kate's reading. It's called *Hollywood Wives* by Jackie Collins, and Kate says it's filthy. She borrowed it from her older sister. She says she knows exactly where all the dirty bits are because they're the most well-thumbed. They all laugh. Mrs Minor delivers a disapproving glance over her specs, but remains seated at her desk, reading through an art book. Dust particles hover in the strip of light that cuts across her scarred wooden tabletop.

'How are we meant to learn how to paint, when all she does is read her bloody Van Gogh book every lesson?' asks Kate.

'My mum says she's past it,' says Marianne, surprising everyone with her contribution. 'She says if Mrs Minor really loved her job, then she'd be a better teacher, but she obviously hates it.'

'She hates us,' says Sarah.

Mrs Minor stands up behind her desk.

'Look at her,' says Kate. 'She's the same height standing up as she is sitting down.'

The girls snigger, and Mrs Minor glares at the group, never moving from behind the desk. The more she glowers, the more they try to stifle their laughter, covering their mouths with their floppy jumper sleeves. Tina snorts like a pig. Mrs Minor frowns and marches back down the classroom to see what the fuss is all about.

'So, not much progress in this corner, then. As usual.' She stands at the edge of the group, as they all chomp down on their cuffs, blinking away tears.

'We're stuck, miss,' says Kate, sniffing.

'Stuck?'

'Well no one's ever taught us how to actually paint properly. We don't know what to do next.'

Mrs Minor frowns, shaking her head. Her bowly copper hair moves with her head. She looks like a Playmobil man. Finally, she tuts and walks to the back of the room and into the art store cupboard.

'What's she doing?' asks Sarah.

A few minutes pass, and they exchange puzzled glances as they wait for Mrs Minor to return with more cutting remarks. The lunch bell is due to go off in ten minutes.

Kate puts down her paint board. 'Let's go and have a look.'

Marianne and Natalie look worried, but Tina and Sarah follow Kate to the cupboard and bunch together peering around the corner. Mrs Minor is up on the stepladder with her back to them, rearranging the powder paints. She's just tidying up. Kate puts her finger to her lips, then slams the door shut, turns the key in the lock and claps her hands together. The girls dash back to their seats, grab their bags and escape from the classroom for an early lunch.

'Well, that's a detention,' gasps Tina as they take refuge in the toilets that back out on to the field. Tina drops her bag by the sinks and goes into one of the cubicles.

'She deserved it, the witch,' says Kate, wiping smudged eyeliner from beneath her bottom lashes. 'What she said about Sarah's hair – it's just totally out of order.' She meets Sarah's eyes in the smeary mirror.

'Thanks,' says Sarah, holding her sleeve against her nostrils to mask the overpowering stench of disinfectant from the damp floor. 'You didn't have to say anything to her.'

'I did.' Kate bends over and brushes her hair in fierce, noisy strokes. She flips her hair back, picking up sections to backcomb from underneath. When she's finished, she offers the brush to Sarah. 'Sorry, Sar. About Dante and everything. About New Year.'

Sarah pauses, biting her lip.

Kate smooths her jumper down over her breasts, turning to check out her reflection from all angles. She continues to look in the mirror, poking and prodding at her hair. She turns to face Sarah square on. 'So, can we be friends again? I've really missed you, Sar.'

Sarah finishes brushing her own hair and hands back the brush. 'Yeah, why not?'

The loo flushes and Tina comes out of her cubicle. She fills her mouth with water from the cold tap, swills it around noisily and spits into the sink.

'Cool,' she says, giving them both the thumbs up. 'Everything's back to normal.'

Kate stands between them, putting an arm around each of her friends. 'Cool,' she says.

'Yeah,' Sarah says, relief rushing through her as warm as sunlight. 'Cool.'

~

After work on Saturday, Sarah goes to Kate's with her overnight bag. When she arrives, Tina answers the door and beckons her in with a flick of her head. She's holding the biscuit tin in her chocolatey splayed fingers and she has to finish her mouthful before she's able to speak.

'Kate's in the shower,' she says, pushing the tin back on to the shelf and washing her hands at the sink. 'She said to help ourselves to anything.'

Sarah drops her bag by the fridge and looks out of the window at the dark garden beyond. She can still see the edge of one of the tree stumps poking out from behind the large shed. 'Clocks'll change soon,' she says.

Tina opens the fridge and reaches in for a Diet Coke. 'Want one?' she asks, snapping back the ring-pull and strolling over to lean against the warm oven.

Sarah takes a can and does the same, hiccuping as she swallows the first fizzy mouthful. She laughs, putting her hand to her mouth just as Jason walks in, tucking a smart black shirt into his jeans with the flat of his hand. He's wearing black Chelsea boots, which have been polished to a high shine.

'Hello, Sarah, love. Glad to see you're making yourself at home.' He gives her a bright smile, making a final adjustment to his jeans with a tug of the belt loops.

'Oh, sorry – ' she stutters, holding up the can.

Jason wrinkles his eyebrows in a frown. 'Don't be a daft mare!' He walks across the kitchen and stretches one arm around her shoulder so that they're standing side by side, facing Tina over by the oven. He gives Sarah a tight, jostling squeeze. 'What do I always say, Teen? *Mi casa es su casa*, as the Spanish say. Help yourself!'

Sarah's muscles go rigid, and she stands beneath the weight of his arm, uncomfortably gripping her can of Coke and staring blankly at Tina.

Tina laughs, blushing, and takes another swig from her drink. 'What's that other one you always say? *Que sera, sera*,' she says.

'Very good!' Jason says, abruptly releasing Sarah and striding towards Tina.

In that instant, Tina stiffens, appearing small, her eyes uncertain. Jason stops and reaches into the cupboard above her head. He brings out a glass and carefully pushes the door shut. Tina stares at her feet.

He stands between the two girls, juggling the glass loosely from one hand to the other, regarding them both expectantly.

'Well?' he asks, his hands held wide. 'Aren't you going to say anything?'

Tina and Sarah look at one another, baffled, trying to stifle their embarrassed laughter.

Jason lets his shoulders fall, as if disappointed. 'About how dashing I look? I'm taking Patty out tonight for our anniversary.'

'Oh! You look very nice,' says Sarah, smiling politely.

Tina keeps her bony hand clasped over her mouth.

'Sixteen years we've been married,' he says, filling his glass at the cold tap. He turns towards the kitchen door conspiratorially. 'You'd get less for armed robbery,' he whispers with a wink.

Sarah doesn't know how to react, so she smiles and runs her hand through her hair. She hopes Kate won't be too long. Maybe they could just go up to her room and wait.

'Right!' says Jason, looking at his watch, 'I'd better go and give Patty a kick up the bum.' He drinks his water down and sprints into the hall and up the stairs without a backward glance.

Sarah frowns at Tina and they break into silent laughter, folding their arms across their bellies and hiding their faces behind their loose hair.

'He's barmy,' Tina whispers, when she's sure he's out of earshot.

Sarah nods, finishing her drink and dropping the can in the swing bin. 'He's quite a laugh, really. He's nothing like my dad.'

Tina shakes her head. 'Nor mine! Nothing like him at all.'

Five minutes later, Kate comes down looking blow-dried, and her parents leave through the front door.

'Be good!' Jason shouts as he closes the door behind him.

'And you!' Kate calls back. She freezes for a moment, with her hand cupped to her ear, listening for the sound of the car pulling away. '*Yes*!' she says when she's certain they've gone.

She brings out the cider and whacks up the volume on the kitchen hi-fi, bopping her head in time to the beat. 'Who's hungry?'

The others nod.

'Oh, I love this album,' says Tina.

'Who is it, then?' asks Kate. She's always trying to catch her out.

'It's Prince, isn't it? *Purple Rain*.' She rolls her eyes at Kate. 'I'm not a complete div, you know.'

Kate laughs. 'Yeah. Who was the one who got A Flock of Seagulls mixed up with ABC? And you didn't even know who Ian McCulloch was!'

Sarah doesn't know who Ian McCulloch is either. 'This album's great,' she says, pulling out a chair at the kitchen table. 'Can I tape it?'

Kate picks up the oven gloves and opens the door to lift out a large macaroni cheese. 'Sure. Dante hates Prince; he can't believe I like him. He calls it my plebby music.'

'You should listen to whatever you like,' says Tina. She points at the food. 'Has that got any meat in it?'

'Fuckin' hell, Teen! It's a bloody macaroni cheese! Since when did macaroni cheese have meat in it?'

Tina's neck shrinks into her shoulders as if she's been caught in a cold wind. 'Alright, alright. Anyway, you should listen to whatever music you want. I'd never let a bloke tell me what to do.'

Kate drops the oven gloves on the side and tuts. 'Like you're suddenly the world expert on men or something?'

Tina looks wounded. She starts furiously scratching at the palm of her hand. 'No. I'm just saying. I wouldn't let a bloke tell me what to do.'

'What, and you think I would?' Kate's hands are on her hips now, and she looks ready for a full-on fight.

Sarah shifts in her seat awkwardly. 'I don't think she meant – ' she mumbles.

'And if I'm such a pushover, how come I *am* listening to Prince, even though Dante hates it? I don't let him tell me what to do. I do whatever I want to do, whenever I want. I've got my own mind, thank you very much.'

Tina puts her hands up in surrender. 'Al*right*! I didn't mean it like that. I know you've got your own mind.'

'Shall I get some plates out?' Sarah asks, getting up from her seat. 'Where are they, Kate?'

Kate looks at Tina and Sarah and sighs. She points to one of the cupboards. 'Sorry,' she says. 'It's bloody Dante again.'

Sarah turns to the cupboard, clenching her teeth. She's sick to death of hearing about Dante.

'We went shopping in Tighborn today, and we ended up having a massive argument in Our Price. He kept going on and on about my crap taste in music in front of the whole shop, so I told him to shove his Velvet Underground up his arse and I stormed off. I got the bus back on my own.'

Sarah pinches her lips between her finger and thumb, to stop herself from laughing. Tina stares at her feet.

Kate notices and breaks into a reluctant smile. 'Yeah, I suppose it does sound funny when you say it out loud. Anyway, he just really pissed me off.' She picks up the oven gloves and lifts the macaroni cheese on to the table with a thump. 'Right. Let's eat.'

Later, when they're all asleep, Sarah hears Patty and Jason returning downstairs. She can distinguish the sounds of discarded shoes thudding on the soft carpet, of keys being dropped on the kitchen floor. In the silence of the house she can just make out their muffled argument.

'Fuck it,' Jason says. They must be in the living room.

'What d'you mean, "fuck it"?' Patty's words are slurred.

A cupboard door slamming.

'I mean fuck it. It's the same old thing with you. You never change your tune. Day in, day out. Poor me, poor me, poor me. Change the record, Pats.'

There's a long pause. Sarah holds her breath in, afraid she'll miss something if she breathes out.

'Well, actually, yes, poor me! The shit I've had to put up with, living with you all these years! Disappearing down the youth club whenever it suits you. Playing about with your bloody records all the time, when you should be home. Making us move house willy-nilly whenever things don't work out for you. It's a wonder I'm not a nervous wreck.'

'What d'you mean, "it's a wonder"? You *are* a bloody nervous wreck! Look at you, knocking back your happy pills right now! No wonder you look so bloody knackered all the time. You're half-asleep.'

There are sounds from the kitchen, more moving about.

'I've had enough,' Patty says, her voice growing clearer. 'I'm going to bed.'

Her footsteps move unsteadily up the stairs and past the girls' room. After a minute, the toilet next door flushes, and the door to Patty's room clicks shut.

Sarah lies motionless on the futon bed beside Tina, who's deep in sleep, her skinny white arm draped high above her head. Sarah hears the light switch going off downstairs, and the clunk of metal as Jason pulls the deadlock on the front door. She hears him sigh heavily at the foot of the stairs, before his tread becomes audible as he reaches the top step and passes their door.

'Happy fucking Anniversary,' she hears him mutter, and when his bedroom door clicks shut the house falls silent again.

~

Sarah has study leave on Friday afternoon, so she finishes school after lunch and heads home via Selton High Street, stopping off at the Co-op to pick up a madeira cake for Dad to have with his afternoon tea. The steady drizzle has soaked through her school jumper by the time she reaches town and she decides to take cover in Shattered Records before making the ten-minute walk home.

The owner looks like an overgrown teenager, with long unkempt blond hair and a thin gingery beard. He's wearing a Black Sabbath T-shirt and a pair of bleached jeans which are frayed and torn around his heavy boots.

He looks up from the rack of second-hand albums he's sorting through beside the counter. 'Alright,' he says with a convivial nod.

'Hi,' Sarah replies.

The tiny box-shaped shop feels claustrophobic and muggy, appearing windowless and dark behind the posters and gig flyers that cover every inch of the glass shop front. The wall-to-wall album racks are painted entirely black, starkly contrasting with the grubby white walls and flaky ceiling. A life-sized poster of Alice Cooper stretches up the wall behind the counter, disguising what must be the door to the back room. She recognises the music playing as Bob Marley, which seems strangely incongruous in a shop like this.

She walks slowly around the rows of albums, checking out the handwritten A–Z tabs, trying to think of something she wants to look at. Her mind goes blank, and she starts thumbing through the sleeves aimlessly, starting to wish she hadn't come in. There's no one else in the shop. It's just her and the beardy man.

'Looking for anything in particular?' he asks, moving behind the counter and easing on to a high stool. His voice is soft and slow.

Sarah looks over her shoulder at him. 'Not really. Just looking, thanks.'

'Just shout,' he says, popping open his Golden Virginia tin and placing the lid gently on the counter. 'We've got loads more out the back.'

She tries to remember the name of the tape that Dante gave Kate for Valentine's. It began with a Z. She moves along to the Z section, and flips the album covers over one by one. ZZ Top. Ziggy Stardust. The Zombies. Zappa. *Frank Zappa* – that was it. There are a few different albums of his, and she lifts one out and turns it over in her hands.

'Classic,' says beardy. He's finished rolling his cigarette. He leans back to push open the stock room door and lights the roll-up with a snap of his brass lighter. '*Joe's Garage*. Classic.'

She looks up again and nods, just as John walks in through the entrance. Sarah is partially obscured by the middle rack of albums, so John doesn't notice her immediately. She watches him as he walks across the small shop towards the till.

'Alright, John,' says beardy.

'Alright, Sol.'

Beardy slowly scissors his fingers along a thick lock of drab blonde hair and pushes it behind his ear. 'I've got that King Crimson album you were looking for, John-man.'

'Nice one.' There's a bar stool on the customer side of the counter, which John pulls out and sits on.

'It's in mint condition, man. Hardly been played, I'd say. I gave it a little spin myself, when it came in. *Classic.*' He reaches under the counter and produces a freaky-looking album cover which he carefully slides across the desk.

John picks it up by opposing corners and spins it neatly between his hands, surveying it with respect. 'The sleeve's in really good nick, too.' He nods, impressed. 'How much do you want for it?'

Beardy reaches for a small notepad at the side of the till and places it on the counter between them. He writes a figure down in pencil.

John rubs his chin. He takes the pencil and writes his own figure on the pad.

Beardy rubs his chin and jots one last number on the paper. John nods, stands, and shakes him by the hand. They both grin broadly, and John reaches into his back pocket for his wallet.

'Hiya, John,' Sarah says, coming out from behind the stand.

He visibly jumps. 'Sarah!' he says, looking delighted.

'Hey, man,' says beardy, 'I forgot you were there.'

Sarah smiles.

'What are you doing here?' asks John, tipping her album sleeve forward so that he can see it. 'Zappa?' he says, looking perplexed.

'Why not?' she replies. She's uncomfortably aware of her school uniform.

He takes the album sleeve from her and turns it over. 'Have you ever listened to Zappa before?'

She feels the blood rising to her cheeks. 'No. Someone told me it was good.'

'He's a misogynist sex-maniac. That's what all his songs are about. There's all this hype about Zappa, and I just don't get it. Anyone who writes songs about genital lice and wet T-shirt contests can't be all that talented.'

Beardy laughs behind his till. 'Come on, man. Lighten up a bit. Zappa's a classic.'

'It's classic crap,' says John. 'Whereas this, on the other hand – ' he holds up his King Crimson album ' – is something else altogether.'

Beardy purses his lips.

'OK,' says John. 'You've got to choose one album, Sol. If you were on a desert island. One or the other – *Joe's Garage* or *In the Court of the Crimson King*. Which is it to be?' He holds out the two sleeves for scrutiny.

Beardy pinches his chin hair. 'Alright, man. You're right. It's gotta be the Crimson.'

John turns back to Sarah, flicking the ponytail from his shoulder triumphantly. 'See? I'll do you a tape, if you like. Forget about the Zappa – it's a waste of time. Really.'

Sarah laughs and slides the Zappa album back into the racking. She didn't really want it anyway.

They leave the shop together, and John walks her to the end of the path where the High Street turns into Tide Road. The drizzle has disappeared now, and the sun is trying to break through the strewn clouds.

'See you at work tomorrow?' he asks, holding the white carrier bag protectively against his chest.

Sarah nods. 'Don't forget my tape,' she calls back as she walks away.

Deborah's purple Escort is on the driveway when Sarah arrives home. She looks at her watch; it's just after three.

She crunches over the gravel and pauses at the door, wondering which room they're in. Faint laughter travels through the living room window at the front of the house, and Sarah clenches her jaw as she wiggles her key into the lock. She pushes the door closed behind her, noticing Deborah's strappy leather sandals sitting side by side beneath the coat rack. She bought them in Corfu, she told Sarah. They were made to measure in an open market, to fit her small wide feet perfectly.

The hallway smells of fresh cooking: fish and vegetables, at a guess. She glances into the kitchen, where pots and pans are stacked up on the side, waiting to be washed up. Ted comes out to meet her, carrying one of her stripy socks in his mouth.

'Oi!' she says, pinching his nose and retrieving the balled-up sock. 'Mine!'

Ted's body wags excitedly, as if he's hinged loosely in the middle. He trots into the living room, looking back, wanting her to follow.

'Aha,' Dad calls out before she can escape to her room. 'Here she is! Look who's here, Sarah-Lou!'

Sarah grinds her teeth together, attempting to push back her intense irritation. In the living room she holds her school bag across her body and smiles stiffly. 'Hi, Deborah.'

Deborah and Dad are sitting on opposite sofas, an open bottle of wine on the coffee table between them. There are dessert plates and forks beside their glasses, alongside a large bowl of fruit salad and a little jug of cream. Ted jumps up to sit beside Deborah.

'Hello, darling!' Deborah says, trying to get up off the low sofa without disturbing Ted. Her loose kaftan top catches beneath her heavily jewelled hand, and Sarah can see it's a bit of a struggle.

She waves her hand. 'Don't get up. I'm off to do my homework anyway.'

'Oh, Sarah! Come and say hello for a few minutes, at least!' Dad stretches over to the coffee table to pick up a large glass of red wine. He twists round to look at her, hooking his elbow over the back of the sofa. 'Come and tell us what you've been up to.'

Sarah gives him a disapproving stare, as Deborah reaches for her own glass. 'I thought you were meant to be working on your Selton project today?'

'Uh-oh,' he says, turning to Deborah with a melodramatic expression. 'Looks as if I'm in trouble. Naughty, naughty.' He takes a drink from his glass and widens his eyes at Sarah. He's clearly had one too many.

Deborah smiles and shakes her head. 'Ignore him. He's only trying to wind you up.'

'Nothing new there, then.' Sarah crosses over into the dining room where the glass doors to the drinks cabinet have been left wide open. She pushes them shut with a loud rattle, picking up the discarded wine foil and cork from the side. She marches back into the living room and drops them into the bin in full view of Deborah and her father.

'Actually, I don't think he's used to drinking during the day. Are you, Dad? Well, *I've* never seen you drink during the day, anyway.'

Dad gives her a patronising smile and turns to Deborah on the opposite sofa. 'I think someone's being a bit of an old stick-in-the-mud, if you ask me.'

He pushes out his bottom lip and looks at Sarah as if he's a five-year-old.

'Oh, my God,' she says, still clutching her school bag. She looks at Deborah, and gestures towards him with an upturned hand. 'Deborah, how can you bear it?'

She doesn't wait for an answer. She leaves the room and thumps up the stairs where she won't have to endure his embarrassing attempts at humour. Outside her bedroom door, she pauses to eavesdrop on their conversation below.

'Do you have to provoke her like that, James?' Deborah says, sounding exasperated.

'She knows I'm only joking. She's known me long enough to be able to take a joke, for heaven's sake!'

'Well, if you really want me to get to know Sarah better, that's not going to help, is it?'

There's a pause, and the sound of a glass being placed on the table.

'Maybe I should go up and see her?' Deborah says. 'I can't help feeling I should do something to help.'

Sarah makes a little fist and pushes open her bedroom door.

'No, no. Leave her. She likes to be left alone when she's in one of her moods. I'll speak with her later.'

Silence.

'Trust me, Deborah. She'll be fine.'

Sarah clicks the door shut behind her and flops on to her single bed. She thinks about the old times, when she and Dad would buy fish and chips on a Friday night and settle in front of the TV, just the two of them. She kicks her shoes off the bed and blows hot air between her lips.

'Just go,' she whispers up towards the dusty rattan lampshade. 'That would help.'

~

In the last week of term, one of the office staff interrupts Sarah's Maths lesson with a message calling her out of class.

'Sarah Ribbons, you're to go to Mrs Jensen's office. Take your bag with you,' she says.

As Sarah stands up from her desk her chair scrapes noisily across the wooden floor, and everyone turns to look.

'*What've you done*?' Kate whispers as Sarah quickly stuffs her books into her bag.

She hurries along the silent corridors and up the stairs towards Mrs Jensen's room. Without the usual sounds of footsteps and chatter, the Victorian building takes on an eerie quality. Its wood-panelled walls seem to sigh with each step she takes along the worn parquet floor. *Clack – sigh – clack – sigh*. Her mind is leaping through all the possibilities, causing her heart rate to double as her speed increases. By the time she arrives at the Head of Year's room, she's almost running. She knocks.

Mrs Jensen opens the door and invites her in. 'Sarah. How are you?' She places her hand on the centre of Sarah's back and guides her into the orange plastic chair that faces her desk. She's uncharacteristically gentle, so Sarah knows that something really bad has happened.

Her throat feels as if it's closing up. The room is tiny, pinned in by chipped bookshelves, which bow under the weight of files and staple guns. The messy paperwork on the desk is excruciating.

Mrs Jensen walks around to her own side of the desk and sits, clasping her hands together on the desktop.

'Sarah, we've had a phone call. About your father.'

Sarah thinks she might faint. She stares blankly at the teacher. The window behind Mrs Jensen is made of reinforced glass, with metal bars across the lower half. It's like a prison window. It reminds her of the old Victorian workhouse they visited in the third year. Scary shop dummies were dotted around the old building, dressed in authentic clothing, posed with chimney brushes and milk pails. One of the child dummies had its nose missing, broken off at an obscene slant to reveal the grey plaster beneath.

'He's been taken to St Jude's,' says Mrs Jensen, 'with a suspected heart attack. Now, he's doing fine, but they need to keep him in until he's stable. Sarah, do you understand?'

Sarah nods. What about Ted? He'll want feeding. She'll have to go back home and sort him out. She needs to think about all this; she can't do it here. Mrs Jensen is still talking and Sarah realises she hasn't heard any of it.

'What?' she says, frowning irritably.

Mrs Jensen looks affronted. 'I said, you'll have to stay with relatives for a few days.'

Sarah feels the panic rising through her ribcage. 'I haven't got any.'

'You must have some,' Mrs Jensen replies briskly.

Sarah shakes her head. 'But I'll be fine on my own. It won't be a problem.'

'No, no. We can't have that, Sarah. You're just fifteen. It would be wrong of me to allow you to do that. So you've *no* living relatives at all?' She seems to think Sarah is lying.

'No.'

'Right, so we'll have to arrange for you to stay with a friend. Who would you like me to call?'

'Um.' Sarah can't seem to work it out. She shakes her head. 'I'm mostly friends with Kate and Tina in my class, so one of them, I suppose.'

'Right. I'll phone their parents and sort something out. It will only be for a few days, Sarah, until they let your dad go home. In the meantime, Mrs McCabe is going to run you down to the hospital. You can stop off at home and pack a bag, and I should have something sorted out by the time you get back. You go and wait down by the front office, and we'll be with you shortly.'

Mrs Jensen stands and walks around her desk to open the door to see her out. 'I'm sure he'll be fine, Sarah,' she says, patting her firmly on the shoulder.

Sarah walks down the hushed stairs towards the front office, the numb sound of her school shoes echoing softly in her wake.

When Sarah sees her father lying flat against the starched white of the hospital bed, she has to suppress an involuntary shriek. His eyes are closed and he has wires stuck to his exposed chest, a tube taped into his nose. He must sense her there, because he turns his face towards the door and smiles weakly.

'Sarah-Lou,' he says, lifting his hand from the coverlet.

She walks towards the bed, winded by shock, and takes his hand. It all feels wrong, standing here like this, looking down on him. 'What happened?' she asks in a whisper.

'You can sit down, you know,' he says. 'I won't break.'

She perches on the side of the bed.

'It's all my own fault, of course,' he says when she asks him what happened. 'Thought I'd get myself walking again, you know, lose some of the excess baggage and all that.' He pats his stomach, pausing as his breathing becomes laboured. 'Pass me a drink, Sarah-Lou?'

He takes a sip and she returns the glass to the bedside cabinet.

'Just took it a bit far. I was going for the eight-mile circuit, up to West Selton along the seafront, then back through the farmland and into town.'

'Dad! I can't believe you could be so stupid! You haven't been on a big walk like that for years. You can't just launch straight into a big hike, for heaven's sake!' She swipes at her forehead; the ward is uncomfortably warm.

'Anyway, I did quite well – got as far as the town centre, before I had a bit of a funny turn. Right outside your chemist's, as it happens. Nice young man with a ponytail came out and helped me, got me off in an ambulance in no time.'

'They want me to go and stay with friends until you get out,' Sarah says, scratching at a small dot of dirt on the hem of her skirt.

'Good idea.'

'Well, I don't want to go! Why can't I stay at home? Get it ready for when you come out?'

'It'll only be a few days, Sarah. Just go along with it, and you'll be back home before you know it.'

'What about Ted?'

'I'll phone Deborah. See if she can have him for a few days.'

'He doesn't even know her!' Sarah's face feels as if it's on fire.

'Yes, he does. He'll be fine with Deborah.' Dad pats her hand.

Sarah can see how weak he is. 'Sorry,' she says.

She looks back towards the door, where Mrs McCabe is waiting on the seat outside. She sits neatly, reading a magazine with her body turned slightly away from the doorway so as not to appear intrusive. Sarah watches as she runs her hand over her small baby bump, resting her fingers beneath its curve as if to hold the weight. She told Sarah to take as long as she needed. No rush.

Sudden tears spring into her eyes. 'I'd better get going,' she tells her dad, flicking her head in Mrs McCabe's direction.

He indicates for Sarah to fetch his wallet from the drawer beside him, and hands her two five pound notes. 'In case you need anything.'

'I'll bring you a bar of Bournville, after school tomorrow?'

He smiles approvingly and squeezes her hand. 'Good girl,' he says.

Sarah zips the money into the front of her bag and kisses him goodbye.

Mrs McCabe drops them at Kate's house after school. She lifts Sarah's bags out of the boot, and stands beside her car as the girls walk up the path.

'Let me know if you need anything, Sarah,' she calls after them.

Sarah turns to look at Mrs McCabe and sees the warmth in her eyes as the light spring breeze ripples through her blonde waves. She feels light-headed. 'Thanks,' she calls back.

The school nurse stands watching until Sarah steps over the threshold and clicks the door shut behind her.

Kate's mum is home, chopping onions at the island unit in the middle of the kitchen. She stops when they walk in, her knife hovering over the work surface. Sarah is struck by how much older she seems than Jason. Her hair has more grey streaks through it than she remembered, and she looks so tired.

'Alright, Mum,' says Kate, picking up the biscuit tin and prising it open against her chest.

'Hello, girls. How are you, Sarah?' She wipes her hands on a tea towel and walks round to stand with them. 'Have you visited your dad yet?'

Sarah feels an immediate rush of emotion flood up through her lungs. She gasps back a sob, and Mrs Robson embraces her, holding her head protectively against her own shoulder. Sarah's body heaves haltingly as she attempts to stem the tears. After a minute, she pulls back from Kate's mum and gratefully accepts the kitchen towel that Kate thrusts into her hand.

'I'm sorry, Mrs Robson. I really don't want to be a bother. They wouldn't let me stay at my place.' She blows her nose and exhales through pursed lips. 'But they think he'll be out on Saturday morning, if he's doing OK.'

'It's *Patty*. And it's no trouble, love. Make yourself at home.' She returns to the onion chopping, and the girls take Sarah's things upstairs.

Kate throws herself back on her big puffy double bed. 'She never hugs me like that,' she says.

~

For the last few days of term, Kate and Sarah walk to and from school together. There's no Dante as he's gone to Florida for Easter; it's as if he never existed. Most evenings they take their meals up to Kate's room to watch TV and listen to music. They hear Patty's soft tread on the stairs every night around nine, followed by the sounds of her brushing her teeth and the quiet click of her bedroom door. It's because of the sleeping pills – that's why she's like a zombie every morning, Kate says. They lie in bed talking into the early hours, laughing quietly and gossiping about the other girls at school. They've never been closer. Jason's smile lingers on Sarah over breakfast when no one else is looking, and her stomach flips as their eyes meet.

On Friday evening, Sarah returns from the hospital on Kate's bike, just in time for supper. The family are in the kitchen, serving up lasagne and salad as she comes in through the door.

'Sarah, sweetie! Just in time for grub!' Jason's got a plate in one hand and a can of lager in the other.

'How's your dad?' asks Patty. She's wearing a large pair of shiny red spectacles.

Sarah's cheeks feel pink from the cycle ride. 'He's really good. They think it was a very mild attack – he's doing well. But they don't think he'll be home tomorrow, more like Sunday.'

Patty hands her a plate and she starts to help herself to lasagne.

'That's great news, love. Just in time for the Easter holidays. Bet you're pleased?'

'Wanna Coke?' asks Kate, holding open the fridge.

Sarah nods and smiles in answer to both questions. The tension behind her eyes has lifted, and everything feels right. Kate's place is so warm and comfortable, but Sarah is excited about the prospect of being back in her own home with Dad and Ted, with all her own things around her.

Kate brings out two cans and snaps open both ring pulls. 'What d'you think of Mum's new specs?'

Patty rolls her eyes.

'Very nice,' says Sarah smiling.

'Nice?' says Kate. 'She looks like Timmy Mallett!'

Jason grins. 'Don't be mean, Katie. She looks more like Su Pollard. *Hi-de-Hi!*'

They both snigger. Patty pulls open the cutlery drawer to fetch a bundle of knives and forks.

Kate slaps at the worktop with the palm of her hand. 'Or – I know, I know – what's his name, the one who does the weather?'

Jason laughs hard. 'Ian McCaskill! Now, that's just nasty!'

Kate screeches with laughter, pushing Sarah to encourage her to join in.

'Well, I think they're really nice,' says Sarah, smiling at Patty.

'Thanks, love.'

'Creep,' says Kate. She flicks a ring-pull across the worktop. 'Oh, Mum! – I'm supposed to be going over to Gail's tomorrow morning. Can you phone Auntie Linda and let her know I can't make it?'

'Don't be silly, Kate,' Patty says as she walks through to the living room. 'You've had Sarah with you for the last few days. It won't kill you to be parted for one night! And Auntie Linda's looking forward to seeing you.'

'Oh, Mum!' Kate kicks her heel back against the kitchen cupboards.

'Katie,' says her dad. 'Come on. You've had your cousin planned in for weeks. You can't let her down at short notice. You can have Sarah back over any time.' He joins Patty in the living room, and the girls take their food upstairs.

'I've got to work all day tomorrow, in any case,' says Sarah, trying to make Kate feel better. 'Maybe Tina's around – I could see her after work?'

Kate places her tray on the bedside table. 'She's babysitting the twins. To be honest, she's really getting on my nerves at the moment. She's constantly on about how great it is to be a vegetarian, and telling everyone else that they're murderers 'cos they eat meat. The other day I flicked a slice of Spam in her face at lunch break, just to make her shut up.'

Sarah laughs. 'She wrote on the blackboard in Geography the other day, before Miss Tupper came in. *Chickens are Friends NOT Food.* Miss Tupper asked who had written it on the board, and when no one owned up she said, "I rather like them with a few potatoes and a bit of gravy, myself." Tina nearly went mental. She was raging and whispering about it all lesson. Miss Tupper must've known it was her.'

'She's a right pain in the arse these days. I'm gonna give her a bit of a wide berth until she stops going on about the bloody veggie stuff.'

Sarah pulls up a pillow and sits on the edge of the bed with her tray on her lap.

'I'm really pissed off I've got to go to my cousin's,' Kate says. 'Gail's a complete square.' She hops between the channels on the portable TV until she settles on *The Cosby Show* and sits back on the bed with her legs up. 'She's sixteen, and she's into horse-riding and playing the violin. God, you should see some of the clothes she wears – it's embarrassing. She's still got a ra-ra skirt!'

Sarah laughs and wiggles back up against the padded headboard to get comfortable. 'Maybe you can give her some fashion tips.'

'Yeah, right. I'd die if anyone knew she was my cousin.'

'Well, at least she doesn't go to the same school as you,' says Sarah, stretching across to put her can on the bedside table.

Kate eats the last mouthful of her lasagne and downs the rest of her Coke in one go. She turns and prods Sarah, before letting out an enormous belch. '*Be – el – ze – bu –b*,' she growls deeply.

Sarah shrieks. 'You freak!'

Thank God for Kate.

~

Half an hour before closing time on Saturday, Jason pops into the chemist's to ask Sarah if she'd like a takeaway curry. She's busy filling up the flannel basket beside the bubble baths.

Jason picks up a tightly rolled pink flannel, and juggles it from hand to hand. 'I'm having a rogan josh, and Patty usually has a tikka masala. What d'you fancy? My treat.'

Sarah's never had an Indian takeaway before. 'I don't like anything too hot,' she says, trying not to sound ignorant. 'I can't remember which ones are less spicy.'

'Oh, you'll want a korma, then. Chicken?'

Sarah's aware of John at the back of the shop, where he's running the till roll off for cashing up. He hovers around the counter, glancing in their direction every now and then.

She turns her back to him.

'Yes, that's the one I like,' she tells Jason. 'Great, thanks. Do you want some money? Dad gave me ten pounds in case I needed anything.'

'No! I said, it's my treat. I'll pick up something for pudding, if you like. I guess you like chocolate?'

Sarah smiles,waiting for him to leave. She can feel John behind her, still watching.

Jason waggles the flannel in the air and drops it back in the basket. 'Righty-ho. What time d'you finish?'

'Half-five.'

John brings the empty baskets down from the counter and drops them on the pile beside the door, a couple of feet from where Sarah and Jason are standing.

Jason looks at his watch. 'Why don't I meet you outside, and we can walk back together? Kate's not home, is she, so I expect you'll be glad of the company?'

John wrinkles his nose at Sarah as he returns to the counter.

'OK,' she says to Jason. 'See you then.'

Jason walks out through the shop door, smiling like a fourteen-year-old boy. He turns to look back through the window and gives Sarah a little wave. She turns away quickly, pretending not to notice.

John pulls out the second till tray with a clatter of coins. 'Who's that again?' he asks when she returns to tidy up the till bags under the counter.

'You know, it's Kate's dad. I told you before.'

'He's a bit chummy, isn't he?'

'No, he's just trying to be nice.'

'Yeah, *really* nice, by the looks of it.'

'Don't be an idiot, John. I'm staying there at the moment. Because of Dad. He just popped in to see what I wanted for supper.' She tuts, and pushes the paper bags back into place.

John looks embarrassed, and he stares into his tray distractedly. 'Sorry. I didn't realise – you know, that you'd had to go and stay with Kate. I mean, you could've stayed with us, if you'd wanted.'

Sarah bends to pick up a ten-pence piece which has dropped from John's tray. She plops it into the right compartment and starts to polish the worktop.

'That's alright. Anyway, thanks for helping Dad when he fell outside the shop. He said a nice young chap had helped him. I knew it was you when Dad described the dodgy ponytail.' She turns away, smiling, and puts an excess of energy into polishing the Vicks stand.

Still balancing his tray, John prods her calf with the toe of his boot, causing her to buckle at the knees.

'You – !' she gasps, laughing and swiping at him with her cloth.

He flicks his head theatrically, causing his ponytail to swish. 'They call me the Horse-tailed Hero! Where there's trouble, I'll be on hand to save the day!' He stamps his foot like a pony and neighs, galloping out the back with the day's takings.

For a moment, Sarah stares at the space he leaves, half expecting him to return. She carries on with her polishing, counting down the last fifteen minutes till home-time.

When the shop shuts, she rushes off as fast as she can to avoid John seeing her with Jason again. She peels off her pinafore, rolls some tinted balm across her lips and leaves through the fire exit, shouting a quick goodbye behind her.

As she hurries down the alleyway, she spots Jason crossing the road towards her with a carrier bag of shopping from the Co-op. They walk along the High Street, out on to the suburban roads that run parallel to the sea. It's a mild April evening and the sun is low and bright above the houses and bungalows of Tide Road. The gulls are out in numbers this evening, calling and bombing over the rooftops, to and from the sea. There must be some activity down at the seafront; perhaps the fishing boats are drawing back in to the shore. She can smell spring in the air. The salty tang of sea spinach and wet shingle circulates on the light breeze like the promise of a long summer. The branches of an enormous cherry tree hang over the old stone wall of the big house on the corner, laden with newly formed pink blossom flowers. They'll flutter like mist for a week or two, before the tree starts to shed its petals, carpeting the pavements with a blanket of rippling pink. Sarah thinks of the bare, gnarly branches of the winter cherry tree. All that waiting, all that hard work, growing and blooming, for just one short moment of beauty.

Halfway home, Jason slows down outside the Old Sailor and peers in through the low window. He looks at his watch.

'We must have time for a swift one? The curry won't be ready till seven. What d'you reckon?'

Sarah feels uneasy. 'What about Patty? Won't she be expecting us home?'

'Patty? She'll be sitting in front of *Neighbours* or whatever that rubbish is she watches. Come on, we'll have a quick drink then head straight back.'

Jason strides ahead into the dim-looking public bar. There are old glass lifebuoys and dusty ropes hanging across the bar and into the corners. The treacly wood-panelled walls are adorned with lobster pots and anchors, all of them looking as if they need a good clean. Sarah feels the tacky texture of the wooden floor beneath her sensible work shoes.

'How-do, Jase,' says the man behind the bar. He's got the biggest beer belly Sarah has ever seen.

'Afternoon, Stan. Pint of my usual, mate, and a half of cider for my friend here.'

Sarah smiles flatly, terrified that the landlord will know she's not eighteen.

A group of men enters the bar. They stand at the other corner, bantering noisily and arguing over whose round it is, looking as if they've come off a building site, all of them in muddy boots and dusty clothes.

'Jase,' says one of them with a smirk. He drapes his oily eyes over Sarah. He's about Jason's age, and his shoulder-length hair grows back from a deep widow's peak. If Kate were here she'd say he looks like a pikey.

'Dave,' replies Jason, leaning into the bar on his forearms.

'That's not your Katie, is it, Jase?' asks the landlord, flipping down two cardboard coasters and placing their drinks on the bar in front of them.

'No, this is Sarah, she's a friend of Kate's, aren't you, love? She's staying with us for a few days.' He pats her on the back and pulls out a bar stool for her to sit on.

'Is that right?' says Dave in the corner, with a dirty leer across his face. 'That's nice, innit, Jase? Eh? That's nice, mate.'

'Yeah, that's right, Dave.'

One of the older men moves closer and gives Sarah a little nudge. 'Don't mind Dave, love. He's a bit touched,' he says, tapping his temple.

'I went to school with him,' Jason adds, keeping his voice low. 'He used to be a right mental case, you know, really aggressive. Then he had an accident on his motorbike, down on Sheepwash bend. He's just a bit slow now, that's all. No harm in him, though.'

Sarah drinks her cider, deciding she won't look at Dave again. He gives her the creeps.

'So, where's Patty tonight, then, Jase?' asks Bert, the older guy.

'Back home. We're picking up a takeaway later on, so me and Sarah thought we'd stop off for a swifty.'

'Hope the missus don't find out!' caws Dave from his corner. He snuffles into his bitter. 'Wouldn't like that, eh, Jase? Wouldn't like that.'

'Yeah, got yourself a younger model, Jase?' chuckles the other man. 'Traded in the old one, eh?'

All the men are laughing, even Jason. Sarah tries to look as if she's amused too, so they can see she can take a joke, but she just wants to get out of there.

'Well, it had to happen sooner or later,' says Jason, putting his arm round Sarah and giving her a squeeze.

Sarah frowns at the group to show them it isn't true, shaking her head. She glugs back the rest of her cider and hops off the bar stool to pick up her bag.

'Looks like you're off, Jase, mate!' says Stan the landlord, picking up Sarah's empty glass and leaning under the bar to put it in the dishwasher tray.

Jason slowly drains his pint and eases himself off his stool, to show he's in no hurry.

'She's already got you well trained, mate. Look, she didn't even have to say a thing, but he knew it was time to go!'

Laughter fills the bar, as Jason grins at the group and opens the door to show Sarah out of the pub. 'See ya later, lads!' he calls over his shoulder.

'Don't do anything I wouldn't do!' Dave yells after them as the door closes.

They walk away from the pub and Jason puts his arm around Sarah's shoulder again, squeezing her upper arm with firm fingers. The sun is lower than before, casting a rose tinge across the pale skyline. 'Take no notice of that lot. They've got nothing better to talk about. Tell you what, bet they were all wishing they were in my place, though. Sitting next to the prettiest girl in town.' He lets his arm drop, and gives her a little bump with his shoulder.

'Hardly,' she says, pushing her fists further into her coat pockets. She looks up at Jason, who's squinting against the strange sky. His face is bathed in pink light, and the blue of his eyes appears almost unnatural. 'How old are you?' she asks, regretting it immediately.

He laughs, surprised. 'Thirty-nine. Why?'

'Just couldn't work it out, that's all.'

'Why, d'you think I look younger?'

'Yeah, I suppose so.'

'You're a darlin'!' he says, giving her a swift peck on the cheek. 'I know I feel it, sweetie. That's for sure.'

Sarah, Jason and Patty are sitting down to watch a film and eat their takeaway by half-seven.

Jason brings out a can of Strongbow for Sarah, and a lager for himself. He eases himself into the armchair nearest Sarah and pulls the coffee table closer for his feet.

'What's the film?' asks Sarah, puffing up a cushion behind her back.

Patty's beside her on the sofa, with her feet curled up underneath her bottom. She's got her food on a tray, and a glass of water sits on the table alongside two little pills.

'Remind me to take those in an hour, love,' she says to Jason as she snaps a poppadum in two.

'It's *National Lampoon's Vacation*,' says Jason. 'Chevy Chase. It's meant to be really funny.'

Sarah's pleased it's a comedy. She can't stand the horror films that Dante used to go on about. The more she thinks about Dante, the more she hates him.

'I could do with a laugh,' says Patty. She's already eaten half her curry before Sarah's even started.

Sarah kicks off her slippers and Jason turns off the main light. He passes her a poppadum, his fingers brushing hers as she takes it. She looks up at him as he sits back in his seat. He smiles furtively, knowing that Sarah is blocking Patty's view of him. Sarah wriggles down into the cushions and eats her korma, acutely aware of Jason's proximity as the film trailers run.

Halfway through, Jason pauses the video to fetch more drinks. Sarah visits the toilet in the break, and when she returns Jason passes her another Strongbow. She picks up the first can she's been sipping slowly for the past hour and knocks it back quickly. Patty doesn't seem to mind that Sarah's drinking cider; Kate must be able to drink at home whenever she wants to. Patty takes her tablets and stretches her legs out on to the coffee table, flexing her toes and rotating her ankles. She's wearing those special socks with rubber pads on the bottom to stop you slipping. Slipper socks. They're a faded aqua colour with pink pigs knitted into the design, bobbled around the tops where they're worn.

The film is so funny that once or twice Sarah almost spits her food across the living room. Jason's roaring, clapping his hands and covering his eyes at the toe-curling embarrassment of the Griswold family's blunders. Patty gives little 'ha-ha' laughs as she grows visibly sleepy on the sofa beside Sarah. Her eyes begin to sag a little, and eventually she pushes herself up out of her seat and clears the plates.

'That's me done for,' she says. 'Sorry to desert you, love. I can't keep my eyes open a moment longer. I'll see you in the morning, won't I?'

Sarah shifts on to the edge of the sofa. 'I'll probably get off quite early, to get the house ready for Dad. They're sure he'll be home tomorrow afternoon.' She smiles at Patty, who's vacantly running her fingers through her wiry hair.

'That's good. Well, night-night.'

Sarah hears Patty put the plates on the side in the kitchen and trudge up the stairs with weary footsteps and a yawn. The upstairs toilet flushes and Patty's bedroom door clicks shut.

As they continue to watch the film, Sarah becomes intensely aware of her own breathing. Jason nips out to the kitchen and returns with a box of Matchmakers. He sits in Patty's place, but he's closer to Sarah than Patty had been. He rattles the box in front of her, and starts to unpeel the outer layer of packaging.

'I love Matchmakers,' Sarah whispers, her eyes still on the TV.

'Thought you might,' Jason replies, sliding open the tray and removing the inner paper.

They watch the rest of the film crunching on chocolates and laughing together. 'That was good,' sighs Sarah as the credits roll up the screen. She laughs again. Jason hands her another Matchmaker, and they sit quietly munching, gazing across the living room. She knows she should go to bed now.

'Show you a trick,' says Jason, pulling up one knee so he's facing Sarah on the sofa. 'Hold this between your teeth and close your eyes.' He puts a matchmaker between her lips, so that it sticks out in front of her face horizontally. 'No peeking. Just keep your eyes closed until I say.'

She closes her eyes, the tip of her tongue feeling at the centimetre of rough chocolate stick held carefully between her teeth. Time seems to freeze, and her neck grows hotter with each passing second. She imagines she feels Jason leaning in, not touching her, just breathing into her skin as she sits there, waiting, waiting. Is he watching her? The chocolate in her mouth slowly softens, exposing the sharp embedded mint crystals. Her tongue returns to roll around the stick in a circular rhythm; round and back, round and back. She's sure that the Matchmaker is starting to tremble between her lips, but she keeps her eyes clamped shut, hearing nothing but the blood that rushes through her ears. Jason's mouth gently grazes her lips with moisture before his teeth bite the chocolate stick off at the base. The click of their teeth is fleeting, but audible, huge in the now silent room. Sarah gasps, but still her eyes remain closed. She can feel the pressure of Jason's chest against hers now, his lips lightly feeling their way down her neck and into the dip of her throat.

'OK?' he sighs into her skin.

'OK,' Sarah replies and her limbs wilt against the cushions of the sofa. She lets him kiss her, doesn't remove his fingers as they unbutton her clothes and slide beneath the layers of thin fabric. Her desire is crushing, and when he lifts her from the sofa, and lays her across the deep pile carpet of Kate Robson's living room floor, Sarah gives herself up.

~

Deborah's car pulls into the drive around teatime. Sarah stands over the kitchen stove, feeling sick with the weight of her secret. So much has changed in the space of so little time.

She's been at home alone since seven this morning, having risen early to cycle back before Jason or Patty woke. When she'd walked in through the front door the house had felt damp and hollow, having been shut up for several days, and dust motes rose in illuminated billows, surprised into action as she walked through the dreary hallway and up the stairs. She threw her bag in through the bedroom door and ran a deep bath, scrubbing herself clean and sobbing into the vapour, replaying the scene over and over in her mind's eye.

'So, you're not such a good girl after all?' Jason had said as he pushed himself up from the carpet, buttoning his flies, still breathing heavily. 'I could tell the first time I laid eyes on you.' Sarah had scrabbled up on to her knees, hugging a cushion to her lap to cover her dignity. Her eyes kept wandering back to the chicken korma smear on the glass coffee table. She was overwhelmed with self-loathing. Jason winked and switched off the TV, which was buzzing grey where the video had run to its end. She pulled on her leggings as quickly as she could, inwardly cursing them as they hooked on her toes, causing her to stumble against the sofa.

'Time for bed,' Jason said as he flicked off the side light and left the room. 'And no creeping into my room asking for more.'

Sarah takes the pan off the stove now, and walks down the hall to open the front door.

'Sarah-Lou.' Dad smiles as Deborah helps him out of the passenger seat. He's lost weight.

Ted leaps out of the back seat and sprints towards Sarah, jumping up on his back legs to be picked up. Deborah opens the back door of the car and lifts out Dad's overnight bag.

'We got him back in one piece,' she calls over to Sarah.

'Who? The dog, or me?' asks Dad as he shuffles across the gravel, waving Sarah away when she moves to help him. Anger buzzes in her fingers as he passes.

'I bought some cod in butter sauce for dinner,' she says, careful to control her voice. 'It's the boil-in-the-bag kind that you like. Would you like to eat with us?' she asks Deborah, hoping she'll say no.

Deborah smiles appreciatively. 'I'd love to, Sarah.'

She makes a pot of tea, and they sit in the living room and talk lightly for a while. Dad produces a leaflet called *Advice for a Healthy Heart* along with a bottle of pills. 'Rat poison,' he says.

'Do they know what caused it?' Sarah asks, taking the leaflet from him and scanning the information.

'The good life,' Dad chuckles. He finishes his tea and sinks back into the sagging sofa.

Sarah scowls. 'It's not funny, Dad.'

'Sorry. I've got to change my diet, so no more chocolate biscuits for me. Or butter. All puts a strain on the heart and that's what brought it on. They said it's a good job I don't smoke as well. I should thank my lucky stars it was a mild one – more like a warning than a proper heart attack, really.'

Deborah pours him another cup of tea from the pot.

'Got any cake to go with that?' Dad asks with a stony face, turning to raise an eyebrow at Deborah.

'God, Dad! You're not taking this seriously at all! You could have died!' Sarah's face flushes with rage. Stupid, *stupid* man.

'I'm off to the little boys' room,' he says, easing himself from the sofa. He slaps Sarah's hand as she tries to help him from his seat. 'Get away, woman!'

Deborah and Sarah sit in silence until they hear the door to the toilet bolt shut. Sarah shakes her head at Deborah, still fuming inside.

'It's all bravado,' Deborah says. 'It scared the living daylights out of him, Sarah. He just doesn't want to let on to you.'

'I know. Bloody stubborn old fool.'

Deborah smiles. 'Yep. Want a hand with supper?'

Dad's in bed by six, barely able to keep his eyes open after eating. He could only manage a child-sized portion of fish and mash, and didn't even touch his vegetables. Deborah and Sarah return to the living room after settling him in his room.

'I could murder a drink,' says Deborah. Her voluminous purple tunic flutters as she walks across the room.

Sarah opens the drinks cabinet in the adjoining dining room. 'Port? Sherry?'

Deborah joins her to choose from the various dusty bottles. 'A sherry should do it. I expect you could do with a small one too?' She unscrews the cap and reaches up for two small crystal-cut glasses, brushing them off on her shirt.

‘OK,’ says Sarah, returning to the sofa and letting Deborah pour the drinks. She watches her as she places the bottle back in the cabinet and shuts the glass doors. She seems so at ease.

‘Tell me about Dad, when you used to work together,’ Sarah says when Deborah sits on the sofa opposite.

Deborah smiles wistfully, as if she’s remembering something amusing. ‘Well, when we met, we were both in the same boat. We started at Stokely around the same time, and, even though it wasn’t a first teaching job for either of us, the older staff used to treat us as if we were still green young things. It was all a bit stuffy. Your dad was such an irreverent young man; I remember laughing a lot whenever he was around. I was thirty, so that would make your dad about thirty-five. We worked together for fourteen or fifteen years, before he left for the university at Tighborn.’

‘So he must have met my mother when he was at Stokely?’

‘*Yes*,’ says Deborah with hesitation. ‘I could do with a top-up.’ She crosses the room and returns with the sherry bottle, refilling both glasses as she sits back.

Sarah picks up her glass. ‘Why don’t you stay over tonight? I can make you up a bed on the sofa?’

Deborah smiles, and wiggles her sherry glass. ‘Might not be a bad idea.’

It’s still quite bright outside; yet the living room always seems so dusky, no matter what the weather or time of day. The early evening light highlights the grimy fabric of the net curtains which cover the windows along the length of the living room wall. They look filthy. Sarah leaps up and drags a chair beneath the window, unhooking the nets in one quick movement.

‘That’s better,’ she says as she bundles them up into a small ball. She places them next to the doorway, so she’ll remember to stick them in the laundry basket on her way to bed. ‘So, did you work with her?’ asks Sarah, determined to prevent Deborah from shutting the subject down.

Deborah sighs. 'I feel uncomfortable talking about your mother without James here, Sarah. It doesn't seem right.'

Sarah leans on to her knees with her palms held up plaintively. 'But that's the thing! He never talks about her; it's as if she never existed. All I've got is one photograph of her when she was really young, and that's so blurred you can hardly make out her face. There's not even one of her and me together. I've asked and asked over the years, but he just gets upset and shuts himself in his study. I deserve to know about her!' She doesn't dare blink, for fear that the tears in her eyes will spill over.

Deborah reaches out and touches Sarah's wrist with the tip of her fingers. 'Oh, you poor thing. Look, I can tell you that your father was very much in love with your mother. Which is probably why he finds it so difficult to talk about. When they got together at Stokely they were the talk of the staff room. I used to rib him about it at every given opportunity, and he'd get all flustered and tongue-tied. I'm just sorry we lost touch for so long.'

'Dad said it was her heart – that her heart failed soon after I was born. Maybe I should know that kind of thing, in case I ever have kids?'

Deborah rubs her face with both hands. 'I don't know about all that. Really.'

Sarah lets a large tear plop on to her lap, and looks imploringly at Deborah. She's seen her cry now; she might as well make the most of it.

'Oh, darling!' Deborah leaps up and moves on to Sarah's sofa. 'They'd both left Stokely by the time you were born, and we just lost contact.' She embraces Sarah, breathing in deeply, and out again, like the tide. 'You know, they made a lovely couple. The lecturers were always having flings with their students, but it was different with James and Susie.'

Sarah pulls away sharply. 'She was his student?'

Deborah looks appalled. 'Of course. He was a good twenty years older than Susie. Maybe more. You knew that?'

Sarah shakes her head and leans back against Deborah, who squeezes her and produces a clean tissue from her pocket. Sarah has never been hugged by anyone as large as Deborah before. She feels soft and yielding, like a warm pillow after Ted's been sleeping on it.

'Maybe he's ashamed,' Sarah whispers, 'about the age difference. I mean, it's not right, is it?' She turns to look at Deborah.

Deborah tugs on the little gold studs in her earlobes. They're tiny pieces of jewellery for such a large woman. 'Darling, they were both grown adults. Your dad had been on his own for a long time, and Susie was old enough to make her own choices. The age gap never seemed important. And they loved each other! Now, I think we should stop here – and when your dad is feeling better I'll have a chat with him. See if I can persuade him to talk to you?'

Sarah sinks back against the cushions, exhausted. The sherry is making a fuzz of her head, and she closes her eyes, feeling herself drift. She's awake, but she has the sensation of being somewhere else, far, far away from her own body. Deborah remains quietly beside her for a few minutes, before breaking the silence as she rises from the sofa.

'Off to bed,' she urges, helping Sarah to her feet. 'Don't worry, I'll find the sheets and things myself.' She kisses Sarah on the cheek and sends her up the stairs.

As she lies in the cold dark of her cheerless bedroom, Sarah can see Jason standing over her, buttoning his flies, his smile now a sneer.

An emergency siren sounds off in the distance, from an ambulance or fire engine passing through the town. As the noise dims to nothing, Sarah turns on to her side and draws herself up like a ball. Uninvited pictures hurtle through her mind: Dante and Kate at New Year; Dad lying deathlike in his hospital bed, his pyjama shirt unbuttoned to the waist; Jason's fingers on hers in the chemist's. Tina giggling in Kate's garden at the bonfire party as the firelight dances in the moisture of

Kate's eyes. Sarah stares wide into the night-dark room. She pushes the heels of her hands into the sockets of her eyes, as she tries to expel the swarming images. The sherry pounds behind her eyelids, and she flips over fitfully to face the other way, grasping the covers tightly around her ears. She visualises the faded old photograph on the wall outside her door and lets her mind travel to another place, a place of calm and peace where her mother is waiting.

Summer Term 1986

Back at school after the Easter break, the days seem unbearably long. Spring is in full bloom, and the scent of cherry blossom and jasmine lingers on the cool breeze. Spring is Sarah's favourite time of year, but this year it is muted, the colours and fragrances somehow toned down, shaded grey. At registration she gazes through the windows of the classroom, out across the field where crows pick away at the gardener's freshly sown grass seed. She imagines Deborah tending to Dad, taking him soup in bed and reading to him from the daily newspaper. Each day, she arrives just as Sarah leaves for school, staying on in the evenings to make supper for them all before she returns home. Her cooking is good, and she is kind and generous in all her actions. Sarah knows she should be pleased, but she doesn't feel it.

Mr Settle finishes taking the register, slams his briefcase shut and strides from the classroom to teach his morning lesson. Most of the girls start to gather up their bags to go on to their next class, but Sarah's limbs have turned to lead, and she sits passively in her seat, reading the blackboard beyond the teacher's desk. There's a Chad drawing that someone has chalked up the night before: *Wot no decent teachers?* it says.

Mr Settle didn't even notice it when he breezed in to take the register. Or, if he did, he chose to ignore it. Sarah can feel herself sliding back inside her head, and she closes her eyes briefly, just to rest them for a moment.

'You alright, Sar?' Tina asks, pausing by her desk. 'We've got Geography next.'

Sarah looks up and smiles blindly, feeling as though her thoughts have separated from her body.

'Sar?'

She picks up her bag and follows Tina across the room, shielding her nostrils from the stench of chalk dust which dances across the desks and chairs. 'I'm alright,' she says, and she walks gingerly down the main staircase and out into the sunlight of the foyer.

~

As the first fortnight of term progresses Sarah's spirits revive, and at lunchtimes she and Tina sit out by the steps to the dining hall sunning their legs and talking about *Saturday Live*. Sarah's been recounting some of the jokes, and Tina laughs uncontrollably, slapping her shins, leaning over from time to time to let other girls pass up the steps.

When Kate returns from a lunch detention, Tina is wiping the tears from her face.

'Kate, you've got to hear this! Go on, Sar! Did you watch *Saturday Live* at the weekend? Ben Elton was hysterical, going on about the royal family.'

Kate shakes her head, and stands back against the brickwork of the wall, closing her eyes against the glare. She folds her arms and crosses one ankle over the other.

'Nope.'

'Oh,' says Tina. 'Well you probably wouldn't get it, then.'

The carefree atmosphere has gone.

'What detention did they give you?' Sarah asks.

'Bloody algebra.' Kate tuts. 'But I don't have to go back tomorrow now. The dwarf must have something better to do, because she said I don't need to go back again.'

'Mrs Minor?' Sarah laughs. 'She's shorter than I was when I was nine.'

Kate huffs.

'Maybe she's shrinking,' Sarah adds, pulling her sock up and pushing it down neatly. 'Maybe she used to be normal-sized, but old age is shrinking her.'

Tina jabs Sarah with her elbow. 'You're cracking me up today!'

Kate looks down at them with scorn; a quick, nasty flash. 'Oh, my God!' she suddenly shrieks.

'What?' Tina and Sarah ask together.

'Your *legs*! Urggh! They're so hairy! Look, Tina – *look*! Don't you shave, Sar?' She stands over Sarah, hands on her hips.

Tina jumps up, leaning on the railing to get a better look as Sarah tucks her knees up under her skirt. She snorts and stand beside Kate in the sunshine.

Sarah can feel her cheeks roasting. 'What? They're not that bad! My dad says if I shave them now, I'll never be able to stop.'

'Your *dad*? What would he know about shaving legs. Oh, my *God*!'

Two of their classmates pass through the group and up the steps.

'Look at Sarah's legs!' Kate's finger hovers over Sarah's downy tanned knee. 'That's not normal, is it?'

'Rank,' Zoe Andrews says, pulling a disgusted face.

'You have got to do something about that, Sarah,' Kate tells her, shuddering.

Sarah pushes herself up from the steps and joins Tina and Kate where they lean against the warm, rough brickwork. They stand like this for a while, the three of them uniformly posed, arms folded, ankles crossed, absorbing the warm spring sunshine. Sarah closes her eyes and wishes for rain tomorrow. Then she can wear her thick black tights to conceal her revolting animal-pelt legs. If only they could wear trousers.

'Oh, I nearly forgot,' says Kate, bending to open up her school bag. It's a new raffia basket with a pretty floral lining and a tiny handle – a bit like a dolly's bag Sarah had when she was little. Kate turns over the contents, dropping make-up and tissues on to the concrete floor until she finally unearths what she's looking for. She passes it to Sarah without looking up.

It's a small blue jewellery box, with the word 'Ratners' embossed in gold. Sarah looks perplexed.

'It's yours,' says Kate over her shoulder. 'You left it at ours when you stayed.'

Sarah frowns.

'Earrings. Dad said they're yours. Apparently you left them when you stayed over.' Kate repacks her bag as Sarah opens the box.

Inside is a pair of brand new gold hoops. They're just like the kind Tina wears, and Sarah wouldn't be seen dead in them.

Kate stands up and takes the box from Sarah. 'I told him you didn't even have your ears pierced, but he said you bought them for when you do. He reckons they look quite expensive.' She turns and faces Sarah squarely. 'I can't believe you're finally getting them done. It doesn't hurt, does it, Teen?'

Tina shakes her head, running her fingers along the edge of her own ear. 'I'm gonna get another one at the top. In the cartilage bit. When I can afford it.'

Sarah stares at the little earrings and nods, feeling the panic gather in the centre of her chest.

Kate looks delighted. 'Great! We can go in together if you like?' she says. 'Blackman's is best – they use a proper gun and sterile studs. That's where we got ours done, isn't it, Teen?'

'Uh-huh,' says Tina, distractedly twiddling the hoops in her own ears. She puts out a finger and tips the little box towards her to get a better look, then rubs her nose with her knuckles. 'Nice.'

Sarah pushes the Ratners box down into the inside pocket of her bag and zips it shut, feeling the bile rise in the back of her throat. She wants to get the earrings as far from her as possible, to forget all this ever happened. And she knows what her dad will say if she tells him she wants to get her ears done. 'You'll look like a gypsy,' he'll say, and that will be that.

'Come on Teen,' says Kate, picking up her bag. 'We've got Dance now, haven't we?'

The two girls link arms and amble away together, along the edge of the dining hall and into the main building. For a fleeting moment, Tina looks back at Sarah with a puzzled expression, as if she's looking right through her. Sarah tips her head and frowns; Tina looks away.

'See ya later, Sar!' Kate raises her hand through the glass.

Sarah stands with her palms pressed hard against the gritty wall, watching as Kate and Tina pass through the glass corridor and out of sight.

~

On Saturday night, while her father watches the news, Sarah shaves her legs with a disposable razor she bought from the chemist's. She vigorously rubs a bar of Pears soap between the palms of her hands, smoothing the white foam down the length of her legs before drawing the razor back up against the grain of her leg hair. She holds her breath as the soft blonde hairs collect in the blade and disappear down the sink. Afterwards, her legs are smooth and hairless, the skin desensitised beneath her fingers. A little nick on her knee just won't stop bleeding, and eventually she tiptoes down the stairs and into the kitchen to find a plaster. The volume on the TV is turned right up, and she pauses in the doorway of the living room to see what Dad's watching. Footage of a smoking industrial plant fills the screen, and Dad sits on the sofa, leaning on to his knees, shaking his head.

'*The scale of the disaster at the Chernobyl power plant is still uncertain*,' the BBC news reporter says. '*Reports that several thousand people have been killed are as yet unconfirmed.*'

Breathtaking plumes of dark smoke billow and drift from the ruined power plant. Dad shakes his head again and rubs his brow.

'Night, Dad,' Sarah says.

He turns and smiles, sadly. He looks so old and tired. 'Night, Sarah-Lou,' he says.

~

Every second Thursday, the fifth years have a two-hour session called 'Personal Development', led by their form tutor, Mr Settle. They each have a folder containing coloured A4 sheets with sections such as 'Career Planning', 'Relationships' and 'Further Education', and they're expected to work through the sheets alone, completing the various tick boxes and commentaries. Some of the boffs have finished writing up all their sheets by the end of the first term and now spend each session quietly polishing their work for final hand-in at the end of May. Sarah's group sits at the back of the classroom stifling their laughter as they try to outdo each other with increasingly ridiculous answers to the worksheet questions.

> ***Q: What plans do you have in place for your further education next term?***
> A: Hopefully if I get enough O-levels, I'll be starting an apprenticeship as a petrol pump assistant in September.
>
> ***Q: If you are going straight into paid employment, have you started your applications?***
> A: Yes. I recently sent a topless photograph of myself to the *Sunday People*, and I await their reply with anticipation.
>
> ***Q: What will you wear for any potential job interviews?***
> A: My pink leotard, purple pixie boots, and a gorgeous set of glitter deely-boppers.

Q: Who inspires you?
A: Mr Settle. Definitely.

Q: Where do you see yourself in ten years' time?
A: Collecting trollies at Sainsburys.

At the end of each session they hand the folders in, and Mr Settle returns them a fortnight later with his dated signature in the box at the front. It's a great sense of shared accomplishment every time they receive them back from him without punishment. Safe in the knowledge that they won't be read, the girls grow ever more confident in their responses.

In the second session after Easter, Mr Settle takes the morning register and tells them to gather their belongings and line up by the door. He stands in the doorway in his shiny brown suit, his briefcase in one hand, his oily doughnut bag in the other. 'Right, everyone! Now that the engineers have finished with the boiler, we are *finally* moving back into the hut.'

'But we'll be leaving in a few weeks,' Kate calls out. 'It's hardly worth it.'

Mr Settle pushes his spectacles along the brow of his nose. 'Thank you, Kate! For your information, they want us out of this room as soon as possible so they can decorate before the end of term.'

There's a rally of cheers and whoops from the class, who have missed the independence of their old hut. It'll be good to move back; the huts are separate from the main building, and the 5G hut looks directly out on to the sixth form common room where the older boys and girls are able to mix freely between the two schools.

'So, this morning I want you to transport all your belongings OUT OF your temporary lockers in the corridor and INTO your new lockers in the hut cloakroom – without disrupting the rest of the school in the process! Is that clear?'

A murmur of agreement ripples through the distracted group, who are anxious to get on with it.

'Marianne, you are responsible for collecting up the old locker keys and returning them to the front office. Got that, everyone? Off you go. QUIETLY!'

Mr Settle leads the way, forking off towards the staff room as the girls run along the corridors, chattering excitedly as they pass the occupied classrooms on the way to their lockers. The sound of metal doors clanging rattles along the hallway, as they drag out their books and PE kits, unpeel posters and feel around for lost pencils and rubbers.

'Look at this!' shrieks Kate, holding up what looks like an embalmed banana. 'Grim!'

Tina is stacking her books in a pile, trying to work out how she'll be able to carry it all back through the school and out to the huts. Kate picks up Tina's school leotard and catapults it at Sarah like an elastic band. It lands on Sarah's face like popped bubble gum.

'Urghh! That's disgusting. I don't want Tina's sweaty gusset in my face, thank you very much,' she says, holding it out at arm's length.

Tina snatches it from her and pushes it into her PE kit. 'It's clean, you know,' she says grumpily.

'I was only joking, Teen,' says Sarah, still dragging out a bundle of books from her top shelf.

As she turns to place them on the floor, the small blue Ratners box slides off the top and on to the ground between her and Kate. She'd completely forgotten about it; pushed it to the back of her locker, and pushed it from her mind.

Kate picks it up and opens the box to reveal the tacky gold hoops.

'That reminds me,' she says. 'You were gonna get your ears done.' She purses her lips and holds the box out in her open palm.

Sarah blinks, caught out. 'I just haven't got round to it,' she says, taking the box from Kate and ramming it down inside her bag. She turns her back on Kate to give her empty locker another inspection.

Kate grabs her by the shoulder and spins her round roughly. 'Right, that's it! I've had enough of this. I've sussed you out, Sarah Ribbons.'

Sarah's breath stops in the back of her chest as she recoils with a gasp. She bends to pick up her other belongings. 'What?' she asks without looking up.

Kate taps her on the shoulder so she has to turn and face her. 'We know, don't we, Teen? About the *earrings*.'

Tina folds her arms and shrugs. Sarah stands between them. The blood rushes to her face. She can feel her ears burning and she wants to lean against the lockers for support. Kate reaches out and tugs Sarah's soft pink earlobe.

'We know why you haven't had your ears pierced yet.' She smiles. 'You're scared it'll hurt. Aren't you? You big chicken! So, I've decided for you – we're going into town straight after school today, and you're gonna get them done.'

Sarah is so relieved that tears well up in her eyes, and she has to turn away so the others don't see. 'OK,' she says. 'You win.'

Once they've packed away their things, Mr Settle asks the girls to carry on with their Personal Development folders. There's a large box of his belongings on the desk at the front, beside his briefcase and doughnut bag.

'Right! You've got half an hour before first break – and I don't need to remind you that these folders have to be completed and submitted by the end of May!'

He starts to unpack his box, carrying items back and forth into the cupboard in the corner behind his desk.

Kate points to the clock above the blackboard. 'At ten to ten he'll sit down and eat his doughnut, just you watch. It's like clockwork.'

Sarah nods, laughing. 'It's the same every day. You'd think he'd get bored of the same thing.'

'Dare you to take a bite,' says Kate, looking at Sarah.

She pulls a face. 'No way! You do it.'

'I always do stuff. You're such a chicken, Sar.'

'What about Tina? She never does anything like that either!'

'Yes, she does. You're such a goody-two-shoes.'

Sarah flicks through her folder, trying to think up something funny to change the subject.

After five minutes, Mr Settle comes out of the cupboard to fetch another pile of books. Sarah watches him as he disappears into the cupboard. She looks up at the clock.

Kate widens her eyes. 'Go on,' she says. 'I know you're dying to.'

Sarah sprints down towards the table, unwraps the white bag, takes one huge bite and returns it to its packaging as if nothing had happened. She tiptoes back to her desk, chomping down on the greasy dough. The smell of it is repulsive.

Kate silently bangs the desk with the flat of her hand, as Tina laughs and laughs behind her folder. Mr Settle comes out and fetches another batch of books.

'OK, watch this, then,' says Kate as he returns to the cupboard. She takes her lipstick from her pencil case and dashes down to the front desk.

Removing the doughnut from its wrapper, she swiftly outlines the bite mark with a thick layer of Twilight Teaser, rolling the colour around and around until it's clearly visible. She holds it up to the class with a grin, then slides it back inside the bag.

At 9.50 precisely Mr Settle sits behind his desk and arranges the remaining items, straightening his ruler along the top of his A4 lined pad, the pencil along the top of that. He moves his glass of water closer, so that it's level with the top of the pad, and places his pencil pot on the opposite side for balance. Once everything is organised with perfect symmetry, he reaches for his morning snack. The eyes of the class are on him, and Sarah thinks she might burst from the tension of it all. Her stomach is rolling in spasms of repressed laughter, and she can hear Kate's little gasps beside her as she tries to hold it in. Tina's resting her head on her folded arms, quietly drumming her bony fingertips against the scored wooden desktop. He's going to go mad. He's going to flip out, and give them detention, and they're all going to die of laughter asphyxiation before he even opens the bag...

'Ten minutes to go,' Mr Settle tells the class. He opens the wrapper and pulls out his doughnut. He turns it over between his forefinger and thumb, inspecting the size of the bite, the shade of lipstick used. He looks up over his glasses and rolls his eyes across the class, passing over every girl until he reaches Kate, who's not even looking at him. He slips the doughnut back in its bag and drops it into the wastepaper basket with a hollow thump.

Sarah notices for the first time just how frail and old he seems. His skin and hair merge into one indistinct sandy colour.

He pushes the items on his desk apart, breaking up the order. 'Finish the section you're on and leave your folders on my desk. You can go early.'

Dad is in his study when Sarah gets home, working on his Selton project. The back door is open and Ted lies panting in the sunlight as she bends to pat his chest. He lifts a back leg towards her and smiles in the white light. The scent of the Solent grows stronger as spring rolls towards summer on Seafield Avenue. Gulls circle in the sky overhead, moving in graceful formation as they soar towards the shoreline beyond.

In the kitchen, Sarah shoves a pile of Dad's dirty pots into the corner and fills the kettle. She rests her face in her hands to stem the tears, running her fingers along the contours of her brow, around her eye sockets, across her cheekbones, until they rest on the newly pierced earlobes which throb faintly beneath her touch. Everything's wrong.

'Cup of tea?' calls her dad from the study, pushing the door open just a crack. 'I'd love one!'

'Coming up!' she replies, slapping her cheeks sharply. She pours the tea and gets down a new packet of biscuits for him.

As she pushes through the door, Dad twirls round in his chair and reaches out to take the tea and biscuits. He smiles at her with such pure warmth that she can't hold it in any more. She crumbles on to his lap, her slender limbs awkward across his, her face pushed hard into his shoulder to conceal her fractured expression. 'I'm sorry,' she cries through heaving sobs, 'I'm so sorry. I'm so sorry.'

He holds her, his arms around her waist, his tone soothing and low. 'What is it, Sarah-Lou? What's happened?'

As her breathing slows and her tears ebb, she lifts her creased face and gazes into her father's old eyes. Without thinking, her hands reach for the newly pierced earlobes, and she sees in that split second, as he notices the sparkling diamante studs and gives a sad little smile, that he thinks that's it. That it's the ears she's crying over.

'Oh, you silly girl,' he says hugging her closer. 'You silly, silly girl.'

She presses into his baggy wool cardigan and cries, and cries.

After a long fitful struggle into sleep that night, Sarah dreams that she's at school, where Kate and Tina are trying to make her look at something inside one of the lift-up desks in 5G. But Sarah doesn't want to look at it. *It won't bite!* Kate laughs. Then they hold her, one on either side, pushing her closer and closer to the desk, forcing her head down to look inside.

When she wakes, her throat has closed up and she tries to cry out but nothing will come. The wind is whipping up outside, curling around the trees and rattling the glass of her windows. She pulls the sheets around her neck and listens. Time passes, and she slips from her bed, dressing rapidly before crossing the hallway to ease open the back window towards the sea. The moon is perfectly round and still, and Sarah can hear the distant crash of waves against shingle down on the shore. The smell of wet stone rushes in at her, as the breeze spreads her hair like a fan. Pausing to listen to her father's deep breathing, she sprints through the dark house with the sound of dragging pebbles clear in her ears, and with growing exhilaration she slips out into the night. She runs towards the beach on light feet, her jacket flapping and snapping in the high wind, along Seafield Avenue and down through Sandpipers Lane, a moonlit shadow trailing her all the way, until she comes out at the beach. The giant water pipe is vast and clear in the white light, buffeted by thick foaming waves which greedily lap and crawl up its supports. The sea drags the water away from the pipe, sucking it back like a breath, before hurling it skyward in great arcs of fury. Sarah walks down across the pebbles, slipping and steadying herself as her trainers slide over the wet stones. She walks along the sodden wooden framework, bracing herself against the force of the wind, until she's balanced at the head of the pipe, one foot on either wooden strut.

The clouds pass the moon's face in rapid movements, so that for a moment Sarah really believes the moon is travelling across the skyline. She turns her head to look along the upper beach, towards the darkened beach huts, still standing strong after all these years. A wave slaps hard against the pipe's legs, sending spray and mist over Sarah's face and body.

Her tears flow, and she slides down on to the iron-cold head of the pipe, allowing the salt water to rage and spit around her legs as they dangle precariously low. She watches the water lap and growl, feeling strangely soothed by its unrelenting fury.

The cold starts to seep into her bones. She pushes the tears away with the backs of her hands, rising to her feet. As she retreats up the shifting bank of stones, she looks over her shoulder, where the white tide continues to thrust and drag at the impotent shoreline.

~

The fifth years have a lot more freedom once the final exams start. Much of their time is spent lying around on the playing field in the sunshine, or huddled together in the library, pretending to revise.

After the Geography exam, Sarah and Tina collect their bags from the front of the school gym and go straight into town, where they're meeting Kate in Marconi's.

Kate waves at them from the back of the café, where she's bagged a four-seater in the shadowy smoking area. There's a used cup and plate on the table in front of her.

'Have you been here long?' asks Sarah, checking her watch.

Kate wrinkles her forehead. 'A while. Dante's being a dickhead, so I left him and Ed pissing about at the memorial.'

'Oh, my God,' hisses Kate as Tina slides across on to the red vinyl seat opposite. 'There goes Lilo Lil. I don't know how she's got the nerve to show her face in public!'

Sarah sits down next to Tina and turns to follow Kate's gaze.

The three girls watch as Jo Allen passes on the other side of the glass, her shoulders slumped over a pram, her pallid skin the colour of dough. To Sarah, it seems as though it's all happening in slow motion; she feels as if she can see every pore of Jo's skin, every hair on her head.

'Everyone knows she's the town bike,' Kate adds, breaking Sarah's thoughts. 'It was only a matter of time. So, you seen anything of Ed, Teen?'

Tina's trying to keep her face blank. Ed chucked her last week. 'No. If he can't handle the fact that I'm a vegetarian, then he can stick it for all I care. Meat-head.'

Kate smiles mischeviously. 'Dante said you dumped Ed's burger in the bin when you met him in town last week.'

'Yeah, well, I'd already told him I didn't want to be around him when he was eating dead animals. He knew that. And he laughed in my face and went and got one anyway. So, I knocked it out of his hand and stamped on it.'

Sarah and Kate splutter. 'No way!' says Sarah.

'So, is that why he finished with you?' asks Kate.

Tina shrugs. 'I like your top,' she says.

Kate plucks at her new T-shirt. It's black and floppy, hanging off one shoulder to reveal a purple vest underneath. 'Thanks. So, how'd it go?' She looks at them both expectantly.

'What?' asks Sarah, looking confused.

'Your exam, stupid!'

'Oh, that. Crap. Ungraded probably.' Sarah rubs her eyes. 'I never wanted to do Geography in the first place. They only made me do it because I wasn't good enough to take another language.'

'Won't your dad mind if you fail it? God, I was up till midnight all last week, revising for History. I swear, I've been dreaming about Jethro Tull's seed drill ever since.'

Tina and Sarah exchange a puzzled look and burst out laughing. Kate tosses her hair. 'If you did History you'd know what I was on about.'

Tina and Sarah queue at the counter and order hot chocolates and flapjacks, returning with them precariously balanced on a grubby-looking tray.

'Ugh,' says Sarah pointing out a jammy splodge on the corner.

'It's rank in here,' agrees Kate. 'Dunno why we even come here.' She looks around at the other customers with a sneer. 'It's full of Casuals. *Saddos*.'

Tina eats her flapjack hungrily, her knobbly hands poking out of the frayed edges of her school jumper. She's like a mouse, with her sharp little nose and whiskery movements.

Kate lights up a cigarette and blows the smoke into the air between them. Dreary windows run all the way down the external wall of the café, looking out on to the alleyway which leads to one of the main car parks in town. The daylight streams across the tables on that side, bathing the crumbs and tea slops in white light. On the table adjacent to theirs, someone has left an empty cup of tea and a half-eaten sausage roll. Sarah can see the grease on the pastry, shining wetly in the sunlight. She can almost smell it from here.

'You alright?' asks Kate as she cradles her own mug. 'You've gone all greenish.'

Sarah bites down against a sudden rush of nausea, and runs her hands through her hair distractedly. 'I think I'm just hungry,' she says, breaking her flapjack in half and taking a small bite.

'You've got to keep your strength up. That's what my mum keeps saying.' Tina says, wiping her mouth. 'She's always fussing. The other day she started pulling down my eyelids and talking about how menstruation makes you need extra iron because of the blood loss. We were having steak and kidney pie at the time. Well, *they* were. My dad was so embarrassed he picked up his plate and went and ate in the other room.'

Kate snorts and runs her finger around her plate, picking up the sugar residue from the doughnut she's eaten. 'At least she's not a miserable cow like mine. Don't suppose *you* have to put up with all this, do you, Sar?'

Sarah sips her drink. 'I know I've only got my dad to deal with, but sometimes I think he's twice as hard work as two parents.'

'Are you gonna leave that?' Tina asks, pointing at Sarah's half-eaten flapjack.

Sarah pushes the plate towards her.

'So what was your mum like, Sar?' asks Kate.

Sarah feels a sickening rush as the hot chocolate hits her stomach. 'I'm not sure. You know, she died soon after I was born.'

'But your old man must've told you about her? It was a heart attack, wasn't it?'

'Yeah. Apparently it was brought on by the pregnancy, some really rare sort of heart condition. But I don't know all that much about it – Dad always tries to change the subject when I ask him. He's not very good at talking about that kind of thing.'

Kate puts down her mug dramatically. She leans in, talking low. 'Oh, my God, Sar. You don't think he killed her or something? Maybe she didn't die of natural causes and that's why he's so secretive.'

Sarah frowns. 'Don't be stupid. He just doesn't know how to handle it, that's all.'

'Mmm. Do you believe in the afterlife?'

'What, like ghosts and that?' asks Tina, looking suddenly interested. 'I do. My aunt used to go to a medium, and she got all sorts of stuff right about her, like how many kids she'd have and how her husband would get ill. She even knew about his fallen arches.'

Sarah doesn't answer.

Kate stacks the plates in the middle of the table. 'What if your house is haunted, Sar? Your mum might still be there, floating around the house at night. Wouldn't that be creepy?' She laughs, giving Sarah a little push across the table.

'I wouldn't mind,' says Sarah. 'Maybe she is there. Sometimes I hear things at night, or when I'm on my own in the house. The other day, I couldn't find my keys anywhere. They turned up on the upstairs landing, near her photo.' She pauses dramatically. 'I didn't put them there.'

Kate and Tina look at each other and both let out a little scream.

'I can't believe you've never said anything before!' says Kate. 'That's so cool!'

Sarah shakes her head. 'It's probably nothing,' she says, gazing across at the window beyond, pleased to give Kate something new to think about.

~

The Spring Disco is the first time that the two schools have brought the boys and girls together for a shared event. Designed as a reward and incentive for all the work towards their O-levels and CSE exams, the disco is exclusively restricted to the fifth years, to be held in the girls' gym on the last Friday before half-term.

Sarah's dad drops her off at the top of School Lane just after six, where she'd arranged to meet Tina and Kate ten minutes ago. Neither of them is there, and she wonders if they've gone ahead without her. Already, a steady snake of fifteen- and sixteen-year-olds makes its way through the iron gates of the school, whooping and chattering impatiently. A pair of teachers ushers them in, checking them for alcohol and cigarettes. There's an untidy tangle of confiscated cans on the floor at Miss Tupper's feet, which another teacher is transferring into a cardboard box. Dad hasn't noticed. He bends low to speak to her through the passenger window.

'It's alright, Dad, you can go,' she says with hushed urgency. 'I do know my way from here.'

'So, I'll meet you here at ten. It was ten o'clock? Not a moment later!' He stretches across to wind up the window.

Sarah wraps her arms around herself and taps her toe on the pavement as she waits for him to go. He toots the horn as he turns the corner and vanishes from sight. She looks down at her outfit critically. This afternoon, she went through everything in her wardrobe until she found something that looked OK, opting for an oversized white shirt and cropped blue jeans. A wide black elastic belt pulls the billowing shirt in, and she's crimped and backcombed her hair so that it's just like Debbie Harry's. She looks at her watch: 6.20. They must be inside.

Sarah joins the line of kids wandering towards the entrance, surveying the crowd for a glimpse of Tina or Kate. Once she breaks from the mass, she finds Tina waiting outside the wide exterior entrance to the gym, in snow-washed jeans, ankle boots and an off-yellow 'FRANKIE SAYS RELAX' T-shirt.

'Where's Kate?' Tina asks as Sarah approaches. She's scowling, sounding miffed.

'I thought we were all meant to meet out the front,' Sarah replies. 'I've been out there for fifteen minutes and she's not there.'

Tina's hostility appears to melt away.

'Maybe she's made up with Dante,' she says, tutting. 'Maybe they've made up and she's decided not to come after all.' She scans the faces as they walk past. 'I've never known a couple to fall out so much.'

Sarah shakes her head. 'Even if they have made up, she'd still come. She was going home to dye her hair straight after school and she had her outfit all planned. She wouldn't miss this for anything.'

Tina nods, and they stand side by side, arms folded, watching the pupils crossing the netball courts to file in through the entrance beside them. 'So what's she gonna wear, then?' asks Tina. 'She changes her tune so much, I've lost track.'

'She said she'd bought a black leather waistcoat when she went to Tighborn market with Dante. I think she's going to wear that with some leggings.'

Tina utters a disgusted sound from the back of her throat. '*Leather*. That is so gross. What is wrong with the world?'

'What's wrong with leather?' asks Sarah.

'It's all butchery. Just because you wear it on your feet or whatever, it doesn't mean an animal didn't die for it!'

Sarah pushes away from the wall and stands in the entrance to the gym trying to spot Kate. 'Isn't leather a by-product? I mean, the animal died for meat in the first place, but then they use the leather for shoes and stuff to save throwing it away. It's better than wasting it.'

'You'll never understand, Sarah,' Tina sighs. 'Meat is Murder. So is leather.'

'Leather is *lovely*,' says Kate, sneaking up on Tina and grabbing her by the shoulders so that she yelps. She caresses her black leather waistcoat and gives them a twirl. Her stripy grey and black leggings taper down into a pair of black winkle-picker slingbacks, and her loose white vest top drapes low over her rounded bosom. 'Whaddayathink?'

'You look great,' says Sarah, wishing she'd worn something else. 'I love the waistcoat. And the hair! It's really dark!'

'Damson, the packet said.' She leans out to check her reflection in a glass panel.

'Looks more like plum to me,' says Tina.

'A damson *is* a plum, you pleb! So, who's here then? Have you seen what Marianne's wearing? Oh my God, I don't know why someone doesn't say something. She's got this pale blue jumpsuit on, and I swear it's two sizes too small. Her bum looks massive!'

Kate slips between Sarah and Tina and links arms, leading them into the gym. It's crowded out now, and the multicoloured lights flash and strobe from the DJ desk at the back. The DJ is a thin young lab technician from the boys' school, and he's fussing over the decks, looking strained, checking the plug sockets, scratching his temples.

'Oh, for God's sake,' says Kate, dropping the girls' arms and striding towards him.

She talks to him for a moment, fiddles with a few cables and places a record on the turntable. He smiles, wiping his brow and offering to shake her hand. Kate waves a hand through the air, jumps off the platform and sashays towards Tina and Sarah, turning back once to smile broadly at the technician.

Billy Idol's 'White Wedding' plays out into the hall, met by the grateful screams and cheers of several hundred Selton teenagers now crowded into the gymnasium. There's a sudden surge as girls rush towards the DJ desk to dance and shriek and laugh.

'Should've asked my dad to do the DJ-ing. That bloke up there hasn't got a clue.'

They make their way over to the refreshments area at the far side of the hall, and buy crisps and cans of drink. Kate ushers them into a corner, and slips a hand inside her big cotton bag to pull out a half bottle of vodka. They all drink a few mouthfuls of their Coke before she pours a good slug of spirits in through the opening to each can. They stand at the edge of the room, watching, discreetly assessing the outfits and hairstyles of their peers; absorbing the attention of every Selton boy who passes by.

'How are things with you and Dante?' Tina asks.

Kate rearranges her vest top so that it shows off her bust to best advantage. 'So-so. We're still together. But that doesn't mean we have to live in each other's pockets, does it? He likes to go out with his mates, and I like to go out with mine. Which is how it should be, you know?'

Sarah and Tina nod in agreement. Sarah notices Simon Dobbs across the room, who Kate's always had a big thing for. When she was new to the school in the fourth year she used to loiter around the entrance gates, hoping to bump into him. She even tried hanging about the playing field on weekends when she knew he had a rugby match on, but he was never interested; never even looked in her direction. It used to drive her insane.

She crushes her empty can and throws it into a plastic bin. 'Right, I'm off for a nosey. See you back at the dance floor in half an hour?'

They watch her parade across the room, squeezing past groups of boys, meeting their eyes intimately as they turn to let her through. Her laughter travels back across the floor.

'Simon Dobbs,' says Tina, cramming her mouth with crisps as she bops her head in Kate's direction.

Sarah laughs, watching Kate's effortlessness as she meanders through the rippling crowd. She draws in the attention of every boy in the room. She's not what you'd call beautiful; there's just something about her.

'Back in a minute,' Tina says, and she jogs over to the makeshift refreshments bar. Mrs Whiff is on duty, serving fizzy drinks and snacks to the pupils. They've placed it near the entrance to the loos, probably so that she can keep an eye on the comings and goings of girls and boys as the evening goes on. Tina seems to be buying up the shop, and when she's paid she vanishes through the corridor and into the loos.

The gym is crammed with kids now, and the heat in the room is rising rapidly. They've all been told that they can congregate around the netball courts and on the first stretch of field, but that's their limit. They don't want pupils wandering around the grounds unsupervised at night time. Sarah edges along the side of the gym, trying to locate Kate or anyone else from her form. It's still light outside, and she steps out through the wide doors and stands against the wall sipping her Coke. A small group, two boys and two girls, clusters a little way from her. The girls are laughing at everything the boys say, and the boys exchange pleased glances every time the girls laugh.

'You look much older than fifteen,' says one boy.

Giggle. 'Do I?'

'Yeah, you really do. You both do.'

Boy Two: 'Eighteen, I'd reckon.'

Both girls: 'Really?' They both laugh, leaning into each other as if they're attached.

'We're both getting motorbikes at the start of the summer, aren't we?' says the second boy.

'Yeah. 50cc. Don't know what kind yet. Maybe Suzuki or Yamaha.'

'Depends how much we can save up between now and then.'

'Have you got a job, then?' asks one girl.

'Yeah. Down at Shoreside Packaging. We can get all sorts of perfumes and stuff, really cheap.'

Both girls: 'Really?'

'Yeah. We'll get you some if you want. What d'you like? Poison? Obsession? They do loads.'

'Oh, my God! I love Poison! It's *lush*!'

'Yeah,' says one of the boys, his eyes flickering towards his friend mischievously, 'it's really sexy.'

The girls fall about, covering their mouths and shrieking, their plastic handbags swinging and swaying with every movement.

Sarah looks away. Everyone must think she's got no mates, standing out here alone. She's started to walk back towards the entrance when she spots Marianne sitting on one of the wooden benches further along the wall towards the field. She's on her own, staring at her soft yellow shoes.

'Hi, Marianne,' Sarah calls out, strolling over.

Marianne looks up and smiles. 'Hiya. What are you doing?'

'I've lost the others, and it was getting a bit hot inside.' She sits down on the bench beside Marianne. 'What about you?'

'I can't find any of my friends in there, and I felt a bit faint so I came out here for a bit. There are too many people.' She sits stiffly with her elbows at her side.

Sarah notices the dark sweat rings spreading from beneath the armpits of Marianne's pale blue jumpsuit.

'That's a nice colour,' says Sarah, pointing to the jumpsuit.

Marianne flushes. 'Wish I'd never worn it.'

'Why?'

'Oh, you know. People always take the mickey. If I stick to my normal clothes, they say I'm square. If I make an effort, they laugh.'

'Who laughs?'

Marianne gives a small meaningful smile. 'People like Kate. I hate her.'

There's a pause between them, as both stare out across the field without speaking.

'She doesn't mean to be like that,' Sarah says.

Marianne laughs, a little hard cough. 'How can you not mean to be like that? *You're* not like that. Loads of people aren't like that. She never stops. Every day, it's something. My hair. My shoes. My height. My big hands.' She turns her hands over on her lap.

'Maybe I could have a word with her?' suggests Sarah. She puts her empty can under the bench behind her feet.

'No,' sighs Marianne. 'It'll only make it worse. Honestly, I'm fine. I'll be back inside in a minute. Honestly.'

Sarah stands to go. 'I could – you know. Have a word with her?'

Marianne shakes her head. 'It's fine. *Really*!' She smiles and turns away, and Sarah returns to the gym.

Tina meets her at the entrance, looking irritable. 'Have you seen her?'

'Who?'

'Kate! I've looked everywhere, and she's completely disappeared.' Tina scratches away at her fingers, frowning hard.

'She'll turn up,' says Sarah. 'Wanna dance?'

'No. The music's shit. I was gonna get Kate to get them to put on some better music. They always do it for Kate – ' Her face clouds over momentarily. 'Hey! I bet she's with Simon Dobbs!'

'No!' exclaims Sarah, her eyes wide. 'She's still going out with Dante. She wouldn't!'

'She would! Come on, let's find her. I bet she's in the main building. She's definitely not in the gym or the loos.'

They dash around the edges of the crowded gym, testing the door handles to the rest of the school. They're all locked. They slip out through the fire escape at the end of the corridor and roam about the exterior walls, looking for a way in. The light is dimming now, and they whisper and snigger as they run along the side of the building like cat burglars.

'Here!' Sarah calls.

There's a low window to the library, open just enough for them to squeeze through. They can reach up easily by standing on the flower trough below, dropping on to the parquet floor on the other side.

Sarah puts a hand on Tina's arm and they pause for a moment, listening into the silence. 'Do you think they're here?' she asks.

Tina shrugs and they tiptoe around the place, peering through the inner window to the librarian's tiny office, sprinting up the dark wooden staircase and checking in all the classrooms above the gallery. There's no one there.

'What now?' asks Sarah.

Tina stands at the balustrade, looking out over the library below. She sits, cross-legged, and presses her face up against the bars.

Sarah joins her. 'She's a funny one, Kate,' she says, gazing down at the shadows cast by the heavy bookcases as the sun goes down.

'How?'

'She can be such a good laugh one minute, then – well, quite nasty the next. I was just outside with Marianne. I don't know what Kate said to her, but she was a bit upset.'

'But Marianne is a right saddo. It's really funny, when we're in French together, Kate hums the theme tune to *The Addams Family* every time Marianne walks in or says anything. It cracks me up.'

'That's what I mean. She *is* funny, but it's not all that nice, is it?'

Tina shifts position. Her thin white arms protrude sharply over her crossed knees. 'I know what you mean. She took the piss out of my Frankie T-shirt earlier. Said I was always miles behind the trends. She's always saying that, but I still like this T-shirt, so why shouldn't I wear it?'

'Maybe things aren't that good at home. Her parents seem to argue quite a lot.'

Tina snorts. 'Well, Patty's on those nut-nut pills, isn't she? Then there's Jen and all her problems.'

'Her sister? Oh, yeah, Kate says her boyfriend's a dope-head.'

'And the abortion.'

Sarah leans back to take a better look at Tina. 'Who? *Jen*?'

Tina looks astonished. 'Yeah. Oh, my God, don't you know? She was only fifteen, that's why it was such a big deal. Nearly split the family up, it did. That's one of the reasons they moved here, to get away from it all. Apparently, Patty wanted Jen to keep the baby, and Jason wanted her to get rid of it. Can you imagine?'

The hush of the library crushes in on Sarah. She can just make out Tina's breaths, which come in short, audible bursts.

'Let's go back to the gym,' she says, rising.

In the gym 'Agadoo' is playing, and hordes of pupils are dancing around the DJ desk. One of the really square girls from Sarah's French group dances madly at the edge of the crowd; she seems to know all the moves.

'*Push pineapple – grind coffee*!' Tina sings as she leads Sarah over towards the gym cupboard in the corner. 'What d'you reckon?' she smirks.

She pulls open the cupboard door, and there, on top of a high pile of sweaty gym mats, are Kate and Simon Dobbs, looking as if they're in the middle of a championship wrestling match. Kate's white vest top is pushed high above her lacy black bra, and Simon's got his hand stuck down the back of her leggings.

Sarah gasps.

'Piss off!' Kate hisses as she turns to see them in the doorway.

Simon blinks blindly. 'Uh?' he says. He seems half-asleep.

Tina pushes the door shut, and they sprint over to the dance floor, screaming.

Half an hour later, Kate finds them dancing to 'Uptown Girl' by the speakers.

'I'm not a tart,' she insists, shouting over the music to be heard.

The love bite on her neck is the size of a plum.

~

On the first Saturday of half-term, Sarah cooks her dad a full English breakfast.

'Good God!' he cries out as he trots down the stairs. 'I do believe I've actually died and gone to heaven.'

He stands in the kitchen doorway, puffing his chest out as he breathes in the warm bacon aroma that wafts into the hallway and up the stairs. He buttons up his tatty grey cardigan and pats his stomach. 'Of course, it could finish me off altogether.'

Sarah tuts. 'None of it's fried, Dad.' She scoops the poached eggs on to their plates and pulls out the grill pan to serve up the bacon and sausages. 'Go and sit down. I'll bring it in.'

'Lord! And a newspaper too! You're spoiling me, Sarah-Lou.'

She opens the back door to let out the cooking smells and joins her dad in the dining room.

'So, what's the special occasion?' he asks as she sits down opposite.

'Nothing, really. Mrs Gilroy's given me the next few Saturdays off, because of exams. So I thought I'd cook you breakfast, seeing as I don't have to be at work.'

'Well, it's greatly appreciated, whatever the reason.' He cuts into his sausages, carefully dabbing a slice with mustard and popping it into his mouth. 'Mmm. Divine!'

The breeze from the back garden drifts through, sending a whisper of roses and sea spray into the dining room. She wonders about Deborah. She hasn't been round since Sarah told Dad about their conversation. 'She said Mum was one of your students,' Sarah had told him, hoping it would encourage him to tell her more. 'Did she now?' he'd replied.

Dad spreads the Saturday paper across the centre of the table so that he can read and eat at the same time. Every now and then he chuckles or grumbles, giving Sarah edited highlights of the world news.

'Good God. They're still going on about building a tunnel to France. It was madness when Napoleon suggested it, and it's madness still! Whatever next? A bridge to Switzerland? Waste of bloody money, if you ask me. They'll end up tunnelling halfway there and giving up after they've spent millions in the process. Just you watch.'

Sarah nods and agrees.

Dad scrapes his plate with the side of his fork, and pushes it to one side. 'Are you alright, Sarah-Lou?' he asks, suddenly looking at her with intensity. 'You're terribly dark under your eyes.'

'I'm fine. Just a bit tired, that's all. You know, all these exams.'

'Well, don't overdo it. You saw what happened to me when I pushed myself too far.'

She eats quietly, gazing out of the window on to the gravel drive at the front. It's true she's been tired. Yesterday afternoon she fell asleep in front of *Neighbours*. One minute she was eating a bowl of Frosties and kicking off her school shoes, and the next she was waking up with a crick in her neck and the remote control still in her hand.

She feels the calm warmth of the day blowing in, and looks forward to walking Ted on the beach after she's washed up. She gathers up the condiments and takes them back into the kitchen while Dad continues to read his paper.

As she returns for the plates and mugs, Dad puts his arm around her waist.

'I know I don't tell you enough, but I love you, Sarah-Lou.'

She gently tries to pull away, but he holds on for a few seconds longer, before releasing her and pushing out his chair. 'Wait here a moment. I've got something for you. Just stay there.' He removes his reading glasses and drops them beside his mug.

Sarah hears him in the hallway, opening the door to his study. She perches on the seat next to his, resting the dirty plates on the edge of table. When he returns, his face is earnest, almost nervous. He's clutching a small item in his fist.

'What is it?' Sarah asks, her eyes fixed on his hand.

He sits beside her, replacing his glasses. 'I've been having a bit of a clearout. And, well, I came across something that I think you ought to have.'

He opens his hand to reveal a gold ring, delicately studded with three little pearls.

'It was your mother's engagement ring,' he says. 'She told me she preferred the pearls, which was just as well, as I couldn't afford a diamond on an academic's salary.'

'It's beautiful,' Sarah says, slipping it on to her wedding finger for size. It's just a little too loose.

He steeples his fingers over his stomach and smiles gently. 'You have hands just like hers.'

Sarah lays her hands flat against the table and studies the ridges and dips of her fingers. She removes the ring and closes her hand around it. 'I'll wear it on my silver chain,' she says.

'She would have been so proud of you,' he says, his eyes moistening.

Sarah wraps her arms around his shoulders.

'I'm so sorry, Sarah-Lou.' His voice cracks with emotion.

'For what?' she says, pulling back to look at his face.

'For all this.' He sweeps his hand through the air, gesturing at everything and nothing.

She embraces him again, to conceal his weakened face.

'And I'm sorry I haven't been a better father,' he whispers into her sleeve. 'I know things have got to change. I've got to change. I promise I'll try harder, Sarah-Lou.'

'*Idiot*,' she says softly, rubbing her hand over his bobbly grey back.

The sea is calm and flat, and Sarah has to shield her eyes against the bright strip of horizon that runs from east to west. The tide is way out, and the top pebbles are dry underfoot. When she digs the toe of her shoe deep into the shingle, she reaches the small wet stones below, where polished glass and yellow periwinkles can be found. She squats down and widens the hole with a short length of weatherbeaten wood, scooting the larger pebbles to one side and stirring around to explore further down. She finds a smooth piece of brown glass, the size of peach stone, and rubs away the sand between her finger and thumb. Brown glass is rarer than green or clear. She slips it into her jacket pocket to add to her jar when she gets home.

Down at the water's edge, Ted has met another terrier. Sarah blinks into the sunlight, cupping her hands to whistle him back. The younger dog is leaping and frisking about, and Ted just wags his tail and trots on the spot, letting the other dog sniff and circle him. She whistles again, and Ted turns, cocking his head. He starts to run back, a little silhouette against the silver sunlight. The other dog continues to frolic at his side, until his own master calls him and he bolts across the wet sand to fall in step.

'Good boy,' Sarah says, bending to scratch Ted behind his ears. She pulls her white cotton jacket around her torso, and walks into the sun, across the sand towards West Selton.

As the coast gradually curves round, the breeze picks up. Turning to look back the way they've come, Sarah sees how she and Ted cast two distinct shadows across the sand. She wishes she had her disc camera with her. Ted is keeping up, but he looks tired, narrowing his eyes against the spray, his silky little ears waving in the wind.

'Want a rest?' Sarah asks, picking him up to climb over the high wooden barrier. She tucks him under her arm and jogs to the next breakwater where they sit, nestled into the side, sheltered from the wind. She closes her eyes and rests her head against the smooth grey wood, enjoying the warmth of the sun on her face. Ted is draped over her lap, his head nuzzled under the crook of her elbow. Overhead, the seagulls squawk and crow, their volume moving in and out of focus as they drift and return from the water. Summer's coming. Sarah drops inside herself, her hands relaxing around Ted's salty coat, her breathing growing heavy. The heat of the sunlight permeates her clothes, thawing out her inner chill. Summer's finally coming.

The crunch of boots on the pebbles rouses Ted, and he kicks Sarah in the side as he tumbles from her lap. Sarah sits up, twisting round, holding her arm over her forehead to focus on the man walking down the shelf of stones.

'Hello, you.' It's John.

'What're you doing here?' asks Sarah as he sits down on the pebbles beside her.

He turns and nods to the large stretch of grass that leads away from the seafront. Beyond the grass are the grand houses at the border to West Selton, screened by great yews and box hedges.

'I've got the day off. And that's our place,' he says, pointing to the property directly behind them. He looks a little embarrassed.

Sarah takes a long look at the large house looming beyond the hedge. 'Really?' she says, smiling at his Led Zeppelin T-shirt. 'You seem so – well, ordinary.'

He gives her a shove. 'Thanks a lot. I know what you mean, though. I don't think the neighbours think I should live there either. I'm sure they all think I'm a smack-head or something. The way they look at me, it's as if the sixties and seventies never even happened.'

Sarah smiles again and closes her eyes, easing herself back against the stones. She feels John lie down beside her.

'I guess I won't be seeing you in the chemist's for a while. Mum says you're revising for your exams.'

Sarah sighs. 'I'm *meant* to be revising, but I can't seem to take anything in at the moment. I think my brain's gone on strike. I've just about given up.'

The gulls return, hovering above them noisily. Ted paces about and gives a couple of small yaps. The birds move on, and for a while Sarah and John lie silently in the sunlight.

'I saw your mate in town,' John says. 'You know, the one who's going out with your ex-boyfriend.'

'Kate and Dante.'

'Yeah, them. They were at hanging around at the war memorial, arguing.'

Sarah's hands paw at the stones involuntarily. 'Really?'

'I think she was accusing him of getting off with someone else. I couldn't help but overhear – it got a bit heated. He called her a stalker.'

Sarah laughs. 'What did she say to that?'

'She told him to piss off, and then she ran off crying. Looked pretty terminal to me.'

'Blimey,' says Sarah.

'Told you,' he says. '*Karma*. Works every time.'

Ted falls down beside her, stretching out along her body.

'Do you miss him?' asks John.

Sarah burrows into the stones with the knuckles of her right hand, irritating Ted enough to make him move. 'Dante?

Not really. I think we're all better off on our own in the long run. Other people just let you down, don't they? I'm not so sure we're meant to be in pairs. Maybe we should be more like birds. They always seem happy enough, flying here, there and everywhere. They don't have to worry about the bother of relationships, do they?'

'Swans mate for life.'

'Well, I bet they're the exception.'

John props himself up on his elbows, squints at Sarah in disbelief and drops back against the stones. 'Not everyone's like Dante,' he says. 'And life would be a pretty lonely place if you spent it alone.'

'I dunno. It sounds quite appealing,' she says, pulling Ted back towards her. 'Maybe it's just me who's better off alone, then.'

They lie there a while longer. She can hear the movement of stones as John's hands rake them into piles by his side. The sun seeps into the layers of her face and neck; she could stay here all day. John's hand brushes hers, and wavers uncertainly, the tips of their smallest fingers still touching. She senses his breath pausing, his uncertainty hovering in the wide sea air.

'I really like you, Sar,' he says quietly.

She presses the pad of her little finger against his, then draws her hands together across her chest. 'I like you too, John. But not like that.'

A gust of wind batters against the far side of the breakwater. 'I know,' he finally says. 'I was just checking.'

The phone rings soon after Sarah gets back from the beach. It's Kate, inviting her over for the evening.

'Mum and Dad won't be home till after midnight. Dante was meant to be coming over, but that's it, as far as I'm concerned. He's history. The bastard.' She starts sobbing down the phone.

'I'm not sure I can make it.'

'Please!' Kate begs. 'I'll be all on my own!'

She's really howling now.

'Is Tina coming too?' Sarah asks. 'Why don't you ask Tina too?'

'Yeah, OK,' she sniffs.

'Alright, I'll come. But I can't stay the night, because of my dad. I have to be here just in case. What time shall I come over?'

'Seven?'

'See you then,' says Sarah. She stares at her reflection in the tarnished hall mirror. She wants to feel pleased about Kate's distress, but she can't.

Dad pushes open the door to his study. 'Did I hear you say you're making a cup of tea?' he calls into the hallway.

She tuts and kicks off her sandy shoes. 'No!'

'That'll be lovely!' he replies. 'Bring it in when it's ready!'

Ted sprints along the hallway and slips into the study before the door pulls shut. Sarah fills the kettle and switches it on. She wonders what Dante's doing right now. Dirty Dante. She smiles to herself. That'll cheer Kate up. *Dirty Dante*.

When Sarah and Tina arrive at seven, Kate seems determined to show them that she's not bothered about Dante. After ripping him to shreds for the first ten minutes she seems happy to drop the subject altogether.

'The worst thing is, I can't believe I let him come between you and me, Sar,' she says, looking ashamed. 'I'm such an idiot.'

'No, you're not,' says Sarah.

Kate throws her arms around Sarah and squeezes her tight. 'You're such a good friend.'

Tina looks on, scratching her fingers. 'You've still got us,' she says, self-consciously stretching across to rub Kate's back.

Kate smiles bashfully, picking up her purse. 'Who fancies fish and chips?'

'Can I have a pickled egg?' Tina asks.

Sarah and Kate look at each other in disgust. They burst out laughing, slapping Tina on the arm as they push through the front door.

'What?' says Tina, a bemused wrinkle forming between her eyebrows. 'What's wrong with pickled eggs?

After they've eaten their fish and chips in front of the TV, Kate pulls the coffee table closer to the sofa. 'Let's do a Ouija board.'

'What's a weeji board?' asks Tina, scrunching her chip paper into a tight ball.

'It's where you call up ghosts,' says Sarah, dropping her half-finished supper on the coffee table with a plop. 'I don't think I like the idea of it. It's creepy.'

'Oh, don't be a wimp, Sarah. It probably won't work anyway.'

Kate gathers up the chip debris and scoots from the room in her fluffy socks. They hear her flip open the kitchen bin with a bang. Tina dashes to the loo, leaving Sarah alone in the living room. She draws her feet up off the floor, away from the spot where she and Jason had been. Her eyes scan the room, running over the big TV, the *faux* log fireplace, the wall to wall immaculate carpet. There are no pets, no piles of newspapers, no kicked-off shoes or socks. It's all too neat and orderly.

Kate returns with sheets of paper, a black marker pen and a wine glass. She kneels at the table, just as Tina comes back and settles on the carpet beside her.

'I like your necklace,' says Tina, pointing at the ring hanging from Sarah's chain.

'Thanks. It was my mum's.'

Kate sniffs the air. 'Urgh! What's that smell? Have you just chucked up, Teen?'

Tina looks mortified. 'No! It's probably just the chip wrappers or something.'

'No, it's definitely your breath,' Kate scowls. 'You ought to get yourself some mouthwash.'

She tears the paper into equal-sized squares, marking each one with a letter of the alphabet. She arranges them on the coffee table in a circle and places the wine glass upside down in the centre. She sits back on her heels to view her work, then quickly scribbles out a 'YES' and 'NO' sheet and adds them to the circle.

'So, here are the rules. We all have to place our finger on the base of the glass, and we start off by moving it in small circles. There's no point in trying to make it move in a direction you want it to go in, because we'll all be able to tell. If a spirit comes into the glass, it'll spell out messages to us. I'll do the talking.'

She jumps up and flicks off the main light, so that the room is in shadow, illuminated only by the hall light on one side and the kitchen light on the other. Tina widens her eyes at Sarah and exaggerates a noisy gulp.

Kate moves closer to the table. 'Fingers on? So, we'll just get it moving a little. Yep, like that. OK. Spirit in the glass, spirit in the glass. If there is a spirit in the glass, tell us of your presence by moving to "YES".'

The glass rotates a few times, then swerves to 'YES' and halts. Tina starts to squeal, but Kate thumps her with the back of her free hand. The glass starts to move round again.

'Stay calm. Spirit in the glass, are you a good spirit or a bad spirit? Go to "YES" if you are good.'

The wine glass starts to circulate again, slowly at first, increasing in speed until it violently stops at the 'NO'. The girls gasp.

'What should we do?' asks Tina, sounding scared.

'Burn it out,' replies Kate. She sprints into the kitchen and returns with a lighter, lifting the glass and placing the flame inside the upturned goblet. 'There, it's gone. Let's go again.'

The glass rotates inside the circle and after a few minutes they find a good spirit. Sarah's concentrating hard on figuring out if Kate is guiding the glass, but the movement is so light and independent, it seems impossible that any one of them is responsible.

'Good spirit, do you have a message for any one of us here? Indicate by moving towards that person.'

The glass spins about the circle, slowing down and eventually stopping in front of Tina.

'Spirit, tell us your message.' Kate rises up on her knees, her back straight, her voice authoritative.

The glass slowly spells out Tina's message, as she watches on in horror.

F. L. U. F. F. Y.

She appears to be speechless.

'Does that mean anything to you, Teen?' asks Kate. Sarah suspects her concern is phony.

Tina's tongue darts in and out of the side of her mouth. 'He was my first kitten. Remember I told you? We think he fell down the back of the plasterboard when the builders were putting the kitchen in. By the time we realised where he was it was too late. They'd already rendered the wall and started sticking up the wallpaper.'

'God, that's awful,' says Sarah, thinking of the little kitten tumbling down the back of the wall. When she locks eyes with Kate it suddenly seems funny, and she has to bite her lip.

'Yeah. Dad said we couldn't afford to take it all down again, especially as the wallpaper came from Laura Ashley. And anyway, Fluffy would've been, you know, dead, by the time we realised.'

'Poor Fluffy,' says Kate, with water in her eyes. A nervous smile quivers at the edges of her mouth. 'Right! Fingers on!'

The next message is for Sarah. Without realising it, her other hand reaches for the ring and she runs her finger over the bumps of the three little pearls.

'What is your message for Sarah?' Kate demands.

The glass circles a few times and starts to spell out a word. The girls' lips move in unison, as the message appears.

W. E. D. D. I. N. G. R. I. N. G.

Sarah's hand flies to her lap. She throws Kate and Tina an angry glare. 'It's her *engagement* ring.'

'What is?' asks Kate, appearing perplexed.

Sarah feels light-headed and furious. She shakes her head. 'What else have you got to tell me?' she demands, taking over Kate's role.

Tina and Kate look at each other sheepishly. The glass circles, spelling out a new message for Sarah.

B. E. G. O. O. D.

Sarah puffs air through pursed lips. 'Well, that could be for anyone.'

The glass continues to spin, pulling their fingers with it, becoming more frantic all the while, threatening to spill over at any time. The girls chant out the letters as they come:

A. L. W. A. Y. S. W. I. T. H. Y. O. U.

The glass comes to an abrupt halt in front of Sarah, and topples over dramatically. It lies on its side rolling in gentle semi-circles until it slows to a stop.

Tina draws breath slowly.

Kate picks up the glass and returns it to the middle of the table. 'Was that your mum, Sar?'

Sarah's eyes move from Tina to Kate. Tina looks terrified.

'Probably not.' There's a slow tremor building up inside her organs, and she needs to get out of here before she starts to shake all over. She feels sick. She feels sick all the time.

'Another one?' asks Kate, returning her finger to the glass.

Tina shakes her head and edges away from the table.

'I'd better go,' says Sarah. 'It's gone eleven. Dad'll be waiting up, no doubt.'

Tina and Kate stand at the back door with the patio light on, so Sarah can wheel her bike out through the side gate. She hears the back door clunk shut as she leans over the gate to draw the bolt behind her. Her thoughts are racing. She tries to replay Kate's movements as the glass sped from letter to letter. Was it Kate?

'Hello, stranger.'

Sarah spins round, almost losing grip of her bicycle. It's Jason, standing right beside her, jangling his car keys. Sarah hears Patty's voice as she enters the house around the corner, out of view.

'You made me jump,' she says, stepping back against the gate, her hands gripping the bars of the bike.

'Long time no see.' He throws a furtive glance over his shoulder and slides his hand up past her waist, cupping her breast firmly.

She flinches.

'Bloody hell, sweetie. You've filled out since I last saw you.' His second hand comes up to take the other breast, and he gives them both a squeeze, his eyes moving from one to the other like a greengrocer weighing up produce.

She shoves past him, her head firmly down as she wheels her bike on to the path.

'Night, sweetie,' Jason calls after her.

Sarah cycles as fast as her legs will go, feeling the blood pumping through her body, the wind in her ears. Tears whistle across her cheekbones, flying out into the night.

~

The first morning back after half-term Sarah enters the toilets next to her form room and finds Kate and Tina bunched together at the far end. They've all got exams scheduled after lunch, so the morning is meant to be spent revising. Tina is leaning over the far basin, her white knuckles gripping the edge, as Kate forces a small gold stud through the ridge of cartilage at the top of Tina's ear.

'What are you doing – ?' asks Sarah as she moves closer.

Kate turns and smiles.

'Fuckafuckafuckafucka – ' Tina chants, her sharp body held rigid against the basin.

'There! Let me just pop the butterfly on,' says Kate, looking delighted with herself. 'Da-dah!'

Tina looks side on at her reflection in the mirror. 'Shit,' she mutters.

'It'll be fine!' Kate steps back into one of the toilet cubicles and returns with a wodge of toilet paper for Tina to press against the mess. 'Cool, eh? You know Siouxsie's got them all the way up her ears.'

Tina cautiously peels the toilet roll from her ear for another look at the swollen purple-red mass of skin. 'Who's Suzy?' she asks.

'Siouxsie and the Banshees, you plank.'

Sarah has a closer inspection. The skin pulsates grotesquely around the tiny gold stud. Drying blood is caked into the vertical creases of her ear.

'We should go and register or they'll put us down as absent,' Sarah says, pulling open the door.

The girls pick up their bags and return to the form room, Tina still pressing the toilet tissue to her mutilated ear.

By mid-morning, it's still bleeding, and Tina says the throbbing has become unbearable. The three girls sit in the far corner of the library, trying to revise, with Tina growing increasingly neurotic about her ear. She keeps removing the tissue and assessing the blood loss, which she believes has reached a critical stage. Sarah and Kate are struggling to keep from laughing. 'I've got to get it sorted before one o'clock,' she says desperately. 'I've got my Home Ec. exam! You know what Miss Norman is like about hygiene. She won't let me in looking like this!'

Kate decides to take her to see Mrs McCabe to get it seen to, and they scurry off towards the front office, leaving Sarah alone in the library. She leans back in her chair and gazes up at the high Victorian ceiling and dark panelled balcony which looks out from the first floor classrooms. She'll go and see Mrs McCabe herself later, as soon as Tina and Kate go off to their afternoon exams; she'll know what to do. Sarah's exhaustion seeps through her veins like mud, and she slides down against the top of the desk, closing her eyes and resting her head on her forearms. The library is so quiet she can almost hear the dust falling from the balustrades above. Occasionally, she hears soft footsteps walking through the corridor, but no one knows she's here, tucked away behind the high bookshelves in the furthest corner of the room. She dreams of the spring tide, gently lapping at her toes as she sits at the water's edge. In her hands she holds a small chain of slipper limpets which she prises apart, one at a time. One. Two. She tosses each mollusc into the retreating water. Three. Four. Five. She's left with the final limpet, turning it this way and that, trying to coax the living creature out. But the sun is too bright and all she can see is the ear-shaped contours of its interior, its smooth septum gleaming pinkly in the white light.

She's startled by the sound of Kate's bag clunking against the desktop. 'What?' she says, sitting up.

'What, what?' replies Kate, grinning, pulling out the chair opposite. In the shimmering shade of the library her skin looks flawless.

'Where's Tina?' Sarah runs her hands through her hair and blinks a few times to refocus her brain.

'Down at the front office being patched up. They wanted her to take the stud out, but I told them it's more likely to get infected if they do that. So they're soaking it in surgical spirit and they said they'll put a dressing on it for the afternoon.'

'Didn't they have a go at you for doing it?'

'Don't be stupid. We told them she got it done in a proper salon. They said it's disgusting that places like that are allowed to operate. I don't know how I kept a straight face. I'll do yours if you want.'

'No chance, you butcher.' Sarah laughs, tugging on her own cleanly studded lobes. 'So was it Mrs McCabe you saw?'

Kate drags out a second chair and puts her feet up. 'No. When we got to the office, we asked for her, and they told us to wait. Then Mrs North came out instead. She said Mrs McCabe went off on maternity leave just before half-term.'

Sarah remembers how tenderly Mrs McCabe had taken care of her rounders injury, and how much she'd wanted to stay in her calm little office.

'Shame,' says Kate. 'I quite liked her.' She draws a length of hair through her mouth. 'It's probably for the best. She'd only have gone mental if she'd stayed, working with all those other nutters. You never know, she might even be in the funny farm right now. Poor cow.'

'Yeah,' Sarah replies, gazing up at the dark oak gallery above, 'poor cow.'

After school, the girls stop off in town for ice creams. They each buy a Mr Whippy '99', and wander over to the war memorial to sit in the sunshine and chat. They spread out over the top step of the stone structure, gazing across the High Street and watching as people come and go. Seagulls cry out overhead, casting passing shadows as they dip and soar. Tina's already managed to get a big dollop of ice cream on the green nylon of her school skirt, and she licks her fingers and rubs at the stain as it spreads and smears.

'How was the Home Ec. exam?' asks Sarah.

'Fine,' replies Tina, still scrubbing with the heel of her hand.

'What about RE?' she asks Kate.

'Fine.'

There are hordes of Selton High School kids wandering about the town today, many of them celebrating the end of their exams. Sarah's just got Maths left to do next week, then that's it. 'It's almost over,' she sighs, licking her ice cream in a neat, smooth line around the top of the cone.

Kate slowly curls her tongue around her flake and smiles flirtatiously as she bites it off at the root. 'See that sixth former over there by the newsagent's? Look at him staring. He's been eyeing me up for weeks. Every time he passes our hut he has a look through the window to see if I'm there.'

'You're outrageous!' Sarah laughs. 'The way you're licking your ice cream!'

Kate smiles contentedly and scoops up a little white peak on the tip of her pink tongue. 'I know.'

The sixth former turns away and pushes through the entrance and into the shop.

'Ahh,' says Kate. 'He's a shy boy.' She gathers her hair up behind her head and lets it fall as she stretches her arms out in a wide theatrical arc. 'I'm gonna finish with Dante tonight.'

Sarah raises her eyebrows in disbelief.

'Really,' says Kate. 'I can't be bothered with him any more. He's chucked.'

Tina stands up and brushes herself off, scattering crumbles of cornet across the pavement.

'Have you eaten your ice cream already?' says Kate. 'I've never known anyone stuff their food in quite like you, Teen.'

Tina sits and pulls her knees up, shaking out her new poodle perm. 'Anyone see *Prisoner Cell Block H* last night?'

Sarah's not sure what she's talking about.

Kate nods. 'Yeah, it was really funny. Have you ever seen so many ugly women together in one place?'

'Well, the same can't be said for you lot, that's for sure.' Jason's standing at the foot of the war memorial, in a pair of massive aviator sunglasses, his suit jacket hooked on to his thumb so that it's casually tossed over his shoulder.

'Oh, look! It's *Top Gun*,' says Kate, laughing and pointing at his glasses.

'Yeah, yeah,' he says, grinning broadly. 'Except Tom Cruise doesn't look as good in them as I do. So, what are you ladies up to?'

Kate pops the last piece of cornet into her mouth and brushes her hands together. 'Hanging about.'

'That looks nice,' he says, nodding at Sarah's ice cream.

She hasn't even got down to the cone yet, and she can't lick it with him standing there. The ice cream starts to glisten and slide.

'You'd better eat that, before it melts,' he says.

Kate and Tina turn to look at Sarah. She licks it, a quick, flat-tongued motion, to catch the drips and make them stop staring at her.

'So, I take it you'll all be coming to the Summer Disco at the youth club? It's gonna be a blast.'

'When is it?' asks Tina, scratching at her fingers. She's kicked her shoes off and Sarah can see she's got eczema between her toes too.

'It's on a Friday, love. It's the Friday before the World Cup final, so if England make it through we'll have even more reason to celebrate!'

Kate rolls her eyes. 'What is it about blokes and football? Anyway, back to the disco. I think it's the week before Signing Out Day, so we'll all have finished our exams by then.'

Tina and Sarah sit stiffly on either side of Kate, smiling politely at Jason.

'So?' he says, taking his glasses off in a cheesy smooth action. 'Whaddya say? You coming?'

The girls exchange quick glances and nod.

'Why not?' says Kate, crossing her arms across her low-cut blouse.

'Excellent,' says Jason and he swaggers away, breaking into a jog as he crosses over to the estate agent's office on the opposite side of the road.

He turns and raises his hand. Sarah is gripped by a sudden rush of forgotten panic.

'You alright?' asks Kate.

Sarah smiles and gathers up her school bags. 'Indigestion,' she says, patting her chest.

Tina puts her bag over her shoulder and winces. 'Bet it doesn't hurt as much as my ear,' she says. She lifts her hair up to reveal a thick wad of cotton wool and white tape.

'Surprised you didn't need a blood transfusion, Teen,' Kate says, smirking at Sarah as they drop down from the memorial stone and head off along the High Street.

Sarah laughs, forgetting her anxiety, and waves her friends off as they walk home in the opposite direction.

~

On the day of Sarah's final exam she leaves the house early, optimistic about the freedom of summer ahead. After today, she only has to return for Signing Out Day, when the school takes the final leavers' photograph before the girls stream out, heading into the streets and parks around town.

The morning is bright and windy, and as she nears the corner of Seafield Avenue Sarah has to shield her eyes from the sun to make out the figure perched on the street sign up ahead. It's Dante. She's suddenly aware of her every movement, the way she's holding her bag, the tightness of her school jumper across her chest. She flicks her hair over her ears, and wishes she hadn't. She read somewhere that fiddling with your hair in front of someone of the opposite sex is a sure sign of attraction; and in this case it's not true. She can't stand the sight of him.

He stands up and waits for her, his hands plunged deep into his pockets. 'Alright, Sar,' he says, falling into step as she walks past. 'I was hoping I'd see you. Got an exam today?'

'Yep.' She shifts her bag on to the other shoulder.

'Suppose you heard about me and Kate?'

'Uh-huh.'

They don't speak again until they turn into the road leading up to the school gates. Dante puts his hand on the crook of her elbow, forcing her to stop and look at him.

'Look, I was a complete dickhead with you, Sar. I don't know what was wrong with me. I was new to the area, and I just – well, I just fucked up.'

Sarah frowns at him. 'Was that an apology?'

He looks really pissed off. 'Yes, actually, it was. But if you want to hear the words: I'm sorry. There, is that better?'

'A bit,' she replies, halting suddenly. She holds her wrist up between them, and looks at him directly. 'Did you give this to me, or not?' The tiny seashells rattle along the leather cord as the bracelet settles on her arm.

Dante runs his hand up through the underside of his hair, rubbing the crew-cut section beneath his floppy dark layers. '*No.*' He glances at the school. 'Look, I really like you, Sar. I didn't realise just how much until I'd screwed it all up. I can't believe I've been such a pillock. Really.' He holds her shoulders to make her look at him.

A horn sounds from an approaching car, and they both turn to see a silver Cortina slowing beside them as it passes. Jason glares at Sarah through the windscreen, his face obscured by black sunglasses. *Tut-tut*, he mimes, waggling his finger in the air. He revs the engine twice and accelerates up the road at hazardous speed.

'Who the fuck was that?' asks Dante. 'Dirty fucker. Did you see the way he was looking at you?'

Sarah looks up the road where the car had been. A cold chill runs through her body.

'I don't know,' she says, and she walks in though the school gates, leaving Dante standing on the corner gazing after her.

After the exam, Sarah returns home to spend the afternoon with her father. It's his birthday, and she finds him in the garden, sitting under the willow tree at the far end, smoking a pipe and drinking coffee.

'What's that?' Sarah asks, pulling a disgusted face. She now sees it's not even lit.

'What? This? It's my old pipe! I was having a bit of a tidy-up, and I came across it in my college things. I used to smoke it to make me appear more debonair. I think it works, don't you?'

'It makes you look like even more of an old duffer, if that's what you mean.'

He laughs, and puffs at the stem theatrically. Sarah returns to the house to fetch his card and present, and to bring out the birthday cake she'd secretly baked last night. It's been hidden in the drinks cabinet all day. As she passes through the dining room she spots a ripped envelope and card in the top of the wastepaper bin. She pauses, resting the cake on the table, and retrieves the card. It's from Deborah, so she reads it swiftly and puts it back in the bin, shoving it to the bottom out of sight. Best forgotten. Ted is lying in the triangle of sunlight by the back door, and he rises and stretches, following her lazily to the end of the garden. He falls over in the half shade of the tree.

Dad is delighted with his cake, throwing his hands in the air and blowing out the candles with gusto.

'Victoria sponge?' he asks.

'Naturally,' she replies. 'I know you're not meant to, but it's your birthday. After today it's back to normal.'

They sit in the deckchairs and eat their cake, quietly chatting about the flowers and fruits which have started to show themselves in the garden. White anemones have spread throughout the lupins and buddleia on the sunny side of the lawn, and the flowers gently ripple with the light movements of painted ladies and industrious honeybees.

'So, that's it now,' says Sarah, picking crumbs off her school skirt. 'I've just had my last exam. So once we've signed out next week, I'm free.' She holds her arms aloft in a cheer.

'Jolly good. So what's next?'

She sighs. 'I've put in the application to do A-levels, like Kate.'

Dad stretches his legs out and clasps his hands across his belly. He closes his eyes against the sun. 'I don't remember signing the forms.'

Acute exhaustion washes over her. 'No, you don't need to these days. I think it's a new thing, because I'll be sixteen when term starts.' She hates lying to him. 'But, if I don't do that well with my O-levels, I thought I could maybe do some shop work for a while? Like Tina – she's got a job at Boots in Tighborn. Just until I make my mind up about something else? I mean, they always have last minute places at the Tech. I could do hairdressing or something.'

'Over my dead body,' he grunts, his eyes still closed. 'That reminds me. That young chap from the chemist's phoned, said his mother wanted to know if you'd like to work over the summer holidays.'

'I don't know. I think I've had enough of the chemist's.' She turns to look at him in profile. 'You know, I'm not going to do that well in my exams. I'm not expecting to pass anything, really.'

He opens one eye, his face scrunched up. 'We'll cross that bridge when we come to it,' he says. 'Now, I'm thinking a few weeks in Dorset might do us both some good. So, if you're not working it makes it all a bit more straightforward.'

Sarah frowns, cupping her hands above her eyes to look at him better.

'Remember Jim Porter? Old head of department at Tighborn. Well, he's got a nice little cottage that he's putting up for sale after the summer; said we can make the most of the place while he's still got it. Right down at the seafront it is, near Lyme Regis. Beautiful piece of coastline.' He smiles and waits for her response. 'Actually, it's free for the whole of July and August, so we can stay for as long as we like.'

Sarah closes her eyes and breathes deeply. 'What about your work?' she asks.

'That can wait. I think a change will do us both good, don't you?'

She wriggles down into her deckchair, stretching her toes out to rub Ted's upturned tummy. 'Yeah. It sounds great, Dad.'

~

The Health Centre gives Sarah an appointment with a female doctor at one o'clock on Monday. She's less likely to bump into anyone she knows at that time, as most people are either at work or school, or eating lunch.

Her hands trembled as she made the phone call and they shake again now as she approaches the clinic at the back of the main parade. She feels exposed to every car which passes, and she avoids eye contact with other pedestrians, staring intently at the cracks in the pavement as she walks. She barely slept at all last night. The bright June sunlight makes a mirror of the glass-fronted clinic, and Sarah catches her own reflection as she reaches for the metal door handle. She comes to a dead halt, barely recognising herself. It's indistinct, but she looks different. She pulls back the door to the entrance porch. Once through the next set of doors she will have to communicate with the middle-aged women behind the desk, announce her name and the name of the doctor she's seeing. They might know her, or her father. Perhaps they'll know why she's here; even worse, perhaps they'll speculate between themselves, checking her medical notes once she's gone. She doesn't want to go through too early, to sit in the waiting room under the scrutiny of other patients and medical staff.

She pauses in the airlock between the two sets of doors, checking her watch and scanning the health notices on the wall. *Measles is Misery.*

A faded poster shows an image of dark brown tar being poured into a glass bowl. It reads: *No Wonder Smokers Cough.* The visual provokes her gag reflex. She looks away, searching over the other posters by way of distraction. She looks at her watch again. She's got a few minutes. The largest poster of all is a shiny new one, royal blue with a yellow bolt of lightning running through it.

> *TAKE CARE. AIDS is caused by the HTLV III virus. This virus is found in blood, semen and vaginal secretions. So sharing needles or having unsafe sex puts you at risk. PLAY SAFE – LEARN THE FACTS.*

She stares at the poster, reading the words over and over again.

The inner door swings back and John strides out from the reception area.

'Hello, Sarah!' he says with a big smile across his face. 'What are you doing here?'

She flinches, her eyes flickering towards the big blue poster. 'Nothing,' she says, horribly aware of her defensive tone.

'Nothing?' he says with a little laugh.

Sarah returns a guarded smile.

'So, aren't you going to ask me what I'm doing here, then?' John looks as though he's about to burst with exhilaration.

'OK,' replies Sarah. She frowns at him as if he's lost his marbles.

'I've been getting my vaccination boosters. I'm going travelling again at the end of July! I'm going to start off in Turkey and take it from there. You know Sol from Shattered Records? He's coming with me. He's getting a mate to look after the shop for a few months so he can get away. Man, I can't wait to get out of this dump!'

'So you won't be working in the chemist's, then?' Sarah can hardly hear her own words.

A woman in a pink velour hat passes between them, bustling through the front door and out into the street. Sarah's eyes search the noticeboard beyond John, as she tries to make sense of the moment. *Straight Facts about Sex and Birth Control.*

''Fraid not. It just can't compete with Turkey, I'm sorry to say.' He grins, pushing his hands further down into the pockets of his straight black jeans.

Sarah looks at her watch. One minute to one. *PLAY SAFE – LEARN THE FACTS.*

'You got an appointment?' asks John, suddenly appearing concerned. 'Is everything alright?'

Her insides tremble with alarm, and cold dread washes over her skin.

'Sar? What's wrong? Sarah?' He reaches out to her.

She gasps, biting down on her lip as she pushes past him and on to the pavement outside the clinic. He follows her, reaching out to touch her shoulder and spin her around. She feels the blood drain from her skin, and the words in her throat constrict and choke as she tries to break free.

'Sarah!' he says again, this time with authority. 'Talk to me! Something's not right!'

She steps back, feeling an angry flash of hate rushing up through her body. 'Just leave me alone, John! You just go off on your travels and have a fine hippy time, dossing about and smoking dope, and leave me alone to get on with my life! OK?!'

John stands with his palms upturned. He tips his head to one side, squinting as he tries to make her out. Sarah gazes into his deep amber eyes, and for a brief moment she wants to collapse against his chest and tell him everything. She turns and runs; away from John; away from the clinic; away from it all.

~

Kate, Tina and Sarah arrange to meet at the oak tree on Signing Out Day, an hour before the photograph is scheduled outside the gym. Sarah is sweating profusely by the time she arrives, having remembered at the last minute to clear her locker and pick up her PE kit. She slides into the shade of the tree, kicking off her shoes and fanning her shiny red face with a notebook.

'Blimey, did you run here?' asks Kate, budging along to give Sarah more space. 'Your face looks like a radish.'

Sarah shakes her head. 'No, I'm just boiling.' She removes her jumper, pulling it up over her head and chucking it on the grass in front of them.

Kate stares at Sarah's breasts. 'What's going on there, Sar?' she asks, pointing.

Sarah looks down at her chest. Her white shirt is pulled tight across her torso, key-holing where it's become too small. She grabs at the hem of the shirt, trying to straighten herself out and make her chest seem less obvious. 'What?' she says.

'Your knockers! You were flat as a pancake this time last year. We used to call you fried egg tits, didn't we, Teen?'

Tina laughs, spitting a mouthful of crisps across her lap. She nods, apologetically.

Kate prods one of Sarah's boobs. She recoils; they're so tender she can hardly stand to touch them herself.

'Wow, they're pretty impressive,' laughs Kate.

Sarah scowls at her. 'Weirdo,' she says.

Kate has brought a hip flask of vodka and lemonade, and Tina has an old bottle of Malibu she nicked from her kitchen cupboard.

'So, what happened to you on Friday?' she asks Sarah. 'Thought you were coming to the Summer Disco?'

She offers Sarah the flask and she takes a swig.

'Urghh,' she shudders, still fanning herself frantically. The heat is spreading up her neck yet her hands feel cold and damp. 'I wasn't feeling well. My dad got us some fish and chips for supper, and one minute I was feeling fine and the next I was chucking up. I think the fish was off. It smelt vile, like the fishiest fish you've ever smelt.'

'Oh, you really missed out, Sar. It was a right laugh,' says Tina. 'Your dad was being a complete loony, wasn't he, Kate?'

Kate kicks off her shoes and wriggles up her skirt so that the sun can get to her legs. 'He was all overexcited about the quarter-finals on Sunday, so he kept making everyone shout "Engerland!" every time he put on a new track. It was funny. Mind you, he's not in such a good mood now.'

'Why's that?' asks Sarah.

Kate looks incredulous and pokes her with her toe. 'Well, they lost, didn't they? Honestly, you should have heard my dad when it happened. I thought he'd lost the plot altogether, and he's still not over it. He was reading the paper last night, going on and on about Maradona. "Hand of God?" he said. More like "Hand of Cheating Argey Sod".'

Sarah searches through her bag, looking for some tissues. She finds a crumpled handkerchief and wipes the sweat from her face. The heat in her skin is unbearable.

'Try a bit of this,' offers Tina. 'It's lush. It's all coconutty. Mmmm.'

Sarah tries the Malibu, swallowing a large gulp. The sickly liquid slides down her oesophagus like snot, and the nausea is instant.

'Oh, that was horrible,' she mutters, pushing herself to her knees. Her head feels as if she's buried in cotton wool, and her vision has diminished to a small pinprick of light. She manages to crawl away from the tree just before she throws up.

Kate jumps to her feet and stands over Sarah. 'Jesus! What happened? It can't be the drink – you hardly had any! You must have a bug or something.'

Sarah groans and shakily returns to the tree, taking her water flask from her bag. 'Don't know. I have been a bit off-colour lately. I think the heat got to me.'

Tina puts the Malibu back in her rucksack. She glances over at Sarah's vomit pile and slaps her palm across her mouth. 'Can we go and sit somewhere else?' she mumbles through her hand.

They pick up their bags and walk back down the field, stopping halfway between the tree and the school building. The chairs are being counted out for the back rows of the fifth year photograph, and Mrs Whiff and Mrs Jensen are directing the photographer as he unpacks his equipment. Sarah sips water from her flask and sits down on the grass beside Tina, curling her feet beneath her legs.

Kate unwraps a scotch egg from a square of tinfoil and bites into it, revealing a grey-yellow yolk at the centre. 'You don't half look pale, Sar,' she says, accidentally dropping a greasy lump of sausage meat into her own lap.

'Murderer,' Tina mutters.

Kate shakes her head irritably. 'Veggie *freak*.'

The eggy stench hangs in the air and Sarah averts her eyes, fighting the rising bile. She lies back against the warm grass, running her fingertips over the springy carpet of cloverleaf.

'What are you doing after the photo?' she asks, gazing at the clear sky overhead.

'Nothing much,' replies Tina. 'My mum said she'll treat me to a hot chocolate in Marconi's. So I said I'd meet her in town.'

'What about you, Kate?'

'Dad's picking me up. I'm helping him redecorate the youth club. We're painting the main hall, because they don't have enough cash to pay to get proper decorators in. They're so lucky to have my dad there. They don't appreciate just how much he does.'

Sarah's eyes are closed against the sunlight, and she feels as though she's slipping away, losing consciousness as she lies here. Kate and Tina flop out on the grass beside her and everything goes quiet for a while, as if someone has muted all sound. She's aware of the sun singeing her skin and pinning her limbs down with liquid heat.

It's all over; no more exams, no more school.

January 2010

John and Sarah step out of the old Citroën and into the damp January night.

She tugs at her coat collar and shudders, as John locks the driver's door with his manual key.

'Don't desert me in there, will you?' she says.

He smiles, pushing his hands deep into the pockets of his heavy wool jacket.

'Not unless you want me to.'

There's a strange shyness between them, the result of so much time passed, and they walk stiffly, side by side, approaching the gaudy-bannered opening to the school gymnasium.

Inside, the large hall is already filling up. Directly ahead, there's a DJ desk on a raised platform against the wall bars of the gym, with coloured flashing lights just like the ones on the system Kate's dad used to operate. The smell of plimsoll rubber is overpowering, clean and sweaty all at once; Sarah flinches as a strobe light circulates the room and pierces her eyes. The DJ looks at least fifty, and it's clear he's trying to model himself on Gary Numan, judging by his shiny black hair and heavy eyeliner. He rifles through the record collection, chewing gum and bopping his head to each beat of the music as Elton John's 'I'm Still Standing' blasts from the giant speakers on either side of the mixing desk.

Sarah and John locate the makeshift bar in the far corner, next to the gym cupboard where Kate was caught snogging Simon Dobbs at the fifth year Spring Disco. The drinks are set up on low school tables so that it looks more like a cake sale than a bar. Sarah feels suddenly furtive, certain she shouldn't be here, as she tries to work out if the women serving are teachers or ex-pupils.

'You OK?' asks John, handing her a large plastic tumbler of red wine.

A man in his forties walks past wearing a frilly black shirt and face paint. He grins and gives the thumbs-up to a group of Bowie impersonators beside the bar.

Sarah cringes. 'I'm starting to think this might be a terrible mistake.'

'What?'

'*This*,' she says, sweeping her arms wide. 'We must be the only people not in fancy dress.' She looks down at her own outfit, a simple striped top and black jeans. She readjusts the little red scarf at her neck, wishing she'd worn a dress after all. 'God, it's going to be a nightmare.'

'Forget about it,' he says, running his hand through the back of his hair. 'You look fine – you look like *you*.'

'Do I?' she asks, tipping her head. 'I must look a bit different.'

John leans against the climbing bars and shrugs. 'Only a bit. I mean your hair's different. It was blonder before and shorter, and of course we're all a bit older. But you still look like you. I know I'd recognise you if I passed you on the street.'

'I don't know if I'd even recognise me.' She tucks a lock of tawny brown hair behind her ear.

He smiles. 'You would. So, tell me about Dorset.'

Sarah joins him against the wall, perching on a low bar. She takes a sip of the cheap red wine, grimacing at the sharp tang. 'What do you want to know?'

'Well, how come you ended up staying there?'

She scans the room. There are people everywhere; hundreds and hundreds of people. 'Dorset? I don't know really. We just did. We went there that summer, after my exams, and we stayed in a cottage belonging to one of Dad's old college friends. It's tiny, right down by the sea. Anyway, it was up for sale and after we'd been there for a week or so, Dad said, "How about we stay?" And that was that. He put the Seafield Avenue place on the market and bought the cottage.'

'Wow,' says John. 'He never struck me as the impulsive type.'

Sarah runs her thumb around the rim of her plastic cup. 'He wasn't.'

'And what do you do for a living?' he asks, bending to place his bottle of lager on the floor between his feet. 'This feels so weird,' he says, shaking his head. 'I don't know a thing about your life now.'

For a moment they are locked in an intimate gaze, unobtrusive and comprehending.

Sarah pushes her hands together, feeling the knuckles of her middle fingers crack. She looks across the room. 'I went up to London when I was twenty, for a trainee job at the Natural History Museum. I ended up working in the education department, you know, taking kids around the museum and running workshops. It was great fun; I really loved it.'

'So, you don't do it any more?'

'No. I had to move back to Dorset a couple of years ago, when Dad got very ill, and after he died I just stayed on.' As Sarah speaks, she realises how intently John is listening. The noise of the room subdues as the party fades in and out of focus. 'I know I don't want to go back to London,' she says with a lurch of startling urgency. 'I really do need to decide what I'm going to do next.'

John rubs his chin, frowning. 'I'm sorry to hear about your dad. I only met him a few times, in the chemist's, but he seemed really nice.'

Sarah picks up John's empty cup and leaves him beside the wall as she joins the queue at the bar. After a moment or two, she realises that it's Jo Allen in front of her, with her best friend

Bev Greene. They've put their hair up in backcombed single side bunches, and they're both wearing red plastic earrings and off the shoulder tops. Sarah takes a backward step, folding her arms across her body and dropping her chin as she listens in on their conversation. She hasn't seen Jo since that afternoon in Marconi's, when she walked past the window with her new pram. Sarah recalls the pallor of her skin, the detached expression etched across her face.

'Which one's the vodka and Coke?' Bev asks the woman serving, indicating towards the two plastic cups on the table in front of her. She raises her voice over the music. 'Here, put a slice of lemon in the Bacardi, will you, so we don't get mixed up? Don't wanna go mixing our drinks this early, do we, Jo?'

Jo reaches for her own drink and turns round to see Sarah standing a couple of feet behind her in line. Jo's eyes are made up with shimmering blue and green eyeshadow and her lips are a thin slick of iced pink. As she meets Sarah's startled gaze, she shows no sign of recognition whatsoever.

'Here, Bev, get us some crisps, will you?' she says, stretching across to look at the selection. 'Cheese and onion. My stomach thinks my throat's been cut.'

They pay and leave the queue, drinking from straws and nudging each other as they spot old faces. Sarah imagines Jo thrashing about in the emergency room, before that poor little baby popped out and got the shock of its life. 'Toyah, they called it,' Tina told her that day in the chemist's. *Toyah*. Sarah orders her drinks and returns to John at the climbing bars.

'So, what about you, John?' she asks, handing him his drink. 'The last time I saw you, you were off on your travels again. Turkey, wasn't it?'

He nods thoughtfully. 'Yeah, I travelled for about six months or so, then I came back and worked for Mum so I could concentrate on my music. Remember I was in that band with Sol from the record shop? Well, we kept that going for a bit, gigging in local pubs and bars, that kind of thing. We really thought we could make it big.' He laughs, shaking his head.

'Must have been good fun, though? I wish I could have heard you.'

'Yeah, it was. But we were stony broke most of the time, and that wasn't such a good laugh. I finally got my act together when Mum paid for me to complete my piano diploma. Anyway, about ten years ago I met this media guy through my music teacher, and he gave me my first break, writing little bits and pieces of music for TV and films. And that's what I do full-time now.'

'Really? Any films I'd know?'

He scratches his head distractedly. 'A few documentaries.' He looks at his feet. 'Um, that last Spielberg film…'

Sarah laughs and claps her hands. 'John, that's amazing!'

He bobs his head modestly.

'Where do you work from?' she asks.

'I'm still at Mum's place,' he replies.

Sarah can't hide her surprise. 'In West Selton?'

John's thumb moves in a small circular motion over the top button of his waistcoat, clockwise, then anti-clockwise.

'Mum passed away five years ago, and she left me the house. I set my studio up in the top room, so it looks out over the sea.'

'But it's huge,' says Sarah. 'I can't imagine you there on your own.'

He stretches his legs out and wriggles back on to the horizontal bar. 'It's nice. It's quiet.'

They gaze out across the crowded room.

'I really missed you, Sar,' he says, still facing ahead.

A hard knot of regret forms in her chest, like a blockage. 'I'm sorry,' she says.

John turns to face her, brushing his knuckles over her wrist so that she has to look up. 'You just never came back.'

The gym is almost wall-to-wall with people now, and the DJ increases the volume to compete with the growing wave of voices that pushes out across the room.

'Shall we have a walkabout?' John suggests.

Sarah follows in his steps, untucking the hair from behind her ears and letting it fall across her face. Hopefully no one will recognise her. Bodies seem to press in from every direction: a crush of hair and skin, of big, tall men, of bony white shoulders and inappropriate necklines. Even now, she feels smaller than most of the other women here, and she's gripped by the haunting sense of once again being outside the action. It's as if she missed an important lesson right at the start of school, when everyone was told how it all works. Where was she when everyone else learned how to be a teenager, a girlfriend; a woman?

Sarah gasps as Mr Settle squeezes past her in his tweedy suit, holding his scotch and ice high above his head. She grabs on to John's elbow so she doesn't get separated from him and he turns, looking at her over his shoulder as if he's hating this too. In the multicoloured light of the disco lamps, Sarah is struck by the sharp contours of his face. His bone structure borders on the gaunt, but he looks so much like himself, so much like John Gilroy, and no one else. Her eyes brim with unexpected tears.

'You alright?' he mouths to her.

She nods, tightening her grip on his elbow as she hears her name shrieked above the noise.

'Sarah *Ribbons*!'

Sarah recognises her instantly. Through the crowd, a few feet away, is Kate Robson. She's a good couple of stone heavier, and her hair is different, but it's her without a doubt. And next to her, almost a head shorter, is Tina, stretching her neck like a terrapin, to navigate the crowd in Sarah's direction. Sarah sucks in her breath, stuck to the gym floor, pinned in from every angle, as Kate and Tina force their way through the mass of people. Kate's arms wave above the crowd, one hand clutching a beaker of white wine. It slops over the edges, splashing the face of a man who stands between them.

'Oi!' he yells, blocking her path.

'Sorry!' she yells back with laughing eyes, reaching up to wipe his face.

He grins. 'Get you another one?' he asks, pointing to her drink.

Sarah watches through the ebb and flow of bodies. Tina stands beside Kate, looking redundant.

Kate runs her hand through her fringe, pulling it down across one eye, as she fixes the other on the stranger. 'Maybe later?'

'Deal,' the man replies, and he moves to one side to let her through.

'Sarah Ribbons!' Kate repeats when she reaches her. She throws her arms around Sarah's shoulders and squeals into her ear. 'Oh, my God! You look great! Look at her, Teen!'

Tina's smile seems fixed to her face, and she stands uncomfortably to one side as Kate commandeers Sarah.

'Wow,' says Sarah when Kate releases her. She's acutely aware of her own stiff body, her awkward limbs. A passer-by bumps her from the left, shoving her into the side of Tina. Sarah puts her hands up to steady herself, smiling broadly. 'Wow. It's been years.'

Kate turns from Sarah to Tina with wide eyes. 'Years? It's been twenty-four years, to be exact! Have you seen anyone yet? We got here early, and we've already seen Mrs Whiff, Mrs Carney, Pervy Potter – '

'Mrs Jensen,' adds Tina.

'I saw Mr Settle,' says Sarah. 'What about pupils? Are there many here from our year?'

'Loads! Come and sit with us – we've bagged a couple of seats over by the food.'

Kate goes to link arms with Sarah, who stiffens again at the prospect. She turns to look at John, who's still standing close by, gesturing towards him so that he steps forward.

'This is John Gilroy. You might remember him from school? He was a few years older than us, though, weren't you, John?'

John gives a little smile. 'Still am,' he says.

Kate and Tina stare at him blankly.

'Sorry, can't say I do,' says Kate. She moves towards Sarah again.

'His mum owned the chemist's shop, you know, where I used to work on Saturdays?' Her voice is strained, and she feels nauseatingly self-conscious as the strobe light catches her eyes again.

Kate and Tina smile politely at John.

'I remember the greasy one with the ponytail, but not you,' says Kate. 'What was his name?'

'John,' says Sarah, trying not to laugh.

'That must have been confusing – ' says Kate.

Sarah looks at John and raises an eyebrow. 'No,' she says to Kate. 'It's him. Without the ponytail. He's the same John.'

Kate looks him up and down, unembarrassed. 'Really? Are you sure?'

'Yeah,' says John, scowling. 'Unless I'm suffering from false memory syndrome, I'm pretty sure it was me. I remember having a ponytail, but I don't recall being particularly greasy.'

'Ha ha,' Kate replies sarcastically. 'Are you two – ?'

The high-pitched squeal of feedback pierces through the room and the music comes to a sudden stop. They all turn to face the music decks, where Mrs Smith is standing on the edge of the platform with a large microphone in her hand.

'Mrs Whiff!' says Sarah.

'Testing, *testing*,' Mrs Smith says, tapping the microphone briskly. Her solid, squat body hasn't changed a bit, but her hair is now completely white.

'Oh, my God,' says Kate. '*Whiffer*.'

The teacher speaks into the microphone. 'Thank you, everyone!'

The room falls silent.

'Good evening, old girls and boys of Selton High Schools!'

There's a murmur and a ripple of cheers across the hall.

'We are delighted that so many of you were able to join us tonight. I can confirm that we have just over five hundred ex-pupils here tonight, all of whom attended the schools during the 1980s. This is the biggest reunion we have ever staged, and I am over the moon to be able to welcome you all.'

Tina leans across and pokes Kate. 'Remember when you squeezed an ink cartridge into her handbag? It leaked right through on to the floor.'

Kate laughs.

'Now, we know how much you all want to meet up with friends from your own year groups, so to make it easier we have stationed around the room ten meeting points, starting with 1980 over in the far corner and working round to 1989 here on my left. So, when the music starts again, simply make your way over to the meeting point which matches your fifth year at the school. There are drinks and snacks over at the bar – and I'd just like to ask you all to refrain from smoking in the school building and grounds at all. If you must smoke, please make your way out through the entrance gates on to School Lane, where we've stationed an ashbin in which you can dispose of your cigarette waste. Needless to say, there will be NO smoking in the school toilets.' She breaks into a coy little smile and laughter travels around the room. 'I'll be here all evening, so please, do come and say hello if you see me! Enjoy your evening, and with no further ado – music, DJ, please!'

'I Need a Hero' blasts from the speakers, as Kate spins Sarah towards her, firmly hooking arms.

'1986 – that's our year. It's over by those seats we've bagsied.' Kate pulls Tina in too, so that she's flanked by each woman, their arms intimately linked.

Sarah turns back towards John, panic rising in her chest. 'I'll find you,' she mouths over her shoulder. She doesn't want him to go.

He puts up his hand and walks away in search of his own year group. Heart lurching, she's chaperoned towards the 1986 area, which bustles with activity as the group increases in number. There are lots of men in the group, boys from her year, but she never had much to do with them back then, so there's no hope of recognising them now. Kate and Tina say hello to a few lads as they pass through, giggling like little girls when the greeting is returned. They haven't changed a bit. Women from their year group shriek and embrace each other, falling into easy conversation, comparing notes on marriages, children, divorces, jobs. They all make it look so easy, as if they've never lost touch, as if they never left Selton High School at all. The strobe light brushes through the 1986 group, illuminating the face of each pupil, briefly painting them naked for all to see. Sarah isn't interested in any of them; she wishes she could excuse herself and find John again. The Potter twins push past in matching devil's horn headbands and red dresses. 'Hi,' they say in unison when Sarah smiles.

Kate tugs her arm. 'Uh-oh,' she whispers, inhaling air through the 'O' of her pursed lips. 'Unfinished business.'

Sarah recognises Simon Dobbs instantly, standing at the edge of the group holding on to two plastic pint glasses of lager. He's wearing three-quarter-length jeans and a white New Romantics shirt which moves like silk as he raises his glass to his mouth. He hasn't seen them yet. The men he's with all possess the over-pumped, beer-rounded physiques of ageing rugby players, and Sarah recalls now that he was a player in the school's top team. In particular, they were renowned for their eternal capacity for drinking and shagging. She never could work out what Kate saw in him, and he causes her to shudder even now. Despite his carefully groomed exterior, he still manages to look grubby. He's broader now, and he's cultivated a strange little goatee beard, but his cocky expression remains unchanged. He makes Sarah think of earwax, which causes her to shudder again. Kate edges them closer, so that they can overhear the conversation.

'What are you up to these days, Si?' asks one of the group.

He takes a large swallow of beer before answering. 'Got my own metal fencing business.'

'Doing alright?'

'Mate, I'm run off my feet. Our problem is keeping up with the orders, not getting them in. Mind you, I'd be mad to complain. It's a good living.'

'Nice one. So what are you driving, then?'

'Silver BMW M3 convertible.'

The other man whistles through his teeth.

'Very nice,' says Kate, just loud enough for Simon to hear.

He smiles out of the side of his mouth as he locks eyes with her across the group, finishing his first pint in a single open-throated gulp. He slips the empty plastic tumbler over the base of the second pint.

'Kate Robson,' he says in his deep rugger voice, tugging on his earlobe.

The other men in the group turn to see who he's talking to.

'Simon Dobbs,' she returns with a confident wiggle of her shoulders. She steers Sarah and Tina away from him, passing through the group with a flirtatious smirk.

Bev Greene and Jo Allen stand beside the 1986 sign on the wall, still sipping their drinks and talking conspiratorially. Jo's wearing a short pink skirt, and her muscular shins are the colour of uncooked chicken.

'Oh, my God, look over there,' Kate mutters under her breath as she halts sharply. 'It's bloody Lilo Lil.' She turns to Tina, looking to her for encouragement. 'I can't believe she came, can you? She's got a bloody nerve.'

'Jo Allen?' says Sarah, glancing over discreetly. 'I saw her earlier. She was up at the bar.'

Kate's grip tightens around Sarah's arm, and she keeps turning her head to look over in Jo's direction. 'What a fucking nerve.'

'I don't think we even knew Jo all that well at school, did we? She was in different sets for most things, I seem to remember.' Sarah tries to manoeuvre Kate in a different direction.

Kate resists, widening her eyes and letting out a small harsh laugh. 'Did you see the way she just looked at me? Cheeky *cow*. Who's she think she is, giving me dirty looks like that? Remember what they used to call *her*? Jo "Bury-me-in-a-Y-shaped-coffin" Allen. *Everyone* knows what she was like.'

'Shhh,' says Sarah, feeling the heat rising into her cheeks. She wishes Kate would let go of her arm. 'She'll hear you.'

'Good.' Kate shrugs. 'What's she gonna do? Lump me one?'

'Probably best to leave it, Kate,' says Tina, who's barely spoken a word since they all met up. 'You don't want to get into an argument here. Not with everyone watching.'

Kate narrows her eyes and glares at Jo, who challenges her, staring back with her head cocked to one side. Jo's mouth moves aggressively, but Sarah can't make out the words.

'How about a drink?' she suggests, nudging Kate. 'Are those your seats over by the wall?'

Kate drops their arms, marching over to the seats to ensure that no one else gets them. 'Good thinking. I want to have a good time tonight, and I'm not gonna let some old slapper wind me up! I'll get the first round in – what's it to be?'

Tina insists on accompanying Kate to help with the drinks, while Sarah sits and saves the seats. She sees Jo Allen and Bev heading away from the 1986 group, breaking into dance as they near the DJ desk. Sarah's relieved to see them go; she's seen Kate in this kind of mood many times before, and it never ends well.

Kate and Tina return with the drinks, howling with laughter.

'We just bumped into Darren Clifford – he's got a face full of Botox, I swear!' says Kate. 'And I reckon he's had his lips filled 'n' all!'

'He couldn't even smile!' Tina screeches. 'Honest to God, he looked like a waxwork.'

Kate hands Sarah her drink and pulls up a chair in a quick possessive motion. 'Well, what about you and that John bloke? Are you and him together? I'm sure he's not the same fella who used to work in the chemist's, you know. The other one was really thin and he used to wear heavy metal T-shirts. This one seems nice.'

Sarah laughs. She recalls how Kate had described John as a saddo head-banging greaser after she'd been in to collect her mum's prescription one Saturday when he was serving. 'What, do you fancy him or something?' Kate had said when Sarah had tried to defend him. 'No!' she'd protested. 'He's just a nice bloke, that's all. Not everyone's as trendy as you, Kate.' That had pleased Kate no end. 'True,' she'd said, running her hands down her hips.

Sarah drinks her wine too quickly and scoops up a handful of Hula Hoops from a bowl that Tina has found. The table beside them is laid out with a long stretch of white paper tablecloth and bowls of peanuts and crisps. Already there are red rings and soggy rips in the paper. On the floor, a green plastic bowl of onion rings has been upturned and left where it fell. Some of them have scattered into the walkway where they lie crushed underfoot. Sarah imagines bundling the whole lot up into a bin bag in one swift movement.

'Oh, my God,' says Kate again, patting Sarah on the knee. 'I just can't believe it! So what've you been doing all this time? Married? Kids?'

Sarah shakes her head. 'I've been busy working. And I looked after my dad when he got ill, so that took a lot of my time.'

'Is he in a home now?' asks Tina, her face creasing. She's aged badly.

'No, he passed away last year.'

'Oh, sorry.' Tina looks down at her knees and scratches her hand. The eczema is red-raw between her fingers.

'No, it's fine. It's been a year since his funeral. What about you two?'

Kate slaps her hands against her own thighs. She's wearing bright purple leggings and a voluminous black T-shirt. 'Well, believe it or not, I did quite well after school. Retail management. I started in the ladies' department at M&S. Then, after having the kids I ended up at Woolies and I was doing really well –

department manager – but of course that all went tits-up when they went bust. So now I'm on the lookout for something new. There's a management job going at the new restaurant on the Parade. Might go for that.'

'Don't you have to have catering experience for that?' asks Tina, stirring her drink with a straw.

'Don't think so,' Kate replies, looking annoyed. 'It's all management, isn't it?'

A tall woman raises her hand over the crowd and starts to walk in their direction. She's statuesque and elegant, with funky cropped hair, and she's at least as tall as most of the men in the room. She moves across the room with confidence, her smile growing as she approaches.

'Who's that?' whispers Kate, watching her intently.

'Marianne?' asks Sarah uncertainly, as she recognises the broad shoulders and heavy jaw of her old schoolfriend.

Marianne breaks into easy laughter. 'Sarah?'

Kate and Tina remain seated, as Sarah rises to hug Marianne. 'You look fantastic,' she says, turning to the others for agreement. 'You remember Kate and Tina?'

Marianne nods without warmth. 'Who could forget? Kate Robson. And Tina Smith-not-Smythe.'

Tina looks as though she can't decide if Marianne's being funny or just taking the piss. 'I can't believe you remember that,' she mumbles.

Marianne throws her a cursory glance. 'I remember all sorts of things.' She taps Sarah lightly on the arm. 'Really good to see you, Sarah. Listen, I'm not staying for long, but I wanted to come over and say hello.'

'I'm really glad you did,' Sarah replies.

Marianne turns her back on Tina and Kate, lightly resting her hand on Sarah's wrist with affection. 'I just wanted to say, I never forgot how kind you were to me back then, when everyone else was – well, you know, don't you? Anyway,' she says, pushing her white-blonde hair up over her forehead, 'thanks.' She kisses Sarah on the cheek and slips smoothly into the crowd, her silvery blouse shimmering like fluid over her large, graceful frame.

Sarah stares at the space she leaves, remembering with clarity the self-conscious Marianne of their school days.

Kate pokes Sarah, who spins round, startled.

'Bloody hell. Well, she really reckoned herself, didn't she?' Kate's mouth is gaping.

Sarah frowns. 'Who? Marianne?'

'Yeah! She goes and gets herself a new haircut and reckons she's the bee's knees!'

'I thought she looked amazing,' says Sarah. 'I can't believe how much she's changed. Remember how embarrassed and awkward she always seemed? She hated PE, because of the changing rooms. She used to make out she was sick just about every gymnastics lesson we ever had.'

Tina grins at Kate.

Sarah scowls at them. 'I always quite liked Marianne. She got a rough deal of it, from what I remember. You two were pretty mean to her.'

Kate snorts and starts humming the *Addams Family* theme tune.

'Yes!' yells Tina. 'That was it!'

Sarah rolls her eyes. 'She was always close to tears after French with you two. You were merciless, now I come to think of it.'

Kate looks confused and drains her white wine. 'We weren't that bad! God, you always were a bit of a goody-goody, Sar!' She laughs and squeezes Sarah's knee. 'Teen, fancy getting another round in while I catch up with Sar?'

Tina stands and picks up the empty tumblers, holding Sarah's in the air. 'Red wine?'

'Thanks,' replies Sarah, watching Tina as she makes her way along the table towards the bar. Her tight snow-washed jeans hang loosely over her skeletal legs, bunching up over black *faux*-suede pixie boots. 'I'd have come in eighties gear if I'd realised everyone else was going to,' Sarah says.

'Oh, Tina's not in fancy dress,' Kate says. 'She dresses like that anyway. Swear to God! She's had those jeans for years.'

Sarah smiles.

'Anyway, you've gotta make an effort.' Kate smoothes out her top.

It's only when she unfolds it from her generous bosom that Sarah realises it has a Blondie image printed across the front. Until now, Debbie Harry's face had been gobbled up in Kate's cleavage, so all you got to see was the yellow edges of her choppy hair.

'But you look lovely anyway,' Kate says quickly, waving a flippant hand in Sarah's direction.

Sarah's pleased to be sitting at the dark edges of the room. It's only a couple of hours since the start of the party, and already lots of the guests seem well on their way to a hangover. She recognises a few more faces from this distance. Many of them just have a familiar something or other, but nothing she can really relate to. She helps herself to another handful of crisps.

'Tina looks very slim,' she says, searching for something to say. 'You wouldn't guess she'd had two kids.'

Kate makes a puking action with her two fingers and raises her eyebrows.

'Really?' says Sarah.

'Uh-huh.' Kate tips her head to one side and lowers her voice. 'Ever since school. Mind you, I didn't know for sure till recently, when I caught her chucking up in my en-suite. She denied it, of course, but, well, you've just got to look at her to know. It's a wonder she ever managed to have kids at all. It can make you infertile, can't it?'

Tina's now at the front of the queue for drinks. She's digging around in her big slouchy handbag, which looks enormous against her tiny frame.

'I had no idea,' Sarah says.

'You know, her mum was just the same. D'you remember her? She always looked like she'd snap if you bumped into her, and she seemed knackered all the time. She's just about bedridden with osteoporosis now. And the worst thing is, Tina's daughter Britta is only nine, and I swear she's going the same way.'

'What, she's got an eating disorder? Surely not at that age?'

Kate pulls her chin in. She looks like Les Dawson. 'Mm-hmm. Won't eat in front of anyone, and she's cut out whole food groups. She won't touch any dairy and she checks everything for sugar. She's got huge bags under her eyes. It's not right for a nine-year-old.'

'That's terrible. Are they getting her any help?'

'Don't be stupid. Tina can't even see it. She's too busy with her own problems to notice Britt. You know her husband buggered off last year, and I think that's what set off the whole eating thing again.' She clears her throat as she notices Tina leaving the queue. 'He went off with the neighbour. She had no idea; one minute he was home, the next minute he'd gone, leaving Tina with the kids. Bastard.'

'Poor Tina,' says Sarah. 'That's awful.'

'You just never can tell, can you?' Kate whispers, plucking Blondie out from her chest again. She looks under her eyelashes at Tina, who's carefully setting the drinks down on the table. '*You never can tell.*'

Tina passes out the drinks and sits on the seat next to Kate, tearing open a large bag of pork scratchings with her teeth. 'I just saw Mr Green,' she says. 'Buying three white wines and a gin and tonic.'

'I don't even remember him,' says Kate, craning to get a better view of the queue.

'You know, Physics in the second year?' says Tina. 'He had a nervous twitch.'

'Oh, yeah!' reply Sarah and Kate together, and they laugh.

Kate starts singing along to 'Karma Chameleon', bumping Sarah and Tina on either side, trying to get them to join in.

Sarah wonders where John is. A lanky bloke in glasses walks past them carrying a tray of beers. He stops suddenly, then turns back and smiles at Tina. It's Ed. He's still got great big gaps between his teeth, as if some of his adult ones never came through.

'Heh-hay! Let me see – it's Tina, Kate and, hang on – hang on – Sara!' He looks pleased with himself for remembering.

'Sarah,' she corrects him.

'Sarah. That's right, now I remember! Yeah, that's it. Small world, eh?' He carries on grinning, his upper body curving over the tray like a wilting flower head.

'Well, not really,' says Kate, pulling a stupid-face.

'What?'

'It's not really a small world. We were all invited to the reunion, weren't we? So it's not that surprising that we've bumped into each other.'

Tina holds her alcopop close to her lips and doesn't say a word.

'Well,' says Ed, raising his tray towards them. 'Better get back. They'll all be dying of thirst by the time I get these to them!' He navigates his way through the throng and out of sight.

The three women look at each other and burst out laughing.

'Oh, Teen,' sighs Kate. 'What on earth did you see in him?'

Tina shakes her head and sucks at her straw.

Sarah wipes her eyes. 'I'd wage a bet that he works with computers.'

'I know! What a mega-geek! We can safely say *he* hasn't improved with age.' Kate indicates to Tina to pass her a bowl of crisps. 'Hey, we should have asked him if he's seen Dante tonight. Not that I particularly want to see him, you know. I bet he's gone all bald and ugly – '

'I doubt he's here,' says Sarah. 'Hope not, anyway.'

Kate shrieks. 'Oh, my God, I forgot you went out with him too, Sar!'

'How could you forget *that*?' Sarah asks. A sharp memory passes through Sarah's body in a rush of lucidity: Dante and

Kate coupled together on the bed at New Year, their wet lips glistening in the half-light. The full emotion of that moment flows in and out of her like a blast of cold wind. She stares at Kate.

Kate looks at Tina and shrugs. 'Dunno. It's a long time ago.'

Sarah squints into the crowd, searching for John. Kate shifts in the seat beside her and leans against the edge of the table, crossing her ankles and stretching out her small feet. Sarah notices how her legs have thickened, starting out stocky at the thighs and tapering down into tiny black pumps.

'So you've got kids too, haven't you, Kate?' Sarah asks.

'Yeah, three. Molly's my youngest, she's just five and – ' She reaches into her handbag and pulls out a wad of photographs.

Sarah's heart sinks. Politely, she sits and accepts the pictures, flicking through them as Kate introduces the children, her husband, their car, the old house, the new house...

Tina holds out her hand for the pictures as Sarah passes them on, glancing at them briefly. 'I've already seen these,' she says. 'Have you seen our class photo up on the wall?'

'No!' says Kate.

Tina drops the photographs on the table and finishes her bag of pork scratchings, running a wet finger around the inside of the packet to pick up all the flavoured dust. 'Over there by the meeting point. Jo Allen was standing in front of it earlier, so I didn't want to go over.'

Kate jumps up, pulling Sarah with her, and the three women hurry over to the grainy colour photograph stuck on to the wall beside the 1986 sign. They huddle around the picture, pressing in to search for their own faces. *'Fifth Year Girls, Summer Term 1986'*. The pulse in Sarah's neck is flickering as she gazes into the image; she feels herself sway back on her heels, her inner balance thrown off. She moves closer, resting her hand on the wall, steadying herself against its solid weight. There they all are, the girls of 1986, with their Rita & Sue haircuts and short, nasty skirts and scuffed white slip-ons and oversized green school jumpers from the M&S men's department. The teachers flank the group, formal and smiling all at once, as the girls squint against the bright sunlight. It was so hot that day, almost unbearable; Sarah recalls the heat on her skin as she lay out on the open playing field, the buzz of summer travelling up through the hard dry ground, all sound muted behind her narrowed eyes. She scans each row in search of her form. She doesn't remember the class names but she can distinguish between the different bands – there's Upper Band One at the back, Upper Band Two in the next row. Down at the front are the girls from Lower Band, the kids the caretaker employed to paint the huts and scrub the windowsills while everyone else was sitting their exams. And sandwiched together in the largest group are the girls from the Middle Band, neither overly bright nor totally incapable, idly-middling average girls, the could-do-betters of Sarah's peer group.

Gradually, faces come forward, along with their names: Marianne Thomas; Shelley Lowe; Zoe Andrews. Sarah's ears feel hot.

'There!' shouts Tina, her finger landing in the middle of the picture.

Sarah shakes her head as the photograph blurs out of focus and she has to turn away momentarily to recalibrate her eyes. When she looks back at the picture, she sees them instantly. Nestled in between all the other faces, the sunlight white on their hair, are Kate and Tina. She stares at their faces, blinking as the image blurs and shifts. It's definitely them. She starts to search for herself in the photograph, scanning the picture from top to bottom, over and over again. Finally, with crashing clarity, she realises her own face is missing.

Of course. She wasn't even there.

Sarah excuses herself, initially maintaining her composure as she walks across the hall towards the corridor. Once Kate and Tina are out of sight, she quickly gains pace, weaving in and out of the other guests as fast as they'll allow. 'Walk Like an Egyptian' is playing, and there's a group of deranged-looking women hanging around outside the toilets trying to do the dance.

Sarah shuts herself in the far cubicle, standing with her back pressed against the closed door. She drops her head, focusing on her breathing until her heart rate drops to a steady thump. *Thump. Thump.* Beyond her door, women clatter in and out of the loos, screaming and laughing and gossiping openly about old friends they've seen. It's all fine. Sarah stares at the toilet. She doesn't really need to go, but perhaps she ought to now she's here. The facilities have improved since her school years, although the graffiti still seems to be a consistent feature. She wipes the seat with a big clump of toilet paper before sitting down. *Mrs Whiff is a man* is scrawled across the back of the door in permanent marker pen. Even the toilet roll dispenser has come up to date, unmarked by the melted cigarette burns that could be found on top of every bog roll box in the school. Don't girls smoke in the loos any more? she wonders. Perhaps not.

At the sinks she washes her hands vigorously, flicking off the excess water as she waits to use the hand dryer. She surreptitiously studies the other women in the mirror, but none is familiar to her. One woman is banging on a locked cubicle, 'Come on. Lorrie! You 'aven't changed a bit – always the last out!' A cackle comes from the other side of the door, before the second woman spills out from behind it, clearly the worse for drink. There's a square of toilet paper impaled on her patent blue stiletto. The women leave the toilets without washing their hands, just as Sarah's dryer shuts off. She checks her make-up and decides to return to the hall to search for John.

She turns the corner from the toilets into the hallway and walks straight into Mrs McCabe. 'Sorry,' she says, putting her hands up in apology.

'Sarah!' Mrs McCabe exclaims. She pauses to scrutinise Sarah's face before embracing her warmly.

Sarah takes a moment to recognise the school nurse. Her blonde wavy bob is now a soft ash tone but she's still just as tidy and compact as Sarah remembers.

'Sarah,' she says again, smiling broadly.

'Oh! Mrs McCabe,' she says. She stands stiffly beside a large red fire extinguisher, as a scattering of women moves past them to and from the toilets. The sound system vibrates through the corridor, causing the framed fire inspection certificate to shake in its casing on the opposite wall.

'How are you?' Mrs McCabe asks with a confiding tilt of her head. As the curls of her hair fall across her face Sarah recalls her more clearly. She was one of the good ones.

'I'm fine. Really good, thanks. And you?' She gazes over Mrs McCabe's shoulder, wishing John would walk past and rescue her.

'Good. Yes, I'm good,' she says, still smiling broadly. 'I remember you so clearly, Sarah. Some girls stand out over the years. I'm sure you must have gone on to do something special?'

Sarah fiddles her neck scarf self-consciously. 'Not really. I mean, I've got a good job, but – ' She doesn't have the energy to explain it all. 'So, what did you have? When you left to have the baby?'

Mrs McCabe looks surprised. 'Oh! I had three eventually – the first one was a girl – she's nearly twenty-five now! And then I had two boys. I came back to the school when they were all old enough. What about you? Any children?'

Sarah shakes her head. 'No. I've been a bit too busy with my career.' She rearranges her scarf again.

Mrs McCabe's eyes narrow sympathetically. 'I remember your father taking ill when I was still at the school.'

Sarah tugs at the hem of her top. 'He passed away last year.'

'Oh, I'm so sorry, Sarah,' says Mrs McCabe. 'And have you seen any of your school friends tonight?'

Sarah scans the corridor, to give the impression of searching for somebody. 'Yes, I was just on my way back to find them. Do you remember Kate and Tina? I haven't seen them since school, so we've got lots to catch up on!'

Mrs McCabe pats Sarah on the elbow. 'Good. Well, off you go. It's lovely to see you after all this time.'

Sarah says goodbye and walks quickly towards the hall. At the end of the corridor she turns to see Mrs McCabe still in the same position, watching her leave. As she raises a farewell hand Sarah grows light-headed with fear. She gazes back along the corridor, and sees Mrs McCabe standing outside Kate's house with the spring breeze gently rippling through the blonde waves of her hair. Sarah steps through the doorway as Kate calls her in, clutching to her chest a single creased carrier bag, packed in haste just minutes earlier. She pauses in the doorway to see the school nurse standing beside the car. Mrs McCabe raises her hand once more, her blonde hair lightly swaying, as the front door clicks shut, and Sarah knows she's gone.

Her head spins as she turns in through the doors to the party. She pushes past the swaying bodies of the spotlit hall and eventually sees John standing at the edge of a small group of men. His posture relaxes as she touches his arm.

'Sorry,' she says as he turns to face her. Her heart beats fast and a small nerve flickers in the side of her jaw. 'I got kidnapped.'

'No probs,' he replies, and he puts his hand on her shoulder and gives it a squeeze.

The other men in the group eye her with interest and she turns her back towards them to avoid their scrutiny.

John tilts his head to see her face. 'Are you OK?' he asks.

'It's too loud in here,' she replies, slipping her arm beneath his. 'Come on.'

Much of the school is locked up, but from the gym they can still access the corridors to the east side of the school. Everywhere is in darkness, lit only by the external security lamps that cast strips of light through the tall thin windows of the building. They tiptoe along the shiny parquet floor in silence. Sarah points to the staircase which runs along the side of the oak library and they sprint up the steps and crouch in the shadows where they can spy down through the galleried balustrade. Cross-legged, they sit side by side, with their faces pushed up against the bars. The toe of John's pale desert boot touches Sarah's knee.

'I used to hide out in the library,' she whispers to John. 'Especially if I'd fallen out with Kate and Tina. There was this one awful time when they thought it would be funny to start following me all over the school. Any time I wasn't in a lesson, they'd be there, right behind me. At one point they managed to get a whole group of other girls involved, chasing after me everywhere I went, chanting my name. It felt as if I was going mad.'

She looks out across the library towards her favourite seat on the far right-hand side. Once they'd discovered her hiding place, they'd started bombarding her with nasty messages, written on jotter paper, balled up tight so they could hit her even from this height and distance. The worst one was only a couple of weeks after she and Dante had broken up; it just said *FRIGID* in large capital letters. She was crushed to think that Dante might have told Kate everything about the time they spent together.

'But I thought they were meant to be your friends,' John says, running his hands down the dowel posts.

Sarah stares across the gallery towards the classroom opposite, where they had Sex Education with Mrs Whiff. *Pee-niss*, she used to say, as if it were two separate words.

'They were my best friends,' she says.

He laughs drily.

'It's complicated.'

'Not really,' he says, shaking his head.

Sarah squints into the darkness below. A few women are creeping around, giggling.

'So, you never got married, then?' asks John.

She laughs.

'Me neither.'

One of the women below is hiding behind a bookshelf. She jumps out at her friend, who lets out a full-lunged scream and runs back into the corridor. 'You cow!' The first one is bent over, as if she's holding her insides together. Sarah and John stifle their laughter, and watch as the group retreat back along the corridor towards the party.

'I recognise her,' says Sarah. 'The one who screamed. You remember Barbara, from the chemist's?'

'How could I forget?'

'That was her daughter, Kim.'

'Really? How can you tell from up here?'

'I could see her gold sovereign rings twinkling in the moonlight,' she replies.

John pulls a face.

'I'm joking. But it was definitely her. She looks the same.'

'Poor her. She was pretty rough, wasn't she? Mind you, just look at her mother; it's no wonder. I still see Barbara around the town from time to time, riding about in her mobility scooter. She lost loads of weight after she broke her hip, and now she's all wrinkly and shrunken. She looks like Davros.' He raises his eyebrows. '*Karma*,' he whispers.

Sarah walks her fingers up the post, smiling into the darkness.

'I really appreciated your friendship, John. You know, when we worked together.'

John wraps his fingers lightly over hers. 'And I really appreciated yours. Of course, I used to wish we could be more than friends. But you were only fifteen.'

'And you were only nineteen. It's not that much difference.'

'It is at that age. It would have been wrong, somehow. But, well, I don't think you thought of me like that anyway.'

'More fool me.' Sarah removes her fingers and places them on top of his, causing her bracelet to brush against his wrist.

'So, you knew it was me?' he says, pulling back to watch her expression. 'The bracelet.'

She rolls a charm between her finger and thumb, shaking her head, suddenly comprehending. 'No, I didn't. I had no idea it was you'

A strong beam of light shines across their faces from a hand-held torch below and they shrink back from its blinding force.

'Ay-ay!' a male voice calls out. 'I think we've stumbled on a couple of young lovers here!'

Sarah and John push themselves out of view, Sarah covering her face with her hands, John laughing and scrabbling to his feet. They run around the edge of the gallery and down the stairs again, passing their intruder on their way back along the corridor.

'*Naughty, naughty*,' he calls after them, making squelchy kissing noises as they run by.

Sarah screams and pulls at John's shirt sleeve to make him run faster. Their shadows rise and fall as they pass the windows of the lower corridor, looming long and high, falling dramatically and rising again. Their footsteps bounce and echo as they run, gradually fading to nothing as they burst through the swing doors and out into the passageway leading towards the gym.

'Drink?' asks John as they return to the noise of the party. He's breathing heavily, pushing the hair from his eyes.

Sarah laughs and covers her face again. 'A large one, please.'

They stand side by side in the drinks queue, their upper arms touching conspicuously.

'Maybe we could go out for a drink or something, before you go back to Dorset?' John fixes his eyes on the space ahead, his hands clasped politely behind his back. He turns to her for an answer.

The space behind her ribcage ripples nervously. 'Sure. Why not?'

'Great,' he says, pulling at a lock of his hair, trying to hide his smile. 'Yeah. That's great.'

Kate joins them in the queue, swiping her brow, her shiny cheeks vibrant and flushed.

'Oh, what a laugh! You've got to come and dance in a minute, Sar. There's a bunch of lads from the boys' school down on the dance floor and they're cracking me up! D'you remember Tom Brant?'

Sarah shakes her head.

'Used to be really tall and skinny? Blondish hair. Oh, well. Get me a vodka and lime while you're up there, will you? I'll be over by the 1986 sign – I've gotta sit down for a minute!' She pinches the front of her T-shirt and wafts it vigorously as she zigzags towards the seats at the side of the room.

John orders the drinks and they carry them over towards Kate, who's sitting on a plastic seat, running a brush through her hair.

'You're a lifesaver,' she says to John with a big grin. 'Sar, I've asked the DJ to put on some of our old favourites. Keep an ear out for them – you'll know which ones they are!'

There are only two seats, and John indicates to Sarah to take the other one. Just as she moves towards the seat, Jo Allen taps her on the shoulder.

'I know you, don't I?' she says. There's a gaping hole above and below her eyebrow where it looks as if she's let a recent piercing close up. She's swaying slightly, her eyes subdued by drink.

Bev Greene stands a little way behind Jo, uncomfortably squeezing and releasing an empty plastic cup.

'Sarah Ribbons,' says Sarah, tapping her collarbone. 'We were in the same year.'

'Oh, yeah. I remember. 'Spect you was a brainbox? We didn't do any classes together, did we?'

'Um, Maths, I think. In the second year?'

Jo looks at Bev.

Bev nods. 'Yeah, I remember. You used to sit behind us.'

'Who'd you used to hang about with, then?' asks Jo, warming up.

Sarah takes a sip of wine. 'Mostly Kate Robson and Tina Smythe.' She turns to look at Kate, but John is blocking the view. He steps aside. 'Remember Kate?'

Jo's expression turns to one of repugnance.

Kate stands, dropping her shoulders and pushing out her chest. She starts to leave, but Jo reaches out and grabs at her T-shirt, causing her to spin round and snatch it away. Kate's rage pushes into the room, and she stumbles backwards to increase the space between her and Jo.

'Alright, Kate?' says Jo with a laughing sneer.

Kate turns to leave again.

'How's your dad?' Jo shouts over the music.

Kate halts, turning on her heel to stride back into the group. 'What did you say?' She pushes her face at Jo's.

Sarah steps back, colliding with John. He steadies her, resting his hand on her upper arm. She wants to vomit.

'I said, how's Jase? *How's. Your. Dad*?'

'How dare you – ?' screams Kate, lashing out and catching Bev with the side of her hand.

'Hey!' shouts Bev moving in behind Jo.

John steps in and guides Kate backwards, as Sarah watches on in horror.

Jo knocks back her drink and hands the empty tumbler to Bev. Her upper body is thrust forward now, as she yells in Kate's face. 'Hey! I bet they miss 'im down the youth club! Tell you what, bet it's not the same down there since he left?'

Kate lunges at her, screaming, flailing her arms as John leads her away.

'They got a youth club where you moved to?' Jo shouts after her. 'Hope not, for everyone's sake!'

Kate ploughs into the dense crowd, raging and sobbing, heading out towards the corridor and the toilets beyond. Jo snatches the empty cup from Bev's hand and throws it over her shoulder where it falls to the ground and rolls beneath the paper-covered tables at the side of the gym. They march off in the opposite direction, shoving their way through the group and out through the wide entrance at the front of the gym. Sarah stands beside John, gripping her plastic cup with frozen fingers, immobilised.

'Who was that?' asks John.

Sarah shakes her head, feeling the thump of music pounding inside her chest. 'Jo Allen,' she replies.

John's expression shifts as something troubled passes across his eyes. 'Jo Allen?'

She can barely hear her own voice over the noise. 'Do you know her?' Sarah watches for the slight changes in John's face: the deepening crease between his eyebrows, the minute parting of his upper and lower lip, the flare of his nostrils, in, out, in, out.

'No,' he says, finally. 'No.'

The opening bars of 'Sunday Girl' play out over the speakers and Tina weaves across the room, waving her hands in the air. 'Knew I'd find you here,' she smiles, her eyes half-closed with drink. She throws her arms around Sarah's neck, falling on to her for support. 'It's your track!' She grabs Sarah's hand and tugs her.

John pulls up a seat and waves her away with a resigned smile. 'Go!' he urges her. 'I'll be right here.'

Tina scurries ahead, jumping up and down, beckoning her on to the dance floor. Sarah mouths an apology to John, and pushes through the throng to join Tina at the dance area below the DJ desk.

'Where's Kate?' Tina shouts above the music.

Sarah pretends not to hear, but scans the room as she dances, trying to catch a glimpse of Kate or Jo. She feels every nerve-ending shake beneath her skin.

Tina pulls a puzzled face as she dances, pulling Sarah closer. 'Kate was the one who asked for this track – 'cos she knew it was your favourite. But then I saw her with Simon Dobbs an hour ago, so who knows?'

'I don't think she's with Simon Dobbs,' Sarah shouts back.

'Mmm. I saw them dancing together earlier, and he had his hand on her bum. She didn't seem to mind much, so I thought I'd better leave 'em to it. Same old Kate.'

'But I saw her a few minutes ago. She wasn't with him then.'

'Whatever.' Tina rotates her neck. It looks like a yoga warm-up.

Sarah leans closer so Tina can hear. 'But she's married, isn't she? Kate? I thought Kate was happily married.'

'Don't know about the happily bit. You know what Kate's like. Grass is always greener. You know she's had a few flings over the years, but she always ends up sticking with Nigel. Dunno why he puts up with it. He's a nice enough bloke.' She makes little maraca motions with her fists as she moves her feet in tiny pixie steps.

'Trouble is,' Tina continues, putting her face close to Sarah's, 'she's never satisfied with her lot. Always wants what everyone else has got. Take me. My husband left me a few months back, with two kids to bring up alone, and she tells me I'm the lucky one, and what wouldn't she give to be in my shoes? It's bloody amazing, really. Here I am, nearly having a nervous bloody breakdown, and Kate thinks she's the unlucky one.'

Sarah shakes her head. 'Do you still see a lot of each other?'

Tina nods. 'We do now she's back in the area. But you know she moved away for a while, after all the trouble. With her dad.'

A cold flush sweeps through Sarah's skin. 'What trouble?' she whispers into the noise.

'Uh?' says Tina, frowning blindly. 'You heard what happened, didn't you?'

Sarah shakes her head, and guides Tina away from the speakers to prevent her from knocking them over.

'I can't believe your mate John didn't tell you. *Everyone* knew about it.'

Sarah looks over to where John is sitting. He's completely obscured by the crush of bodies between them.

Tina blinks. 'It must've been, what, a couple of years after we left school?' She tilts her head as if she's trying to locate the exact date. 'Anyway, you remember Jo Allen? How she had that baby when she was still at school?'

Sarah stops dancing, as she stands and stares at Tina, listening intently, knowing what will come next.

'Well, when the baby was two or three, Jo's mum marches her down the police station and she makes a statement, saying the baby's his. *Jason's.* Jo reckoned they'd been going out together in secret since she was thirteen, and that it was his baby. That's what she said: "going out together", like she was totally in love with him or something.'

'No,' Sarah whispers.

'What?'

Sarah recalls Jo's pallid skin as she passed the grease-smeared window of Marconi's all those years ago. 'You don't "go out with" a thirteen-year-old,' she says.

Tina shrugs. 'So, to cut a long story short, he got arrested, but he said Jo was making the whole thing up. That she just had a crush on him, and he couldn't help that, could he? The police couldn't prove anything, could they? Not back then they couldn't. Patty nearly went completely doolally over the whole thing.'

Sarah runs her thumbnail across her lower teeth, tracing back in time. 'Kate's mum?'

Tina nods knowingly. 'Explains why she was on those happy pills, if you ask me.' She's still bopping around, wriggling her bony shoulders up and down to 'Chain Reaction'. Sarah's chest is pressing in so hard, it feels as if it might crack in two at any moment.

Tina leans in again, so close that Sarah can feel the heat from her clammy skin. Her breath smells of pear drops. 'When the police got involved, they found out about loads of other girls, mostly from down the youth club. Turns out he'd been doing it for years.'

Sarah can barely form the words.

'So what happened to him?' She's standing in front of Tina, swaying lightly from side to side, her breath coming in small, hot stabs.

'Well, I heard he had a friend in the police, and they managed to convince the girls he wouldn't get done 'cos there wasn't enough evidence or witnesses. So when it came down to it they all backed out.' She runs her fingers through her thin mousey hair and waves them above her head. Just like in the Diana Ross video.

'What about Kate? How did she take it?'

Tina looks around conspicuously, checking to make sure Kate isn't within earshot. 'She wouldn't believe it; said they were all making it up. She said Jo Allen was such a slapper it could've been anyone's. She said her dad wouldn't touch Jo Allen with a bargepole. Anyway, Kate and her folks had to move away because of the scandal.'

'What, and Patty stayed with him?'

'Yup.'

The music's deafeningly loud now, and a small drunk man keeps bumping into Sarah from behind, brushing his sweaty wrist against hers. She moves away, pulling Tina towards her.

'What do you think, Tina?'

Tina carries on dancing, spinning in wide circles, swaying her head from side to side.

'Tina!' Sarah shouts into the music. 'Teen! Do you believe he did it?'

Tina stops dancing and clasps Sarah's forearms to stop herself from stumbling. Dark shadows circle beneath her eyes. 'I *know* he did it, Sar. I've known since I was fourteen.' Her careworn expression glazes over and she closes her eyes and sways to the beat of the music.

The DJ desk is thumping, its traffic lights flashing out over dancing bodies and swirls of hair. Images of Jason crowd in, uninvited. There's Tina again, sitting in the bright glow of the bonfire in Kate's back garden, giggling and blushing at Jason's every remark. There's Jason, buttoning up the flies of his jeans, pleasure dancing at the edges of his mouth. There's the fresh greasy smear of chicken korma on the polished glass of Patty's new coffee table, and the gentle indentations of fifteen-year-old fingers on a can of cider. The smell of filth is in Sarah's nostrils. 'Club Tropicana' plays out, and a group of women crowds on to the dance floor, shrieking and whooping in chorus. Sarah takes flight through the stampede, stumbling and breathless as she races out of the gym hall, past the chattering queue at the girls' toilets, deep into the darkened corners at the far end of the corridor, away from Tina and Kate and talk of Jason. She stands in the shadows, her back pressed against the cool metal plate of the boiler room door, fighting back the tears. Her breaths come short and fast, and she wrestles the scarf from around her neck to let the air through, using it to blot away the perspiration which now covers her brow. She squeezes her eyes shut and presses back against the door, feeling for the handle as the red scarf floats to the polished floor like a streamer.

It's Signing Out Day at school, and her eyes are closed against the sunlight. She feels as though she's slipping away, losing consciousness as she lies here. Kate and Tina flop out on the grass beside her and everything goes quiet for a while, as if someone has muted all sound. She's aware of the sun singeing her skin and pinning her limbs down with liquid heat. It's all over: no more exams, no more school.

'Shit!' Kate suddenly cries out, leaping to her feet.

They sit up, shielding their eyes with the flat of their hands. Across the field, by the open doors to the gym, the photographer is fiddling with his camera tripod, as Mrs Whiff and Mrs Jensen move the fifth year girls into position on the edge of the playing field.

'They're all over there! Hurry up, or we won't get in the picture,' Kate says, and she grabs her bags and sprints across the field. Tina follows close at heel, while Sarah rises to her feet, the wooziness folding in over her.

She starts to run towards the group, and has just reached the shade of the building when she feels the first stabbing pain slice through her abdomen. It's acute, and she presses her fingernails into the twisted cord of her PE bag as she fights it, determined not to double over in front of the whole year group. The teachers have their backs to her, and she slips in through the wide doors to the gym and out into the corridor towards the toilets. The pain is intensifying now, crushing and dragging all at once, and as she turns the corner to enter the loos, the blood comes in a excruciating rush.

The door to the toilets is closed; bolted shut. There's a strip of yellow ribbon barring entry: *OUT OF ORDER*.

Sarah gasps, her awareness wavering, as cold perspiration covers her body like a film. She clutches her PE bag to her chest as she staggers along the corridor, her knees clamped together to stem the flow. She's sobbing now, desperate not to be found this way, and when she reaches the door to the boiler room it gives against her weight and she steps on to the splintered wooden stairs into the humid, stone darkness of the basement below.

Down here, nothing has changed. The drip-dripping, churning guts of the boiler continue to roar, as if they've never paused since 1986. Sarah's fingers find the switch on the way down, and the overhead strip light flickers and buzzes above her head.

She reaches the bottom steps, breathing in the damp oiliness of the basement room. Nobody knows she's here; she's completely alone, as all those old pupils dance and drink in the gym overhead. The distant thump of music fades into nothing as she draws closer to the crash and churn of the boiler tank. Sarah presses her back into the cool brick wall and squeezes her eyes shut. She grasps at the fractured memories that flood and rush from every dark corner.

She glances towards the steep wooden steps which lead to the outside world, and slides down the wall, pressing the palms of her hands against the cement floor. The pain of the place jolts through her fingertips. She draws herself into that same position, and she's there again, back in the boiler room where it all ended.

The mechanical rhythm of the water system drowns out her low whimpers, and she lies, small and foetus-like, curled up beside the large main drum of the boiler room, her PE kit hugged tight to her chest like a pillow. There are no lights, but she grows gradually accustomed to the darkness and her eyes can now make out small details around the cavernous basement. It's summer, and the humidity is stifling but the concrete floor feels cool against her waxy face, the sharp sensation of grit on her skin strangely soothing. A metal bucket stands several feet away, and between the groaning strains of the boiler she can just make out the small regular sound of water drops falling from the overhead pipe with a shallow plop. Her abdomen is gripped by a corseting spasm of pain, the contractions intensifying with each wave. She grabs at her school skirt, hitching it up and away from the blood now pooling on the grey floor beside her thighs. She slips in and out of consciousness. The machinery thumps and hisses away, heating the water pipes for the hundreds of girls walking about in the real world overhead. Thump-thump-thump-shhhhhhh. Pain crashes through her like a rolling winter wave, and her solitary grief pours out into the darkness.

The flickering buzz of the overhead light rouses Sarah. Pulling herself upright, she sits against the wall of the basement, straining to put together the remaining fragments of Signing Out Day. She sees herself dousing her PE shirt in the water bucket, sweeping it down the lengths of her legs to wash away the blood. Faintly, she recalls standing at the bottom step, gripping the wooden railing; the wood was rough under her fingertips, unlike the smooth polished banister of her own staircase at home. It must have been late by the time she left, because the school was quiet. But she could tell that the caretaker was around, because he'd propped the fire door open at the end of the corridor; the evening light flooded across the wooden floor, orange and warm. How long had she been down in the basement? She made her way across the hushed grounds, the only sounds coming from the songbirds and the soft whirr of teatime traffic beyond the school walls. But the journey home: there's nothing there at all. As she crept in through the front door and eased it shut, Dad had called from his study, his voice light and playful. 'Cup of tea, you say? I'd love one!' She'd dropped her PE bag in the hallway and filled the kettle, pressing into the sink to stop herself from falling. 'I'm just running a bath,' she called back. That's all; nothing more.

Sarah pulls her knees up, turning her hands over for clues. She drops her head back against the solid brickwork, and exhales, paralysed in the moment.

The door at the top of the stairs opens and in the dim light John's pale desert boots appear on the first step.

'I've got your things,' he says. He sits beside Sarah, his back against the wall, gently wrapping her red scarf around his fingers as if he were winding wool. 'I found this at the top of the stairs,' he says, handing it to her. 'I've been looking for you everywhere.' He draws up his knees too, and she can see little flecks of mossy green and blue in the knit of his exposed socks. 'What happened?' he asks.

She turns to look at him. The set of his face is strong, yet his eyes are full of sorrow. Again, she recognises something unsettling in his expression, and she turns away to focus on the brickwork of the far wall.

'What made you come down here?' he persists, taking her hand in his.

She pulls her hand away and brushes at the dusty floor with the tips of her fingers. 'I thought I remembered something, and I had to come and see. To be sure.' Calm washes over her as she speaks the words, and she looks up to see the tears in John's eyes.

'So, it was here,' he says quietly.

The boiler groans and hisses, obscuring these last words. Sarah looks up and frowns, inviting him to repeat himself, but he turns away, nervously running his hands through his hair. Simultaneously, they stretch out their legs, crossing their feet at the ankles.

John nudges her foot with his. 'Do you remember my old car? It was a Datsun Cherry.'

Sarah shakes her head.

'It was blue. You went in it once,' he says. 'It had a magic tree freshener hanging in the rear-view mirror, and you said the smell made you feel sick.'

All at once, she's there. She's made it to the top end of the High Street, nearest the school, but she still has to get the rest of the way home. She's propping herself up against the wall behind the yew hedge at the corner of Tide Road, and she can't step out because the blood just won't stop coming. She's afraid; she's faint and sick, and deeply afraid. The evening sun casts long shadows across the path, betraying her position. The shops must be closing because the traffic's dying down, and she knows she has to get home, or her dad will start to worry. She swipes at the streaks of drying blood with her stained school jumper, and takes a small step into the street.

John Gilroy is driving up the road in her direction, and as she moves back on to the path to get out of his way he stops, pulling up beside her. She looks through the side window at his horrified expression. He's seen. He leaps out of the car and runs round to her, taking her weight as she feels herself slipping.

'But what about the blood?' she whispers as he helps her in. 'Your car? What about the blood?'

John places an old blanket beneath her and clips the seatbelt in place, his face distorted with anxiety. 'Did somebody hurt you?' he asks as he gets back behind the wheel.

Sarah covers her eyes with her filthy hands and shakes her head. They drive in silence, along the High Street, past the chemist's, past the war memorial, past the estate agent's on the corner.

Outside her house in Seafield Avenue, she tells him he can't come in.

'Just let me walk you to the door, then? I need to make sure you're OK, Sarah.'

She shakes her head. 'Please. No one can ever know about this. *No one*.' She weeps, and John holds her, trembling against his chest until she's ready to go. 'Promise me,' she says as she steps out of the car, her legs trembling with every movement.

'I promise,' he replies, and he sits and waits until Sarah reaches her front door.

She turns and looks back at him, her face an apology.

The boiler lets out a sigh, and Sarah reaches for John's hand, lacing her fingers through his.

'He's dead, you know,' he says, pressing the tips of his fingers against the back of her hand.

Sarah looks up, her heart quickening. 'Who?'

The roaring rush and grind of the water system slows to a hum as Sarah takes in his words.

John nods once, holding her gaze steady. 'Kate's dad,' he says. 'Jason Robson. He's dead, Sarah. He's gone.'

Easing the boiler room door shut behind them, Sarah and John step out of the basement. Screeching laughter carries along the hallway from the ladies' toilets and the walls shudder with every thumping beat from the DJ desk in the party hall. Sarah indicates towards the fire exit at the end of the corridor; John pops it open easily and they escape on to the dark playing field at the side of the gym, running across the frosted grass until they reach the old oak tree which separates the boys' field from the girls'. The mist has lifted, and the stars are now visible in the clear sky. They can see the lights of the party spreading out on the far side of the building, and the occasional flurry of movement as partygoers stray into the car park and the grounds beyond. The pounding music can still be heard from here, sailing out into the cold night, the words gaining clarity in the quiet air.

They stand beneath the tree, their breaths rapid from the sprint. The branches cast shadows across their faces so that John's eyes flicker in and out of the light as he moves.

'I never told anyone,' he says, helping her into her coat.

She fastens the buttons, her head hung low.

'I know.'

He wraps his arms around her, sighing heavily into her hair. 'You didn't have to do it all alone.'

They remain like this for some time, swaying to the music, neither speaking. From the darkness of the playing field, a fox comes into view, just five or six feet from where they're standing, the auburn sheen of his coat bright against the night. He halts, his front paw poised to run, turning his unflinching face to meet theirs.

The fox gazes at Sarah, blinks once with his amber eyes and sprints across the field until he's no longer visible. A momentary hush falls across the field as the track comes to an end.

'Is it over?' John asks, looking at his watch.

Sarah looks back along the playing field, towards the small square of light from the open door of the fire exit. Mrs McCabe leans out to grab the bar of the door, taking a quick scan of the area before she pulls it shut, closing off the light altogether.

They emerge from the darkness of the oak tree, out over the field and into the open.

As they cross the car park towards John's old Citroën, Sarah drops his hand. Little groups mill around outside the entrance to the gym, laughing and shouting as the party comes to an end. The ground is littered with cigarette butts and empty cans, and a few women sit on the kerb at the edge of the car park, singing along to non-existent music. Sarah and John reach his car just as a horn sounds out from the vehicle beside them. She spins round at the noise, to see a man and woman in the silver BMW next to theirs. The driver's seat is reclined so that the woman's feet are hooked on to the steering wheel, while the rest of her body is obscured by a smooth pink backside and a billowing white shirt. An inside-out pair of purple leggings is draped over the passenger headrest, and through the partially open window the woman's familiar laughter lifts out into the cold air.

Sarah gazes at the car, and back towards the old school building. Darkness surrounds the place as the party nears its close.

'See you, Kate,' she whispers. She exhales, feeling the warmth of her breath rushing out into the night.

John leans in through the driver's side of his own car and pushes open the broken door. Still laughing at the tangled scene in the car beside them, he walks round and holds the passenger door open for Sarah to get in.

'All done?' he asks as he slides into the driver's seat beside her.

Sarah winds down her window and they drive out through the high iron gates, up through School Lane towards the High Street. The smell of sea spray is rich in the night air, the sharp, salt tang a nostalgic fragment of home. She closes her eyes and sees her father, stretched out on his deckchair in Dorset, on that holiday in 1986. She's paddling down by the rocky water's edge as he smiles and waves, lifting his tatty straw hat and raising it high above his head like a flag.

The car slows halfway along the High Street, drawing to a juddering halt beneath the salt-bleached sign for the Slipper Limpet B&B. The street is quiet in the late January lull. A tangle of greasy white chip paper drifts along the pavement; Sarah watches as it dances and weaves in the empty street. It flutters once at the junction to Tide Road, where the wind briefly hoists it towards the light of a flickering streetlamp before snatching it away altogether.

John turns to speak, but Sarah puts up her hand as she gets out of the car. 'Wait here,' she says.

She lets herself into the guest house with her visitor's key, looking over her shoulder once, before closing the door with a soft thud. She thinks of John, waiting outside in his funny knitted waistcoat; waiting for her. The house is dark and still. Silently, she sprints up the stairs to her room and gathers her belongings. She places £30 beside the guest book on her way out.

On the front step she pauses, turning her face into the salt breeze as the roar of the incoming tide draws closer. John pops open the passenger door and she throws her overnight bag on to the back seat and gets in, fixing her seatbelt with a solid clunk. She gives him a little nod.

John laughs, pinching his chin thoughtfully between his finger and thumb.

'OK,' she says, her eyes fixed on the road ahead. 'All done.'

Acknowledgements

My thanks go to everyone who has encouraged me in my writing pursuits along the way – you are too many to name, but you are greatly valued.

Particular thanks to Jane Osis and Juliet West, my workshop partners, for their insightful feedback and friendship (and laughter, wine and pasta); to everyone at the University of Chichester for their continued support; to Vicky Blunden, Candida Lacey and Adrian Weston for their frank and sensitive input during the editing and completion of *Hurry Up and Wait*; to Corinne Pearlman, Emma Dowson and Linda McQueen for their enormous contribution behind the scenes; and to Derek Niemann, a generous friend and perceptive reader of my various drafts. A special mention must go to Jacky Newman, my enduring childhood friend, who accompanied me through the endless, painful, poignant and funny moments of our 1980s schooldays. Jacks, I couldn't have done it without you.

As always, my deepest love and thanks to Colin, Alice and Samson.

If you liked *Hurry Up and Wait*, you might like Isabel Ashdown's critically acclaimed début novel *Glasshopper*.

Observer **Best Début Novels of the Year**
London Evening Standard **Best Books of the Year**
Winner of the *Mail on Sunday* novel competition

For an exclusive extract, read on...

WINNER OF THE *MAIL ON SUNDAY*
NOVEL COMPETITION

Jake, November 1984

I love November. I love the frosty grass that pokes up between the paving slabs, and the smoke that puffs out of your nostrils like dragon's breath. I love the ready-made ice rink that freezes underneath the broken guttering in the school playground. And I love the salt 'n' vinegar heat inside a noisy pub, when everyone outside is walking about in hats and gloves with dripping red noses.

This one Saturday afternoon, Dad and me are down the Royal Oak, getting ready to watch the match. Dad tells Eric the landlord that I'm fourteen, so I can come into the bar so long as I only have Coke. Not that I'd want what they all drink.

Dad shouts over, 'Fancy a bag of nuts, Jakey?' and I give him the thumbs-up from the corner seat we've bagged. It's great today because it's just me and Dad. Andy's on some boring Scout trip, and he won't be back till teatime. And Matthew – well, he just sort of disappeared a few weeks back. One morning I got out of bed, and went into Matt's room to wake him up with this fart I'd got brewing. It kills him every time. Anyway, this one morning, I go into his room, and he's not there. His bed was empty. So were his drawers. He'd taken all his clothes and records, so I knew he wasn't planning on coming back any time soon. Even his aftershave had gone. When I went in to tell Mum, she said, 'He'll be back when he's hungry,' and she rolled over and went back to sleep. But he didn't come back. Dad says he's old enough to leave home if he wants to, now he's seventeen. But I know that Dad wishes he knew where Matt was. The thing is, Matt couldn't stand being around Mum any more, and Dad's still in his bed-sit, so he couldn't have him there. It's not ideal, Dad says, but what can you do? The worst thing is, Matthew had only just got on to this Youth Training thing that was going to teach him bricklaying. He was gonna make a fortune, he said. I wish he'd phone or something. I could ask him if they've got YTS at his new place.

'There you go, Jake, lad.' Dad puts the drinks down on the round table, and settles into his seat. 'We should get a good view from here, son. Here, 'ave you seen the new TV Eric's got up on the bar? It's the business – Teletext, eighteen-inch screen, remote control – the works. Reckon I should save for one of them, shouldn't I, lad? Trinitron.'

It's a really nice telly.

'So, what's new, Jakey? How's it going at school? You still in the footie team?'

That's one of the things I like about Dad. All his questions are dead easy, and we never run out of things to say.

'Yeah, it's all cool. Because we're in the second year, we're doing Classical Studies, and it's brilliant. We're learning about Odysseus. He has quests, and he has to kill monsters and cross oceans just to get back home. There's a Cyclops and sea monsters and loads of other stuff. It's brilliant – you'd love it, Dad. I think it's my best lesson now. Miss Terry's giving us Greek names as she gets to know us. Simon Tomms is Poseidon, Emma Sullivan is Artemis. She's still thinking about mine.'

'Your mum got me to read *The Odyssey* when we were courting. And *The Iliad*.' He takes a sip of his beer and smacks his lips loudly. 'You'd like *Jason and the Argonauts*, son. Now that's a good film. There's this one bit, when the Argonauts run into seven skeletons and they rise up from the earth, wielding swords and marching like soldiers of the dead. I tell you, that was one of the greatest achievements of twentieth-century film-making, Jake. And it was bloody creepy too. There's a film to stand the test of time.'

He takes another swig from his glass, wiping the froth from his top lip with the back of his hand as he looks around the pub.

'And Mrs Jenkins chose my bonfire night picture for the corridor display this week. She said that it's "highly original".' I do her high-pitched voice to make Dad laugh. 'It'll be stuck up in the corridor, so everyone will get to see it when they come for Parents' Evening.'

'Parents' Evening,' Dad says, dabbing his finger in the dew around his glass. 'Is your mum going?'

'She says yes. I mean, she signed the slip saying she would. And I gave it back to Mr Thomas.'

'When is it, son?'

'Some time at the end of the month,' I answer. I know what he's getting at.

'Well, if there are any problems, you give me a ring. Here's 10p for the phone box, in case you need to phone from school. Stick it in your pocket. You can get me at the workshop. Alright, son?'

I smile at him, sucking up my Coke through two straws. It feels different drinking Coke out of two straws instead of one. If I had to choose, I think I'd go for one straw. It's less gassy. I wonder what Odysseus would choose, one or two. Mind you, Coke wasn't even invented back then.

'Dad, I don't s'pose you know what Mum's done with our library cards, do you? It's just they won't let me take out – '

'Stu!' My dad shouts across the crowded pub.

Stu's this new mate of Dad's, and he's come to watch the match too. Sometimes, when he comes to the pub, he brings his son with him – Malcolm. Malcolm's the same age as me, and he's mostly OK, but sometimes a bit of an idiot. Once I saw him trip up this little kid in the pub garden, on purpose, just for a laugh. Then this other time we saw some woman struggling with a pram in the paper shop, and he helped her lift it over the step. Dad reckons Malcolm's a bit of an oddball. I think Malcolm's OK.

'Alright, Bill mate!' Stu bundles over with their drinks, grinning at Dad, unwrapping his scarf and hat. 'Glad to see you could make it. This should be a good 'un, eh? Room for two more? Budge up, Jakey boy.'

Dad's pleased to see Stu. 'Just in time for kick-off, mate. Good timing.'

Malcolm's cheeks look all shiny and red with the cold. Like apples. We nod at each other, and then Eric whacks up the volume, and shouts, 'Alright lads!' and everyone turns to the TV as the players run on the pitch and take position.

Stu lights up a cigarette and squashes further into the seat so that I have to budge up to get out of his smoke.

'Should be a good match,' he says knowingly, leaning on to his knees like an excited kid.

Dad agrees and helps himself to one of Stu's fags. 'Just the one,' he says to me with a nudge.

As it turns out, the match is a really boring one, and by half-time it's still nil-nil. In between, Dad and Stu give us each 30p and let us go off to get some sweets from the newsagents. We leave them in the pub getting another round in.

On the way back from the shops, Malcolm tells me about the BMX he reckons he's getting for his birthday next week. They're dead expensive, and I ask him how his dad can afford it. He squats down next to a drain in the road and drops his lolly stick through the gaps, before carrying on along the path.

'It's 'cos him and my mum are divorced. 'Cos I live with Mum and Phil. So Dad always tries really hard to get me a better present than them. Then they say stuff like, who does he think he is, flash git, and then they get me something great too. It's brilliant. Win-win.'

Sometimes I don't get Malcolm, but he's got a point. It does sound quite good.

'Is Phil loaded, then?' I ask.

'Nah. But they get the money from somewhere. That's what counts.'

Malcolm looks like a spoilt kid. He's too big, and too chubby, and his black hair is a bit square. But he talks like he thinks he's cool.

He shoves his hands in his pockets and pulls out a liquorice shoelace, shovelling it all in at once.

'What about your lot?' he asks, an end of shoelace poking out the corner of his mouth. 'Do you get good stuff off them? I mean, they've split up, haven't they?'

We reach the phone box on the corner of Park Road.

'You ever played "Mrs McSporran", Malc?' I ask him, heaving open the chipped red door, releasing the stench of old piss and cigarette burns. Malcolm's frowning at me like I'm a right prat. 'Come on,' I urge him, as he stands outside the glass, chewing.

Half-heartedly he comes inside, which is a bit of a squeeze with his chubby belly.

'It'll be a laugh,' I say. 'Watch the master at work.'

I dial 100. 'Reverse call, please,' I tell the operator. I give her a made-up number and name – 'Yes, Albert' – and we wait for the connection.

Malcolm keeps looking around, to see if anyone's coming. He looks really nervous.

'Hulllooo!' I shout when the operator puts me through. 'Hulllooo? Is that wee Ethel McSporran?'

Malcolm's eyes are like saucers, and his mouth has dropped open like a cartoon.

'Ach, Ethel! D'ye need any haggis, Ethel?' I hoot, as the woman on the other end tries to explain that I've got the wrong number. 'Och, Ethel, pipe down, will ye, wee lassie! Ye dinne wan' iny haggis? Hoo aboot some bagpipes?'

Malcolm has tears welling up in his eyes.

'Eh? Oor hoo aboot a kilt?' This one is so high-pitched that I crack up too, and just manage a final 'Tatty-bye,' before hanging up.

Malc is thumping his fists on the glass, choking on his Hubba Bubba. 'You're nuts, mate – ' he splutters, still chuckling, his shiny cheeks redder than ever.

I offer him the receiver – 'Wanna go?' – but he shakes his head, laughing, pushing out of the phone box backwards. As we carry on back towards the Royal Oak, we see an old dear sat at the bus stop on the other side of the road. She looks quite sweet, with a big shopping bag on the floor by her little brown shoes, and she seems to be smiling at everything. I notice the bag's made of a kind of plastic tartan material. Malc sees it too, because he snorts and shoves me.

She's a little way off, and I come to a stop facing her over the road, hands on my hips, legs wide. In my deepest Scottish bellow I shout over to her, 'Hullllooo, dearie! D'ye wanna haggis?'

The little old lady tips her head to one side, like she's trying to hear better.

Malc tugs at my sleeve, and screeches in a rubbish accent, 'Oor perhaps a hairy sporran!' and we tear off down the street before she has a chance to get a good look at us.

An old man with a poofy little sausage dog waves his newspaper angrily at us as we run past.

'Bloody hooligans!' he shouts, like a character from *Benny Hill*.

I smirk at him, running backwards so he can see I'm not scared of him. His dog cocks his leg and pisses against the litter bin, and the steam rises like smoke as it trickles down the pavement and off the kerb.

When we get a safe distance away we stop, hands on our knees, catching our breath between sobbing laughter. A gob-stopper slips out of my mouth on to the toe of my plimsoll, before rolling along the pavement and coming to a stop by Malcolm's foot. We look up at each other, and now we're almost screaming, holding our bellies and gasping like we've got asthma.

'Was she Scottish, then – ' Malcolm asks as we get a grip of ourselves '– the woman on the phone?'

I shake my head.

'Then what's with all the Scotch stuff?'

'Dunno, it's just kind of funny,' I answer. 'Shit! I forgot the oatcakes! You should always ask if they want any oatcakes!'

As we get closer to the pub, we run out of things to say for a bit.

'Malc, do you do Classical Studies at your school?'

Malcolm wrinkles up his nose, and snorts, 'Yeah. Why?' like he can't believe I just asked it.

'Oh, nothing, really. Wanna jaw-breaker?' I say, offering him the bag, and then we turn the corner, across the road from the pub, and Malcolm nudges me, grinning.

'Fuckin' 'ell mate – look at the state of that!'

And there's this woman, swaying around outside the door of the pub, arguing with Eric the landlord. She looks like she's just crawled off a park bench, wearing a summer dress and slippers. She must be freezing. Eric is shaking his head – sorry, love, no chance – trying to get rid of her. There's a match on, they don't need this kind of bother.

Malcolm's laughing; he doesn't know it's my mum. I try to act normal, pull a face, rummage in my sweet bag.

'Yeah, fuckin' 'ell,' I reply. My head's throbbing. 'Malc, mate – I need a waz. You go on in – tell Dad I'll be there in a minute.' And I pretend to head off towards the pub's outside loo.

Malcolm nods, stuffing in more sweets, looking the drunk woman up and down as he passes her in the doorway. Eric the landlord spots me, shakes his head as if to say, don't worry about it, Jakey. For a moment, I'm stuck to the spot. I just stand and stare at the back of her head. She's like the Gorgon, and I've turned to stone. Quietly, I walk over and slip my hand into hers, and lead her away from the pub.

'I'll make you a nice cuppa, Mum. I think we've got some logs out the back. It's cold enough to make a fire, I reckon.'

Mum shuffles along beside me, shivering silently, till we reach the house. We get inside and she wraps her arms around me and sobs against my shoulder.

'You know I love you, Jakey. Never, ever forget that, darling. I love you.'

MORE FROM MYRIAD EDITIONS

'Ed Siegle's moving and dynamic tale of loss and discovery is a meditation on being seen, and being unseen. Full of surprises, crackling with energy, and with characters bristling with life, *Invisibles* pulled me along from the first page and didn't set me down until the last.'
Kathryn Heyman

Invisibles spans two cities by the sea and four decades of music, torture and romance. From the streets of Brighton to the bars of Rio, Ed Siegle weaves the rhythms of Brazil and the troubles of his characters into an absorbing story of identity, love and loss. At once familiar and foreign, this sweet, sad and compulsively readable first novel throngs with visceral memory and unbreakable ordinary heroes.

ISBN: 978-0-9565599-1-3

SELECTED FOR AMAZON RISING STARS

'A very impressive first novel. This is a fantastic personal read with plenty for a reading group to discuss.' *NewBooks Magazine*

'Within ten minutes I couldn't put it down. There's real dramatic tension in this book and when I got to the end the first thing that I did was to turn back to the beginning again.'
The Bookbag

'A tense and thought-provoking début novel with dark moments. Its portrayal of obsession will send a shiver down your spine and you'll hope that you are never in that position. But don't look for a pat ending, it seems that things never end the way one hopes. This début novel by a police intelligence analyst is certainly well worth the read.'
Shotsmag

ISBN: 978-0-9562515-7-2

MORE FROM MYRIAD EDITIONS

SHORTLISTED FOR THE GREEN CARNATION PRIZE

'Fast-moving and sharply written.'
Guardian

'There is a deceptively relaxed quality to Kemp's writing that is disarming, bewitching and, to be honest, more than a little sexy.'
Polari Magazine

'An interestingly equivocal and quietly questioning début.'
Financial Times

'London itself, in its relentless indifference, is as powerful a presence here as the three gay men whose lives it absorbs.'
Times Literary Supplement

'Drawing inspiration from the life and work of Oscar Wilde, just as Michael Cunningham's *The Hours* drew from Virginia Woolf, *London Triptych* is a touching and engrossing read.'
Attitude

ISBN: 978-0-9562515-3-4

'An intense study of grief and mental disintegration, a lexical celebration and a psychological conundrum. Royle explores loss and alienation perceptively and inventively.'
Guardian

'An experimental and studied look at mourning. Playful, clever and perceptive.'
Big Issue

'Royle's meandering prose – which seems at once anarchic and meticulously arranged – is appropriate to the subject matter: the disarray and isolation a man experiences when his father dies. There are moments of delightfully eccentric humour and impressive linguistic experimentalism.' *Observer*

'Nicholas Royle's first novel is a story of loss and love. He captures the absolute dislocating strangeness of bereavement.'
New Statesman

ISBN: 978-0-9562515-4-1

MORE FROM MYRIAD EDITIONS

SELECTED FOR WATERSTONE'S NEW VOICES

'This reads like an author on their fourth or fifth book rather than their début novel. The prose is masterly, the characters are fully drawn.'
Savidge Reads

'Every single page is full to bursting. Yet every single word earns its place. The whole novel is breathtaking in its scope and originality. This is a multi-layered read. Thoroughly recommended.'
The Bookbag

'Hillyer's meticulous research and gift for atmosphere brings London and its rich history to life; his handling of Brippoki's hallucinogenic episodes is skilfully done and his use of Dreaming is sensitive and understated. The result is a charming, unusual and poignant book.'
All About Cricket

ISBN: 978-0-9562515-0-3

SHORTLISTED FOR THE WRITERS' GUILD AWARD FOR BEST FICTION BOOK

'A beautiful début about a son trying to break free from his father.'
Financial Times

'Lyrical, warm and moving, this impressive début is reminiscent of Laurie Lee.'
Meera Syal

'Passages in this novel made me laugh out loud and others were extremely moving. I silently gave three cheers for Ellis when I reached the end of this book. A poetic, moving and evocative read.'
The Bookbag

'A warm coming-of-age story that tackles family relationships, secrets, belonging and self-acceptance.'
Coventry Telegraph

'A very fine, funny and moving read.'
David Baddiel

ISBN: 978-0-9562515-2-7

MORE FROM MYRIAD EDITIONS

'Imagine Brighton in chaos. Communities are divided – socially, economically and physically. The council is all-powerful, inconvenient people are "dealt with", children are controlled and tolls strangle the transport system. Dickinson creates a world that only vaguely resembles our own. This intriguing story brings the issues of political influence, red tape and corruption to the fore – if only by making us relieved that it seems improbable it could come to this.'
Liverpool Daily Post

'As a satire, it works well, and is completely believable as a "nightmare present" scenario.'
The Bookbag

'I was pleased to find myself rapidly becoming engrossed in the strange world which Robert Dickinson has created.'
A Common Reader

ISBN: 978-0-9562515-1-0

BEST BOOKS OF THE YEAR
London Evening Standard

'Tender and subtle, it explores difficult issues in deceptively easy prose. Across the decades, Ashdown tiptoes carefully through explosive family secrets. This is a wonderful début – intelligent, understated and sensitive.'
Observer

'An intelligent, beautifully observed coming-of-age story, packed with vivid characters and inch-perfect dialogue.'
Mail on Sunday

'A disturbing, thought-provoking tale of family dysfunction that guarantees laughter at the uncomfortable familiarity of it all.'
London Evening Standard

'An immaculately written novel with plenty of dark family secrets and gentle wit within. Recommended for book groups.'
Waterstone's Books Quarterly

ISBN: 978-0-9549309-7-4

MORE FROM MYRIAD EDITIONS

DRAMATISED FOR RADIO 4 WOMAN'S HOUR

'*The Cloths of Heaven* is a wry, dust-dry, character-observation-rich gem of a book with one of the most refreshing comic voices I've read for a long while. This book is a bright, witty companion – values and attitudes in the right place – acute, observant but also tolerant and understanding and not afraid of a sharp jibe or two.'
Vulpes Libris

'Graham Greene with a bit of Alexander McCall Smith thrown in. Very readable, very humorous – a charming first novel.'
Radio 5 Live

'Populated by a cast of miscreants and misfits, this début novel by playwright Eckstein is a darkly comic delight.'
Choice

'Fabulous... fictional gold.'
Argus

ISBN: 978-0-9549309-8-1

WINNER OF THE PEOPLE'S BOOK PRIZE FOR FICTION

'Lesley Thomson is a class above, and *A Kind of Vanishing* is a novel to treasure.'
Ian Rankin

'Thomson skilfully evokes the era and the slow-moving quality of childhood summers, suggesting the menace lurking just beyond the vision of her young protagonists. A study of memory and guilt with several twists.'
Guardian

'This emotionally charged thriller grips from the first paragraph, and a nail-biting level of suspense is maintained throughout.'
She

'A thoughtful, well-observed story about families and relationships and what happens to both when a tragedy occurs. It reminded me of Kate Atkinson.'
Scott Pack

ISBN: 978-0-9565599-3-7

MORE FROM MYRIAD EDITIONS

'Imaginative, clever and darkly claustrophobic.'
The Big Issue

'An exquisitely crafted début novel set in a post-apocalyptic landscape. I'm rationing myself to five pages per day in order to make it last.'
Guardian Unlimited

'Martine McDonagh writes with a cool, clear confidence about a world brought to its knees. Her protagonist is utterly believable, as are her observations of the sodden landscape she finds herself inhabiting. This book certainly got under my skin – if you like your books dark and more than a little disturbing, this is one for you.'
Mick Jackson

'This is a troubling, beautifully composed novel, rich in its brevity and complex in the psychological portrait it paints.'
Booksquawk

ISBN: 978-0-9549309-2-9

This celebration of Brighton and Brightonians – resident, itinerant and visiting – is a feast of words and pictures specially commissioned from established artists and emerging talents.

'I loved writing a piece with crazy wonderful Brighton as the theme... a great mix of energy and ideas.'
Jeanette Winterson

'Give a man a fish and you'll feed him for a day. Give him *The Brighton Book* and you will feed him for a lifetime.'
Argus

Contributors: Melissa Benn, Louis de Bernières, Piers Gough, Roy Greenslade, Bonnie Greer, Lee Harwood, Mick Jackson, Lenny Kaye, Nigella Lawson, Martine McDonagh, Boris Mikhailov, Woodrow Phoenix, John Riddy, Meg Rosoff, Miranda Sawyer, Posy Simmonds, Ali Smith, Catherine Smith, Diana Souhami, Lesley Thomson, Jeanette Winterson

ISBN: 978-0-9549309-0-5

COMING SOON FROM MYRIAD EDITIONS

***4 AM* by Nina de la Mer**

Set in the early 1990s on a British army base, *4 AM* tells the story of Cal and Manny, soldiers posted to Germany as army chefs. Bored and institutionalised, the pair succumb to the neon temptations of Hamburg's red-light district, where they dive into a seedy world of recreational drugs and all-night raves. But it is only a matter of time before hedonism and military discipline clash head on, with comic and poignant consequences. Life-affirming raving soon gives way to gloomy, drug-fuelled nights in fast-food restaurants, at sex shows, and in Turkish dive bars. As a succession of events ratchets up the pressure on Cal and Manny their friendship is tested, a secret is revealed, and a shocking betrayal changes one of their lives forever.

•

***Interpreters* by Sue Eckstein**

When Julia Rosenthal returns to the suburban estate of her childhood, the unspoken tensions that permeated her seemingly conventional family life come flooding back. Trying to make sense of the secrets and half-truths, she is forced to question how she has raised her own daughter – with an openness and honesty that Susanna has just rejected in a very public betrayal of trust. Meanwhile her brother, Max, is happy to forge an alternative path through life, leaving the past undisturbed. But in a different place and time, another woman struggles to tell the story of her early years in wartime Germany, gradually revealing the secrets she has carried through the century, until past and present collide with unexpected and haunting results.